The Beautiful-Ugly
The Trilogy

James Snyder

Bandera Publishing Company ™

Dallas, Texas

Copyright © 2014 by James Snyder

All rights reserved.

ISBN: 0991527062

ISBN-13: 978-0-9915270-6-9

Published by **Bandera Publishing Company ™**

Dallas, Texas

Book design by Richard K. Green @ richardkgreen.com

This is a work of fiction. Any resemblance to actual persons living or dead, events or locales is entirely coincidental.

For Berlin.

CONTENTS

PART ONE: THE BEAUTIFUL-UGLY

1	Forever Lost	1
2	Drop House	14
3	Saying Good Bye	25
4	Pilgrims Mercy	32
5	The School	44
6	The Special	51
7	The Interview	57
8	Churn	62
9	A Special Day	74
10	Fostering Out	81
11	Her New Family	86
12	Learning to Pray	99
13	The Choice	110
14	Losing the Faith	117
15	The Way It All Ended	126

PART TWO: INTO THE ABYSS

16	In the Out Door	140
17	Lillian	152
18	The Hot Drop	158
19	ER	168
20	Gen H Psych	175
21	The Letters	186
22	The House on the Ocean	194
23	Beautiful-Ugly	202
24	The Art School	214
25	Girl of a Certain Age	224
26	A Psychosomatic Diversion	235
27	The Offer	247
28	Crossing America	254

CONTENTS CONT.

29	Roxy	266
30	Jessing	276
31	Things She Never Told Herself	286
32	Bobby	299
33	The Last Jess	309
34	Latin Kings	317
35	What She Found There	329
36	Finding Eric	340

PART THREE: WHERE ALL THE RIVERS RUN

37	A Disturbance of Attachment	361
38	Cousins	373
39	Gone to Texas	382
40	A New Blood-soaked Country	396
41	The Help	408
42	Growing Grass	415
43	Those Other Walkers	421
44	Pulling Calves	433
45	Working Her Art	444
46	The Quality of Things Undefined	456
47	At Buster's	463
48	What Happened When She Died	468
49	A Fan of Frida Kahlo	477
50	Finishing What They Started	490
51	Peddling Her Art	502
	Epilogue: Fourteen Years Gone	513
	About the Author	517

PART ONE

THE BEAUTIFUL-UGLY

1 ♀ FOREVER LOST

*T*he moment she felt her consciousness seeping back inside her, she knew where she was. She didn't have to look. Or listen. No one had to come whisper in her ear. She could smell it that far out, returning. Something she had learned near the very beginning, or at least after the first year or so: When you wake up, don't move so much as an eye muscle. Smell first. Quietly. That is, don't sniff. Don't dare flare a nostril they might see. Just let the odors come to you, as they always do. Establish your surroundings. Your boundaries. Then, if it passes the smell test, you can take a peek. So she lay there, motionless, and let it come inside her...those smells...the rancid, rotten-cabbage attempts at sterility...the blood-and-pus-soaked gauze...the metallic, needle-sharp tinge of stainless steel...the stagnant, stifling, incredibly compressed air of depression, threatening to crush and blow apart her skull all at once...and, of course, (at least according to some funny-at-the-time name-game she'd overheard somewhere) that noxious chemical war between Sergeant Shit and Private Piss and those two ranked and spiffy overachievers, Captain Clorox and Lieutenant Lysol. This was an easy one. Just another cashew clinic, she realized. Another psych ward was all.

And she opened her eyes.

*

In the beginning, it was the Quiet Room they kept her. Or, at least, their version. She knew that. Where she could be alone, away from the others, while they admired their latest freaky-deaky on display.

The Quiet Room.

But like those other rooms, she could still hear the yelling and screaming and the strange mix of voices beyond the walls, so she didn't think it was that quiet. But she didn't say anything. She didn't talk with them at all, in fact. She lay on the bed, or she sat in the chair they placed her, as they came and did what they always did.

Someone—one of the nurses—waved a hand before her face, and she blinked.

"Well, at least she's not catatonic," the nurse said.

Someone else said, "I guess she just doesn't want to talk with us."

She didn't. She knew who they were. And she knew they wouldn't do anything, except talk. But now she was through talking. Besides, she was tired now, so tired she didn't know what, except that she wanted to be alone. So she sat there, seeing them come and go, but not ever looking at them, their eyes, like they wanted, and never saying a word.

They called her Sleeping Beauty, trying to ingratiate themselves. Trying to make her react—some way, anyway.

As she stared out somewhere beyond them, at that faint, red-pulsing light—fading away and returning—just above the steel-door entrance.

*

After what seemed like a week, they removed the restraints and replaced the major dressings, binding her sutured wrists with minor ones. She was healing. She was getting better now.

Then one day he came and sat beside her. He had a clipboard and a bedside smile.

"I was wondering if we might have a conversation."

Oh, you mean one different from those thousand-and-one previous conversations I've had?

He sat there, waiting.

OK then—where would you like me to begin? Perhaps, when I was six—that would be, let's see, ten or so years ago—when my parents were burned to death in their old gray Toyota somewhere down on Highway 1? Or maybe those hot-drops the courts first placed me with that took turns probing and examining my so young, so previously unavailable body, until I just couldn't help myself and ran away? Or maybe that trailer-trash rapist you stuck me with on that rainy night that—on second thought, Doc, I really don't feel like having another conversation right now. I really don't.

"I think it would help if we talked."

That's not what she was thinking. What she was thinking was, she wished there was some way she could take all these soul-searching, so-called caregivers—every psychiatrist and psychologist and psychotherapist and counselor and social worker and know-better-than-thou government lawyer that had ever put her through their maddeningly invasive, mind-numbing routines—and make them actually hear themselves.

"Perhaps it would help if we went back to the beginning," he said. "The very beginning and work forward from there. Why don't we start there and see where it leads us, hmmm?"

She lay there, still ignoring him—actually, blocking him entirely out of her mind, and turning off his switch—but doing that. That is, for just a mind-flashing moment or so, going back to the beginning. The very beginning...

When she was six. And loved raspberry sherbet. And catching fireflies, which she called magic bugs then, racing after them through the twilight, seeing their cool, red-sherbet tummies blinking teasingly on and off around her, as she snapped them up inside her peanut-butter jar. Then her brother Eric, who was nine, three years older than herself, and who thought he knew everything, told her they weren't magic bugs at all. They were just winged beetles. And the glow was just a chemical reaction called bio-something-or-other. But she didn't care. If she wanted them to be magic, then they were, that's all. They were magic just like the taste of raspberry sherbet was magic. And why couldn't Eric understand that? *Why?*

Of course her mother agreed with Eric. Her mother was a researcher in a laboratory. She was smart like Eric. And the two of them would sit side-by-side on the sofa, watching the science programs on television, and discuss them afterward. And when she went to her once and asked her—couldn't they be magic bugs, if she wanted them to be?—her mother only smiled and said, of course, sweetheart, of course they can, and hugged her. But she knew. She knew her mother thought they were winged beetles, just like Eric, and was only being polite.

But her father was more like her. And when he'd say, "Hey, brat, let's go over to the park and catch some magic bugs." She believed him. She really believed he thought they were magic, as she did, and that made running after them through the near-dark and catching them inside their peanut-butter jars even more fun.

Of course he always made her release them, after she watched them glowing inside the jar for a while. And once, when she caught one in her hand and wrote the first letter of her name: C, for Connelly, on her other hand, he told her, "You know, brat, that's how they find each other in the dark, blinking on and off like that, and how they find their way back home. And if you remove the glow from their tummies, they'll be lost, forever, in the dark. They'll never find their way home then."

She had tried then to put the glow back on the magic bug's tummy, but it didn't work. She finally had to let it go, and it flew away, she realized, forever lost.

She remembered that then, waiting outside in the dark on Mrs. Bagleresi's balcony, when she saw the firefly.

Earlier in the afternoon, when Mrs. Bagleresi had her tea, she called her and Eric to the kitchen table for milk and cookies. Then Connelly went back to the balcony to wait. Her parents always came to pick them up not long after their snack, and so she read her book and waited, as the shadows drew long across the balcony, and the light faded.

Twice she had stood and gone over to the balcony railing to peer down the street, looking for their car. Then came the dusk and the evening dark when she saw the firefly glowing on Mrs. Bagleresi's railing; and, frustrated, she went there and grabbed it up in her hand. She carefully touched her right index finger on the tummy, removing just a little of the magic dust, before releasing it to fly away. Then she stood there, looking out over the San

Francisco skyline, and raised her finger, the pale red glow (as she made her wish) showing them both the way home.

Car lights approached. She leaned over the railing and watched until the lights were there below her, before the apartment building.

But it was a police car, instead.

She watched as two policemen and a woman got out of the car and came inside their building.

Connelly went and sat down again, waiting, until she heard the strange voices inside the apartment. She wiped the magic dust off her finger onto her shorts.

Before long, Mrs. Bagleresi came to the balcony door and said, "Connelly dear, you need to gather your things."

She looked up. "Where're mommy and daddy?"

Mrs. Bagleresi's face looked different. "You need to gather your things, darling. You must hurry."

She sat there, unsure.

"Hurry, dear—they're waiting for you."

She didn't know what to do. Who was waiting for her? *Who?*

She followed Mrs. Bagleresi inside and saw them—the two policemen and the lady, standing there.

Now everything seemed a blur to her. She and Eric were gathering their things, glancing at each other. She wanted to say something to him but she was afraid. Everyone was standing there, unsmiling, watching them moving about as if they had done something wrong. She was so confused. And she was afraid. By the time she had everything tucked inside her backpack, and was lifting it on her shoulders, she began to cry. She cried quietly, hoping no one would notice. That's when the strange lady came and put her arms around her. She looked young. Younger even than her mother.

"Connelly, my name's Melissa. We're going to go someplace and talk, all right?"

Her parents had always told her never to talk or go with strangers. But Mrs. Bagleresi was letting them go. And policemen were different, she remembered. She could go with policemen, her parents had told her.

At the elevator Mrs. Bagleresi said, "Good-bye, children. I want you—"

And she stopped, suddenly covering her mouth with her hand and turning away, hurrying back inside her apartment and shutting the door, as the elevator door opened.

*

That was the first time she had ever ridden in a police car. It was funny. There was a kind of plastic wall between the three of them, sitting in the back seat, and the two policemen in the front. And a lady kept talking over the radio very quickly in a low voice she couldn't understand. But she didn't care. She didn't understand anything that was happening, and so she just leaned against Eric, and he didn't try to push her away this time, or tell her to leave him alone. In fact, he didn't seem to even notice her leaning there. No one said a word while they were driving, and so she sat there, leaning against her brother and listening to lady saying things over the radio she couldn't understand.

*

When they arrived Connelly saw a big building with small lighted windows. She wondered where they were. Everything seemed to be happening in a hurry. Suddenly the policemen were gone, and Melissa took them inside and told them to sit down on one of the benches there. Then she left them, going into another room and shutting the door.

Connelly sat there beside her brother, looking around. It was a big room.

She whispered, "What's happened, Eric? Where're mommy and daddy? Why didn't they come get us?"

"I don't know," he said, his head turned away. She heard him sniff. "She'll tell us, I guess."

But he wouldn't look at her. She kept trying to see his face, but he kept looking away, so she stopped. Next, Melissa came and took him away.

"I want to talk with your brother a minute, Connelly," she said. "Just a minute, and then I'll talk with you, all right?"

She watched them walking away hand in hand, disappearing inside another room. After they were gone she looked around the room again. There were desks and chairs, and no one else was there. She wondered where everyone was. Then she remembered it was night, Saturday night, and everyone was probably home. Next she remembered how early that morning her father had picked her up out of bed and carried her, still in her pajamas and slippers, to the elevator. Sleepily, she saw Eric standing there, holding mommy's hand behind them, everyone riding the creaky, early morning elevator up one floor from their apartment to Mrs. Bagleresi's.

Then she heard Mrs. Bagleresi at the door, whispering, "Oh, put her there on the couch. I've made the sheets up. Eric, you go sleep on the daybed. Would you like some coffee before you go?"

She had heard her mother say no thank you.

At the last moment were the familiar hugs and kisses. Even with her eyes closed she could smell the difference between them, leaning down near her face: her mommy smelling soft and sweet like lavender flowers; her daddy like the outside, like the wind on San Francisco Bay on a sunny day. He told her once that was just his aftershave.

Then they were gone, and she snuggled down into the sheets Mrs. Bagleresi had prepared for her and went back to sleep.

She looked up.

Melissa was standing there. "Will you come with me now, Connelly? You can bring your backpack with you."

She stood up, shouldering her backpack, and took Melissa's hand. They walked across the floor into the other room. This room was smaller, with a desk and chair, and there was a couch and stuffed chairs in the corner. She saw Eric sitting in one of the chairs. His face looked different now, surprised different, like Mrs. Bagleresi's face earlier on the balcony.

Melissa said, "Connelly, would you sit down here on the couch with me."

She pulled off her backpack and they sat down on the couch, and suddenly she was afraid again. She didn't like being there. She didn't like feeling how she was feeling and not knowing why.

Melissa was sitting beside her, their knees touching, and Connelly looked down to see the larger hands now holding her smaller ones. She heard Melissa's voice say strangely, "I'm afraid your mother and father had an accident. They were coming home, driving up the coast road, when another car hit their car."

She stopped.

"Oh," Connelly heard herself say, and she felt her face twisting. "Are they hurt then?"

She saw Melissa look at Eric and then back at her. She was squeezing both her hands hard now. She said, almost whispering, "Connelly darling, they were both killed. When the other car hit their car it...it took away their lives."

She didn't know. She sat there and didn't know. Her voice sounded squeaky, saying, "Where are they now? Can I go see them?"

"They were taken to a special place when people die," Melissa said. "A man has to look at them and do a report, and then they have to be buried. When they're buried you and Eric can be with them. You can say good-bye to them then. Do you understand what I'm telling you, Connelly?"

She didn't. She didn't want to understand. She wanted to think of something else. Once, she asked her mommy if she could have a kitten, but she told her it wasn't allowed.

"But Mrs. Bagleresi has Fifi," she reminded her.

"That's because Mrs. Bagleresi pays a deposit we can't afford."

She wasn't sure the difference, but her mommy finally promised, "When we can afford a real house we'll get you a kitty."

"But when?"

"When we can afford it, Connelly," she repeated. "When we have the money."

"We don't have any money?"

"Yes, enough to pay the rent and pay the bills and not starve. But not enough for a whole house. Not yet."

She wasn't sure what all that meant either, except that she couldn't have her kitty then. Instead, she went to her bedroom and played with her doll, Priscilla, telling her: "No, Priscilla, you can't have a kitten. You know very well we can't afford it. We have to pay other things first, so stop asking me."

She remembered waiting, allowing time for Priscilla to answer her, and then said, "No, you can't have a puppy either. When we can afford a real house, then you can have a kitten. A black and white one that we'll share." She had waited, listening. "No, you can't have your own kitten, because I have to take care of it. *You can't take care of it*—you're just a doll." She waited again. "Well, you can cry if you want to, but it won't do you any good."

She had picked her doll up then, rocking her gently back and forth in her arms, humming.

Melissa said, "According to Mrs. Bagleresi, you don't have any relatives nearby, is that right?"

Connelly saw that she was looking at Eric, but he only looked confused; afraid, even. Instead, she told her, "Our grandmother's in the rest home. She has Alzheimer's. She doesn't remember anything, not even my daddy, who was her son."

Now Melissa looked back at her. "But you have an uncle?"

She nodded. "Uncle Boyd. That's mommy's brother. He's somewhere in the merchant marines. He goes all over the world. He likes to drink."

Still, all this talking felt so strange. Why did they have to talk like this?

"Well, the important thing now is to keep you safe," Melissa said. "That's what your parents would want. You see, I work for the Child Welfare department, and that's one of the things we do. The problem is, it's the weekend, and it's late, and none of my emergency caregivers can take you till, at least, tomorrow. So you'll have to sleep here tonight."

Eric said, "Why can't we sleep at our house?"

"Because there's no one there."

Connelly thought about it and said, "Can't we stay with Mrs. Bagleresi?"

"She told me she had a heart condition," said Melissa. "No, the best thing is for you to stay here tonight, until I can make arrangements. We have a security guard here, and the doors will be locked, and you'll be safe, I promise you."

Strange, she thought. Everything was strange now. Ugly and strange. The way everything looked. The way everything sounded. Even herself. She just didn't understand any of it; so, instead, she pulled her hands away from Melissa's hands, fell back on the couch into a tight ball, and began to cry.

*

That night they slept there in Melissa's office. They folded down the couch and made up the bed. Then they put back on their pajamas from their backpacks, brushed their teeth in the small bathroom connected to the office, and climbed beneath the cool sheets.

Melissa stood at the doorway and said, "I'll be here first thing in the morning." Connelly watched her, standing at the door, looking in at them. "I'm really sorry about your parents."

She turned out the lights and shut the door.

Connelly lay there, looking around the dark room. You could see shadowy things, because a little light was coming through the window from the other room. After a while she said, "Well, I don't guess we'll go to Spaghetti Warehouse tonight, will we, Eric?"

He didn't say anything. His back was to her, and he was very still.

She lay on her back, thinking: *Our apartment in San Francisco is very small, and we are very happy.* She wrote that at the beginning of school for her teacher, Mrs. Dougherty. She and Eric went to the same school, which was two blocks from their apartment building. In the morning, sometimes her mother, and sometimes her father, walked them to school. She was in second grade and liked it very much, even though she was not nearly as smart as Eric, who was in fifth grade and wanted to be a scientist like their mother.

She thought how Mrs. Dougherty put a smiling little bumblebee by their name when they were good and a sad bee when they acted naughty. She got a sad bee once when she hit Roland Mellon, who sat behind her, for pinching her bottom. And it seemed like forever, until the following week when she got a happy bee again, and she kept staring at it on the far wall, relieved.

In the afternoon, Mrs. Bagleresi always picked her and Eric up from school. Eric did his homework and she would draw, or watch TV, or go read on the balcony. She didn't play with Fifi because the little dog would sit there and curl her lip if she tried to touch her.

"Fifi, you be nice to Connelly," Mrs. Bagleresi always said, sitting there, sipping her tea and looking at her magazines. "She only wants to be friends with you."

But Fifi would only lower her head in shame and slink up on Mrs. Bagleresi's wide lap, turning around three times, before lying down in a small white circle with her back toward her.

Connelly liked Mrs. Bagleresi, but it annoyed her how the old woman would lean back her head and laugh at the television. She didn't think the program was funny at all, but Mrs. Bagleresi did, and she would lean back her head and laugh, with the skin on her neck jiggling like a turkey neck, and bounce Fifi on her lap.

When she grew tired of watching Mrs. Bagleresi's neck, she always went out on the balcony. She loved it there because they didn't have a balcony at their own apartment, and Mrs. Bagleresi kept all her plants there. It was like a cool dark jungle, sitting there, surrounded by the big leafy plants, and reading.

"Good-bye, Mrs. Bagleresi," she said each afternoon, taking her mommy's hand.

"Good-bye, Connelly. Good-bye, Eric," Mrs. Bagleresi would say, standing in the doorway, watching them walk to the elevator.

"Eric," she said now, looking over at him. "Are you all right?"

He still didn't answer her.

She sighed and lay back again, staring at the ceiling, thinking of...*them*. Her mother was a research assistant and worked in a laboratory. Sometimes she wore a white smock to work. Her father was a graphic artist. He did advertising and showed her pictures in magazines. One was a pretty lady standing there, wearing nothing but high heels and a long silver fur wrapped around her, and holding up a funny glass her father called a martini glass. That was advertising.

At home on weekends her father made paintings he called abstract. She loved sitting in the living room, holding Priscilla in her lap, and watching him paint wonderful, colorful things that made no sense to her.

One time she asked him, "Why don't you paint a cow?"

"A *cow?*" he said in that surprised, teasing voice he used sometimes. "Why a cow?"

"Because I like them."

"A *cow?*" he said, shaking his head as if he couldn't quite believe her.

But hardly a week later she woke up one morning, and on the wall across from her bed was a beautiful painting of a big red cow, staring back at her with grass sticking out its mouth. That was also magic (even though she knew perfectly well her father had painted it and put it there during the night); and she had lay there, snuggling Priscilla in her arms, looking at that cow looking back at her, and sighed contentedly.

Now she shut her eyes, but when she opened them there was only Melissa's ugly ceiling instead. She looked away and thought how sometimes her mother and father gathered up some of her father's paintings, put them in the trunk of their car, and drove down the coast to the weekend art shows. They always left early in the morning and came home in the evening, and she and Eric had to stay with Mrs. Bagleresi the entire day. She didn't like that, but Mrs. Bagleresi told them it was good for her parents to get away once in a while.

"It's so hard being a parent," she said. "Even with wonderful children like you." And she patted Fifi on the head, sitting there talking. "Everyone needs to have some enjoyment once in a while."

Still, she didn't like it.

But when they came home on those evenings, it was exciting all over again. If they had sold a painting, they always went down to Fisherman's Wharf or Spaghetti Warehouse for dinner. If they didn't, they went to McDonald's instead. But she would look up and see them there: all fresh and new, surprising her with their warm good presence each and every time…except one.

She heard something and peeked and saw the door to Melissa's office open. There was a man there dressed in a uniform, looking in at them. She couldn't see his face, but she could see his gray shirt and pants; and then he backed out of the room and shut the door back. Now she laid back her head and listened to the silence, and tried to think again about her mother and father. The thing was she didn't really understand that—being dead. Then she remembered Miss Minnie-Pea, her hamster that died last year. She and her father had driven out of the city and buried her in a tiny box in a field somewhere. And she wondered if that was it, if that was all there was to it. She wasn't sure. But before she could think any more about it, she heard something else. She heard the awful choking little sobs beside her—and she reached over and touched Eric's shoulder, but nothing happened. Nothing changed. He just kept crying.

2 ♀ DROP-HOUSE

In the morning Melissa took them to breakfast at McDonald's.

"We're going to have a busy day," she said, smiling across the table from them. "First we have to go over to your apartment and pack you each a suitcase. Then we'll take a drive down to south city. There's someone there you can stay with until we can make better arrangements."

Connelly saw that Eric was not eating his sandwich. He was just sitting there. She took a bite of hers and said, "How long?"

"What, darling?"

Connelly swallowed her bite of biscuit and egg. "How long do we have to stay there?"

Melissa smiled again. "Well, we have to make other arrangements. You see, you have to be assigned a permanent caseworker, and that person will make those arrangements. Then a judge will have to decide what to do about everything else, your estate and everything. It's all very complicated, I'm afraid."

Connelly looked at her, trying to understand. "You're not going to stay with us?"

"Oh no," she said, taking a bite of her own sandwich. "That's not the way it works."

Next, Melissa's cell phone started singing. She quickly set down her sandwich and answered it. "Hey you," she said, wiping her mouth with a napkin, as she turned her head away from them. "Well, I didn't want to wake you." She giggled. "No, this won't take long, just a stop and drop—I should be back before noon." She listened and giggled again. "Okay, that sounds like fun. Yeah, sure." She listened to something else. "You are so awful, Brad. Just *awful.* Okay, later—bye."

She snapped her cell phone shut and looked brightly over at them. "What—not hungry?"

*

That felt most strange of all. Connelly walked slowly through their little apartment and thought how everything looked just like it did the day before, only different now.

"We'll have to hurry," Melissa called from the front room. "We don't want to be late."

Everything *looked* like theirs, it was everything her mother and father had gathered for them; but everything looked so strange now, as if it didn't belong to them anymore. And she kept expecting to look up and see her mother, with her soft pretty brown hair like Eric's, come into the room, reading work papers; or hear her father, whose hair was long and dark like hers, and his funny voice, calling her down the hallway: "Hey, brat, c'mere a minute, will you. Take a look what we found at the flea market today."

"*Daddy,*" she whispered urgently. "*Daddy, where are you?*"

"Hurry, you two," Melissa said.

In her bedroom she put things into the overnight bag Melissa took from the hall closet. When they went somewhere, her mother always packed her things, so she wasn't sure. Finally, Melissa came to help her.

"Plenty of underwear, girl," she said, taking things from her dresser. "These T-shirts are *so* cute."

"My mom bought them for me. We bought them together."

"Well, you have nice stuff," Melissa said. "Your mom's got taste. Unfortunately, we can only take vital necessities."

She didn't know what that meant, but she watched as Melissa held up two pair of her jeans.

"Choose."

She pointed to the pair with the pink flowers around the pocket hems.

Melissa smiled and winked at her. "You got taste too, girl, don't you."

She put the jeans in the suitcase and zipped it closed.

Connelly wished they could stay there for a while. Even though she knew her parents weren't there, she wished they could just stay there, because she felt that was as close as they would ever be to them again. And she didn't want to lose that feeling. She felt like all her feelings, one after the other, were being taken away from her.

"Can't we just stay here for a while, Melissa?"

"Sorry, kiddo, in my business you always have to stay on schedule. I mean, I never know when my cell's gonna ring and I pick up another case, you know?"

No, she didn't know. She wanted to stay there. That was *their* house, *their* home. Why did they have to leave it? It wasn't fair. Nothing seemed fair anymore. *Oh, Daddy, why? Why?*

"Then can I at least take Priscilla?"

"Priscilla?"

She pointed to her doll, lying back against her bed pillows.

"Sure, sweetheart," Melissa said, looking into her eyes.

She went over and picked Priscilla gently up off the bed and held her tightly to her.

"I love the red cow," Melissa told her, looking at the painting on the wall before her bed. She walked over and read at the name in the lower corner: "Michael Pierce." She looked back at her. "You're father's an artist?"

"He was," Connelly replied, holding Priscilla in one arm, as she lifted the overnight bag with her other.

*

THE BEAUTIFUL-UGLY

Driving south through the city, Melissa mostly talked on her cell phone. She talked to her boyfriend, and then she had a conversation with one of her girlfriends, and then her boyfriend called back. It sounded to Connelly like the two of them were planning a picnic that afternoon at Golden Gate Park. Trying to block out all Melissa's talking, which was annoying her, she thought about the picnics *they* had had—at the park, at the ocean, or at nowhere at all; that is, her mommy would pack their picnic lunch in the big straw basket with the leather straps, and they would drive someplace. It didn't matter. There was no place special they were going. They would just drive until they saw a nice place to stop: at a roadside picnic table or a big field or, once, under a bridge.

"Oh, Daddy, let's eat under that bridge!" she had called out from the back seat.

"Okay," he said, looking for a place to pull off the road.

"Michael, are you sure?" her mommy said, who always had a practical mind, according to her daddy.

It was somewhere in the country, along a narrow twisting road. And there were big trees that ran alongside the creek that flowed under the bridge. They found a path down to the water, and there was a small square of sand there her mommy spread the blanket. The sun was hot that day, but it was dark and cool under the bridge, and they sat there, eating and talking and watching the water go by.

After they ate, Eric and her mother went to make a specimen list, while she and her father took a nap.

"We'll let the two brains go count tadpoles, brat," her father said, stretching out on the blanket. "Meanwhile, we'll count the little black sheep jumping inside our eyelids."

"Oh, Daddy," she said, snuggling against him. And she listened to his breathing against her ear growing deep and steady, until she knew he was sleeping. Once, she heard his stomach growl, and she giggled. Then she slept.

"*Shit,*" Melissa said, taking another call. "Yes, Harold." She listened, and then she said, "Can't Jody take this one?" She listened again. "All right, if that's all it is, but I'm blocking your calls until, at least, Wednesday. Yes, I love you too, Harold. Bye." And she snapped her cell phone shut and looked at them in the rearview mirror. "Sometimes this job can be a real pain, you know?"

*

It was a small brick house in the middle of other small houses, she saw. Children were running and riding bicycles back and forth, everywhere, chased by dogs and other children. There were old cars and old boats in the driveways and between the houses and on the street. Some of the cars were in pieces, left open and raised into the air on big pieces of wood under the front tires. Things seemed piled about, things scattered. There didn't seem to be any order here like she was used to. Like the city. Everything was just piled and scattered and moving about this way and that, as if a big wind had blown it and left it there, all broken and dirty and dizzily spinning, before moving on.

"I tried to get you someplace else," Melissa said, pulling her car to the curb and stopping. She turned and looked back at them sitting there. "But there wasn't a thing. The Johnsons are my go-to when all else fails. They're a little rough around the edges, but it's just until I can find something better. I'm contacting some children's homes in the morning, I promise." And she tried to smile again, but didn't quite make it.

Connelly wanted to ask her why they had to stay there, at that horrible place, but she knew what Melissa would say. She looked over at Eric who was staring out his little window, not saying a word. She knew what his face looked like without even seeing it. She knew how he didn't like things to be different. He didn't like things to change. Everything in his bedroom was exactly in order: his toy models, and his little science trophies from school, and his books; he always drank a glass of milk at dinner, even if they had strawberry soda; and he always watched the same programs on TV, usually science programs, even if he'd seen them before. He and their mother sometimes watched them together, sitting perfectly still, side by side, never changing the channel, and then talking about them when the program ended. She and her father, meanwhile, would pop popcorn in a big bowl and lie together on the couch, jumping from one channel to the next, until they saw something they liked. And they would whisper things together, making jokes about something on TV, or about nothing at all, just making each other giggle, and eating the popcorn and getting bored with whatever was on, and changing the channel again.

"Okay then," Melissa said, "let's go inside."

They walked up the sidewalk to the front door. The sidewalk was broken, Connelly saw, and the grass beside it had holes dug in it. There were other children watching them from the next house. Two boys and a girl stood there, eating purple popsicles, and watching them. She saw the melted purple lines running down their raised, dirty arms, and she looked away.

A woman was at the door. She was a big woman with funny, frizzled-looking hair, and wore a big flowered dress that looked like a sack dropped down over her, and she wore flip-flops on her feet. She was smoking a cigarette, standing there.

"Hey, Melissa," she called out.

"Hey, Eunice," Melissa answered her. "I've brought you two more."

"I see that. Well, that's all right, you know I always got room for more."

"Well, you don't know how grateful I am," said Melissa.

Connelly was afraid to look at anything, going past the big woman, into the dark house. Inside, she stood there, looking down at the floor, wishing she and Eric could be almost anywhere else. She sniffed and knew she didn't like what she smelled. It smelled dusty and smoky there; it smelled like things had been burned there, food and things she couldn't recognize. While Melissa and Eunice were talking, her eyes began to adjust to the dark room. It was a small room with an old couch and stuffed chairs. In one of the chairs, in the corner, she saw a man sitting, looking at her. She looked away, back at the floor, and sighed.

Melissa knelt in front of them. "Okay, you two behave yourselves now. Like I told you, in the morning I'll make some calls and see who has beds open. In the meantime, the Johnsons will watch you."

Then she hugged them both and went out the door, closing it behind her.

Eunice sat down on the couch and spread out her dress on both sides of her. She said, "After I've finished my cigarette I'll show you where you'll sleep tonight." She smoked it and rubbed one hand up and down her other arm as if she were petting herself. "Connelly, you'll sleep in the girls' room, and Eric will sleep with the boys." She smoked again, looking over at her. "How old are you, baby?"

"Six."

"What about you, Eric?"

"Nine."

Connelly knew that was Eric's voice when he didn't want to talk.

"You're a little fellow," Eunice said. "Ain't he little, Arthur?"

The man in the corner grunted.

They both stood there, not knowing what to do.

Eunice said, "You're a real little beauty, girl. Got black hair like a horse's tail. Ain't she pretty, Arthur?"

The man grunted again.

Finally Eunice was through with her cigarette and showed them where they would sleep. She and Eric walked behind her, watching her entire body sway back and forth, moving down the hall.

The house smelled all the same, and it was messy. Their mother would never have let them stay in such a messy, smelly house.

After they put away their backpacks, Eric asked Eunice, "Can we go sit outside?"

"Sure," she said, lighting another cigarette. "Just don't wander off somewhere."

The two of them went outside and sat down on the concrete step. She held Priscilla and watched the children playing loudly in the distance, while Eric stared down at the ground.

"What's gonna happen now, Eric?" she asked him.

He shrugged. "I don't know."

"Then how long do we have to stay here?"

He shrugged again, saying nothing.

"Do you think long?" she asked. "Like a whole year long?"

"I don't know, I told you. I don't know anything about it. So stop asking me, okay?"

She just sat there then, not saying a word about it.

Finally Eric shifted beside her. "I just want to wake up, Con," he said to her, his voice sounding different than she had ever hear it. "I just want to wake up and start everything all over again."

*

There were others there. Connelly was surprised to discover that—other children, like themselves, with no place else to go. There were at least six or eight who seemed to appear out of nowhere when Eunice stood there, smoking and stirring something in a pot for dinner. And she grew dizzy with Eunice calling out their names, telling them to do this or that, and no one paying attention to her.

"She ain't my mama," said one little black boy named Myron, until Eunice threatened him with nothing to eat, and he went off to do what he was told.

Somehow Connelly found herself separated from Eric, and pulled down the hallway, and into the bedroom with some of the other girls, who questioned her. They seemed surprised that both her parents had died together. Listening to them talking, she realized most or all of them still had parents alive, but for some reason they couldn't be with them now. These girls were different from any girls she had ever been around. The way they talked, the way they acted—she had never imagined children could be that way. And she knew her parents would never have allowed that, seeing, hearing everything happening around her all at once.

"You had your own *bedroom?*" A girl named Maria seemed angry and excited at the same time. "Shit, I ain't never had my own bedroom."

Another girl said, "Well, she won't have her own bedroom anymore. We got four beds in this one, and you got to sleep with Cecelia—she a bed-wetter."

All the girls laughed.

"What your daddy do?" Maria confronted her again.

"What he did," another girl corrected her.

"He was a graphic artist and a painter. And my mother worked in a laboratory."

"A what?" someone said.

"She a real princess, ain't she," said a girl who sat smoking before the window she had pried open.

"Not any more she ain't," someone said.

Two of the girls started fighting, pushing each other and saying bad words, about something she couldn't understand. That seemed to divert everyone's attention, for the moment, away from her. She heard Eunice screaming down the hallway for them to come eat. Another girl came into the room and asked if she could hold Priscilla. Everything seemed suddenly to be in movement around her, but none of it made any sense; everyone seemed to be going from one thing to the next without any thought or purpose. She thought of her home again (actually, she had never ever stopped thinking about it): the way the four of them were together, doing the things they did together, the things they loved.

Everyone was rushing out of the room now, leaving her behind. She stood there, looking down at Priscilla where she had been thrown. One of her arms was torn from her and laid a little ways above her head, as if she was reaching for something she couldn't see.

A noise. She turned, and Eric stood in the doorway, looking at her and then her doll. He went over to the bed and picked Priscilla and her dangling arm up, guiding the arm back into the hole, before handing her back. And Connelly held her closely to her.

*

Later that night, after the awful din that was their supper, and the even worse din that followed until bedtime, she crept out of her bed before Cecelia could pee on her, and down the hallway to the front room. There, to her amazement, Eric was asleep on the couch, rolled up inside a blanket, and using a dirty cushion for a pillow.

She made him move over and got inside the blanket with him, snuggling against him. She wanted to talk with him, ask him questions about what was going to happen to them now, but she didn't. She knew he was upset, and he was probably tired from being upset, and so she lay there quietly against him, feeling him warm against her, and remembering how, evenings, the four of them sat around the table, talking and laughing, and eating their dinner. Then, while her mother did the dishes, her father held her in his lap, and helped Eric with his homework. When her mother joined them they sat there talking, or sometimes watching something on television until bedtime.

Then she brushed her teeth and put on her pajamas and someone would read to her. When her mother read, she always read exactly what was there, saying everything exactly, not changing a word. But her father made things up, pretending to read the story, while making up a different story, sometimes funny, and sometimes scary, which she loved the most.

Then when her mother caught him, she would said, "Darling, you're going to give her nightmares again. Let's just stay with the program, okay?"

Then he would wink at her and began reading the book again, just like he was supposed to, except now with a sad face and a funny voice, talking very slowly and sadly, making her giggle still.

Finally, alone, she would stare at her Littlest Mermaid nightlight and think about different things, until she fell asleep. She always tried to catch herself doing that—falling asleep—but she never could. She would wait and wait, hoping she could see what it was like, really like…falling asleep…

Until suddenly it was morning again, with the gray light filtering through the dingy curtains, revealing the floating particles of air-dust. Now she lay there beside her brother, seeing the unfamiliar room, feeling everything around her unfamiliar now, and wondering all over again what had happened to them.

3 ♀ SAYING GOOD BYE

The day they buried their parents, Melissa came early in the morning with their good clothes from the apartment. She brought Eric's dark-blue suit, and her satin gray dress with the tiny red ribbons she wore with her mother to Mass, and, once, when her father got an award for something.

"Your parents have very nice friends," Melissa said, driving there. "Apparently, once they found there were no close relatives, everyone got together and arranged things, the burial and things. People have even called me about taking you in, but all that has to be arranged through the courts. You're both wards of the court now. That means the court will decide what to do with you."

Connelly was sitting beside Melissa, and looked over at her, and then back at Eric. He was looking out the window, and she could see the corner of his right eye where a boy had hit him, breaking his good glasses and bruising his cheek. After that happened, Eric had just looked at the boy, and then turned around and walked away. The others had teased him for being afraid. But she knew he wasn't afraid. He just didn't like to fight. He was quiet, like their mother, but he wasn't afraid. In fact, she thought he was very brave sometimes.

"I talked with the police detective," Melissa said. "They've gone through your parents' papers and talked with their attorney; it looks like they died intestate, or without a will, or any instructions for anything. Not that that matters to the courts, but it would still make things easier." She hesitated and then said, "Anyway, there doesn't appear to be much of an estate."

"What's that?" Connelly asked her.

Melissa smiled at her. "Your parents were very young and very much in love, but it seems they didn't have much else. Not even life insurance. Of course, that's pretty normal, I'm afraid. When you're just starting out, starting a family and having a career, you don't think about that, people don't. They think they'll live a long time, I guess."

She didn't understand any of that. She thought: *Our apartment in San Francisco is very small, and we are very happy.* She had written that for Mrs. Dougherty and got an A, and they had pizza that night to celebrate.

"Eric, wasn't your mother twenty-nine?" Melissa asked him.

"Yes ma'am."

"And how old was your father?"

Connelly saw him look quickly down at his hands, and back out the window. "Thirty."

She remembered her father's birthday party, not long before. Her mother baked him a pink cake, which sagged on one side, with strawberries and blue candles on top. "Okay, kids," she said, smiling, setting down the cake on their dinner table, "your daddy's officially an old man now."

Their father winked at them and said, "That's all right, darling. You'll be an old woman soon. Your birthday's right around the corner."

"Not me, sweetie" her mother teased him back. "I'm stopping the clock *before* my birthday."

Then they sang *Happy Birthday* to him, and her parents had kissed right beside her, and she thought about that now—their kiss, and how it looked with their lips together, and not wanting to separate.

"Just remember," Melissa interrupted her thoughts, "people might say things to you, make promises to you about taking you in, and wanting to take care of you." She shook her head. "I wouldn't pay too much attention to things like that. Grownups are just like kids. They say things all the time they don't really mean."

*

She didn't cry when she entered the big church and saw her mommy and daddy there, or, rather, saw their closed coffins there, side by side. Melissa had already told them: "When the other car hit their car, there was a fire. Still, they'll be right there with you, won't they?" And they were. She didn't cry when she and Eric held hands and walked down the aisle toward them. In fact, she felt almost happy, seeing them there. Oh—*there* you are! She wanted to tell them. You've been hiding from us, and now we've found you both! Almost happy, having them so near again.

She stood there, holding Eric's hand, staring at her mother's photograph on top of the coffin, and then at her father's. Between the coffins was another picture of them together. She knew that was their wedding picture that her mother had hanging on the wall in their bedroom. She wondered who had taken it down; then she remembered walking through their apartment, and how it felt knowing they were not there, and they would never be there again. She remembered that, and pulled her hand free from Eric's hand, and stepped forward, slowly, carefully, and touched the hard edge of one of the coffins, and then the other. She heard the music playing somewhere. It was such strange music, oddly slow and sad; not at all like the music her parents listened to: her father's jazz, or her mother's classical.

"Can't we agree on anything?" she remembered her father teased her mother once.

"Well, I don't know how this whole thing happened," her mother answered him. "This whole marriage thing. We have no points of commonality. You must have fixed my drink or something."

"Oh, we have points," her father said, smiling.

And the way he came behind her then, when he touched just the tiny point of her elbow, making her mother shiver.

*

She watched the other people crying and laughing. She sat there, leaning against Eric, and listened to them talking. She knew some of them—friends of their parents, people they worked with, that came to their house sometimes. Some she had never seen before: "I'll never forget the time Michael and Emily drove up to the Valley of the Moon with us, and we stopped at that winery near Jack London's Wolf House…"

When everyone was through talking, Melissa drove them to the cemetery, behind the two long black cars that carried her parents. At the gravesides, while the priest talked some more and read from his Bible, Connelly thought about what the two of them would think about this. Her mother would have cried, like she always cried at the movies. Her father would have made a joke about it. Her mother was a serious Catholic, her father always said, a Catholic scientist. Her father wasn't serious about much at all.

"I think it's all a setup, brat," he said to her once, as they lay on the living room carpet, looking through magazines, and just talking about things. "I think everything they give you coming out the chute you got to give back when it's over."

She still wasn't sure what he meant by that.

All she knew was that (like Melissa and Eric told her might happen) three different people, at three different moments, pulled them aside and whispered to them they wanted to do something for them, they were looking into that. They would soon come see them. And the way they looked at them, at her and Eric, with their smiling, sad faces.

Then everyone got into their different cars and drove away.

*

A few days after the funeral, Melissa came and took them to another place. Connelly was glad to go, even though she and the girl named Maria had become sort of friends; that is, Maria, who was ten, let her hang around her sometimes, and they talked about things.

"Little girl, you a *real* orphan," Maria told her. "The rest of us here got at least one mommy or daddy, but you got *both* dead; so you need to watch out for your *own* self, you understand me?"

Connelly nodded, trying to pat down Priscilla's hair, which was beginning to get all tangled up in her new life. Her own hair, in fact, was getting tangled, as no one had combed it since the funeral, until Maria said, "C'mere, girl." She took out her own comb, and sat behind her, combing it out.

"You got you some pretty hair, girl," Maria said, combing. "You could be in one of them hair commercials on TV—you cute as anything, and got long wavy hair like this—*mmmm, mmmm.*"

"Is your mother alive?" Connelly asked her.

"Oh—she alive all right."

Connelly hesitated. "Then why don't you live with her?"

"'Cause she a crack-head like her no good boyfriend. And he don't wanna do nothing but get inside my drawers."

She didn't understand any of this. "What about your father?"

"He in the same place your mommy and daddy is, 'cept he been there a lot longer. That man was shot to death when I was two."

"Oh," she said, unsure.

She heard Maria sigh, as she worked on untangling a tangle. "Girl, you sure you ain't got no aunt or uncle or no cousin even?"

"Just my Uncle Boyd in the merchant marines. But he lives on ships."

"That's a damn shame. But that's all right, little doll face like you, some rich white folk gonna snap you up quick."

"What do you mean?"

"Adoption, girl—don't you know nothin' about adoption?"

"A little, I guess." She was learning about that, and about something called fostering, listening to Melissa.

"Well, that's when some nice family come along and decide they want to take you in. And they go to the judge, and then he signs a paper, and you in a new family then."

"But, Maria, I want my old family back," she said, swallowing, feeling the sudden ache rise up inside her again. "I want it like it was before."

"Shit," Maria said. "Then you better start having a conversation with Jesus. He about the only one that can do something like that. You believe in Jesus, girl?"

She told her she thought she did.

*

On the day Melissa came and took them away, they had visited their apartment one last time. When they arrived, Connelly was surprised to see men taking away all their things. She and Eric stood to one side and watched them carry away their sofa, and their table and chairs, and then her mother's favorite stuffed chair she always sat in, making notes on her work papers with her blue pencil, or typing something on her laptop. She saw Melissa talking to one of the men, and then she came over by them.

"Melissa, what are they *doing?*" she asked.

"Well, Connelly, they have to clear out the apartment so someone else can live here."

The three of them stood there watching.

Eric said, "Where are they taking it?"

Melissa looked back at him. "They'll probably store it for a while. Then a judge will have them sell everything and pay off any bills, or expenses, or whatever. Then, if there's anything left, they'll put that into a trust for you and your sister, until you're both eighteen."

"Everything?" Connelly asked, not wanting to believe it.

Melissa nodded and said, "I told the supervisor we needed to get some more of your clothes. But we'll have to use garbage bags to put them in, because they've already taken the suitcases. And we'll have to hurry. There's a painting crew arriving as soon as the movers are gone."

THE BEAUTIFUL-UGLY

It was all very frightening and confusing to her, and it was all happening so fast. Melissa gave each of them a garbage bag from the kitchen and told them again they must hurry. When she was walking down the hallway to her bedroom, a man passed her carrying her red cow painting.

She stopped and watched him carry it down the hall.

"Hurry, Con!" Melissa called out to her, before taking another cell call.

She sighed and went into her bedroom, which, she discovered, was torn apart as well. Her clothes were piled in one corner, and she saw her bed was already gone, and a man was pulling the drawers from her dresser to take it. Hurryingly, she ran over to him. In the top drawer, sitting now on the floor, she saw the gold locket and chain, with the tiny key inside that her parents told her was the key to their hearts. They had given it to her on her fifth birthday. And when she grabbed it up, the man looked at her and smiled. Then she turned away and went slowly back to the corner where her clothes were piled, and began putting what she could carry into the garbage bag.

Afterward, she met Eric in the hallway.

She said, "Did you get anything?"

He held out the small gold medal, attached to the blue ribbon, he'd won at the science fair.

"What about you?"

She held out her hand, showing him her chain and locket, and he nodded.

Then Melissa came and told them they had to get out now, because the painters were already there.

4 ♀ PILGRIMS MERCY

*L*ying *there day after day, seeing them come and go from her room, asking her the same questions she never would answer, she began to put together her own process of evaluation, her own cognitive behavioral therapy (as she had learned from them). Analyzing the tortuous pattern of her thoughts about who she was, or had become, and the world, or worlds, she had inhabited. Still did. It wasn't easy. It wasn't really something she wanted to attempt. But her mind was so jangled and torn she was terrified of what would happen next, if she didn't do something. And so it came—at first, in jarring splashes of time-dulled memory and fresh-hot, stabbing pain, all mixed together. Starting with the unconscionable fact that it had happened at all.*

Who decides that? How is anything like that decided? You have all the life in the world right there in your very hands, and the next instant it's gone. It's taken, or smashed, or ripped apart and thrown into that crazy-terrible wind and scattered into the nothingness of time and space, as if you never existed to begin with. That is, except for those still alive and bearing the burden of your memory. Because it wasn't nice. Remembering who they were and what she had once but didn't any longer wasn't nice at all. It was the cruelest thing imaginable, asking someone to do that. Remembering. Going on with your life, and remembering, and knowing you'll never know why. The cruelest thing.

Then all of a sudden, when you're still so young and barely able to peek over the kitchen counter, you're given a blank slate. That is, concerning your own life now. So forget everything that happened before. Everything. That doesn't matter now. Never did. So forget it. Wipe it clean from your mind like the blank slate you're now holding and start over. Don't worry about it. And don't ask any questions. Just do it. You're nothing now but a goddamned burden to everyone else, anyway, so just do it and don't complain. Besides, you need a platform to complain—called a family—which you no longer have. Perhaps never did. So just shut the fuck up, Connelly Pierce, and go with the flow, okay? Just write down what we tell you on the slate and don't worry about it, okay? There you are. There you go. You're learning now. You're doing better, aren't you?

So you see this is all about altering those unwanted behavior patterns you've developed along the way, those terrible mood swings you're subject to. And after everything we've given you. Why, you should be as grateful as any starving dog given its bone, or pitiful, fur-mangled cat rescued from its tormentors. You should. Damn you, you should, as Richard would say. Instead, look what you've gone and done to yourself. What would your mother think? Your father? Your over-the-edge, fucked-up brother? Oh, that's right. I forgot. Sorry. Still, you've made a mess of it, and you don't have anyone to blame but yourself. And now that I think of it, maybe those behavior patterns, those mood swings, aren't so far-fetched after all. Maybe they're right in line with everything else scratched right there on that slate, for the whole wide world to see. To know what you've done. After all those lovely roads you've been down, all those wonderful choices you've made, and now this. Now this...

That day, they drove a long way before they stopped. It was while they were driving that Melissa told them another woman had been assigned to their case. She reminded them that she was normally only an investigative caseworker; she started the ball rolling, she said, and then a conservatorship caseworker was assigned to handle them. But she told them not to worry, that whoever had them would take good care of them, and make sure everything went all right. This was just the way the system was set up.

"And like it or not," she said, "you're both in the system now."

Connelly didn't care. No, that wasn't true, she thought, looking out her window, she *did* care. She liked Melissa a lot, and Eric liked her too. And they didn't want to go with anyone else. They wanted her to stay with them, that's all. They wanted things to stop changing for them, even for a moment. Everything was changing now, so fast, every day, every minute it was different, and they never knew what to expect next. Besides her mother and father being dead, that was the hardest thing. There was nothing they could depend on now, even little things, like what bed they would wake up in, or where they would brush their teeth next. It was all moving so fast, and she didn't see why it had to be that way; but she knew it wouldn't do any good to complain to Melissa. Eric knew that too. They just had to be quiet and do what strangers told them to do, because there was nothing else they *could* do. And she wanted to cry again, thinking about Melissa leaving them. But she knew if she cried every time something happened now she didn't want to happen, she would be crying all the time. Anyway, she was becoming tired with that, like Eric said he was, just tired crying herself to sleep at night, sleeping out on the Johnsons' dirty, smelly sofa, or listening to him crying in the dark beside her. So she sat there and stared silently out the window, watching everything pass by, and didn't tell Melissa at all what she was really thinking: *Please, please, don't leave us again.*

They were in farm country now: flat and open. They stopped at a little restaurant beside the road and Melissa fed them lunch. Eric had a hamburger. He was beginning to eat again; at least, a little, Connelly noticed. She had half a tuna sandwich and a Coke and listened to Melissa talking with Brad on her cell. Oh, *Brad!* Oh—you're just so *awful,* saying that! And she rolled her eyes, listening, and ate a French fry. She wondered if the food would be any better at the new place than at the Johnsons, which really had been just *awful.* She hoped it would.

In the afternoon there was a little town called Rio Valero they drove through, small and dusty and hot-looking in the sun. Not far beyond the town, Melissa turned off the road, and they drove down a gravel road, passing under a big sign that stretched over the road, and read: Pilgrims Mercy, California State Children's Home.

"Well, we're here," Melissa said, trying to sound happy.

There was an island of shade trees, Connelly saw in the distance, surrounded by endless fields and pastures. It was a small farm. They drove slowly up the crunching gravel driveway, past a pasture with several cows in it. One of the cows, the black and white one, raised its head and stared suspiciously at her as she went past. Next they passed a big white barn with the doors open like a big mouth, yawning. She saw two men inside, working on a tractor. The driveway made a circle before a two-story white wooden house, surrounded by white cottages. Melissa stopped the car before the house.

A young woman in khakis and a white blouse and sandals came down the steps, holding a clipboard. She waved, smiling, and said, "Hey, you, I've been worried."

"We swung by their apartment for more clothes," Melissa said, getting out of the car. Connelly looked back at Eric, exchanging glances, and then they got out as well. Melissa and the woman were hugging and talking, and then they both turned to them.

"Anne Wright, this is Eric and Connelly Pierce," Melissa said.

"Well, hello there," she said, shaking each of their hands. "We're so glad you've come to stay with us for a while. I'm one of the residents here. That means I'm here to get you settled in, and make sure everything goes okay for you. Connelly, I'm actually your First Resident; so we'll be seeing a lot of each other. Eric, you'll be assigned one of the men residents—I think, Joe Hardy. He's pretty cool. He used to work in a circus before he went back to school and finished his degree."

She stopped now, looking into both their eyes. Connelly was starting to get used to that. To strangers looking like that into her eyes, as if expecting something from her, which she could never understand. She stood there, waiting.

"So," said Ann, "are we ready to go inside?"

The four of them carried backpacks and garbage bags up the steps into the house. They entered a large round room, with a high ceiling, and an old iron-hoop chandelier hanging down in its center.

Below the fixture was a seating area—couches and stuffed chairs, facing each other around an enormous round wooden table that looked to Connelly like one of her mother's thread spools. Along the left wall, a curving staircase ascended to the second floor, where the edges of other doorways could be seen.

Anne said, "This is our great room where everyone sort of meets and greets, and we just hang out sometimes."

Connelly sat with Eric on one of the couches, while Anne and Melissa went into another room that, she saw, looked like an office, and shut the door. Occasionally, sitting there, they saw people pass by and look at them. Two residents, a man and a woman in the same khakis and white shirts Anne wore, passed by, smiling at them, and disappeared down a hallway. An older woman, plump and nervous in a white uniform and cap, came past them, smiling and saying, "Hello, children." And they told her hello back as she went on. Then a short, squat, black man, with a towel hanging around his neck, passed by, pushing a mop bucket forward by the mop handle he was leaning on, humming a song. He had bright brown eyes that made him look ready to smile, and he stopped before them, just beyond the intimate seating area, and stared suspiciously at them. Then he chuckled and said in a low deep voice that sounded to her like her feet when she scuffed them over gravel: "Hey there, lil' pilgrims, what you two got to say for yourselves?"

When they both just stared at him, unsure what they did have to say, he chuckled again, shaking his head, and continued on past them out of the room.

Finally, a girl passed them carrying a basket of folded clothes, and Connelly held her breath. The girl did not really look at them, going by—just a glance—but that was enough. In that instant Connelly saw something in her delicate, white face, her dark eyes like two pieces of round, bruised fruit, she had never seen before. She felt something inside herself, seeing her pass by, she had no idea what. But all the feelings of things good and warm and safe and familiar she had known growing up with her family seemed to disappear inside her at that moment. It was like a faint cold breeze came and pushed them away into some deeper, darker place where she could not get to them now. Could not reach them. Now she felt oddly cold and uneasy, sitting there, watching the girl go up the stairs, where she stopped near the top and looked back down at her; and they stared into each other's eyes, before she turned away, and went on again out of sight.

"Eric," she whispered and stopped.

"What?"

The office door opened and Melissa and Anne came out.

She shook her head. "Nothing."

Anne took both her and Eric's pictures from the front, and then had them turn one way, and then the other. "We'll attach these to the computer files we'll build for you," she explained. "Then, depending on how long you're here, we'll take new ones every six months or so, because you guys change so darn fast."

Connelly hardly heard what she said, still thinking about that girl.

Melissa came and knelt before them. "Okay, you two, this is it for us, I'm afraid." She stopped and wiped away a tear rolling down her face. "Here, give me a hug and I'm outta here." They both hugged her, and she looked at them again. "You know, sometimes you meet someone special, in special circumstances, and it's very hard. It's harder than usual, you know." She shook her head, then got up and went quickly across the floor and out the front door, closing it behind her, leaving them.

"Okay then," Connelly barely heard Anne say. "So why don't we assign you a bed, clothes drawer, and some closet space; then I'll help you put away your things, before the school buses get here and our afternoon onslaught begins."

*

Anne told her there were eighty-six children at the home, counting her and Eric, but that number changed almost daily, depending on who came and went.

"We're like one enormous, unfixed family," she said, "always changing, never the same. It's something else you'll have to get used to."

There were five boys' cottages on one side of the main house, and five girls' cottages on the other side. Each cottage had eight beds, and Anne assigned her to Cottage Six, Bed Eight, upon which she was sitting alone, holding Priscilla and looking around at stuffed animals atop pillows, and celebrity posters adorning walls, that first afternoon the other girls came storming through the door before her, talking and tiredly fussing, throwing down their green, Pilgrims Mercy backpacks on their beds, with one or two glaring suspiciously toward her, another glancing indifferently her direction and away, the rest seeming not to notice her at all.

Fortunately Anne came through the door behind the girls, making them go sit on their respective beds, quieting them. As Anne introduced them, Connelly saw they were almost all older than her. Names flew in one ear and out the other, as Anne stood in the center of the room, pointing: "Kathy, Julie, Maribel, Martha, Yolanda, Camerina and Beatrice. And, everyone, this is Connelly Pierce from San Francisco. This is her first…outside home, so I want everyone to behave themselves and help her get settled in."

Everyone stared at her now, as if they expected something from her, or was slightly angry by her sudden presence among them.

"All right then," Anne said, "now let's get settled ourselves, and get that homework done. And those of you on duty roster, make sure you're on time, or it's five points."

One of the girls groaned and fell back on the bed.

Anne looked over at her. "Camerina, how many points do you need for a mall run?"

"Ten," said the girl glumly, staring at the ceiling.

"Then I suggest you make a little better effort than you've been making."

"Yeah, Camerina," said another girl, who Connelly saw was very fat, and had the bed next to hers.

"Beatrice," Anna said, now looking at her, "you've got that history makeup tomorrow, so I suggest you buckle down as well."

The other girls laughed.

Now Anne came over and knelt before her. "Well, Connelly, I'm one of the early birds tomorrow, so I'm going home now."

Connelly looked back into her eyes. "You don't live here?"

"No, I live in Fresno. That's about a half hour from here."

"Oh," she said.

Now Anne squeezed her smaller hand inside her own, and suddenly Connelly recalled the moment Melissa had also squeezed her hands, telling her both her parents had been killed. Then something else flashed inside her mind, and she could see the shadowy policemen milling about Mrs. Bagleresi's living room through the balcony door. "Tomorrow," Anne was saying. "Tomorrow we'll get you registered in school, okay?"

She nodded.

As soon as Anne was gone, some of the girls fell back on their beds, complaining about this or that; others began milling about the room. One girl ran to the bathroom, saying, "I've *so* got to pee." Everyone was occupied and had already forgotten her.

After a while Beatrice looked over at her from her bed. "That's sure a pretty blouse you got on. Can I wear it sometimes?"

Connelly saw she was much too large to fit inside her blouse, but she said, "I guess."

Beatrice smiled and then asked if she could hold Priscilla.

"I don't think so," Connelly told her, remembering the girl that tore out Priscilla's arm when she held her. "She doesn't like anyone else to hold her."

Beatrice looked at her, still smiling. "But she's just a fucking doll," she said. "She doesn't know who's holding her."

Then she turned away from her, opening up her backpack and removing books. "Selfish little *bitch*," Connelly heard her say.

Another girl came and sat down beside her, hugging her. It was the black girl named Yolanda. She was also big like Beatrice, although she wasn't fat. And she had her hair twisted into pigtails and said, "Oh, little biscuit, don't you mind Miss Bea—she always trying to push everyone, trying to see how far she can go."

"Go to hell, Yolanda," said Beatrice, with her back humped, and pretending to read her schoolbook.

Yolanda laughed and looked at her, playfully squinting her eyes. "It ain't so bad here, long as you mind the rules. You see, they give you fifty points when you get here, and that goes into what they call your bank account. Then when you obey the rules and do things right they give you more points, and when you don't they take them away."

"What are points?" she asked.

"Points like money or privileges," said Yolanda. "You want to watch TV or go to the movie or do the mall run to Fresno on Saturdays, you got to give up points."

"You ain't got the points, you don't make the run," another girl said, whose name she couldn't remember.

At dinnertime, she went with her cottage group over to the dining and recreational hall behind the main house. Yolanda showed her how to get her tray and go down the food line, where she watched the two chatty ladies there plop a scoop of mashed potatoes, a spoon of string beans, a piece of chicken, and a Jell-O cup on her plate.

"That's our table over there," Yolanda told her.

She started to follow her over there when she saw Eric across the room, sitting at another table, and went there instead.

All the boys at the table looked up at her, standing there, holding her tray.

"What are you doing, Con?" Eric asked.

"Can't I sit beside you?"

"No, you have to go back."

She saw some of the boys laughing and whispering to each other.

One of the men residents came over to her. "Young lady, you need to go back to your table."

Eric motioned his head for her to leave, and finally she did, walking slowly back to her own table.

"Where you off to, little biscuit?" Yolanda asked her. "Didn't I tell you the group got to hang?"

"Dummy," Beatrice said. "Boys and girls can't sit together; it's not allowed."

"But he's my brother," she explained.

"Doesn't matter," Beatrice said, "there're rules we have to obey. Don't you know about rules?"

Of course she knew about rules, but she still didn't see why she couldn't sit beside Eric. He was all she had left from her family, and now they had to eat apart. It wasn't fair. But then nothing seemed fair anymore, and so she sat down in her chair and began to eat. The food was a little better than the Johnsons', but not as good as her mother's. She thought about her mother's stuffed meatballs and mushroom sauce and wanted to cry, sitting there, eating two or three bites of her pasty potatoes. Next, she took a bite of her chicken, but it was dry; so she ate her string beans instead, before pushing away her plate.

"Can I have your chicken?" Beatrice asked her, and she nodded.

Beatrice's big hand came swooshing past her, and the piece of chicken disappeared.

Now, slowly, sadly, she ate her Jell-O cup, and was little comforted that was still the same. It tasted like her mother's Jell-O, except there were no peaches. And she thought she would have given anything in the world at that moment to find a slice of cold sweet peach, hidden inside, she could mash between her teeth and tongue.

*

Yolanda explained to her that after dinner was free time until nine, when everyone had to be back in their cottages for the count. "You want to be with your brother, you better go do it now. But make sure you're back on time. The night res'll be by with her clipboard and take away points if you're late."

She had decided she hated points, she thought as she went looking for Eric. They could have all her points—she didn't care.

When she found him, they wandered about until they found a bench beneath an old crooked shade tree, farthest away from everyone else they could find, and sat there reading the small brass plate on the upper slat: *This bench has been donated to the Pilgrims Mercy State Children's Home by their friends at Fiesta Markets in Fresno, California. It was made from over 5,000 recycled Fiesta plastic shopping bags to help save our environment. We hope it also helps make your life a little easier.*

"What's your cottage like?" she asked him.

"Same as yours, I guess."

"What about the other boys, Eric? Are they nice?"

He didn't want to talk about it.

They sat there listening to the surrounding noises. She heard a train horn somewhere and people talking and someone playing hip-hop music, which she was starting to like.

She looked at her brother. "Do you think we'll ever have a real home again?"

He shrugged. "I don't know, Con. I guess we will. It's hard to say."

Now she thought about that: being in a new home, a new family. She liked that, and, yet, she didn't. She wanted her old family back. She wanted her real mother and father. She didn't care if other people said they were dead. *She* hadn't seen them dead, so they might still be alive. They could be, couldn't they?

She said, "What if mom and dad came here right now, out of the dark, to take us both away. Would you go with them?"

"Of course I would," he said. "Wouldn't you?"

"Yes." She sat there waiting, staring into the darkness before her, but nothing happened. She sighed and listened to the music instead.

"The important thing," Eric said, "is that we stay together. As long as we're together, we've still got our family."

THE BEAUTIFUL-UGLY

Now she looked at him again. She had never considered that before—that, for some reason, they might not be together, always. Now she held his arm, leaning against him. When the music stopped playing, silence momentarily surrounded them. On one of the tree limbs overhead a bird appeared, a blue jay, her father's favorite bird. Shortly, another jay joined it, and she watched the two fret and dance about the limb, looking down at them. She noticed the way one of the birds turned its head to the side, curiously watching her, and a chill went through her, as she squeezed Eric's arm, and the two birds flew away together into the night.

5 ♀ THE SCHOOL

In the morning Anne drove her and Eric over to Rio Valero Elementary School and enrolled them. Connelly thought this school was so different from Hawthorn-Regent, their school in San Francisco. It was a flat brick building at the edge of an enormous field filled with dry-looking weeds.

There was a moment of confusion when the lady in the office argued with Anne about what grade to put them in.

"The girl should be in first grade and the boy in fourth," she said.

"But their records indicate they were moved to the next grade," Anne said.

The lady looked at them standing there and said, "Well, it isn't fair to the other children."

Anne said, "Well, it isn't fair to them either. Obviously there's a reason they were moved ahead."

The lady pinched her mouth together and went to get the principal. He was an older, smiling, white-haired man who invited the three of them into his office and said, "So we've got a couple of scholars on our hands, have we?"

Connelly watched him, sitting behind his desk, looking through their yellow, children's-home folders. Then he had them both read from their primers—first her, then Eric. Finally, he called in the lady from the office and told her to let them stay in the grades they had been assigned.

"Yes, Mr. Ramirez," the lady said, pinching her mouth again.

Afterward, Anne told them they were on their own now. "Good luck," she said. "Your lunch tickets are paid automatically. And make sure you get on the right bus. Most of them come by the home. Just find the kids in your cottage group and go with them. I'll see you after school, okay?"

Then she was gone.

Now Connelly and Eric were also separated. She watched him go down the hallway one way, his new green, Pilgrims Mercy backpack on his back, following the monitor. One of the older girls came and took her the other way, and she adjusted her own backpack and followed behind her. She wanted to ask her something—anything to calm herself; but the girl didn't say anything to her, and at the classroom door she just pointed and walked away.

Connelly swallowed and opened the door. The room was filled with faces that now turned toward her. The teacher stood in front of the class, looking at her.

"You're from the home," she said, sounding disappointed. "Did the office give you a paper?"

She shook her head.

The teacher sighed. "Then go sit down—there." She pointed.

Slowly, Connelly walked between the rows of desks, feeling everyone's eyes on her, passing.

"Hurry," the teacher called. "You're disrupting the class, moving so slowly."

There was a titter of laughter, then a noise in another part of the room, when she heard the teacher say angrily, "Alberto—*deje de jugar!*"

"*Chingalo,*" a boy's tired voice replied.

Everyone laughed.

She removed her backpack and sat down, placing the pack by her feet. As soon as the teacher began talking again, someone poked her from behind. She turned around, and a big, flat-faced boy sat there, smiling. He ran his tongue slowly over his lips, still smiling, and she turned away. He poked her again, and she didn't turn this time. She heard another voice whisper: "*Chinga, chinga, chinga.*" And then she heard the quiet laughter around her, when the voice came again: "*Chinga, chinga, chinga.*" Like a scratchy tinkling bell.

She listened to the teacher. They were doing numbers, which, she realized, she already knew. They went very slowly, she saw, first in English, then Spanish. She remembered Mr. and Mrs. Rodriguez were Spanish. They lived down the hall from their apartment and would talk noisily to each other, going back and forth to the elevator. They owned a small restaurant on Market Street, and one time her father took the four of them there to eat. They ate something very hot and spicy, and her father and Mr. Rodriguez talked in Spanish and English. And after they ate, Mrs. Rodriguez brought out her and Eric each a small ice cream cone, which felt wonderful to her mouth, still burning from the food.

The boy behind poked her again. "*Chinga, chinga, chinga,*" he said in a deep whisper.

That's when she heard someone else quietly say, "You fucking pilgrims."

*

At lunch she was relieved to discover her cottage group in one corner of the cafeteria. Yolanda said, "Hey there, little biscuit, you come sit with your homeys, awright?" And she hugged her and Connelly felt a little like when her mother hugged her, and she hungrily ate all her food, except her roll, which she gave to Beatrice.

When someone asked her how she liked her class, she said okay. That wasn't the truth, she knew, but she didn't want to complain. Still, she felt they knew anyway.

Yolanda said, "The town folk here don't care too much for the orphanage kids. They think we a burden, even though the state pay them good for letting us use the school and all."

"Even the local Mexicans don't like us out-of-town Mexicans," said Camerina.

"That's the truth," Maribel said. "Shit, and they mostly just fruit pickers and tannery workers. Half of'em ain't nothin' but wetback border-orphans themselves."

"Just don't let no one touch you, girl," Julie told her. Julie was beautiful, with long blond hair and blue eyes. She seemed like an angel. "You do know about touching, don't you?"

Now all the girls at the table hovered near her.

Yolanda said, "Your mama ever teach you about touching, little biscuit?"

"Yes," she said, embarrassed. "She told me to tell her or my father if someone touched me there."

"Where's there?" Camerina insisted.

She reluctantly pointed down to her private area.

"That's right," Yolanda said, hugging her again. "That sweet little joy-box belong to you and no one else, and don't you ever forget it, hear me?"

She nodded.

All the girls were giggling and whispering around her.

Maribel said, "That's right, cause some day some boy's gonna come along—"

"That be the right boy," Yolanda said, "at the right time."

"And he'll want to touch you there," Camerina added.

"And then you'll have to decide," said Julie, winking at her. "Is he the real thing or not?"

Yolanda began to sing and sashay back and forth: "*Oh, he the real thing...*"

The other girls joined in singing and swaying, "*Yeah, the real thing...*"

Everyone was laughing and talking now, Connelly noticed, except Beatrice, who, to her surprise, sat there with her head down, eating her chocolate pudding and crying.

She asked her, "What's the matter, Beatrice?"

Beatrice shook her lowered head, quickly spooning another bite of pudding into her mouth.

Yolanda put her arm around her again, squeezing her. "Oh, little girl, Miss Bea awright. She just thinking about something else, that's all."

But the happy spell was broken, and the girls began to talk about other things, until the bell rang, returning them to classes.

*

That night Martha was gone. They went to dinner, and when they returned, her bed had been stripped.

No one else seemed surprised, but Connelly asked Yolanda what happened to her.

"She got fostered out, baby. What—you think we all gonna stay together like one big happy family?"

She didn't know what she thought, except the suddenness of change, surrounding her now, made her feel a way she had never felt before. Her home, before, living with her mommy and daddy, had never been like that. They would never have allowed that: changing, changing constantly. Everything always different than the moment before. Nothing you could get used to. Nothing you could count on—ever, not for one *breath,* it seemed. She didn't know what she thought. She was afraid even to think, in fact, because the next moment would be something different, and she would have to think something else. Instead, she sat on her bed, holding Priscilla and staring at Martha's bare bed. She wondered where she went. And who had taken her there. And what would her life be now. She wondered that, looking at the other girls, moving around the room, doing the little things they did each night, as if their lives there would go on forever.

*

In the morning at school, with the teacher yelling in Spanish at the boys across the room, and the other boys, around her, poking her back and whispering things to her she couldn't understand, another older girl appeared at the door with a note.

The teacher said simply, "Connelly Pierce, you go with her. Take your things with you."

The girl, saying nothing, escorted her to the office. There, Mr. Ramirez brought her into his office where she saw someone else sitting.

"Connelly," he said, "this is Mrs. McDonough. She teaches our best second grade class here, and I'm putting you in her care."

Connelly barely heard what he was saying. She was looking instead at Mrs. McDonough's hair, which was prettily long and brown and parted on the side, just like her mother's.

"Hello, Connelly," Mrs. McDonough said, standing up and coming over to her, taking her hand. "It's so nice to meet you. I've heard you're a good reader. That's great, because we do lots of reading in our class."

Connelly wanted to swoon, because the way Mrs. McDonough stood, a little to the side, with her hair coming down over one eye was also like her mother. So pretty like her mother.

She felt dizzy, walking down the hall, holding tightly to Mrs. McDonough's hand, watching her out the corner of her eye. The teacher was telling her all the things they did in class, but she really didn't hear her. Finally, Mrs. McDonough stopped and asked her, "Connelly, is everything all right?"

She felt her face go hot, as she nodded.

Mrs. McDonough stood with her in front of the class and introduced her, and everyone said hello. Then she showed her where to sit—in the very center front-row seat. "This is our new kid's desk," Mrs. McDonough explained. "So you don't miss anything. Then, once you're comfortable, you can move somewhere else if you'd like."

She sat at the desk, setting her pack aside, and listened to everyone read, and looked at the blackboard on which someone had written: *A noun is a person, place, thing, or idea.* But mostly she watched Mrs. McDonough move about the room—the way she moved, the way she talked, the way she smiled—dreamily watching her, until she realized the teacher was standing right in front of her, saying, "Connelly, are you still with us? Everyone would like to hear you read the next page. Would you do that for us?"

"Yes ma'am," she said, her ears burning, turning the page and beginning to read.

6 ♀ THE SPECIAL

That afternoon when Connelly got back to the cottage, Martha's bed was made up. The other girls looked in her drawer, and there was underwear and a few tops. They all ran to the long walk-in closet, next to the bathroom, and there were things hanging in Martha's spot: A ragged blue-nylon coat and sweater and two old dresses. Dirty sneakers sat on the floor beneath.

"I know them things," Yolanda said. "Them's that Sara girl's. What's her name?"

"Gill," said Camerina. "Sara Gill. She's one of the specials."

Everyone stood there, staring at the clothes.

"Special what?" Connelly asked.

"Special cases," Beatrice said. "Like I was."

Now everyone went slowly back and sat on their beds, waiting.

Yolanda said, "I hear she come up from Patton State."

Everyone sat there quietly, Connelly saw, as if they were all drifting away, wrapped up in their own thoughts.

"I don't understand," she interrupted the silence. "What's going on?"

"Little biscuit," Yolanda said, "when you come to Mercy, and you real bad off, they don't put you in the cottages for a while."

"They put you in the big white house," said Camerina, "where they can keep an eye on you."

Beatrice said, "They wanna make sure you're not too suicidal, or that you'll stab everyone else in the cottage in their sleep. So they keep you there, and keep you doped up, and let the doctors and nurses and therapists poke around you, until they think you're ready."

They continued to sit there, quietly mulling over this or that, until Yolanda stopped them. "Remember now—when the res bring her over, we can't be acting like nothing at all. We all got to be just cool and every-day, y'all hear?"

"Just pretend like it's nothing different," said Julie, "no matter how much a nut case she is."

"Like my therapist says," said Beatrice. "It's not a matter of crazy, it's degrees of insight, like mind geometry."

"That's right," Yolanda said. "And some folk got more geometry than other folk do."

Now everyone began doing other things. Connelly watched them curiously, and then began to comb what was left of Priscilla's hair, which had sections missing now; and she could see the tiny holes where the hair had once been, hoping Priscilla wouldn't notice.

"You still look very pretty," she whispered, combing, when the door opened, and she looked up.

Anne came in, her right hand holding someone else's hand that came in slowly behind her. "Everyone," she said, smiling. "We have a new group member."

Connelly's breath hung still inside her for a moment. It was the same girl she saw the first day, when she and Eric were sitting in the great room, waiting for Melissa. She had passed, carrying a clothes basket, going up the stairs, and had looked back at her. Her face. Her eyes. Still the same. Except now she looked like a little wild animal ready to run away.

"Does everyone know Sara Gill?" Anne said, and then began going around the room, introducing each of them.

When they came to her, Connelly saw Sara look at her, then quickly away.

"We awright, Miss Anne," Yolanda said. "Now we got two little biscuits to look after, that's all."

Sara went and sat on her own bed, her head down, hands clasped together.

"I'll check in on everyone before I leave," Anne told them, and went out, closing the door behind her.

Everyone sat there in silence for a moment, until Beatrice said lowly, "She's medded to her eyeballs."

Yolanda shushed her, putting her finger to her lips, then motioned with her hand, and everyone became busy with normal things: talking among themselves, doing homework, taking their bathroom turns.

Meanwhile, Sara Gill didn't move at all, Connelly noticed. She sat perfectly still on her bed, dressed in her yellow, worn-out top and blue, worn-out pedal pushers and white sneakers as raggedy as the black ones she had in the closet, as if that was all she would ever do. Connelly thought about it only a moment, and then she got up off her own bed, and went over and sat next to Sara.

Everyone in the room had stopped what they were doing, she saw, staring over at them; then they simply ignored them and looked away. She sat there, wondering what to do next. She said, "My name's Connelly."

Head down, Sara said quietly and a little mockingly, "I already know that."

"Oh."

They sat there.

Finally, Sara said, "But I don't know *her* name."

"Who?"

She indicated the doll.

"Her name's Priscilla."

Now Sara glanced sideways and then away. "What happened to her hair?"

"I'm not sure. I think the Johnsons' cat ate it." She looked over at her. "Would you like to hold her?"

Sara's mouth made a funny little smile. "No thanks, I don't play with dolls anymore."

"Oh."

Sara looked up at her now. Her eyes seemed two large black pools of something both hard and soft, melting about the edges, while deeper inside—at their center—they seemed to quiver, as if tiny bursts of fire were erupting, Connelly couldn't quite see. Then Sara said, "The first time I saw you, when you were sitting with that boy, and you looked at me—I knew."

"Knew what?"

"That you were my guardian angel I'd been asking for and asking for and finally got."

Once again, the funny little smile, as she lowered her head.

Connelly stared at her a moment, and then looked at Priscilla instead. First she looked into her startled eyes, staring back at her. Slowly, she tilted her back, until her eyes closed, and she held her to her chest, rocking her.

*

That night she was dreaming the same dream again, when Sara's crying woke her. The four of them were having another picnic under the bridge. The day was pretty again, and Eric and her mother were wandering among the tall grasses alongside the water, while she and her father sat on the picnic blanket, talking about things she couldn't quite hear. But they were funny things, because she was laughing, and her father rolled over, making silly noises and holding his tummy, and she was saying something else to him—when she woke up, hearing Sara cry out.

Now she lay there, listening first to Beatrice, then Yolanda, then Julie, go sit with her to quiet her. She listened to them, talking quietly across the room, and tried to go back to sleep. She wanted her dream back; she wanted to be with her mommy and daddy again, even if it was just dreaming. It felt so wonderful having them so close she could almost reach out and touch them. That Sara.

Why did she have to have such nightmares? And she tried to sleep, knowing she couldn't, when it was suddenly early in the morning, and someone else woke her, saying: "*Oh, Sara!*"

Everyone was awake now, jumping out of bed, running into the bathroom. She grabbed Priscilla and ran there, pushing her way between the other girls to see. Her mouth fell open when she did.

Sara was crouched naked by the toilet, and she had made such a mess. She had gone potty on the floor and smeared it all over herself and the toilet and walls. And she was crouched there now, as if sleeping.

Maribel said, "I came in and found her like this."

"We better get the res," said Kathy.

"No," Yolanda said. "We get the res, they'll ship her back to Patton."

"Well maybe they should," Beatrice said. "Then maybe we could get some sleep."

Instead, Connelly watched while they put Sara in the shower. Kathy and Julie took off their tops and scrubbed her down, then shampooed her hair, with her saying: "Ow, that hurts!", and everyone else saying: "Shut up, Sara!" Meanwhile, the other girls cleaned up the toilet and walls.

When they were finished, everyone sat in a circle on the cottage's brown carpet floor and talked about what they should do. Sara lay tucked into her bed, sucking her thumb and listening to them.

"First place," said Yolanda, "from now on we got to take turns sleeping with her. That way, if she wakes up, we'll already be there to quiet her."

Camerina said, "Uh-huh, and someone has to be with her in the bathroom, no matter what. I know I ain't cleaning her shit off the walls again, I don't care how cute and helpless she is."

Now everyone looked over at Sara, and she smiled her funny little smile again, sucking her thumb, and turned away from them.

"She gone back to sleep," Yolanda said.

They were all still sitting there, tired and complaining, a few minutes later when the morning res came by with her clipboard, counted them, and told them to get ready for school.

7 ♀ THE INTERVIEW

On Saturday she and Eric met their new caseworker in one of the offices in the big house. Her name was Mrs. Morton, she told them, looking around the room as if she were in the wrong place, and telling them to sit down. Then she talked with them only a few minutes, writing down little notes, Connelly watching her hand and pen moving carefully over the page of the small blue-leather notebook she'd taken from her purse.

"I told them I didn't want any cases out of the city," she complained. "Certainly not the children's home. But no one seems to listen anymore." She shook her head.

She was older than Melissa, she had short silver hair, and wore a lady's blue suit, rather than blue jeans and old shirts like Melissa wore. And she had a string of pearls around her neck that she touched with her left hand whenever she became upset, which was often.

"I told them I was cutting back. My husband wishes me to cut back. So instead they give me two Mercy children and apologize. I don't need their apologies," she said, putting her book and pen back into the purse, and snapping it shut with both her hands. While Connelly counted the four rings on Mrs. Morton's fingers, the caseworker said, "I have only one foster interview arranged for you today. This is all becoming so difficult. I can't remain here that long, of course. Your residents will introduce you. Just remember, it is you that has to prove you are worthy of someone else's time in all this. They're not responsible for your situation, that's your responsibility. So my advice is to be on your best behavior, and use your manners. Your parents did teach you manners, didn't they?"

Afterward, when Mrs. Morton had driven away, they went out to the same bench they'd discovered their first day there. Connelly called it *their* bench now, because no one else ever seemed to sit there. And they met there almost every night and talked. She liked that—that Eric was talking to her again, almost like before, except (and she couldn't quite understand why) he seemed different now. Just a little. Maybe it was the way his eyes would look away when she told him about something, as if he wasn't quite hearing her; or the way, when he told her something, his voice was quieter now, even when it was something he used to love—like a book he was reading, or something he saw on television. She wasn't sure.

Now she was explaining to him how, for some reason, living at Pilgrims Mercy reminded her of when she took a bath and put her head under water. How, when she opened her eyes under water, everything looked different, everything sounded different. She knew the real world was only inches away, above her; but there, in that new world, nothing was the same anymore. The only difference was she couldn't raise up her head now; she couldn't go back to her normal world, like she did when bathing. She was underwater, where everything looked and sounded so strange, but now she would have to stay there, forever. That's the only way she could think about it, and she asked Eric if that's what he thought too.

"I don't know, Con," he said, looking away. "I'm not sure how I feel."

"But it's more than that, Eric," she said. "I mean, more water—a lot more. Like before, the bathtub's only half full, because mom didn't want me making a mess, remember? Or even when we went with them down to San Luis Obispo and stayed at the motel, and went swimming there. It's even more water than that, Eric—do you understand? It's more like the ocean now, I think. I mean, it's like the water's everywhere, and it's very deep, and we're just stuck underneath it, and we can't get out."

"You mean like fish?"

"Maybe, except how do we know how fish feel? Do you think it's like fish, Eric?"

He sighed his frustrated sigh. "How should I know, Con. Fish aren't mammals like we are. They're cold-blooded aquatic vertebrates. Their brains work differently than ours?"

"So how do their brains work then?"

But he didn't want to talk about it anymore.

*

As they were told, Saturday was visitors' day. There was a special room in the main house for the interviews. For some reason, the other girls in her group called them cattle calls, but that didn't make any sense to her. They weren't calling any cattle; they were just talking with people who may want to take them home with them.

That's how Anne and Joe Hardy explained it to her and Eric before they went in. Joe was Eric's resident, and he told them just to be themselves, to always tell the truth, and, most importantly, not to worry.

That's when Eric said, "But why can't we just stay here, Joe? We both like it here."

She saw Joe and Anne look at each other, and Joe said, "Well, Eric, you see, Pilgrims Mercy is just an emergency home. It's available for kids who, for whatever reason, get hung up in the system and don't have any place else to go. But, unfortunately, there're lots of kids like that, and we only have so many beds. So they have to go to the worst cases."

Anne said, "Fortunately for you two, there's a good chance people will want to foster you. You're both nice kids, and we're pretty sure someone will take you. Then some other kids who aren't so lucky can have your beds."

"We call it churn," Joe said, frowning. "In one door, out the other. No one likes it, but we have to do the best we can with it."

Then, when it was time, Joe brought them into the interview room. Connelly saw the tables and chairs set up in each corner. Grownups were on one side of the table, talking with the home kids on the other. At one of the tables she saw Julie talking to a lady. The lady was smiling and holding one of Julie's hands, but Julie wasn't smiling. She was looking out the window.

Joe introduced them to Mr. and Mrs. Gunderson. Then he left them there, and suddenly they were alone with these two strangers, sitting up straight as chair-backs, staring at them.

"Well, Father," Mrs. Gunderson said, "they certainly look healthy enough."

"I don't know, Mother," said Mr. Gunderson. "Boy looks runty."

"We can feed him up," Mrs. Gunderson replied. "Young lady, can you make beds?"

"She's only six," Eric told her. "Our mom always made her bed."

The Gundersons both looked at him, as if they were surprised he could speak at all.

"We own a dairy farm," Mr. Gunderson explained. "Everyone has to pull their weight. We've no time for slackers."

While Mrs. Gunderson read their background sheet aloud to Mr. Gunderson, Connelly sat there trying to understand how they could be each other's mother and father. They both looked old and a little mean, and she couldn't understand it.

When Mrs. Gunderson was finished, Mr. Gunderson asked Eric to hold out his hands. Then he examined them with his big rough-looking hands and said, "Soft as rose petals, Mother."

"Hands toughen, Father."

"Well, boy seems a might tetchy, don't he?"

"A might," Mrs. Gunderson agreed.

"I don't abide by no tetchy boys," Mr. Gunderson added. "I work 'em hard, and they can have off every other Sunday for privates. Milking stock don't know nothing about shutting down. Got to stay lively. No place for a tetchy runt."

The Gundersons stared at them a while longer, before Mrs. Gunderson said, "Well, we'll talk about it. You can go now. Bye."

Eric held her hand tightly all the way out of the house, as if afraid he might lose her there, or they might somehow become separated, if he let her go.

Outside, he did let go of her hand, and she silently followed behind him all the way back to their bench, where he plopped down and said, "Sometimes I just hate them."

She sat next to him. "Who, Eric?"

"Mom and dad, that's who."

She looked at him, amazed. "But why?"

"Because they left us here, Con." He looked at her, his anxious eyes moving back and forth behind his glasses. "Don't you ever get mad because they left us, and now we have to do everything we don't want to do?"

"I don't hate them," she said. "I'll never do that."

They sat there, when Eric said, "All I know is, we're here and they're not."

"That's because they're both dead, Eric," she said, wishing he wouldn't talk like that. She knew he didn't hate them. Not really. And she wished he wasn't so upset. But she didn't know what else to do, so she held his arm, leaning against him. And they sat there, wondering what would happen next.

They were still there an hour later when Joe came looking for them and told them the Gundersons had decided they would keep looking, and were gone as suddenly from their lives as they had arrived.

8 ♀ CHURN

In spite of what Eric had said, she could feel the changing about them—with their brand new lives at Pilgrims Mercy, and their new school, and with everyone new surrounding them—that seemed a little less frightening, with each day passing.

At the same time, she realized she wasn't thinking constantly of *them* now; that is, her mother and father: constantly looking for them everywhere, expecting to see them, and then wondering was all her life now just a bad dream that wouldn't end. Of course, she still thought about them, almost everything she did or saw reminding her of them; but it wasn't like the very beginning when she knew every suffocating breath would be her last if they didn't come back to her right then. It wasn't like that now; although, she still missed them, and her heart still ached, and her stomach still hurt, thinking about them, at least a hundred times a day.

*

New lives, she thought at night, lying in bed, listening to one of the girls trying to quiet Sara. They both had new lives, whether they wanted them or not. That was what she was beginning to understand. There was the before, and there was the now. And the before was gone, and she couldn't get it back. Ever. Except what she had in her mind and could remember. And the now, which seemed to be everywhere at once, unstopping, some things nice, some not.

At school, her favorite time was finger painting. That was her favorite time in her old school as well, letting her fingers swirl the colors about the paper, trying to make it come out like her father's paintings, although it never quite did. Still, when she brought her paintings home, her parents always held their hands over their mouths with surprise, and her father would hang them on the wall beside one of his paintings, even though she knew they weren't nearly as good.

Now when she brought a painting back to the cottage, sometimes one of the other girls would notice it, and sometimes not. And once, when she painted a red cow like her father had done, and taped it on the wall above her bed, Beatrice said, "What's that—a dog?"

"No, Beatrice, it's a cow," she told her.

"Well, it looks like a dog to me. A deformed one at that."

Still, she kept it there where she could see it when she woke up each morning.

*

Another day she and Eric were sitting on their bench, talking, when some boys from the older boys' cottage came by and began teasing them. One boy took Eric's glasses, and he chased him. Then another boy tried to put his hand down her shirt, and she screamed, slapping at him.

That's when a voice made everything stop: "Hey now!" it came from somewhere behind, startling her. "Hey!"

It was the same odd raggedy voice she'd heard their first day there, like feet dragging over gravel. Then she saw him come around the bench and stand there, hands on hips. It was that same old black man, short and round as a barrel, the same towel still draped around his neck, except now he wasn't smiling. He looked mean, in fact.

He said, "Y'all c'mon over here. C'mon now."

All the boys lined up before him, except Eric, who came back and sat beside her on the bench. Now they both watched the man.

He looked at the boys meanly for a moment, then said, "What y'all got to say about it?"

"Nothing, Mr. Pete," one of the boys said.

"You damn right, nothing," he said. "'Cept messing with my lil pilgrims." He shook his head. "How many you boys want me to go tell your res about this?"

"None of us, Mr. Pete," said another boy quietly.

"Say what?" the man growled.

Then all the boys shouted: "None of us, Mr. Pete!"

She watched him still look meanly at all of them, like he would go tell the res right at that moment.

Instead, he said, pointing, "You—give the boy his glasses back."

The boy who took Eric's glasses came over to the bench and handed them to him.

"Now tell him you're sorry."

"I'm sorry," the boy mumbled.

"You—" He pointed to another boy. "You lose something down that young lady's blouse?"

"No sir."

He glared at him. "You do something like that again, I'll break your damn fingers first, *then* go tell your res—you understand me?"

"Yes sir."

"So what you got to say?"

The boy looked over at her and said, "I'm sorry."

The man said, "Now y'all go on, before I put a whupping on you your granddaddies gonna stand up and feel."

When they were gone she was surprised to see the meanness in the man's face disappear. He chuckled and came over and sat down on the bench, lighting a cigarette and telling them, "They ain't mean boys, no. Just bored with bad coming on top of worse, I reckon."

As he smoked, they watched a tiny tractor moving through the middle of the big field before them. A cloud of dust followed behind the tractor, dissolving into the blue sky.

He said, "If the good Lord don't provide us some rain soon, that wheat's gonna up and blow away. Then I might not get my Wheaties." He looked over at them. "Y'all like Wheaties?"

They both nodded.

He said, "I got to have my Wheaties every morning, first thing, with a cup of good chicory coffee—mmmm, mmmm."

He looked at them again. "Now how 'bout that chicory coffee—you like that too?"

Eric said, "Our parents never let us drink coffee."

Now Connelly added, "Only our father drank coffee. Our mother drank tea."

"Well, that's all right," he said, nodding his head. "And you always want to listen to your folks now, don't you."

She saw Eric lower his head, and she didn't say anything either.

Meanwhile, the man was looking at them both, and finally said, "Lookee here now—anyone around here cause you any more problems, you come see Mr. Pete, you understand?"

They nodded again.

"Meanwhile, I got to get back to work," he said. "Mercy don't pay me to sit here all day long and socialize with our lil pilgrims." Then she saw him hold out his cigarette before him and twirl it between his fingers. He saw her watching him and said, "That's called field-dressing a cigarette. Learned it in the Army. Either you two ever field-dress a cigarette before?"

"Not hardly," she told him, amazed he would even ask them that.

"Not—what?" he said, sounding surprised. Then he laughed, his laugh sounding deep and happy inside himself, standing up and walking off, still laughing and shaking his head, talking with himself.

*

Once, when she had to talk with a therapist, Anne told her, "Don't worry. They just want to see how you're doing. She'll talk with you and Eric, and do a report. You know, some people pay lots of money for that."

She didn't see why. The lady was nice and asked her how she was getting along? Did she think about her parents much? Were things bothering her? Did she have good dreams or bad dreams? What did she think about this or that? She didn't tell her much. Actually, she preferred just talking with Anne or Mrs. McDonough at school, or the girls in her cottage group, or sometimes Mr. Pete, or, mostly, Eric, who understood her—the way she saw and felt things now—better than anyone.

"We got to be careful who we trust, Con," he told her once, near the end of school. "Mom told me that, not long before she died. She said her and dad were the only people we could ever really totally trust. She said other people weren't the same as parents. They had their own lives. But parents' lives and their kids' lives were the same. There wasn't any difference. So you could trust them."

"But they're dead now, Eric," she told him.

"That doesn't matter. Other people are still the same. We've got to be careful, that's all."

And the look in his eyes, sitting beside her on the bench, and the moon shining down, and the insects singing like waves of noise, seeming to wash over them, before going somewhere back into the dark.

*

Another time, Anne took her with her on an "emergency run," as she called it. That was a trip to the wholesale warehouse in Fresno, where she bought things the home needed, until the delivery trucks could come.

It was a wonderful trip, riding in the van to the big brightly lit warehouse, and all the things she saw and wished she could have, and all the people around them, the excitement seeming to fill up the entire room.

THE BEAUTIFUL-UGLY

Then afterward, Anne brought her over to the little café in one corner of the warehouse for a strawberry soda, just like her father sometimes did. That's when the thought came over her. And for the very first time she really, really understood that she could never do anything like that with him—with either of them—again. Then she thought of all the other things she could never do with them. For her whole life. And it was suddenly like a terrible knife, cutting through her stomach, into her heart, and she caught her breath.

"What's the matter?" Anne asked her, looking over.

But she couldn't help herself. So Anne moved over beside her and held her, letting her cry against her, surrounded by the enormous, bright, happy, colorful room, not stopping.

*

One day Julie had to leave. She was upset because school still wasn't over and she didn't know what would happen. Her caseworker didn't know either, but she still had to go. So she packed her things, crying, as all the girls in the cottage tried to calm her.

Yolanda said, "Con, you go watch Sara." Who was also crying, because Julie was her favorite, and knew better than anyone there how to keep her quiet at night.

"Julie, can I go with you?" Sara cried, sitting beside her on the bed, watching the others.

"Sara, please don't start," Julie said from the closet.

Connelly watched Sara hold her breath and begin to pull her hair, and told Yolanda, "She's doing it again."

"Awright, Sara," Yolanda called out. "Let's go take us a cold shower."

"No, I don't *want* a cold shower," Sara said, not stopping.

"She's still doing it."

"Miss Bea," Yolanda said, "go strip her skinny little ass down and *throw* her in."

But when Beatrice took a step toward her she stopped immediately, lowered her head, and began pinching one of her legs, as if that interested her more than anything else now.

Finally, Julie was packed and all the girls were hugging her. Then she sat on the bed, holding Sara, who cried quietly in her arms. "My damn mother," she said. "She promised me I could come home this summer, and now she's back in rehab. Goddamn her."

Connelly saw the look in Julie's pretty blue eyes, which had confused her in the beginning, but she was getting used to it now. She saw it almost every day around the home, on the faces coming and going, of not believing what was happening, and then having to believe it.

The res came in to get her. "They're here," she said, meaning the new family Julie would live with now.

"My goddamn mother," she said, kissing everyone one last time, and disappearing out the door.

When the door closed shut, no one moved, no one said a word or made a sound, except Sara, who was curled on the bed, holding the pillow against herself, and making little noises into it that could have been crying or something else, Connelly wasn't sure.

Next, Anne broke their mood, not an hour later, bringing over the new girl that took Julie's bed. She was tall and horribly thin and wore shorts and a top that were much too small for her. Her eyes, Connelly saw, were staring off as she stood there.

"Everyone, this is Meredith," Anne said.

She began going around, introducing them, and when she brought her into the closet to show her her space, Beatrice whispered: "*Special.*"

And they all nodded.

*

On the last day of school, when the bell rang and the other children were gone, she stayed behind and gave Mrs. McDonough the watercolor she had done of her parents.

The teacher was sitting behind her desk, and caught her breath and said, "Oh, Connelly, I'm going to have this framed and take it home with me—is that all right?"

She could only nod, thinking about that. At that moment, realizing she wished she could go home with her too. Her and Eric. Live with her and Mr. McDonough, who she knew must be very nice, or Mrs. McDonough wouldn't have married him.

But she only stood there and said, "Can I see you next year then?"

Mrs. McDonough looked surprised and said, "Of course you can, Connelly. You can see me any time you wish. I *want* you to come see me."

Mrs. McDonough hesitated then, looking at her, and then suddenly pulled her to her, hugging her. She whispered in her ear, "It's going to be all right for you, darling, I know it will. Because that's the kind of girl you are."

She couldn't help it. In Mrs. McDonough's arms, smelling her perfumed hair against her face, Connelly shut her eyes and—just for that moment—pretended it was her mother holding her again. All of her mother's presence, every time she had held her, filled her up then. And she grew dizzy, feeling her, having her so close.

When she ran out of the classroom she heard Mrs. McDonough say: "Good-bye, Connelly. I hope you have a good summer."

But she didn't answer her, running all the way to the bus stop before she stopped.

*

The first week of the summer, both Kathy and Maribel left. Kathy went home again, and Maribel was fostered out. The second week, they took Sara away. Apparently she had done something with one of the new girls that wasn't allowed, but Connelly never knew what.

"She gone back to Patton State, little biscuit," was all Yolanda would tell her, sitting on the bed behind her, braiding her hair.

Then Camerina fought with one of the new girls and was grounded for a month.

"That sucks, Anne," Camerina said when the res came and told her. "She started it."

"She's grounded as well," Anne said.

But Camerina still wasn't happy, and she fought with the girl again, upsetting everyone in the cottage.

Connelly realized the only good thing was she and Eric could spend more time together now, which they did, every chance they got; sitting on their bench and talking; or taking long walks on the path that ran along the edge of the field; or watching television in the recreation hall when it wasn't so crowded; or spending their allowance on a Saturday mall-run.

Once, at the mall, Eric bought a small plastic chess set, and began teaching her to play. After that, they sat for hours on their bench, as he taught her. She thought it hard, because once you made a move—that was it; and you always had to be thinking, close and far, which Eric called tactics and strategy, and which confused her. And she always lost except (she knew) for the times he let her win.

She told him, "When mom and dad played, she let him win too. Remember how dad would complain, 'Honey, you don't have to pity me,' he'd say—remember?"

Eric nodded. "You and dad are the same. You have different concepts than mom and I have. You're thinking with the other side of your brain."

"What side are you thinking with?"

"The logical side. The side that lets you hold several things out at once, and sort of go between them, and look at them."

"I can do that," she said.

"No, your concepts are more general, like shapes and patterns and colors. Remember how dad always saw strange shapes in clouds, or how a street sometimes looked different to him than it really was?" He shook his head. "Mom could never see that. It was always just a cloud or just a street, but things like chess made sense to her."

She made her move.

"You can't do that," Eric said.

"But you said a knight moved three spaces."

"Not along the same line, Con. It's one and two, or two and one."

She sighed and put back her piece. She cautiously moved something else, watching Eric's eyes, and saw immediately it was a mistake.

He made his move and said, "Check."

"But they're all just moves," she complained. "They all look the same to me."

"But they're not," he said. "They're all different. Every move is different, and when you make them, everything changes with them."

They played until time for dinner, and she still didn't see the difference; but she did see the way the clouds moved over the field of wheat, with the breeze shifting it, and the enormous sections of it, growing darker and lighter, swaying. She saw everything in her mind there at once. And it made perfect sense to her, without really thinking about it.

*

Mrs. Morton came on Saturday, with a couple from Fremont. Connelly wasn't sure where that was, and didn't ask. They said their name was Keleman or Kelemer; she wasn't sure about that either. Apparently Mr. Keleman or Kelemer was a teacher, high school biology; and he and Eric talked about that, and she was bored, moving about in her chair, with Mrs. Morton shaking her head disapprovingly, sitting just behind the couple.

Meanwhile, *Mrs.* Keleman or Kelemer asked *her* questions: what kinds of things she liked, what was her favorite this or that, what, what, what. It reminded her of the therapist. And suddenly she remembered the moment, once, when she and her father were talking, and he said, "I got to be honest with you, brat. Painting's the only thing that ever made any sense to me. Everything else is a struggle. Just the art, that's it. I'm a one-trick pony, I'm afraid." So now she told her: "Art—that's all I really like."

"Art?" the woman said.

"Yes, you know, like painting and stuff. Art." She looked away.

When the interview was over, she and Eric sat on the porch and watched Mrs. Morton talking with the Kelemans or Kelemers, and then they drove away.

Mrs. Morton came over to them and stood there, saying, "Well, they are interested and said they would call me next week. I'm surprised, considering the perfectly awful way *someone* acted." She looked down at Connelly and then away. "In any event, let me have a word with the office, and I'm off. I'll be in touch."

And as soon as she was inside, they both ran, as fast as they could, toward their bench.

*

There was a day the summer heat seemed to descend upon them like a giant invisible smothering blanket. Everything moved slower now, while almost every day she saw the same kids and residents come and go. That surprised her, noticing. Because in the beginning, when everything was new and every face a stranger, she didn't think she would ever understand it at all. But now, being at Mercy was almost like being at home had been. Of course, she didn't like it nearly as much, but at least she knew it now. She knew how it looked and felt, and even smelled, at different times of the day and night; she knew the faces, and when someone was missing, or someone was new, and she felt, not so much that she belonged there, but that—since she had to be somewhere—it was not so bad after all. And that surprised her as well.

One day she saw Melissa dropping off a boy. She was so happy, seeing her, she screamed out her name, and ran in her summer shorts and sandals over to her. They hugged.

"Look at you, long-legged girl!" Melissa said, surprised. "Got your hair in cornrows, got your ears pierced, and got the bling thing goin'—look at you!"

"Yolanda did my hair," she said happily. "And Anne took me to the mall and got my ears done and bought me the hoops."

Melissa laughed, shaking her head, and hugged her again, asking, "So how's your case working, baby?"

"Oh, she's all right," she told her, "but I'd rather have you back."

"I'd rather that too, but you know how that goes." She turned around to the boy standing behind her. "Connelly, this is Bryan."

"Hello," she told him. "It's not so bad here."

He was small and dirty, and she saw the too-familiar look in his eyes, trying to be a little angry about it, but mostly afraid. And in one brief flash, she knew exactly what would happen: most likely, what cottage group he would be placed, and what the boys there would do to him, and how he would reach the point he would have to find some way to fit in, to find his place, or they would take him away again, looking for another place to put him.

"Try and get him with Joe, ok?" she told Melissa.

"Sure," she replied. "Promise me you'll keep an eye on him for me."

"Sure."

Then Melissa's cell phone rang, and Connelly stood there, watching the boy casting a cautious eye about himself, listening to her talking with someone named Mark.

Afterward, she asked her, "So what happened to Brad."

"Old news, girl." Melissa winked at her. "Mark sells sports cars. You know how that goes."

She didn't really, but she hugged Melissa again, and watched her take the boy's hand and go up the steps into the big house. Then she turned away and went to find Eric and tell him who she saw.

9 ♀ A SPECIAL DAY

July. Each new day the blue sky sat atop them like a giant, still ocean. Everyone woke up a little early, eating an early breakfast, and then tried to get their chores done, before it got too hot, before noon.

She worked in the laundry, which was in a large red-metal shed behind the rec hall. Her job was to sort the towels and washcloths from the folding machine, and then do the count. That was separating them and tying them into stacks for each cottage, while another girl would rack them. It wasn't so bad, because she was inside, with the giant ceiling fans turning high and slow overhead, listening to every different kind of music and talk—mostly Spanish—around her, and watch the hoppers of dirty linen rolling into the shed from one end, the racks of clean linen rolling out the other end.

Eric, meanwhile, had to water the garden, which he told her he liked, going out into the cool morning and see how things had changed overnight. The garden rows were long and straight, with the black soil running between the plants. And he told her how he would first walk down the rows, lifting up this and that leaf or limb to peek underneath and see what was growing. It reminded him, he said, of the walks he made with their mother, and how sometimes he pretended she was there with him, still discovering little things with him, and the look on her face when they did. It was that look he remembered most of all, he said. The way her face would soften, almost smiling, as her eyes opened wide and alert to see what was there, new and unexpected.

Then he would lay out his hoses and begin the watering.

*

On the 4th of July they had a special day. Everyone got up early and they ate a pancake breakfast, before the first red blisters of light appeared over the eastern fields. Then everyone rushed about getting their chores done by mid-morning.

By ten a.m. the rolling barbeque grills had already been set up out under the stand of elms, and there were to be fireworks that evening. Everyone was excited when the riding academy brought over two long trailers of horses to ride, and a watermelon farmer delivered a pickup load of melons, which they placed inside the walk-in cooler, until the afternoon.

There were volunteers from the different churches, and it was open-house as well, and the parking lot was soon overflowing. Connelly thought it almost like a carnival her parents had brought her and Eric to once. There were sack and foot races, and tug-of-war, and water games. She dunked both Anne and Joe Hardy in the dunking booth, with them pleading her not to; but she did, and then hugged them afterward, apologizing. Meanwhile, Eric was her partner for the sack race, and they won a yellow ribbon, which he pinned to her shirt, kissing her hot forehead.

After lunch they signed up for the horse ride. Eric got a pretty spotted horse, because he was older; but she had to ride an old brown horse that seemed more asleep than awake; and she kept talking to it, promising it sugar and apples if it kept up with the other horses, which it barely did. Meanwhile, they rode all the way around the big field, where she saw the rabbits and birds flushing from the thick wheat, and the black gliding hawks high above them.

After the ride they had to walk their horses around in the shade and give them water. She gave hers an apple, like she'd promised it, but the old thing didn't seem so impressed, looking suspiciously at her sideways, and blinking at her, wanting more. So she gave it a carrot stick, and that seemed to satisfy it, its mouth moving comically sideways, as it ate the carrot.

In the hottest part of the afternoon they ate cold watermelon and homemade ice cream, sitting on the grass under the trees, and listened to the music groups from the churches that played on the little stage set up that morning. She liked the music, especially the choral singing (which she thought, if her parents were in heaven, they might be listening to as well), and Eric said he did as well; and she lay beside him on the grass, until she suddenly woke up, and one of the residents was on the stage, making announcements. She looked around and Eric was gone. She looked and looked and didn't see him anywhere.

Evening was approaching now, and the res was saying everyone had to go back to their cottage for the p.m. attendance roster, and everyone moaned.

"All right, all right," said the res. "But then you're on free time, until fireworks over at the ball field. And don't forget we also have movies and burgers and stadium dogs in the rec hall, till bed count."

Now everyone cheered.

She found Yolanda and Beatrice, who were the only girls left from their original group, and they made their way slowly back to the cottage, singing one of the songs they'd heard on stage.

A gray van passed them and Yolanda said, "Mmmm—mmmm, there go another van from Patton State. Things be turning round here real quick now."

Beatrice said, "That's the only thing good about being a fat, ugly, psycho white girl. Nobody wants to add me to their collection. No turnin' and churnin' for me."

THE BEAUTIFUL-UGLY

"*Turnin' and churnin',*" Yolanda sang, starting to sway, and Beatrice joined her—with Connelly between them, swaying back and forth together. "*Turnin' and churnin', oh turnin' and churnin'.*"

Now Beatrice hugged her. "I just hate the thought of someone taking our girl away."

Then Yolanda hugged her as well. "Ain't no one getting our little biscuit without a fight, girl."

Connelly felt warm and good inside, thinking about the day, winning the ribbon with Eric, the horseback ride, the feel of the two girls' arms around her now, making her feel protected and wanted again. After the count she went over to Eric's cottage, looking for him. She saw the other boys coming out the screen door, heading for the fireworks. She asked them if Eric was inside.

One of them shook his head. "Res already picked him up. They went over to the office."

"The office?" she said. "What for?"

Another boy, passing by her, said a little meanly, "'Cause that's where they take you when you're being turned, I think."

She stood there, unmoving, watching them walk away, laughing and talking among themselves, leaving her behind. *Turned? What was he saying—turned?*

Next, not really thinking about anything at all, not believing any of the thoughts that were gathering inside her head, she began to run toward the big house. She ran past everyone, also laughing and talking and going to see the fireworks, across the lawn, and around the corner of the house—and then stopped.

Mrs. Morton's long white sedan was parked there, along with another car that looked familiar to her, but she couldn't recall. Then she remembered the couple that interviewed them several weeks before: the Kelemans or Kelemers. It was their car parked beside Mrs. Morton's car. And she tried to understand everything that was coming inside her head now, even as she didn't want to understand.

Then she saw Anne coming down the steps toward her through the dusky evening. And suddenly she knew. She knew everything.

77

"Connelly," she heard Anne saying, coming up to her, "there's something I have to tell you."

"Where's Eric, Anne? Where is he?"

"Mrs. Morton's here, Connelly, and the Kelemans are with her."

"Where's Eric?"

She was standing there, looking up into Anne's face, when she saw her reach out to touch her, and she pulled back.

"He's not going with them, Anne," she said. "I won't let them take him."

"It's just for a while, darling, until Mrs. Morton can make other arrangements."

She stared up at her, disbelieving. "There are no other arrangements, Anne. You know that."

"Connelly—" she began.

But she didn't hear anything else. She ran around her, toward the house, feeling nothing now, really seeing nothing. She must have been crying, because she had to wipe her eyes, which were blinded, and then wiped them again, running. She reached the stairs and ran up them without stopping, pushing open the big front door and rushing inside, leaving the door open behind her. There were people there—visitors, she saw, and some of the residents and home kids, and they all looked at her. She ran across the great room to the offices on the other side. She looked in one, and there was someone else there—another resident and caseworker, talking. She ran to the next office and opened the door...and saw them all: Mrs. Morton and Joe, sitting in armchairs before the couch, upon which sat the Kelemans, with Eric between them.

Smiling, Joe said, "Hello, Connelly, we were just talking about you."

"You're not taking him," she said, looking at the Kelemans. "You're not taking him away."

"The Kelemans can only take care of one of you, Connelly," she heard Joe say.

Overcome, she burst into tears again, throwing her hands up over her eyes. There were people around her now. She heard Anne and Joe talking to her; someone had their arm around her. Then she heard Mrs. Morton's voice say, "I have children from the state hospital that must be placed, Connelly. You understand about the other children, don't you?"

"I don't care about them," she said. Now she was holding Anne, tightly, her arms around her, saying, "Please, Anne. *Please.*"

Only then did she feel the other hand on her. She heard his voice, whispering in her ear, "I'll come back, Con. I promise. No matter what, I'll come back and we'll be together again. I promise. I *promise.*"

She couldn't say it. What she was really feeling and thinking. That was—if they took him away from her now, that would be it. It would be forever, forever lost, just like her firefly without its glow. Like her parents dying. She felt that. She *knew* it. But she couldn't say that to him. She only turned and pulled him to her, feeling his thin arms and his body against her. She felt him crying, as well, and held him tight against her.

Finally, she made herself look at him. Her parents' death had taught her that, so quickly, it seemed. And Melissa and Anne taught her. How some things happened that could not possibly happen, but they did. And it was all right to feel bad about them, feel horrible inside. But then you started over with something else. You didn't go on with what you had, because that was over. That was gone. Instead, you started over with something else, they said, because you had no other choice, little by little, first by saying good-bye.

So she said, "I love you, Eric. I'll always love you."

She saw him nod and say, "Me too, Con."

"And we'll be together again, because that's what mom and dad wanted, isn't it?"

He nodded again.

She said, "But let's not say good-bye then, because we *are* going to be together again. And they won't be able to stop us then."

"All right," he said. She saw him hesitate and then say, "So why don't you go sit on our bench for a while."

She looked into his eyes, wiping her own eyes with her hand, understanding. "All right."

"And don't cry."

"All right."

Softly, she kissed his lips again. Then she pushed away from him, going between Joe and Anne, out the door. But once she was out of the house, going down the steps, she did cry again, crying hard as she ran, all the way out to their bench, and crying there with her head down, and her arms folded around her.

She was still like that when she heard the first explosion, then another, larger one. She sat up now, raising her head and looking back through the trees, toward the ballpark, and seeing the reds and blues and golds and greens bursting into the black sky.

She stood up now and began to walk slowly out into the wheat field, leaving behind her and Eric's spot. That night she walked a long way into the field. She wasn't afraid. It was very dark, but she didn't care. She even heard noises—things scurrying about her—and kept going. Until she found a spot where something had pushed the wheat down and she lay down there, rolling over and staring into the night sky, afire with all the bursting colors she could imagine, wondering why it had to happen so, just when things were becoming a little nicer for them again. Why? Then she remembered she had asked herself nearly the same thing when her parents were killed. Why? Because they weren't bad people. They weren't mean at all. They were just trying to have their little family. And they were killed. She thought then how her mother might have told her she could ask God about that. And, in fact, she had once, in the deep night, out on the Johnsons' dusty couch beside Eric. But nothing happened. Nothing or no one told her anything. Now it was the same thing. Why? She listened and only heard the insects around her. And the final burst of fireworks, before the long, deep silence ensued.

But nothing else.

10 ♀ FOSTERING OUT

The rains everyone wanted finally came. A front moved in off the Pacific Ocean, and it rained softly and steadily for almost a week. The things that had been brown and withered began to show hints of green again. But when the sun returned, it was even hotter than before.

"I don't think we'll ever get it right," Mr. Pete told her, sitting beside her on the bench, having a smoke. "First it's too hot, then it's too wet, and now it's too hot again. I guess we may all as well just settle down and live with it. Nothing else to do."

He laughed his rumbling laugh and smoked, but she didn't say anything. She watched him wipe his face with the towel he had around his neck.

She said, "Are you married, Mr. Pete?"

He looked at her sideways, and she was afraid she had said something wrong. But then he winked at her, and got that little smile around his mouth he did sometimes, and said, "Oh, lil pilgrim, I had me a *fine* woman. Married forty-three years, and she found a different way to fuss at me every single day of'em."

"But you're not married now?"

He looked at her and tapped the side of his head with his finger. "Right here I am, darling. Now, the missus died almost ten years back, but I'm still married right here. Always will be: tasting all her good cooking; seeing her first thing in the morning, with her long pretty fingers wrapped around her coffee cup; the sound of her voice; the sound of her in another room, putting things in their place. I'm still married, baby. Always will be." He looked away, smoking.

"Well, I've decided I'm never going to marry," she said. "I've decided, one day, Eric and I are going to have a house somewhere, a big house near the ocean, where it's cool, and I'm going to have a kitty, and he'll have a dog, and we'll go walking by the water every day, and no one will ever separate us again. Ever."

She sat there.

Finally, Mr. Pete said, "Well, lil pilgrim, there's all kinds of ways to live a life. And I can't say one's any better or worse than another. I think just the living's enough. Just figure out which way you're headed and go there. Everything else is just more gravy on the rice, as my missus would say." He chuckled again, field-dressing his cigarette and going back to work.

*

Once, in August, Eric wrote her a letter, saying he was doing okay, the Kelemans were okay. They had two sons, both older than him, and one of them let him ride his bicycle sometimes. The school he would go to in September was not that far from their house. He could walk to school, he told her. And Mrs. Keleman said she would buy him some new pants, or he might get some clothes from the older boys, he wasn't sure. He never watched TV now, because someone else was usually watching it, and all they watched were dumb comedy shows, which he hated. But he read a lot. The library wasn't far away, either. So he mostly stayed in his room and read. He missed her, he said. He missed her a lot. And he told her to take care of herself and to be careful. And don't forget mom and dad. Ever. I love you, Con.

Eric.

She wrote him back that same day. She told him how everything was going at the home, and everyone that said hello, and how much she missed him too. She missed him so much, it was almost worse than before, when Melissa told them what happened to mom and dad. It was almost worse than that. But soon school would start again, and she would have something to do. She would work hard in school, even though she wouldn't have Mrs. McDonough this year. But she could still go talk to her anytime she wanted. Then she told him about her dream: the big house they would live in one day, on a high hill looking down on the ocean, and everything they would do there. That was the only thing that made her happy now, thinking about that. I can't wait, Eric, she told him. I can't wait for that to happen.

Love, your sister, Connelly.

Then she put four large X's below her name for kisses.

Anne mailed the letter for her, and then she waited and waited, but he didn't answer her back. So she wrote him another letter, asking: *What's the matter, Eric? Why won't you write me? Why?*

Anne mailed that letter as well.

Then one day Mrs. Morton came to check on her, and while she was there she told her that Mrs. Keleman had called her and told her she didn't think it was a good idea if she wrote Eric, at least not for the time being. "Apparently, your letter upset him very much, according to Mrs. Keleman. So she wants to give him some time to get settled in. She said she would let you know when you can write him again."

She didn't see what would upset him. She was only writing him what she felt, and what made her happy. What, she knew, would make them both happy. She didn't understand it. And she thought they were lying to her; so the following week she wrote him another letter, and Anne mailed it. Two weeks later it came back with a large blue stamp on it that said: *Return to Sender.*

*

All through August different people interviewed her. She didn't pay much attention to any of them, except Anne told her they were from other children's homes, or people looking to foster, or, perhaps, adopt.

"Would you like that to happen?" Anne asked her.

"No."

She frowned at her. "Then what would you like to happen?"

"To stay here. And bring Eric back."

"You mean, you wouldn't like a real nice family to adopt you and make you part of their family?"

"No."

One day a couple interviewed her. They were a very quiet couple, older than her parents, but not too old. The man was a big man, with a deep, slow voice; and the woman was small and talked in a voice so low Connelly had to lean forward sometimes to even hear her. Mostly it was the man that asked her questions, most of which she wasn't sure how to answer; but near the end of the interview, the woman glanced at the man, then leaned forward and said, "Connelly Pierce, do you believe in the redemption of your soul through the Bible's inerrant word?"

"I don't know." She wasn't sure what that meant.

The lady blinked and smiled, sadly, as if she were sorry for her. "But you do believe in God, don't you?"

Connelly sighed and looked away, at other tables where people were talking. She looked back. "Sometimes, I guess. Like when I was with my mother at Mass, and she looked so pretty when she prayed. Like an angel. But sometimes not, because I've asked Him for things—to help stop things from happening—but He never answered."

She saw the man and women look at each other in a funny way.

They left soon after.

*

They came back the following week and talked with her again. Not long. And they didn't ask her about God this time. Instead, the man asked her if she was ready to have a new life. A new way of living that was so wonderful, she couldn't even imagine. She didn't know what to say. She just shrugged.

Then he smiled and said, "There's a whole world of things for you to discover, Connelly Pierce. His world is everywhere for us, just waiting to be discovered, if we know where to look. We just have to decide we want to do that. Each of us has to decide that."

He smiled again, while the woman only looked at her, unsmiling, as if she were at unease of something.

*

On Monday they came and took her away. Mrs. Morton was there to arrange everything for her. When she was finally ready to leave, Anne and Joe hugged her and told her they would miss her. Next, Yolanda and Beatrice hugged her. Everyone seemed to be crying. But she didn't. She didn't know what to think, or do.

"You take care, little biscuit," Yolanda said, wiping her eyes.

Both of them ran away then, back toward the cottage, not looking back.

Mr. Pete stood a little ways back, behind the others, smoking and saying, "So long, lil pilgrim, you take care now, hear?"

She sat in the back seat of the car, and someone shut the door, and they drove away. Going down the long gravel driveway, they passed the same cows she had passed, arriving. She looked at the cows, standing by the fence, looking back at her. Then she sat back in the seat, holding tightly to Priscilla, fingering the golden heart necklace around her neck, and stared ahead, as they passed under the high overhead sign that said Pilgrims Mercy, pulled out onto the narrow farm-to-market road, and drove away.

11 ♀ HER NEW FAMILY

*S*he knew instinctively it was not going well for her there. She knew all the signs by heart: the changing parade of doctors and counselors and caseworkers; the changing array of medications they gave her, trying to break her down, trying to make her give in to them. She knew it all so well, and ignored it, which she also knew, in the end, would not be good for her. At some point, she realized, they would give up on her. May had already done that. But when that happened, she knew there was only one thing left to do. They would find a place for her. And not just any place, either. But a special place. A special hospital where they put special cases like hers, and then forgot about them. They would put her someplace they didn't have to deal with her anymore, and they would keep her there for the rest of her life. Like the story she read once about poor Zelda Fitzgerald, F. Scott Fitzgerald's wife. The Beautiful and the Damned, as she recalled. Anyway, they would put her there, and she would grow old there, and, if she were lucky, maybe one day she would be consumed by fire there, just like poor Zelda was, in the end.

    She knew this now, very well. And it was as if she were watching it happen to someone else—not to her at all—but someone else entirely. Like reading the book about Zelda, she was seeing this happen, and it was about someone else. It had to be someone else. Because there was no her now. She didn't exist any longer. Somewhere along the way, she had actually seen herself starting to fade about the edges. And then the fading continued inward, until her entire self was *fading and fading, till no more. The invisible girl now. Right before her eyes. No more.*

So when they came and talked with her, and gave her their various pills and liquids in those tiny white paper and clear plastic cups, she could only laugh deep and hard inside herself. How stupid they were! How stupid! Doing all this—for what? Can't you see there's no one there? Can't you see that? She's not there anymore, and you're doing all this? For what? Why don't you go help poor Zelda instead? Pull her from those flames before it's too late. Can't you hear her screaming for you? You put her there, and now she's screaming for you to help her. Why, I can hear her screaming right now. You fuckers. You absolute fuckers locked her there, and then forgot her, and now she's screaming for you to help her.

Meanwhile, the girl in the bed next to her cried all the time and read from her tiny, blue-leather tome of Gospels. And at night, when Connelly turned her back away and curled herself into a little ball to try and sleep, she could hear the whispers, pleading and fervent, behind her. Sometimes, to try and make herself sleep, she followed along, almost subconsciously, against her own fading will, never missing a beat: *"Tell us, when shall these things be? And what shall be the sign when all these things shall be fulfilled?"* She held her breath, listening, letting her mind go, when she whispered: *"'Verily I say unto you, whosoever shall not receive the kingdom of God as a little child, he shall not enter therein.'"* And then she grimaced, shutting her eyes and waiting...

They lived along the farthest fringe of that hot endless valley city, in a brand new neighborhood, in a brand new two-story brick home, with a wooden plaque over the door that read: *The Cardswell Family*. Below it was another plaque: *God Bless This Home*.

"Noah made those in woodshop," Mrs. Cardswell told her in her quiet, sad voice. "Aren't they pretty?"

The brick the house was a funny, muddy-yellow color. The three of them stood there, at the edge of the small dry square of yard grass, looking at it.

"They call it squash," Mrs. Cardswell said sadly. "Apparently, the original buyers saw this brick in a catalogue and thought it looked unique. Then, when the contractor built it, they thought it was the ugliest thing they had ever seen, and told the developer they'd changed their mind, and they forfeited their entire deposit."

"We got it for a steal," said Mr. Cardswell, smiling broadly and winking at her.

Mrs. Cardswell sighed.

The two-hour ride there from Pilgrims Mercy had been uneventful. Connelly sat in the back seat, holding Priscilla, staring out the window, and occasionally turning to observe the two back heads of her new foster parents. They seemed all right. They were quiet and polite, calling each other Mother and Father, just like the Gundersons had done, and everyone listening to the radio, where a man was yelling: *"The time draws near, Sisters and Brothers! The time is creeping and crawling its way to our doorsteps—and are we ready? Are we right with our lives and with the Lord for that moment? That beckoning? Are we?"*

She could occasionally hear one or the other of them whispering something. At first, she thought they were whispering to each other, but then she realized they were whispering to themselves, or perhaps to the man yelling on the radio, she wasn't sure. But they both sat there, perfectly straight before her, whispering and hissing little words or sounds she couldn't make out. And after a while she just turned away, ignoring them and the shouting man, and stared out the window again.

Once, Mr. Cardswell stopped and put gas in the car. While the gas was pumping, she watched him go around the car and carefully clean all the windows, which were already clean, and then check something under the hood.

"Mother, would you like something to drink?" he finally asked, leaning inside through his open door.

"I certainly would!" Mrs. Cardswell said, happy-voiced, as if that was the most wonderful idea.

"How about an ice tea?"

"Ice tea would be just fine, Father."

"How about you, Connelly?" he said, now looking back at her.

"No thank you," she said.

THE BEAUTIFUL-UGLY

Mrs. Cardswell turned and looked back at her, smiling.

Mr. Cardswell said, "Young lady, when we interviewed you, you said you liked strawberry soda. I'll bet you'd like a strawberry soda."

She didn't really, but somehow she felt she should say yes, and nodded.

When he walked away, Mrs. Cardswell said, "Connelly, Mr. Cardswell enjoys buying things for us. That's one of the ways he tells us he loves us." Still smiling, she turned away.

Soon, they were driving down the road again, sipping their sodas and listening to the yelling man.

*

Now inside the squash-colored house everything seemed cool and neat. Oddly, they made her stand in the front room, at the base of the stairs, as, one by one, they called their children down to meet her.

"Rebecca," Mrs. Cardswell said, and a pretty teenage girl descended the stairs from somewhere above, dressed in a long beige skirt and white, long-sleeved blouse, black pumps, and around her neck—backdropped by the whiteness of the blouse—hung a tiny gold cross from a gold chain.

"This must be Connelly," she said, smiling and coming up to her and embracing her. She held her at arm's length, her eyes flickering over her, as if trying and failing to fix upon some point. Then smiling again, a little sadly. "Welcome to our home, Connelly."

She stood aside.

Mr. Cardswell said, "And now Matthew."

A boy younger than the girl, but older than Eric, appeared and came down the stairs and shook her hand. "Hello, Connelly," he said, glancing at her and away.

He went and stood by the girl.

"Noah," said Mr. Cardswell.

Connelly was surprised to see the same boy she had just seen coming down the stairs. They were twins, she realized, as this boy shook her hand, his eyes cast down, saying nothing, and stepped to the side.

"And finally our little Suzy," said Mrs. Cardswell, sighing again.

A chubby girl, perhaps a year or so older than herself, came down, giggling in her pretty yellow dress, and her yellow ponytail swinging behind. She awkwardly hugged her and announced: "You're staying in *my* room. We each have a bed. You have my old bed, because mommy and daddy bought me a brand *new* bed, with a new princess spread."

Connelly looked at her, not knowing what to say; only knowing she wanted so badly to be back at Pilgrims Mercy with Yolanda and Beatrice, and with Anne and Mr. Pete.

Next, another curious thing happened. With no one saying a word, everyone formed a circle there, at the base of the stairs, taking the hand next to them. Rebecca quickly and silently took Priscilla from her, and set her down on one of the steps, then took her hand. Suzy held her other hand. Suddenly everyone was bowing their heads, and, remembering the prayers she said with her mother at Mass, she did the same.

"Father," said Mr. Cardswell, "we thank you for this blessing you have brought us. It was through your guidance we were given the need of one of those lost and abandoned, and now pray we are fulfilling that need as you requested. Oh Lord, we ask your blessing of our home and family, and we ask you to bless the newest member of our flock, little Connelly Pierce. Oh Lord, ours is not to question why you took it into your heart to call home her mother and father; only to ask that you now fill this young heart and soul with your presence and love, as you have each of us. In Lord Jesus' name, amen."

"Amen," said everyone else around her.

Now everyone stood looking at her, everyone smiling, as she looked down at the squash-colored carpet, unsure.

"Mother, why don't you go grill us some boloney and melted cheese sandwiches," Mr. Cardswell said, rubbing his hands together.

Everyone seemed suddenly excited by this, moving about her. The twins disappeared back up the stairs. Meanwhile, at Mr. Cardswell's direction, Rebecca and Suzy grabbed her hands to show her around her new home. Instantly, in some unfamiliar, uncomfortable manner, she now felt she was part of the family; everything in the past being swept away by some unseen momentum; the new future arriving and surrounding her, smothering her with its pressing novelty.

*

As the days passed, she found each of them had their own manner, even as they tried very hard to somehow seem the same.

At night, little Suzy tried to lie perfectly still in her new bed across the room and go right to sleep.

"I don't want to talk," she whispered. "Father says nighttime's for sleeping. That's what God made night for, so we shouldn't talk, because He can hear us."

"Who can hear us?" Connelly asked, rising up on her elbow.

"Shhh—God can. He can hear us now."

She saw her lying perfectly still on her back and not moving.

Connelly lay back down, sighing and remembering how, at night, all the girls in the cottage would talk until no one had anything left to say. Of course, Beatrice talked the most, trying to make everyone laugh, which she usually did, but everyone talked until they were tired, and then they always went to sleep, until somebody had a nightmare, or Sara acted up.

"I don't see anything wrong with it," she said to herself.

"Shhh," Suzy said, otherwise motionless.

Mornings, before she did anything else, Suzy would kneel by her bed and pray. Connelly watched her, snuggling in her own bed with Priscilla. In their bathroom Mrs. Cardswell had placed her own glass and toothbrush, and her own tube of toothpaste, opposite Suzy's. "Don't ever use my things," Suzy told her. "Father says clean habits are the sign of a clean mind."

"At Mercy," Connelly told her, brushing her teeth, "if you didn't have something, like a toothbrush or something, you just used someone else's."

"That's disgusting," Suzy said, looking over at her, with the toothpaste foam covering her mouth.

Meanwhile, there seemed to be a rule for almost everything. The first morning, Mrs. Cardswell told her, smiling, "You just follow Suzy and you'll be fine. She's God's perfect little soldier, aren't you, Suzy?"

In their bedroom, Suzy told her how she should act: To always be polite, and say yes sir and yes ma'am. And, if she wasn't sure about something, to always ask permission first.

"Father says people who have to say they're sorry are sorry people," Suzy told her.

Connelly was amazed at Suzy's doll collection. Dolls covered the bed and small divan in her bedroom, and there was a glass-door cabinet in the corner where she saw small painted porcelain dolls, and dolls carved from wood, and, according to Suzy, real ivory from elephants.

"Mother and father were missionaries before I was born," she told her. "They went to Africa and South America and other places I forgot, and they always brought home dolls. And now I have *all* of them. Rebecca doesn't like dolls. Just remember—don't ever touch any of them. Father says some of these dolls are irreplaceable. That means they can't be replaced."

Connelly lay on her own bed, holding Priscilla, thinking how she didn't care about ever touching a single one of them.

Suzy looked at her and Priscilla and said, "That's the ugliest doll in the world, Connelly Pierce. Where on earth did you get it?"

"From my parents."

"Well it's ugly as sin. It looks like it has some sort of disease. Like cancer or something. I hope it doesn't get *my* dolls sick."

"It won't." She rocked Priscilla against her body.

THE BEAUTIFUL-UGLY

One day they brought home a new doll for her. Mrs. Cardswell came with it into the bedroom. It had long golden hair, and said things to her if she pushed a button.

She thanked her for it, and laid it beside her on the bed.

"You can give me that dirty old thing, Connelly," said Mrs. Cardswell, indicating Priscilla, "and I'll get rid of it for you."

"No thank you," she told her. "She would miss me too much."

Mrs. Cardswell looked at her, surprised. "Well, I guess, at least you have a choice now."

"Thank you, Mrs. Cardswell," she said again.

Mrs. Cardswell looked down at her. "Connelly, Ron and I talked about it. You can call us Mother and Father if you'd like. Would you like that?"

She nodded, although feeling funny about ever doing that.

Mrs. Cardswell stood there a moment longer, as if she wanted to say something else. But then she just turned and went out of the room, saying nothing.

When Suzy came home from her friend's house, she saw the new doll sitting in the chair beside her old bed where Connelly had placed her.

"That's not fair," she said. "I wanted the new chatty doll—that's not fair."

"You can play with that one," Connelly told her. "I don't care."

After a while, Suzy came and carried the doll to her bed, and laid her down among the other dolls. "There you go, Ruth," she said. "I'm going to call you Ruth."

Connelly watched her, moving about, arranging her things.

"I think she likes *my* side better," Suzy finally said. "I think she should stay with me instead." She looked over at Connelly, who was softly smoothing down the remaining strands of Priscilla's hair, and said, "You don't mind, do you?"

"No, I don't mind."

Smiling, she continued on, arranging her dolls here and there, making them just so.

*

Rebecca, who told her the first day she was sixteen, was happily nice to her at first, and then seemed to pull back, growing quiet again, as if that were her normal way. Watching her, Connelly thought she was the saddest person she had ever known. It was Rebecca who removed her cornrows her first evening there, before dinner, and took the gold hoops from her ears, telling her to put them away somewhere.

She said, "Father told me to do this, Connelly. I'm sorry. But he doesn't allow things like this in the house. Actually, I think it's all kind of cute on you. You're a very pretty girl."

Connelly sat there, wishing she could keep her hair plaited, and keep the hoops. It reminded her of Yolanda and Anne. But she didn't want to be rude. She remembered how Anne had told her every family would probably have their own little rules that were different from what she had before, and to try and follow them. Try and get along. Because being a foster parent was not easy to begin with, and if there were misunderstandings, that only made things worse. So she sat there, feeling Rebecca unravel the tight links of her hair, and feeling her long hair falling familiarly about her shoulders again, when she suddenly felt her lean down, whispering in her ear, "One day, I'll bet you're gonna be a real heart-breaker." Before kissing her on top of her wavy-haired head.

There seemed to be some kind of problem between Rebecca and Mr. Cardswell, Connelly saw, but couldn't understand. They always seemed to be a little angry or upset with each other, even when they were being nice about it. Rebecca seemed to try to avoid him, avoid everyone in fact, spending most of her time in her room, unless she had to come out. But she did have to reveal herself more often than not, because Mr. Cardswell always wanted everyone together for meals, and for saying prayers, which they did a lot.

At meals, Connelly observed everyone mostly quiet, except Mr. Cardswell, who asked them all questions in turn: how they were coming with this or that, and questions about the Bible. She was amazed how much each of them knew about that: who was the father of such-and-such; and who killed such-and-such, and why; and who said such-and-such, and what did it mean to them. What did God mean by saying it? And did they truly understand that in their heart, where God had placed it? It made her dizzy, listening to them, since she could hardly answer a single question he asked her, except those simple things she remembered her mother had told her about.

"So your mother was a Catholic?" Mr. Cardswell asked her once at dinner.

She nodded. She had already told him that, she remembered, during one of their interviews.

"And your father? What about your father? What was he?"

"He was nice to me," she answered without thinking. Then she caught herself, looking down, and then back up at Mr. Cardswell. "He made me laugh."

He looked at her a moment, then turned and asked Rebecca something about one of the deadly sins instead.

One night after dinner, out of nowhere, Rebecca grabbed her and pulled her into her bedroom, which she jokingly called her sanctum, asking her what kinds of music she liked, and what all the girls talked about at the home, and did they talk about boys and things? They were sitting, facing each other, on the carpet floor, near the bed; and seeing her face, the way she leaned forward, excited and secretive, Connelly had the impression of some kind of very hungry lost animal, ready to eat her up, if necessary.

Rebecca seemed amazed, hearing how at Mercy they could listen to pretty much whatever kind of music they wanted, which was a little of everything, since everyone seemed to like something different; and they could wear whatever they wanted, or could find to wear, including makeup, as long as it was not, what Anne called, demeaning to them; and sometimes they talked about boys, and sometimes not.

"Mostly, we just talked about girl things," Connelly told her. "Things that bothered us, and our problems and things. There were lots of problems, I remember."

Rebecca listened to her and then said, "Well, here you can't do any of that, and you need to understand that. Everything has to be sanctioned—music, clothes, talking, thinking—everything."

"What's that—sanctioned?"

"Well, our church has these strict rules of conduct that everyone is supposed to obey. You'll see, since we go to church at least three times a week, you'll see. School too. You'll go to their school, and most of the teachers are members of the church. They've got all the bases covered, little girl." She saw Rebecca seemed upset now. Her face was upset, and she was wringing her hands, as if something was on them she was trying to get off, but couldn't. She leaned toward her, whispering, "He even follows me on the web sometimes."

"Who?"

"Father. You see, only certain web sites are sanctioned, Christian chat rooms and stuff, and he knows I'm Jesus' Valley Girl, and he tries to catch me. He calls himself Dark Disciple 3280, which—duh—is his social security number, and he pretends like he's this mysterious young spirit, looking for a soul mate or something, and he tries to arrange meetings and things. Of course, I knew it was him right away, because I know exactly how he thinks and says things, so I just play along. I always tell him I'm not that kind of girl and to leave me alone, and that satisfies him, I guess. Anyway, the chat rooms are as boring as those sanctioned Christian concerts, which are the only ones I can go to, with everyone swaying back and forth with their eyes closed, and those stupid grins on their faces, and silly hands in the air. So I just pretty much avoid all of it now."

She sighed, seeming sad about all of it; but finally they started talking about music and clothes and boys again, and she began to relax, when suddenly the door flew open, and Mr. Cardswell was standing there, smiling down at them. "So what's going on, girls? What are we talking about?"

"The Gospels, Father," Rebecca said, sweet-voiced, smiling back at him.

Mr. Cardswell stared at her now. "And the particular lesson?"

"The law of Christ, Father," she replied. "Matthew 5:44. *'But I say unto you, Love your enemies, bless them that curse you, do good to them that hate you, and pray for them which despitefully use you, and persecute you.'*" She continued smiling sweetly at him.

Slowly, Mr. Cardswell backed out of the bedroom, shutting the door after himself.

Rebecca looked back at her, again leaning curiously and excitedly toward her, reaching out and taking up her hands into her own, whispering: "So have you ever heard any Snoop Dog?"

*

The twins were something entirely different. And they were different from each other, as well. Noah reminded her a little of Eric, the way he liked to read, and how quiet he was, unless Mr. Cardswell asked him something, telling him, "Sit up straight, Noah, and stop your mumbling."

Which seemed to only make him slump down lower, and mumble even more.

"You need to learn to be more decisive," Mr. Cardswell told him one night at dinner. "Of course, Timothy tells us that piety is good and acceptable before God; but remember as well that our Lord of hosts sends lean among the fat, and under His glory He shall kindle a burning fire. God wants His soldiers strong and ready for the coming battle, Noah. You do understand that, don't you?"

"Yes sir," Noah mumbled, slumping even lower.

Matthew, meanwhile, always sat up straight, and didn't mumble at all, but Mr. Cardswell reminded him that God also hated too much pride and arrogancy and the froward mouth, causing him to slump down a little as well.

Connelly observed how that they both seemed determined to please their father, especially Matthew, who always told him about something he'd done well, and waiting, when Mr. Cardswell would only shrug and remind him of something he had recently done *not* well, leaving the boy to promise he would certainly try and do better in the future, as both boys' chins dropped down against their chests.

As taken as they were with trying to please their father, Connelly noticed that her presence among them didn't seem to matter either way. Occasionally, she would try and talk with one of them, only to be ignored. If anything, they seemed a little embarrassed by her, as if she wasn't really supposed to be there, she didn't really belong there. And she *so* wished they would just talk with her like Eric used to do. It was their *boyness* that attracted her, especially Noah, who did small boy things in a quiet thoughtful way, especially when his father wasn't there, criticizing him, telling him to try and be better. Sometimes, in fact, the way he moved or looked at something or said something was exactly how Eric would have done it or said it. And her heart ached, seeing that, hearing it. But one time when she just went up to him and asked him something, Noah told her to leave him alone.

"You're just some stupid foster kid," he said. "You're something my parents want to do, because it makes them feel better; but don't try and be part of our family, because you're not."

That was the most he had ever talked to her, even though he was mean about it, and she told him she was sorry, and went to lie down on her bed with Priscilla, thinking about Eric, wondering where he was right then, and what he was doing and thinking at that exact moment. That was something she did a lot, even though nothing ever happened. She never knew what he was doing or thinking, or anything about him. But she still did it. She couldn't help herself.

12 ♀ LEARNING TO PRAY

One of the first things Mrs. Cardswell did was to buy her her very own half-sized Bible, with her name—*Miss Connelly Pierce*—inscribed inside the front cover. It was white imitation leather, with a zipper to close and open it, and all of Jesus' words in red. It was very pretty, and Mrs. Cardswell sat with her at the kitchen table the first evening she had it and explained it to her, the difference between the Old and New Testament, and how they were divided up, and what they were trying to tell her.

"My favorite books are the poetical ones," she whispered to her as a secret. Connelly noticed that Mrs. Cardswell whispered things a lot, especially when she talked about God, or when Mr. Cardswell was around, as if talking in a normal voice might bother them. She whispered: "Before she died, my mother was an English teacher, and we always had poetry around. But Ron thinks it's pure sinful to call the word of God pretty, as if that might interfere with its true purpose. But I don't think so—do you?"

Ron was Mr. Cardswell, just like Beth was Mrs. Cardswell; and Connelly could always tell when they weren't getting along, or disagreed about something, because they called each other those names then, instead of Mother and Father, when they seemed to like each other more; or, as Mr. Cardswell would say, "Mother is behaving herself now."

"Father would like you to learn your verses," Mrs. Cardswell whispered to her. "That's the way we hide God's word inside our hearts, and help protect us against the enemy. And Father wants you to hide lots of verses there, and be a good little soldier for God. Do you think you can?"

She nodded, not really understanding what she was talking about. "Who's the enemy?" she asked her.

"Oh, the enemy is everywhere," Mrs. Cardswell said, speaking a little loud and breathless now. "But you'll learn all about that in Sunday school. And that's where you'll learn how to be a soldier of God, just like the early Christians were against the Romans. Do you think you can do that too, Connelly?"

"Yes," she told her, because it seemed so important for her.

*

Actually, it seemed important to everyone in the family, and especially to Mr. Cardswell, who seemed to watch them all so carefully when he was around, as if one of them had already made a mistake about something, and now he had to find out who and what it was; or they were about to make a mistake, and he was there just in time to stop them and correct them.

Connelly noticed that as well: How everyone in the family was one way when Mr. Cardswell was not there, and another when he was. How no matter what they had been doing before—watching TV or reading or listening to music or just talking among themselves—as soon as he arrived home from work (where, as Rebecca mentioned, he was a manager in some sort of machinery factory), everything changed. She saw it was the exact moment his car turned into the driveway, and the garage door opened. No one said a word, but they all immediately stopped what they were doing, and became quietly involved with something else instead.

Once, Mrs. Cardswell explained to her, "When Father gets home he likes to get settled in without interruption. So you go with Suzy to your bedroom, and wait there."

So that's what she did, following her there, where she played with Priscilla, while Suzy decided which of her dolls she would play with; and they waited, sometimes until dinner if, according to Suzy, "He must have had a bad day.", or sooner if he came into the room, whistling and smiling and questioning them about what "my girls" had been up to.

If he had had a bad day, dinner was always quiet and almost sad, she saw, with everyone's head down, and answering his questions as quickly and quietly as they dared. Or if he was having a good day, everyone laughed at the jokes he told (which she never did think were that funny at all), and said "Yes, Father" this, or "Yes, Father" that, seeming happy and excited just to be noticed by him.

Then every evening, at eight o'clock exactly, everyone would gather in the living room for what they called Family Bible. That's when Mr. Cardswell would say a prayer, and one or more of them would be chosen to read something from the Bible, and they would talk about it awhile, and finally Mr. Cardswell would say another prayer; after which, they could go back to whatever they were doing before, depending.

Connelly usually enjoyed these little meetings, because everyone always seemed so excited about being chosen to read, and then having Mr. Cardswell tell them all what it meant, with everyone leaning forward intently, and sometimes raising a hand after to ask a question, which, she saw, Mr. Cardswell enjoyed very much answering.

In fact, it was at Family Bible one evening that she first learned, amazingly, of the coming Apocalypse, which, according to Mr. Cardswell, *they* were certainly all prepared for at a moment's notice.

"That's when everyone in this room—that is, if their house is *still* in order at that moment—will be raptured from the face of this sinful earth," Mr. Cardswell said, leaning toward her, his dark eyes filled with the bright hopeful light of the table lamp beside him. "And those that remain—and you'd better pray and confess you sins with every breath you take, you're not among them—will endure seven long painful years of tribulation beneath the hands of the Antichrist. That is, until our Lord returns to lead us in the battle of Armageddon, and begin his thousand-year rule, finally casting that agonized, teeth-gnashing bunch into the burning lake of fire—*forever.*" Then he straightened himself in his armchair, relaxing, and said, "Meanwhile, those of us, select and wonderful, will get to abide, also forever, in the house of the Lord." Now he looked at only her. "Those are the two roads, Connelly Pierce. And you have to choose which one you'll be on, and stay on, when the feathers finally hit the fan, as my dear mother was fond of saying."

Later that evening she went to Rebecca's room and asked her more about the rapture. She did that whenever they talked about something in Family Bible she didn't understand, which was almost every day; and she saw that asking too many questions kept Mr. Cardswell from talking about what *he* wanted to talk about, which seemed to frustrate him; so usually she just sat there and asked Rebecca about it afterward.

They both lay stretched out on her bed, where Rebecca told her, "Sometimes I imagine it'll be like this giant Hoover vacuum cleaner nozzle coming out of the sky and sucking up all the true Christians, and then these big drums will roll, and horns will blow, and the Antichrist will walk the earth, wreaking havoc among the sinners."

"But won't that hurt? I mean, being sucked up into the sky."

"I don't think so, but it's still kind of scary, imagining it."

"Rebecca, if I get sucked up, do you think I can be with my mother and father again?"

"I don't know, sweetie—were they good Christians?"

She thought about it. "My mother maybe, but I don't think my father."

Rebecca shrugged. "Then he might have to deal with the Antichrist."

"Even if he was nice?"

Rebecca shook her head. "It's not about nice, it's about confessing your sins, and hoping God and Jesus know you're on their side."

"Oh."

Then Rebecca softly patted her head, lying beside her. "Don't worry, little girl, everyone's scared about it. Even the Pope and all the preachers in the world. They're all scared silly, 'cause no one really knows who's getting sucked up at that moment of reckoning, and who's not. There's no way to tell, really, because then you'd presume reading Jesus' mind, you'd be second guessing him, and that's sort of a sin itself; at least, according to Reverend Billy. So everyone prays and prays and waits for the moment, and they're all just scared nearly to death. Of course, they pretend they're not, everyone smiling and full of Jesus' love, but they are. Actually, it's really kind of weird, if you think about it too much."

*

Sundays, she saw, were different from all the other days. On Sundays they went to church twice: in the morning, after which they had Sunday school and brunch at the pancake house, and again in the evening. Then, depending upon how he felt, Mr. Cardswell sometimes called another Family Bible at the very end of the day, with everyone stumbling to bed bleary-eyed and exhausted by the end of it.

Her first Sunday church was a little frightening. In the first place, she had never seen such a place (thinking it more like the enormous covered stadium she had once seen a circus, or the arena her father had taken her and Eric to see a hockey game), with its endless rows of colored lighting, hanging high into the heavens of indecipherable darkness above; and the brightly lit stage far below, revealed in glaring detail on the giant overhanging TV screens, surrounding the stage, and jutting out in every direction; but not really like a church; and certainly not like her mother's narrow little cathedral, which, she thought, could fit into one corner of it. And she remembered the close warm way the cathedral had made her feel, with her mother beside her, both of them together holding the rosary her grandmother had passed on to them, just before she got that unfamiliar glint in her eyes, looking at them, and had trouble remembering who they were.

Then she was sitting there, between Mrs. Cardswell and Rebecca, watching Reverend Billy on the overhead screens, jumping and oddly jerking and running from one end of the wide stage to the other, listening to him warning everyone about the deceivers among them, when he suddenly threw his hands into the air and began to make sounds, she had no idea what they were. After a moment, the lady behind her—startling her by leaning forward and grabbing the back of her seat with her clenched hands, and her mouth coming close beside her ear—began to talk the same way: *"Baa-baa nonna. Baa-baa meeno. Nosh-me-toka-muh. Toka-baa-baa-meeno."*

Suddenly people around her started standing up, people throughout the ocean of heads below and around her, with their hands outstretched, and their eyes shut tight, talking that way. Even the Cardswells stood up, even little Suzy, and began doing it. Mrs. Cardswell and Rebecca, pulling her up with them, were whispering the words or noises, she wasn't sure.

After a minute, when Rebecca seemed to grow quiet, only swaying back and forth, she leaned against her and whispered urgently, "What's going on, Becky? What's happening?"

Her eyes closed, Rebecca shook her head, as if in a daze, and whispered back, "They're talking in tongues, baby. It's the heavenly language, the sounds of angels coming to them from God. Isn't it wonderful?"

She didn't think so, it sounding like the greatest noisy babble she'd ever heard; as if something fearful and strange had come over the entire giant space, holding it and not letting it go. And she was glad when it was over, and everyone began sitting down, seeming satisfied with the event and themselves, and Reverend Billy went on talking about the deceivers again.

Then near the end came something else. When she heard Reverend Billy asking everyone if it wasn't their time to stand before their neighbor, and with their neighbor, in God's judgment, again, people in different parts of the arena started standing up and going toward him.

"It's the altar call," Rebecca whispered to her. "This is where you reveal yourself a sinner, and ask God for forgiveness."

Music was playing, filling the air: sad, mournful music, reminding her of when her parents had died; and people were standing up everywhere again, and making their way to the long isles, and going slowly forward; some of them were crying, and some smiling, but most had no expressions at all; while everyone else sat there, watching them.

Eventually, there were so many people there, other men in dark suits—all of them, moving back and forth across the TV screens, looking lean and dark-eyed and hungry about something—had to go help Reverend Billy sort them out. Then the dark-suited men were talking with people, one by one; then she saw the men in two's grabbing the sinner's hands and gripping their foreheads, pushing them backward; and most of them just stumbled backward, but remained standing; but a few fell down on the floor, twisting about like the worms she'd seen the Johnson boys drop on to the sunbaked concrete. Meanwhile, the music was playing, and people lay on the distant floor, twisting and turning, and Reverend Billy was yelling, "Praise the Lord! Praise the Lord!" And then he began speaking in tongues again, along with the old lady behind her, shoving her red lipstick-covered mouth near her. And Rebecca was also whispering something urgently in her ear about being "slain in the spirit." And she finally decided it was a grand spectacle, after all, like the circus or the hockey game; and not really that scary; although, she had no idea what any of it meant.

*

Rebecca had already warned her about Sunday school, during one of their talks: "Everyone takes it real serious, little girl. I think it's how they rate your allegiance and everything. You see, all the church children are God's little Spartans. And since you're a beginner, you'll be a Spartan soldier of God's fortune."

"What are you?"

"I'm a general, the same as the twins. We've all witnessed, and I teach summer Bible camp."

"Oh. What about Suzy?"

"She's a captain. She's been working real hard, learning all her verses and lessons and stuff."

"Oh."

Rebecca shook her head and said, "You ought to know, father takes a lot of pride in his little soldiers of God."

Brother Martin was her Sunday school teacher. That first Sunday when Rebecca had dropped her off and she went into the room alone, she recognized him, tall, thin, white-headed, as one of the men that had helped out Reverend Billy during the altar call. But he seemed nicer now, smiling and laughing and jumping around the room, asking her if she was ready to be a soldier for God. He asked her that standing in front of the beginner's class, with the other little soldiers, sitting before them in their circle of chairs, looking on.

"I think so," she told him.

"You can't *think*, child, you have to know," Brother Martin said.

Suddenly, he had that same lean, hungry look, she remembered, from the altar call.

"I can," she promised.

"Can *what*, child?"

"Be a soldier for God."

"Hallelujah!" Brother Martin shouted, his eyes opening wide, and his mouth grinning so that each corner of his lips almost touched an ear. He looked at everyone sitting there, watching. "Did all you little soldiers hear that?"

"Yes, Brother Martin," they all said.

"Then why ain't you clapping? Why ain't you *showing* you heard it?"

Everyone clapped their hands noisily, cheering her.

"And why ain't you hugging her now? She's joining your ranks. She wants to be a soldier for God with you. So why ain't you *hugging* her now?"

Now everyone was up, surrounding her in front of the room and hugging her; and she was smiling, feeling a little wonderful

THE BEAUTIFUL-UGLY

about all of it, in spite of how nervous and odd she felt about it as well.

Next, Brother Martin made everyone sit down, and they began that week's lesson, which was The Armor of God, in Ephesians, and which Mr. Cardswell had already talked about in Family Bible. So she sat there, only partly listening to him explain to them how important it was they all put on God's armor and be able to stand against the wiles of the devil; because she was more interested, and amazed even—watching him jump around a little wild-eyed, and shouting and laughing like God or someone else was tickling him as he talked—how he could keep the Bible raised, one-handed, above his head, slinging it this way and that, and not dropping it once, not even a page ruffling, as he shouted: *"'Stand therefore, having your loins girt about with truth,'"* and holding one hand clenched against his stomach, while his Bible-hand shot toward the ceiling, *"'and having on the breastplate of righteousness.'"* He then struck his chest with his closed fist, his head dropping against himself, and snapped his Bible shut, with it still held high above him, and jiggling only a little. And everyone sitting there clapped for him, much impressed; after which, a lady came and marched them all, single file, into the church cafeteria where they had cartons of milk and cupcakes with purple frosting, crisscrossed with little pink and blue swords.

*

As the summer passed by, she began to more and more understand what was expected of her, what she was supposed to do, and how and why; and she began to try as hard as she was able to do exactly that. This was not long after her latest case worker, a different lady, brought her a letter from Eric that, as soon as she was gone, Connelly rushed into her and Suzy's bedroom, shut the door, and ripped it from its envelope (which, she noticed, had no return address), reading:

My Sister,

How are things going with you? I hope, fine. I am doing fine with Mr. and Mrs. Keleman and their family. They have all really taken me in as part of the family, so I guess that's a good thing—right? Last week we went on a camping *trip into the mountains, and I caught some fish, and we saw a black bear. It was a long way off, but it was still pretty scary. And before school starts they've promised to take us to Disneyland, which we're all looking forward to. I still read a lot, but the other guys are teaching me how to play basketball, so I don't read as much as I used to. I'm bigger now. Taller, I think. But I think you'd still recognize me. At least I hope you would.*

The other thing is the Kelemans have said they want to adopt me, so that will probably happen. They are good people, and I guess I have finally decided about things. What I mean is I've finally accepted that mom and dad are really gone, and I can't keep thinking something will happen, some miracle or something, to bring them back. So I've decided it's a good thing I'm being adopted and I can live a normal life. I hope you can understand that, Con, because I know what we said about getting back together, but I don't think that's going to happen. At least not until we're older, and maybe can take care of ourselves then. Believe me, if there was any way I could figure out to do it sooner, I would. I hope you believe that, because it's true. But there's no way. We're both kids, and we can't do anything without grownups helping us. Do you understand that? I hope so.

My caseworker talked with your caseworker, and she told me your family was probably going to adopt you too. I hope that's true, and I hope they're as nice as the Kelemans are.

Well, that's all I know to say about it, except that I love you, Sis. You are my sister, my only real sister, and the only one (besides me) who'll ever know what really happened to us, and I'll always love you, and no one can stop that or take that away from me. From us. Everything else, maybe, but not that. Don't you think that too?

Love, Eric

*

The Sunday after she received Eric's letter she answered the altar call, surprising everyone.

When Reverend Billy asked people to come forward and confess their sins and accept Jesus Christ as their savior, she told Rebecca she wanted to go there.

"Are you sure?" Rebecca asked her, turning and looking at her unsure.

She nodded.

So Rebecca took her down there, tightly holding her hand the entire way; until they were approaching the stage, when Connelly felt her shove her forward; and she was walking into the gathering, not sure what to do next. A man stepped in front of her, his dark form momentarily blocking out the bright overhead lights. He shifted and she saw it was Brother Martin.

"Oh, my little soldier, are you here to confess your sins in the name of the Lord Jesus Christ and be saved?"

She wasn't sure what she said, if anything at all; but she thought she said something, and felt his hand on her forehead, squeezing her head, when she suddenly felt the surge move over her and down through her, as if she would be lifted off her feet. This startled her, and when Brother Martin released her, for a moment she thought she would absolutely fall down. She felt so weak and strange, not knowing whether to stand or fall.

Then Rebecca was there, putting her arms around her; and Connelly saw she was crying; she could see her tears in the bright lights, streaming down her face, and she began to cry as well. And they were there, holding each other, crying, and everyone around them, crying and holding one another, with some falling down in twitches and shivers, and Reverend Billy, standing high and wonderful on the stage above them, eyes shut tight, his urgent voice, everywhere through hidden speakers, reverberating and encircling her: *"Baa-baa nonna! Baa-baa meeno! Nosh-me-toka-muh! Toka-baa-baa-meeno! Namuh-reeshka-tuh!"*

13 ♀ THE CHOICE

They taught her how to witness others, showing her who to give the pamphlets to, and who the tiny gilded testaments, and what to say.
"You just look so darling in that pretty dress, with that long black hair and those dark violet eyes. I don't think I've ever seen real violet eyes before," Mrs. Cardswell said, standing outside the Whole Earth supermarket (where, according to Mr. Cardswell, all the rich liberal sinners shopped), getting her ready. There were two or three of the girls they would send together, because of how beautiful and innocent they looked together, and people would stop, coming out of the market, to see what they were doing.
"Hello, ma'am," she said, stopping one of the well-dressed women with her hand-woven shopping bag over her shoulder. "Did you know that the fear of the Lord is the beginning of wisdom, and knowledge of the Holy One is true understanding?"
"Well—not exactly," she said, surprised. "But aren't you just the most lovely child!"
"Ma'am, to accept Jesus as your savior is the first step away from the path of damnation."

"And someone should be careful," said the lady, kneeling down before her, looking into her face, "because I would just steal you away in a minute, and take you home with me."

Then she looked the lady right in the eyes and said, "Hebrews 11:1 tells us that true faith is the substance of things hoped for, the evidence of things not seen."

"And if I had you," said the lady, frowning, "I certainly wouldn't have you out here, doing this."

For that moment, looking back into the lady's eyes, she recalled the way her mother would look at her when there was something very, very important she wanted to tell her. For some reason, she didn't know what to say now. She held out one of the tiny books. "New Testament, ma'am?"

The lady took it and said, "And every time I look at it, I'll think about you. And I'll hope you're doing all right."

She slipped it into her shoulder bag and stood and walked away. And Connelly watched her walking, until one of the other girls came over and pinched her, whispering, "*You need to witness, Connelly Pierce.*"

She went forward again, stopping an elderly couple dead in their tracks.

*

As the months passed, an idea formed in her mind that if she somehow could become perfect in everything she did (or as near as God would allow her to be), that when the judgment did arrive, both her parents might be allowed to join her. Even with whatever faults and sins they had committed, that God would alleviate their mistakes with her own sheer sinless goodness and belief.

"It doesn't work that way," Becky told her, when she confessed her plan during one of their "whisper sessions," as Mr. Cardswell referred to them. "God doesn't pass out chits that we can slip to someone else at the last minute. We each have to prove ourselves in his name. Sorry, girl."

But she still held to the idea, keeping it to herself now, lying in bed at night when she thought about everything she had done that day, and how many times she had sinned; and every night she said a silent prayer, again asking for forgiveness, again promising to do better. Then she lay there each night, looking about her, wondering if it worked. She never knew for sure; although, some nights she felt better about it than others, she felt cleaner and more forgiven; but she wasn't sure if that was Jesus talking to her, or that was just how she felt then. She didn't know.

However, during the day she *did* know she had the most gold stars by her name in the Fellowship Christian Academy's Third Grade Class, which made Suzy so mad, she hardly spoke to her anymore, except to tell her to leave her dolls alone.

"I don't see why Connelly gets to be in Third Grade like me when she's younger than me," she complained to her mother the day the three of them drove over to the school to register.

"Because that's what her welfare transcripts say, Suzy," Mrs. Cardswell told her. "Besides, that's probably God's way of giving back something of what he took from her."

"Well it's not *fair*," Suzy said, looking over at her in the back seat.

"We can do our homework together," Connelly said.

"No thank you," said Suzy. "I don't want you copying mine."

So they did their homework separately, and Suzy complained to her mother about all the gold stars Connelly was getting by her name, while she only had two silver stars beside hers.

Her mother reminded her again, God was most likely only giving back a little of what he had taken.

Besides Suzy being mad at her and starting to complain to her parents why Connelly had to be there in the first place, the twins were also growing evermore quiet toward her, looking at her now with a new fresh-eyed suspicion.

She wasn't sure, but she thought it had something to do with the way Mr. Cardswell was always referring to her now as his "best little girl," and calling on her the most during Family Bible, and paying most of the little attention he paid to any of them, to her.

One night during dinner Mr. Cardswell announced that he and Mother (referring to Mrs. Cardswell) had decided they would soon begin adoption proceedings to bring his "best little girl" into the family fold. Connelly was surprised. That was the first time she had heard it mentioned; and, when he said that, no one else said anything except Rebecca, who reached over and touched her hand. "Now you and I can be real sisters," she said, smiling.

While Suzy and the twins just looked at her, saying nothing.

Connelly knew Rebecca didn't mind at all Mr. Cardswell paying her the most attention now. "That means he's paying less attention to me," Rebecca told her with a shrug in the bedroom that same night Mr. Cardswell had made his announcement. "So, how do you feel about it? I mean, being adopted into our family?"

"It's all right, I guess," she said.

Both of them were lying on the floor, the faint sound of gospel music coming through the radio on Becky's desk, when Connelly saw her roll onto her back, staring at the ceiling. "Well, I think you can do better," she said, then looking quickly over at her. "But don't tell anyone I said so."

*

The very next Sunday, Reverend Billy gave a sermon on The Cost of Jesus' Love, which she barely heard, thinking about something else. It was something she had been thinking about since Mr. Cardswell made his announcement, and Becky told her what she told her afterward; that same night lying in bed and asking God what was going to happen to her now. Was she really going to be adopted by the Cardswells, like Eric was being adopted by the Kelemans? Was that what He—God—wanted to happen? Because she wasn't sure herself, she told Him, and it would be nice if He could tell her something, so she could be sure. He didn't have to do anything, she told Him. She didn't want anything else from Him, unless, maybe, He could tell her something about how her parents were getting along. That would be nice, to know something, anything at all, about them. But she knew He was busy, so if there was any way He could tell her about this—about what was going to happen to her, or what He wanted to happen to her—that was enough. She hoped she wasn't asking too much.

Then Suzy began to snore across the room, and she rolled over on her side and went to sleep.

Now she sat in the middle of that vast auditorium, while Reverend Billy moved back and forth across the TV screens before her, wondering why God hadn't told her anything. She had been trying so hard to be perfect for Him—perfect in school, perfect at church and witness, perfect in every thing, in every moment—and it didn't seem to matter. Or maybe it did matter, but He wasn't going to say anything until the very end, on Judgment Day, which, according to Mr. Cardswell, was going to happen sooner rather than later. She barely heard Reverend Billy shouting: *"'If any man come to me, and hate not his father, and mother, and wife, and children, and brethren, and sisters—yea, and his own life also—he cannot be my disciple!'"* Now she saw Reverend Billy stop dead still and stare out at everyone. "Do you understand what Jesus is saying to you? Do you understand what Jesus is saying he wants from you? He wants your sole committed allegiance above all else—that's what he's saying to you. He wants your wretched sinful forsaken self stretched out before him, and nothing else—that's what he's saying. The question is—are you all listening to him? That's the question. That's what he wants to know."

After the service, everyone separated, going to their Sunday school classes. She was sitting in hers when Brother Martin bounded into the room, laughing and jumping around and slinging out his Bible above his head, announcing, "Today, little soldiers, we are going to recommit ourselves to Jesus. We are going to make the Pledge of Allegiance to Jesus Christ. Are you ready to do that?"

And everyone around her clapped and said, "Yes, Brother Martin, we're ready."

Brother Martin laughed and hopped back and forth from one foot to the other. "All right then, I want you each to stand up, one at a time, and say your pledge with me. Timmy, you go first."

She watched the boy in front stand up, facing Brother Martin.

THE BEAUTIFUL-UGLY

"Raise your hand up, little soldier, and repeat after me."

He raised his hand.

Brother Martin said, "I pledge allegiance to Jesus Christ my savior."

Then Timmy said, "I pledge allegiance to Jesus Christ my savior."

"Above every person and every thing."

"Above every person and every thing."

"Including myself, my mother, and my father."

"Including myself, my mother, and my father."

"I pledge absolute loyalty above all else."

"I pledge absolute loyalty above all else."

"In Jesus' name, amen."

"In Jesus' name, amen."

The boy sat back down and Brother Martin called the next little soldier to stand. Meanwhile, she sat there, growing more and more uncomfortable with each passing moment. She was trying to understand what was happening. What was Brother Martin making them say? And what did it mean? Then she remembered Reverend Billy's sermon and his words about everyone she had to hate, before she could really become Jesus' disciple, and she swallowed.

One after the other, she watched the boys and girls stand up and repeat the words, and sit back down. She thought: They're just words, that's all. They don't mean anything—not really. Do they? And she wondered and wondered, and felt her mind turning and changing in a way she had never felt before. Something was happening she didn't understand. And she didn't know what to think. Or what to do. Until she finally heard Brother Martin say, "It's your turn, little soldier. Stand up and say the pledge with me."

Connelly looked up at him and everyone else, now all turned around and staring back at her.

Suddenly she lowered her head, bringing both of her hands against her forehead, hiding her face.

She heard the gasp erupt from all the other little soldiers.

"Child, what's the matter with you?" she heard Brother Martin say. "Can't you say the pledge to Jesus?"

She didn't move. She didn't know what to say or do now. She didn't know anything, except that they were telling her she had to hate Eric and her mother and her father who always held her in his arms and did anything, absolutely *anything*, he could to make her laugh; as if his very own life depended upon her laughter. And she knew she couldn't do that. Not for Jesus. Not for anyone. And she was scared now, knowing she couldn't.

"Ain't you gonna *stand*, little soldier?" Brother Martin said. "Ain't you gonna say the *words?*"

Overcome, she huddled herself into a tighter ball, as if she could press and squeeze herself to the point she would just disappear.

"Oh, Brother Martin, Brother Martin," came someone's excited voice.

"What—*Timothy?*" came Brother Martin's frustrated voice.

"She's peeing the floor, Brother Martin."

"My—*damn!*" Brother Martin exclaimed. He then quickly apologized to all his little soldiers and sent someone for the church janitor.

*

By the time they led her out of the church, and put her in the car, and drove her away from there, she knew that everyone else there knew what had happened. She could see it on their faces as she passed them by, although she mostly kept her head down, sorry and ashamed.

The ride home was silent, except for the man on the radio, screaming at them all they must prepare, *prepare*. And perfectly still. Except when Rebecca reached over and squeezed her hand.

14 ♀ LOSING THE FAITH

At home, Mr. Cardswell told everyone to go to their rooms, except her. He even sent Mrs. Cardswell away to their bedroom, saying: "I'll handle this, Mother."

Connelly sat in the kitchen chair, wishing she could take off her best dress, which her real mother had taken her to buy, and which was almost too small for her now, and change her damp underwear, which burned against her skin.

Mr. Cardswell sat across the table from her and said, "You've done a very bad thing, Connelly. Brother Martin explained to me what happened, and I just don't understand. Maybe you can explain it so I will, so I'll understand."

Then he sat there, waiting.

She sniffed and lowered her head. "I'm sorry. I'll pray to God and ask for forgiveness, and I'll do better."

Mr. Cardswell's eyes narrowed now, watching her. "No," he said slowly. "I don't think I'm sorry is quite what Jesus would expect now, do you?"

She shrugged.

"Do you think Jesus can hear your shoulders moving?"

"No sir."

"*Listen* to me, Connelly," he said, now starting to sound frustrated like Brother Martin. "I work hard to make a good living for us. Now God came into my heart and my wife's heart, and He asked us if we didn't have a little extra we could share with one of His lost souls, and we said yes, we did. But I don't think this is really what He had in mind, do you?"

She wasn't sure what to say. Since God had never talked with her, not even once, she wasn't sure what He was thinking about. But she knew she should say something and said, "He wants me to do better. I promise I'll do better."

Mr. Cardswell sighed now, in a way, she knew, he still wasn't satisfied. "You've shamed me and you've shamed my family, Connelly Pierce. You've been with us nearly a year now, accepting the charity we've offered, but now in one brief selfish moment you've pretty well destroyed everything that's happened between us during that time. Do you understand that? Do you? You need to answer me—now."

She looked up at him then. "I won't hate them. I'll never do that."

He stared at her, wide-eyed, his mouth hanging open a little, but saying nothing.

Next, he stood up and carried the chair he had been sitting over to the door that led to the garage. He stopped and looked back at her. "You need to follow me."

She got up and followed him out into the garage. It was dark there, except for the light coming from the kitchen and from under the garage door. Mr. Cardswell turned on a small glowing florescent light over his workbench and sat the chair before the bench, facing it. Above the bench, hanging in the very center of the pegboard, among Mr. Cardswell's tools, was a small crucifix of Jesus, with tears of blood streaming down both his plastic cheeks.

"You sit here," he said.

She sat.

He said, "I want you to sit here and consider what you've done and what it means. I want you to understand how you've shamed me and this family. And I also want you to ask Jesus to look into your heart and try and forgive you; although, after the way you've treated him, I'm not sure if he'll do that now. And you're not to leave the chair, for *anything*, do you understand me?"

She nodded.

He stood there looking down at her as if, perhaps, there was something else she should do, or he was thinking of something else to say to her, she wasn't sure. Then he turned and went back into the house, shutting the door a little hard behind him.

She sat there, looking at Jesus on the cross, and looking at all the tools. In an hour she knew all the tools by heart, what they looked like, their particular shape and symmetry, even if she didn't know what they were used for. Her father, she remembered, had never been very good with tools at all; in fact, it was her mother, the scientist, who kept the small green toolbox under the kitchen sink, and who usually made the little repairs necessary. Connelly remembered how she would always become frustrated when her father tried to fix something, and usually made things worse, telling him to put everything down and just leave it alone.

Once, she was sitting at their dining table and saw her father through the kitchen opening saying, "I can *do* this, Emily."

"No, Michael, you're just fucking it up more," her mother said. "Now look what you've done."

"You're being superior again, aren't you?"

"Of course not, dear."

"Then you're being sanctimonious. That's your worst trait. That New England lineage of yours."

"Darling, why don't you just slowly and carefully lay down the screwdriver and back away."

"And why don't you just bite me," he said.

She remembered her mother holding him then (watching them silently through the little pass-through opening), her fingers massaging the side of his head to quiet him, giving him little kisses, which he pretended annoyed him.

Now she looked back at Jesus, looking back at her. She felt sorry for him there, hanging there like that with his arms stretched out and legs pulled up beneath him. And those *nails* through his skin. How that must have hurt, and hanging there in the horrible sun, and being thirsty. His eyes seemed to implore her to help him, and she wished she could. But there was no way; and, besides, she couldn't leave the chair, even if he were really hanging there in front of her, calling for his sup of water. Not even then. And she looked toward the kitchen door and shuddered and looked away, sighing and counting, once again, all the little holes in the pegboard that had nothing in them, whispering, "One, two, three, four..."

*

That night, after evening church, something else happened. When they arrived home, Mr. Cardswell again sent everyone, including Mrs. Cardswell, to their rooms; she started to leave with Suzy, when he said, "Not you, Connelly. I want you to sit on the couch and wait."

So she sat down and waited. Mr. Cardswell had left the room with the others, and he came back in twenty minutes, carrying a coffee service on a tray. She watched him set it down and fix himself a cup, putting in four spoons of sugar and a little cream, and then sit across from her, smacking his lips as he sipped the hot coffee, while looking at her disappointedly. It wasn't long before she could faintly hear a car stopping before the house, and after a minute someone knocked at the door.

Mr. Cardswell opened the door and greeted who was there. It was two dark-suited men from the church, she recognized, but didn't know their names. Becky had told her there was a council of church elders that were the ones that really ran things, not Reverend Billy who, according to Becky, just had pretty brown hair and liked to talk a lot; and these were two of the elders. They were both old, and one was tall and thin and white-haired, like Brother Martin, except he didn't hop back and forth from one foot to the other. He stood very still, always looking carefully about himself, and moved very slowly, not because he was old, but because he seemed to be thinking about everything he did, including moving slowly and carefully to his chair and accepting the coffee cup from Mr. Cardswell, nodding.

The other man was thin too, but shorter, and he was almost entirely bald, and wore gold-rimmed glasses, and looked at her severely like Fifi, Mrs. Bagleresi's dog, when it wanted to bite her. "Thank-you, Brother Ron," he said, when Mr. Cardswell handed him his coffee cup.

"You're welcome, Brother John," said Mr. Cardswell. "Here's the sugar and cream. Would you or Brother Williams care for something to eat?"

Brother John looked at Brother Williams, who sat there like a statue, until he shook his head. "The coffee's fine, Brother Ron," Brother John said.

"All right then," said Mr. Cardswell.

Now the three men sat there before her, as if she was not even there, talking about the church. Brother John asked Mr. Cardswell if he had contacted someone yet about installing the credit card machines in the church.

"They have us on the schedule to be over next week," Mr. Cardswell told him.

Brother John said quietly and confidentially, "I believe tithing by credit card is the best solution, wouldn't you agree, Brother Williams?"

Brother Williams sipped his coffee and nodded. "I believe it's much more effective—that is, I believe it's more in line with our current fiscal direction."

The other two men nodded their heads in agreement.

Brother John asked Mr. Cardswell, "You've got six coming, right?"

"Yes, and we can get more if we need them."

Brother John leaned forward in his chair, patting Mr. Cardswell on the knee, and said, "Why, some of the folks are even joking about using their frequent-flier miles to help them get to heaven."

The three men laughed quietly, sipping their coffee.

Finally they looked over at her.

Brother John said, "You understand, Connelly, when we talk of devotion to Christ, we are only saying everything else must come after. That is the cost of that devotion, and Christ is only saying we should be willing and able to bear it, if we truly believe. You do truly believe, don't you?"

She wasn't sure what she should say. "I just can't hate them, that's all."

There was a moment of silence, with the men making little glances toward each other.

"No one is asking you to hate them," Brother John said.

"But that's what Jesus says," she said.

"Well—" said Brother John.

"He was speaking metaphorically, dear," said Brother Williams. "Doesn't God tell you to honor your father and mother? Isn't that the first commandment?"

She knew it was. But she wasn't sure how she could hate someone and honor them as well. It seemed confusing to her. It seemed like they couldn't agree on what they wanted her to do. She looked up at them. "Can't I just love them both the same—Jesus *and* my parents?"

Then Mr. Cardswell said, "Jesus only wants you with him if you've got your priorities straight." He looked at the other two men, shaking his head. "I told you, she came to us like this. We've had her for a year now, and, after everything we've done, I believe that, deep down, she hasn't changed that much."

He looked back at her, shaking his head discouragingly.

Brother Williams smiled at him and said, "*'Joy shall be in heaven over one sinner that repenteth, more than over ninety and nine just persons, which need no repentance.'*"

She knew that by heart—the parable of the lost sheep, and she knew they were talking about her; but she didn't think she was lost, not really. She said, "If Jesus is really God, then why is He afraid of me loving them as much as Him?"

Brother John leaned forward and said, "In the first place, child, it isn't our place to question Jesus' reasoning. When we do that, our faith dissolves like—like the sugar in this coffee." He held his cup up in the air, then took a sip from it.

"Now that I'm thinking about it," said Mr. Cardswell, "there were signs along the way I should have picked up on."

"Let's not be too hasty," Brother Williams said.

But she saw that Mr. Cardswell was working himself into one of his moods. He leaned toward her and said, "Don't you understand, you could be putting my whole family at risk. I mean, if God identifies you with us, and blames us for your sins."

"But I don't think I'm sinning," she said.

"You *are* sinning if you don't pledge your devotion to Jesus," he told her. "Now I want you—right here and now—to say that pledge before Brother John and Brother Williams."

"But I can't—"

"You won't, you mean."

"But—it's not in my heart, Mr. Cardswell. And if it's not in my heart, won't Jesus know I'm lying?"

"No he won't," said Mr. Cardswell. "I mean—Jesus *wants* you to say it."

"Even if I don't mean it?"

Mr. Cardswell set down his coffee cup and began wringing his hands together, saying, "Don't you understand if you say something enough, after a while, you start to believe it."

She didn't see that. She looked away, only wishing she could go to bed, deciding she would rather listen to Suzy snoring than the three of them. She looked imploringly toward Mr. Cardswell, "Can I please go to bed now?"

"Not until you've said the pledge."

"But I can't."

"You won't."

"No—"

"And stop saying no to me. You know I don't like that."

She looked at him tiredly, distractingly, not really thinking about anything at all, saying quietly, "And Paul said to the Ephesians: '*And, ye fathers, provoke not your children to wrath*—'"

Dark-faced, she saw Mr. Cardswell come half out of his chair toward her, startling her. "Don't you *dare*—"

"Brother *Cardswell!*" said Brother Williams, holding out a hand to stop him.

Mr. Cardswell apologized and sat back down in his chair.

Now Brother Williams looked at her carefully a moment. "We've taught you well, haven't we, child. Of course, Paul also said we should bring you up in the nurture and admonition of the Lord, which is exactly what we're trying to accomplish here."

But she didn't say anything else now. She sat there, sniffing, waiting.

"Brother Cardswell," said Brother Williams, "we shall work this through, by and by."

Mr. Cardswell reluctantly nodded in agreement.

She saw the three of them get up, and Brother Williams shook Mr. Cardswell's hand, but Brother John embraced him, as to offer some greater support.

After they were gone, Mr. Cardswell motioned for her to follow him. They went back out to the garage, and he stood a little to the side, watching her, as she unfolded her metal chair and sat back down before the workbench.

At the kitchen door, Mr. Cardswell turned to her and said, "Oh, and don't even think about us adopting you at this point. You understand there would have to be some major changes for that to happen."

He went out, closing the door.

After that, she remained there the rest of the night, still in her red-satin, black-ribbon Sunday dress and shiny black patent shoes and white stockings, becoming so tired at one point she nearly fell forward off the chair—but catching herself, and sat upright, exhausted, and her body aching so badly she only wanted to lie down somewhere, anywhere, staring hopefully for a while at the

THE BEAUTIFUL-UGLY

hard concrete beneath her; until finally realizing that Jesus must have felt her pain and discomfort as well; must have felt her pain as she had felt his; as it was near dawn when she saw the tears of blood streaming down both his cheeks and dropping onto the metal lid of a small paint can there; which she couldn't see exactly, because it was too high above her; but she heard—the red tears plopping down one, two, three, four upon the unseen lid like the whispering, comforting sound of a softly dripping rain.

15 ♀ THE WAY IT ALL ENDED

She saw it was different now. It was all different, even though she couldn't say exactly what all the differences were. But she could feel things different, although no one said a word, except Becky, who told her she should mind herself. She should take *care*.

That was on the night before she went away to teach summer Bible camp, and Connelly went to her bedroom to watch her pack.

"How long are you gone?"

"A month." Connelly watched her put her favorite red-leather Bible into her suitcase and shut down the lid and zip it. Then she looked over at her, sitting there. "You be careful now. Do you understand me?"

She nodded.

Becky said, "The only reason they haven't sent you away is because they think they can turn you. It bothers them they can't."

"Turn me?"

She shook her head. "Just mind yourself, that's all."

*

In the morning Becky was gone. Becky who had been her best friend and confidant, which was the word Becky had used to describe their relationship. "We're confidants," she had told her.

"That means we have one way we talk to other people, to them, and one way we talk when we're alone."

She understood that. Then Becky said it was like the layers of mystery she felt when she was sitting in church. Like layers of vapor in the air you breathed, when you thought and saw things differently. That is, things said, things understood, depending upon which layer you were in at the moment. And you had to act accordingly, Becky told her.

The day she left, Connelly felt the familiar wrenching emptiness inside her, which she had never known before her parents and Eric left her. Before that, it was like nothing bad could ever happen to her. She was loved too much, protected, for that to happen. In fact, she hardly thought about bad things, before. But now she understood. Bad things could happen to anyone, anytime, no matter how much you were loved and protected. And she missed Becky even more because of that. Because she loved her and because, in the blink of an eye, she knew she might never return to her. It could happen. She knew that now.

Sitting alone with her in the kitchen, Mrs. Cardswell read her Bible to her and tried now and then to explain the importance of sacrifice, whispering, "We must all learn to give ourselves over to God, Connelly. He says in Samuel, *'Wherefore kick ye at my sacrifice and at mine offering?*' God doesn't like it when we tell Him no. He doesn't like it when we misbehave. Neither does Mr. Cardswell."

Who, she saw, spoke to her even less now than he did before. Once he saw that making her sit out in the garage wasn't going to change her much, he more or less began to ignore her, speaking to her only when he had to, or telling Suzy or Mrs. Cardswell to tell her this or that.

"He's shunning you," Suzy told her when they were playing with their dolls in the bedroom. "You're a sinner and he's separating you from his life."

"I'm not," she said.

"You are," said Suzy. "Why do you think they make you sit in the cafeteria now, instead of going to Sunday school?"

She didn't say anything. She lay on her bed, trying to gently rub one of the scratches off Priscilla's face.

Suzy said, "Father says Brother Martin doesn't want you contaminating the other little soldiers with your ideas."

"That's stupid," Connelly said.

"I'm telling father what you said."

"What's he going to do—make me go sit in his ugly garage?"

"I'm telling," Suzy said, and ran off to do so.

But he didn't do anything. She knew he wouldn't anyway, because he had, according to what he announced to everyone one night at dinner, "washed his hands of her." And, after a while, Suzy returned and began rearranging her dolls again.

*

Then one late Sunday afternoon, the week after Becky had gone away, she was alone in her bedroom. They had all returned from brunch an hour before, and were waiting for evening church. She always thought that an odd time for everyone, between churches, with nothing exactly to do; and she was lying on her bed with Priscilla, when the twins came suddenly into the room, both still dressed in their matching dark blue trousers and white shirts and red bow ties, and shut the door behind themselves.

She didn't say anything, but she was surprised. That was the first time either of them had ever come into the room, and now they were both there.

"What's the matter?" she asked them.

Matthew said, "Do you want to be sent away?"

"No."

"Then you need to be quiet or father will send you away. He told us he would."

She didn't know what they were talking about, but then they had never talked to her about anything like that. But the next thing she knew, there was one of them on either side of the bed. She looked up at both of them, and their faces were red, looking down at her.

Matthew said, "I'll hold her down."

She was so surprised, she said nothing as they both sat down, one on either side of her, and Matthew leaned over her and pinned her against the bed with his hands.

"What are you doing, Matthew?" she said, looking at him curiously, not understanding any of it.

He said, "If you're not quiet, we'll tell father, and he'll send you away. He told us he would, so you better be quiet."

"But what are you *doing?*"

"Hurry," Matthew turned and said to Noah, who was lower on the bed, nearer her legs.

She could barely see past Matthew, leaning over her and holding her, to what Noah was doing. But she could feel him, lifting her white-chiffon hand-me-down dress, and pulling down her underwear.

"What are you *doing*, Noah?" she said, catching her breath.

He didn't answer her.

She lay there, staring at Matthew, whose eyes avoided her, and felt what was going on below. She could feel his fingers, first one, then another, like little crooked worms, inside her.

"*Hurry up,*" Matthew said.

After a moment, they changed places. Noah held her, while Matthew went below, and her seeing the top of his head lowered against her like a burrowing beetle; and she again lay still, feeling the gouging fingers. It hurt a little, and she winced, noticing Noah wouldn't look at her either, averting his face.

When Matthew was finished, he pulled up her underwear and pulled down her dress, telling Noah, "You can let her go now."

At the door Matthew turned halfway toward her, warning her again about saying anything. "He'll send you away," he said.

Now they both went quietly out, shutting the door behind them.

Afterward, she continued to lie there. She finally pulled her legs up against her body and held Priscilla tightly against her. She was still lying there when Suzy came and told her she had to hurry, that everyone was waiting to go to evening church.

They came again the following week. Twice. The second time she struggled against them, standing in the middle of the bedroom floor; and Matthew slapped her hard across the face, and she began to cry.

"You better shut up," he told her, giving her a shake.

Then, sniffling, she lay obediently down and let them examine her and probe about her as before.

After they were gone, she lay curled up, thinking about what she should do. She understood they were touching her there, and that was wrong, but she didn't know what to do. She knew if she told anyone, they would send her away. She knew that and was afraid. Where would they send her now? She didn't know. She didn't know anything anymore, except where she was now, which she really didn't like; but she was afraid where they would send her next; that it might be even worse. It was all so confusing now, everything about everything was confusing, and she lay there and cried a little about it, but not much. She thought about the crying, how much she had cried since Melissa had first told her about her parents dying. Then she thought about the twins and what they were doing. She didn't understand it, why they wanted to do it. They would just touch her there with their fingers—always the same: first, one little finger wiggling about inside her, then another. It was silly, all that fiddling about, and why would they do it? What could they possibly be looking for there? She thought it was silly. Boys were silly, doing it. And she lay there for a long while, trying to understand all of it, until Suzy came in with one of her girlfriends, and they laughed at her for lying on the floor like that.

"You look like a snail," said the girl.

And they both laughed at her.

*

When she turned eight and was in the Fourth Grade, she began to notice things. It was mostly the way she thought about things—the new, different ways she was able to think about them. She wondered why, considering it often at night over some months, and thought it probably had something to do with the cost of Jesus' love (at least, as it had been explained to her), which she thought excessive; as well, with the twins fiddling about her, which she had finally stopped, all of a sudden, just by telling them—no. That was the day they pulled her into their room, and, as they fumbled once again with her pants, she stopped them, slapping away Noah's hand.

Then Matthew pushed her hard against the door.

"I'll go tell your mother," she said, wincing, raising her arms, her hands becoming fists before her.

They both looked at her, disbelieving.

Matthew said, "They'll send you away. They'll put you somewhere you won't like."

"Good," she said. "At least I won't have your filthy little fingers inside me anymore."

Now they both stared at her, until Noah said, "We better let her go, Matt."

Matthew continued staring at her, flush-faced and furious. "Get out of here," he said, almost choking, almost ready to cry.

And she left.

*

These months passing, she could see, ever so faintly, she was growing up. She saw it mainly when she looked into the mirror: How her little girl's face was changing, becoming something else; with the softness of her cheeks melting away and her real cheeks appearing; her brows and her chin as well; her nose; all becoming more distinct, more *her*. But it was her eyes that most interested her. Not so much the eyes themselves, with the dark, wet look of them, but the searching way they looked back at her, looking back at them. And there was one moment, for the very first time, she wondered who she was. Who was she, really? Because her eyes, her face, were not telling her much, except that they were changing...into something else. But each time she thought she caught a glimpse of who was there, she was gone, and someone else appeared, also disappearing before she could catch her. It was frustrating, but she did see something after a while that seemed to calm her, or even excite her, in spite of everything.

There were moments she saw bits and pieces of her mother there, of her father, in her very own face. And it was amazing glimpses: her mother's smart thoughtful pretty gaze, or her father's funny wicked glance, at her. She caught her breath. Were they there? Were they really there inside her, growing inside her, and somehow making their way out to look at her and, in their way, talk with her? Or was that God's way (after all this time) of telling her about them? She wondered. She looked again…but saw nothing but herself, disappointed.

*

The way it all ended with them, with the Cardswell family, at first surprised her. And then it didn't. It had been going forward as always, the weeks and months passing, with nothing seeming to change, but everything different at the end.

One night during Family Bible, Becky told Mr. Cardswell that she had changed her mind. She had decided not to go to the Bible college, as they had talked about, and that was only an afternoon's drive away. Instead, there was a liberal arts college, in another state, where she wanted to study medieval history; she was interested in that instead.

Mr. Cardswell stopped his Bible lesson and looked at her. "I thought we had agreed on this, Rebecca."

"I've changed my mind, Father," Becky told him. "I've given this a lot of thought, and this is what I want to do."

"We'll talk about it later," Mr. Cardswell said, opening his Bible again.

"There's nothing to talk about, Father," Becky said. "I only hope you and mother will give me your blessing."

Mr. Cardswell shook his head. "Neither our blessing nor our money. Are you prepared to finance this crazy scheme on your own?"

"I can get aid," she said. "And I'll get a job if I have to. And, Father, this is not some crazy scheme. This is the first important thing in my life I've decided on my own to do, and I'm going to do it."

Connelly also thought that was the first time she had seen Mr. Cardswell so. He stared at Becky, and then he looked over at her. "This is *her* influence, isn't it? We were fine before she came here and disrupted everything."

"This has nothing to do with Connelly," Becky said. "This is *my* decision."

"*Your* decision?" he said. "*Your* decision, Rebecca?" He then lifted up his big Bible and slammed it down hard on the table, making everyone around the table jerk and wince. "Well, *damn* your decision, I say! And *damn* the day we brought her here among us!" He pointed his finger at Connelly, staring severely back at him now, unblinking. "You've done this. You've changed her."

"No, Father," said Becky.

"Yes, it's her all right," Mr. Cardswell affirmed. "I know what you two talk about when you're together, and it's nothing good."

"That's not true, Father," said Becky.

"Oh yes," he replied. He looked back at Connelly. "I remember when we brought her here. With her braided hair. And her cheap jewelry piercing her wanton flesh. I wanted to believe. I felt God was telling me to do that. But deep in my heart I was suspect. I know you can't always turn such bad into good. That is, in spite of our best intentions, the unholy and the ungrateful remain unto themselves."

"Oh, Father—" Becky said.

Mrs. Cardswell said, "Father, why don't we talk about this after Bible."

"There's nothing to talk about," Mr. Cardswell said. "And, Mother, I want you to stay out of this. I've already told Rebecca how it will be, and there's nothing more to discuss."

Now Connelly saw the tears in Becky's eyes. Then she saw her lay down her Bible on the table beside her and say in one of Mrs. Cardswell's whispers, "You're suffocating us, Daddy. Don't you know that? Can you understand that? You're suffocating this family and each person in it, just as you've suffocated yourself."

"Don't you dare talk to me in that manner," Mr. Cardswell told her.

"But it's true, Daddy. Why can't you see that?" She looked around at the others. "Tell him. Tell him what you feel. Tell him what he's doing to you. To us. Mother?"

Mrs. Cardswell lowered her head, her face, as far as she could; pushing her chin deeply into her gray and pink Sunday dress.

"You should go to your room, Rebecca," said Mr. Cardswell.

"I'm going," Becky said, getting up. She picked up her Bible and held it against herself. "What you need to understand is that there are things in life besides what you want and what Jesus wants."

"I'll not have you—" Mr. Cardswell began.

"I'm sorry, Daddy," Becky interrupted him, speaking over him. "I'm sorry for you, and I'm sorry for us. And I'm going to my school."

When she was gone, Mr. Cardswell looked a little lost or like someone might have slapped him. He began reading Scripture to them again, but soon stopped, and told them all quietly that Family Bible was over.

*

The following Sunday, when everyone was preparing for morning church, Mr. Cardswell came and told her not to bother dressing.

"Your caseworker's coming," he told her. "There's something she wants to talk with you about."

As they were all leaving, Connelly sat there in the front room, watching them go out without saying anything. Becky was the last to go and stopped to hug her. "I love you, baby," she said. "I'll always love you."

"What's happening, Becky? What's going on?"

"I don't know. I really don't. He's not talking to me either. But I don't trust him."

Outside, Mr. Cardswell was beeping the horn.

They hugged again. "Oh—please be careful," Becky told her and ran out.

She sat there for maybe half an hour when she heard the car pull into the driveway outside. She sat there, waiting for her caseworker to knock at the door, when suddenly the door opened, and Mr. Cardswell came back inside, shutting the door behind him.

He stood there, watching her. He finally said, "I wanted the opportunity to talk with you, Connelly, without the interference of others. Fortunately, I had to run an errand for the church, so I was able to leave, unattended as it were."

He stood there a moment. Then he stepped once, twice, toward her and stopped. He almost seemed ready to smile, but not quite. He said quietly, "What kind of thoughts do you have? I mean, when you're alone. When you're by yourself in the most secret places. Just you. No one else looking. Or listening. Or watching. What are your thoughts? Knowing you as I do, I can only imagine them impure and…unrestrained."

She didn't say anything. Somehow she felt he didn't expect her or even want her to say something. She swallowed.

He walked across the floor, to the chair opposite the sofa, turned, and sat down. He carefully smoothed out the leg of his blue church pants.

"What I wanted to tell you is this." He looked at her, blinking once, his face seeming to harden like a mask. "No matter what you thought your life has been like to this point, it's nothing compared to what's in store for you next. By that, Connelly Pierce, I mean all the pain and hurt and sorrow you've felt so far is nothing to what you're going to feel now. God's told me that. Yes, He has. He told me that taking your parents from you, taking your brother from you—that's just the beginning. And He's not going to stop until He's taken everything from you like Job. Everything. Until you're entirely alone in the wilderness of His kingdom. Naked and alone and exposed to all the evil that's due sinners such as yourself. And, in the end, you will only spend your days of damnation burning in those liquid, eternal fires, with all the other sinners. Do you understand me? God wanted me to tell you that, privately, just for your benefit." He stopped now and, in fact, did offer her a little smile. "So what do you think of that, child? Don't you feel special? A message from His Almighty, just for you. You should feel special. What I mean is, you are special, Connelly. You—"

When she saw him lunge toward her, she rolled away on the sofa, trying to get to her feet. Trying to get away. She was half standing when she felt him grab her from behind and throw her back down where she had just been sitting. His hands gripped her arms now, his fingers squeezing her hard, as he pushed her into the soft cushion, and she cried out.

"Shut up, damn you!" he screamed at her, his red face just above hers. "Shut up, you filthy little—"

Next, she was gagging, as he pushed his face against hers, pushing his big tongue inside her mouth. She was gagging, unable to breathe, with his tongue filling up her mouth. At last, he withdrew his tongue from her mouth and began to bite her—little bites—on her lips and face, as he made little noises, little moaning noise, like a baby would make, being fed. Then she felt him licking her. The same horrible tongue that had just been inside her was now licking her, like it was licking an ice cream cone. Licking the side of her face, her neck. She lay there, still, her eyes closed, as he licked her face a little more, and then stopped.

Finally, she opened her eyes and looked into his eyes, and she thought at that moment the devil was there, upon her. The look in his face, looking down into hers. The red eyes. *The devil*, she thought, and didn't move at all. Not a muscle.

Now he slowly rose off of her, standing and straightening his suit. Then he turned away and went out the front door, shutting it softly behind. After a moment she heard the car engine start and the car back out of the driveway and drive away.

*

After that, she sat there perfectly still for almost an hour, before she heard the different-sounding car drive up in the driveway.

THE BEAUTIFUL-UGLY

Someone walked up the sidewalk to the front door and rang the bell. She went there and it was a man she had never seen before.

"Connelly Pierce?" he said.

She nodded.

He looked at his wristwatch. "Have you packed yet?"

She stared at him and then said, "I'll do it now."

"Hurry," he said. "We've got to drive all the way back to the city, and I still don't have a shelter lined up for you."

For some reason, she wasn't surprised. As she threw her things quickly into her knapsack, she told herself that. It was Sunday and she was leaving the only home she knew, with a man she had never seen before, and, after today, most likely wouldn't see again. And she remembered how Yolanda once told her it was usually better to be in a bad place you *did* know, than to be going someplace else you didn't.

"That's experience talking, little biscuit," Yolanda had said. "Sometimes experience all you got."

When she was finished she went out and got into the car and the man drove them away.

By nightfall they were driving back across the Bay Bridge, going back into San Francisco, the city looming both dark and bright-lighted before her.

Then she remembered the time she drove across that same bridge at night with her parents and Eric; and her father was in one of his silly moods again, making up silly song lyrics and singing them to their mother in his silly voice.

He sang:

"We love you more than a mountain,
We love you more than the...sea.
Your love fills us like a fountain,
Your love puts us at peace..."

"That's horrible, Michael," she remembered her mother said, laughing. "That's really bad, even for you."

"C'mon, kids," her father had urged them then. "Let's sing it one more time for good old mom!"

And they were all laughing then, singing together and laughing: *"We love you more than a mountain..."*

But she didn't know anything now. She was sitting in the back of the caseworker's car, with everything being left behind, and the dark city looming before her. And she was turning nine in less than a month, and had absolutely nowhere to go, and now she didn't know a thing. Not a thing.

PART TWO

INTO THE ABYSS

16 ♀ IN THE OUT DOOR

*S*he knew almost immediately when they increased her Prozac. She could feel the rise of nausea inside her until she vomited over her bed-clothing and developed diarrhea, and they backed off. Her caseworker, a girl named Sheila, came each morning and tried to question her. She was sweet and urgently empathetic and clueless. Usually, once it was again clear nothing was to be gained by her inquiries, the intern would lean back and begin to prattle on about her own life, as if Connelly was working her case, there being so much to divulge, and so little time.

She talked about her boyfriend, whose name was Fred, and about her university days, and what she liked to eat, and her favorite movies or music, and about her family. How she didn't use to get along with her mother, but did now. And how her father, who had died of cancer two years ago, used to read to her as a little girl, and how much she still missed that.

"Even after all these years," she said. "I still remember him doing that and how much it meant, and how I don't think I ever told him, you know, when I had the chance."

And when she got up, wiping her eyes, and left the room, Connelly lay there, staring after her out the open door, into the long hospital corridor, seeing the frenetic movement up and down its length...seeing...

There was an old tattered green-backed book, with cracked and flaking gold embossing, her own father used to read to her, called, *In the Out Door,* by R.J. Middlebrooks, and it was her favorite book then. It was all about a boy named Freddie Humphrey who, after misbehaving one day (she recalled, hitting his sister, and arguing with his parents, and forking the last dinner chop without permission), was sent early to bed; whereupon, late that night, Freddie was whisked away from everything dear and familiar to him by a good but bumbling wizard named Moglathorp. As it happened, Moggie, as Freddie called the wizard, needed his help to overcome a spell placed upon his land, called Glannamora, by the evil wizard, Benadarne, who, by the way, had also stolen Moggie's beautiful daughter, Diadeara, away to his own mountain kingdom, called Izog, and Moggie was in a fit about the whole thing.

"The Grand Wizard says you're the only one to help me," Moggie informed him, once they landed safe and sound in Glannamora. "He says you're just the right kind of bad little boy I need to do what has to be done."

"But when can I go home?" Freddie whined. "I want to go home."

"When the spell is broken, and I have my daughter back—you selfish little boy," said Moggie. "And not one instant before."

Thereupon, Moggie and Freddie set out to do battle with Benadarne in the wild and horrible Izog; eventually, of course, setting everything right, but not before Freddie is changed in the process. In fact, the last trial he is given is to run in through Benadarne's infamous Out Door, located in the middle of the Forest of the Night, and guarded by the wretched, foul-breathed dragon, Vladiscone, and which, he is told, will break the evil spell and free Diadeara, but will forever destroy his chance of going home again.

Freddie does, of course, run the wrong way through the door—battling Vladiscone in the attempt—and Diadeara is freed, and promptly falls in love with him. But then the Grand Wizard arrives and tells Freddie that, because he has learned such a great lesson about himself, the decision had been made, after all, to allow him to return home; which, amid much weeping and promises to one day return, he finally does.

Time passing, Connelly remembered the odd little book, and invented a game she played in her mind, she also called *In the Out Door*. Playing it, she pretended she had been taken away from her family, as Freddie had been, and was traveling through the evil land of Izog, trying to make her way back to them. And there were many things she had to do, to overcome, in order to make it there: Crazy things. Silly, awful things that made absolutely no sense. But eventually, she told herself, if she did them, endured them, and overcame them like Freddie, she could go home as well.

She played that, and that was how, in the beginning, she kept herself from thinking too much about the other side of it. The side that, she somehow knew if she thought about too much, she didn't know what she would do with herself. She didn't know what would happen to her. So she played this game, on and off, months passing. Then a year passed. Until finally she grew tired, pretending. She knew perfectly well nothing was going to change for her. It was not like Freddie and Moggie's tale, where, once they had endured all the evil trials, their lives would be normal again. It was not like that at all. And she began to think about the other side of it. Which was that everyone and everything she once knew was gone. And all she had left were those crazy things. Those silly, awful things. And nothing else. And what could she do?

"*Oh, Moggie,*" she whispered Freddie's familiar refrain one night to herself, sitting on yet another hard, dirty-orange plastic chair, in the latest harshly bright office, waiting for them to decide what to do with her this time, "*what ever could happen next?*"

Until, moving ahead, she let go of that as well. Or, more exactly, one day it was no longer in that part of her mind she could easily get to; although, she didn't notice at all, in the passing.

*

Where before the changes about her seemed to come in gradual, great heaping waves, gathering up and sweeping down over her (there being the initial cold shocking tumult of her lost home and family, followed by the descending shadows of Pilgrims Mercy, and the more menacing Cardswells), what she felt now was more like an enormous river, pulling her farther and farther out into its swift turgid current, into the center, where she could no longer see the shore; and everything was crashing and churning about her—the wretched faces and broken voices; the stuffy-bright and sticky-dark rooms; the awful cries and menacing whispers and terrible pleas; the choking smells and shrill noises and scenes, unfolding, unimaginable to her—then—tucked safe and sound in her snug bed, with her father closing up their little green-backed storybook and kissing her good night.

At one emergency shelter they dropped her down, just before the doors were locked and barred for the night, an old woman

THE BEAUTIFUL-UGLY

rushed out of nowhere toward her, her eyes bright and anguished, wringing her hands and crying out, "Oh my Margie! My Margie!"

Connelly fell back into a corner, her arms rising to protect herself, as another heavy, older woman lumbered over to intervene.

"Now, Agnes," she said, putting her arm around the other's twitching, scrawny shoulders, "that ain't your Margie, dear."

"Oh my Margie," she said, quieter now, and then broke down into a choking, pleading sob, saying, "She come here, didn't she, Ira? She come here, all right?"

"It's not her night to come, dear," the other woman said. "Now, Agnes, you know she always comes tomorrow night. You *know* that."

"Oh," said the woman, her face now twisting with confusion, as she tried to understand. "Tomorrow then?"

"Yes, dear."

"Well now," she said, turning away, wandering off to another part of the room, still wringing her hands and mumbling to herself.

The big woman looked over at Connelly, still scrunched into the corner. "She don't mean nothing by it, honey. Margie's her daughter, I believe; but she was, best we can tell, killed in a fire—must have been some time back—and every time they try and drop off some other little dark-haired girl here, it's the same thing all over, poor thing." Now the woman was motioning her out of the corner. "We may as well get you settled in, dearie. I reckon it's gonna be another all-nighter."

It was a women-only shelter, and the Child Protection Services caseworker had argued with the attendant about leaving her there; who finally allowed it, with the promise someone would retrieve her in the morning.

"Otherwise she goes out on the street," the attendant said. "That's the rule."

Ira showed her around, introducing her to some of the ladies, who mostly seemed nice, though somehow distracted, to her; as if they were confused about being there, or embarrassed by it, or perhaps had forgotten the reason they *were* there, and were looking for her to tell them.

It was all in one long low-ceilinged room: the rows of narrow folding beds; the three wooden dining tables; the kitchen and food preparation area; the TV and social area, as they called it.

Ira got her the bed next to hers; then showed her where the bathroom was.

"They keep it nice and clean for us," she said, smiling and folding her hands, looking around. She looked at her sideways. "You need to do anything now, honey? I mean, a number one or two or anything?"

Connelly shook her head, and Ira smiled. "I'll get you up early with me. Once the line starts for the showers—forget it. They kick us out by seven, and I don't like being dirty all day, do you?"

"No ma'am," she told her.

Ira nodded. "What happened to your folks, baby?"

Before she could say anything, a bell clanged, and Ira grabbed her hand. "Oh, we got to hurry, or we'll be forever getting anything to eat!"

And Ira took off, heaving from side to side, running and giggling like a girl, clutching her hand.

*

She looked at all the faces, while they ate on paper plates, with plastic forks, wondering how they all came to be there. They were all grownups, and she wondered. She watched two of the women, across from her, arguing over where to sit, until one of the attendants came from behind the counter.

"Martha, you sit there, and, Tillie, you sit there," she said.

She saw neither of them seemed happy about it, watching each other out the corner of their eyes, glumly eating.

Mostly the women were quiet as they ate, concentrating very hard on the dry casserole, as if that were the most important thing at that moment; or some just staring about, eating little.

Tillie was watching her across the table and said, "You look just like Elizabeth Taylor in *National Velvet*. Did you ever see that?"

"No ma'am."

Tillie nodded. "Well, you look just like her."

She ate a bite of her macaroni and cheese, satisfied.

"She don't look like her at all," Martha said, beside her. "She's too young."

Tillie ignored her, her chin stiffening, saying to everyone else. "Well, I don't mean *exactly* like her. I just mean she reminds me of her. Her eyes, especially."

"Liz had darker eyes," said Martha. "And she combed her hair different."

THE BEAUTIFUL-UGLY

Tillie sighed and looked all the way around the room; then, very politely, bent forward and took another bite. "She's got her nose," she said, her head down.

"Well, I don't see that," Martha added.

Tillie ate faster, one bite after another, saying nothing now.

When they were finished, Connelly sat among the ladies, watching television. There was a man on, a handsome detective, and one of the ladies said she knew what she wanted for desert.

Ira giggled beside her, reminding her, "Little pitchers have big ears."

"Now what the hell does that mean, Ira?" said the woman.

"It means we have a child present," Ira told her.

"Well, I didn't mean anything by it," the woman said. "I just said, I know what I want for desert. I'd like some ice cream, that's what."

All the ladies sitting there laughed.

One of them said, "Yeah, Harriet, you want ice cream, all right."

And they all laughed again.

Connelly felt Ira's arm go around her. "Don't worry about them none, baby. They're just a bunch of anxious old nags."

The ladies tittered.

"I just miss having a man around," Harriet said. "What's wrong with that?"

Another woman said, "Well, I don't miss being kicked around."

Several of the ladies agreed with her.

"Well, my man never hit me," Harriet said. "Except for maybe the time I broke one of his fishing poles by accident."

"He hit you for *that?*" Ira said.

"Well, not really," said Harriet. "He just got angry when I broke it, and threw it into the water, and a piece of it hit me."

"Oh," Ira said.

"So, technically," said Harriet, "that's not really hitting me, is it?"

Everyone finally agreed it wasn't.

Then Connelly saw something from the corner of her eye. She looked up, and it was the same woman who had rushed up to her when she first arrived, calling her Margie. She stood off to the side, looking at her.

"Well, there's Agnes," Ira said.

Agnes stood there.

Ira motioned. "Come sit with us, dear, and watch TV."

Agnes sat down on the other side of Ira and stared at the television.

While they watched, Ira said, "Agnes, what in the world are you holding?"

Agnes hesitated and then slowly opened up her hands, revealing a tiny pink doll's brush.

"What *ever* could you do with that?" Ira asked her.

"Agnes, you don't have no doll," said Harriet.

Connelly saw Agnes look at Harriet and then over at her. Everyone was looking at her now.

She felt nervous, and finally she smiled and said, "I think I have a better one." And she ran over to her knapsack, lying on her bed, and took out her old purple brush. She came back and handed it to Agnes, who stared at her a moment, and then stared at the brush, before taking it from her and giving her back the doll brush. Then Connelly sat down on the floor before her, and, without a word, Agnes began to brush her hair so slowly, so gently, she could hardly feel it; and now she closed her eyes…and it was her mother brushing her hair again; and her father was sitting a little ways off, reading his magazine; and Eric was in his bedroom, gluing together tiny model pieces; her eyes closed; stroking, stroking…as she opened her eyes, and they were all there instead, surrounding her, staring silently at the small flickering screen.

*

Night in the shelter. Almost dark. But small yellow lights are glowing, so the attendant can keep watch over everyone. She sees one and then another of the ladies rise up and move off like ghosts toward the bathroom. But it's mostly noises: squeaking beds and groans and whispers and snoring and a voice saying, "It's her eyes, mostly." And the other voice, "Well I don't see that." And then silence, until somewhere across the room, another voice floating in the air above their heads like wisps of fading mist: "Margie? Margie?"

Then nothing, as she was so exhausted, but deep, deep sleep.

*

In the morning the man told her she had to leave with the other women.

THE BEAUTIFUL-UGLY

"They're trying to locate your paperwork," he said. "Where did they have you before?"

It was a group shelter, somewhere south, but she couldn't remember. She thought she would cry, not knowing.

Ira came and rescued her. "First let's eat some of those scrambled eggs before they're all gone. Then you can come with me, all right, baby? I'll show you how I spend my day."

Ira had gotten her up in the dark, and they showered together. Then the older woman gathered up what they had together for dirty clothes and made a wash.

"We're beating them all this morning!" she said gleefully. "Remember, baby, when you don't have much, you still got to keep organized. And don't ever lose any advantage offered you. That may be the last one you get for a while."

She had scrambled eggs and orange juice, and she and Ira shared a Danish. Then she brushed her teeth and peed, and went back to her bed, finishing packing her knapsack.

Meanwhile, Ira got them both box lunches to take with them, and they packed these—she, making room in a corner of her pack, and Ira tucking hers in the enormous canvas arm bag she carried.

"Everything I got left in the world is in this bag," she said, lifting the strap onto her shoulder.

They left the shelter with the other women, everyone heading in different directions.

Connelly watched them all walking away, including Tillie and Martha, going down the street, side by side, arguing as they went.

"Where do they all go, Ira?"

"Oh, they all go different places," she said. "There's a little mall a couple of miles from here they go, or some go to the day shelter; but they keep you locked up there all day, just like the night shelter, and I prefer to stay moving. Of course, if the weather's bad enough, I'll go there, but I like to get away from everyone. I like to be by myself mostly. That's always easier."

They spent the morning at a small marine park along the bay. The sun was shining and from the bench they were sitting she could see the Bay Bridge in the distance, remembering all the times she had crossed it with *them*. She closed her eyes and smelled the salty pungent air and heard the squawking birds, chasing after the fishing boats.

Ira, meanwhile, was rearranging her bag. After a while she took out a small cigar box and held it in her lap, saying, "Well, Arthur, are we ready?"

Connelly looked at her. "Who's Arthur?"

"My husband, dear. Or was for forty-three years. Then his heart gave out with all that working he did. That man was a hard worker. You see, we had us a tailor shop in Brooklyn, and one day, forty-three years after I married him, I found him dead at his sewing machine, letting out some cuffs." She shook her head, looking out over the water. "He looked surprised, lying there like that, like when it was his time—it surprised him. I always wondered." She fingered the cardboard box in her lap, rubbing the lid with her hand. "We were gonna travel. Arthur loved history and different places. He had books—pictures and maps that he followed along with. But that didn't happen. So now I guess I'm traveling for the both of us. That is, I'm doing the walking, and Arthur just sort of tags along."

Connelly watched as Ira raised the lid of the cigar box, and she saw the plastic bag inside, tied shut with a red wire. Ira undid the wire, then stood and walked slowly down to the edge of the water. She stood there for a moment, when she made a waving motion out before her with her hand, and Connelly saw the puff of dust rise up and drift away, disappearing out over the water. Then, a satisfied look on her face, Ira came back to the bench and sat down again. She made sure the wire was snug, closed the lid of the box, and placed it carefully back into her bag.

She sat up, looking out. "We've been all over, and I've left a little bit of him at each place. I think he's liked it, for the most part. At least, when we're alone, and he talks to me, he says he likes it." Ira looked over at her now, smiling. "I think he wants to go up to Seattle next, so that's probably where we'll go, unless he comes up with a better idea."

At lunchtime Ira bought them both juices from a corner gas station with change she kept in a small purse, hidden inside a pocket she had sewn under her dress; then they walked over to a grass-covered hillock, near an office park, and sat beside the flower beds, eating their sandwich and piece of fruit. While they ate, Ira told her about her three children, each of whom lived in a different part of the country, and each of whom had tried to get her off the road to live with them.

"They have this crazy idea that I'm some sort of half-senile bag lady that needs help," Ira said. "My goodness. Now, of course, I won't deny that sometimes it's hard doing this, but I've never felt so free before. And I told them all—I spent my whole life raising you three, going by all the rules, so now leave me and Arthur alone, for Christ's sake. I'll go stay with them every now and then, but, I gotta be honest with you, baby, they drive me nuts after a while. Imagine me and Arthur cooped up in some little room for the rest of our lives—I don't think so!"

After lunch Ira took them over to a small library she knew about, where, while she had her afternoon nap, sitting perfectly upright in a reading chair, Connelly wandered among the isles of books, looking.

She took down some art books and a book of stories and sat at one of the tables in the center of the room. The stories were not very good, but she enjoyed looking at the paintings in the art books, remembering how her father painted; the little details she remembered, now that she was older. She closed her eyes, wishing she could have that moment one more time. Just him and her, one more time, so she could ask him all the questions she had in her mind for him. Just once more.

When Ira woke up, it was nearly four, and she came over and said she felt like a cup of tea. So they wandered down the main highway nearby, until they found a car dealership having a sale, with bunches of stringed balloons bouncing in the breezy air, and bright-colored banners making happy, flapping sounds.

Inside, there was a table with coffee and tea and soft drinks; and Ira fixed herself a hot tea, whispering, "Connelly, there's some nice orange drink. Have yourself an orange."

The showroom was busy, and they enjoyed themselves, wandering among the new cars, looking inside them.

A man came up to them and asked if he could help them.

Ira said, "Oh, no, dear—my husband does all the driving. He's around here somewhere."

She looked around.

The man gave Ira his card, "In case he needs something."

"I'll make sure he gets it," Ira said, dropping the card into her bag.

At one point, Ira looked at the clock on the dealership wall and said they should be getting back. "I have some sewing to do for the ladies," she said. "They'll let us in early, so I can get my work done before dinner. And didn't someone say there was a Gable movie tonight? I believe they did. Oh—let's hurry! I just love watching him make those dark eyes at Harlow like that."

Ira took her hand, shuffling toward the exit door, and recounting little stories to her when she was a girl.

Connelly was at the shelter for almost a week, spending her days with Ira, before the county discovered its mistake and came for her—suddenly one night—just before the shelter closed. Ira was in the bathroom when they came, and she didn't see her again. She told someone to tell her what happened, but there was no way to know if the woman ever did. Regardless, they moved her four times in one month, and she soon forgot about that as well.

*

Just before she turned eleven, she woke up one night and had no idea where she was. Automatically, she sniffed the air, felt the covering, and peeked around herself for clues. Then she moved her legs and felt something different below, causing her to draw her legs up beneath herself, and bumped someone beside her, who moaned.

She got carefully out of bed—still piecing together where she was, who was sleeping where—and made her way to the tiny cramped bathroom, shutting the door and turning on the light. She looked at the other girls' things heaped about, and then looked at herself in the mirror and gasped. Trembling, she sat down on the toilet seat lid and lifted her T-shirt, examining her blood-soaked underwear, and the dark, congealed blood on her leg. She wondered if she was dying. She wondered what she could do.

Slowly the bathroom door swung open. It was the girl she had bumped. She couldn't remember her name. The girl said tiredly, "I have to use that." Indicating the toilet.

Connelly said, "I think something's wrong with me."

"What?"

She raised her shirt.

The girl yawned and shook her head. "You just started your period. Here."

She went over to the cluttered vanity and searched inside a plastic kit, handing her something.

Connelly held the hard tube in her hand, trying to remember the conversations she'd overheard. Once, she had been in another bathroom with another girl, but her back was turned toward her, her hands mysteriously occupied.

"Okay," said the girl. "You take it out like this, and this end goes in first, and, depending on how heavy you are, you change it when it's full. Got it? Now, I really got to pee."

*

There was another place, after she told them no, the other girls surrounded her in the bedroom and made her smoke it anyway. And when she saw the spiders climbing out of the carpet, up the walls, like a creeping army, she told them what she saw.

"That'solright," said one of the girls. "They goin' away from you, ain't they? It's when they turn round and come *to* you, you got to worry."

They were all laughing, except her, because one of the spiders *had* stopped, and was turned around, looking back at her...

*

Somewhere else, *he* would sneak into their bedroom at night from the boys' bedroom and make love with Carmine, who slept beside her. Meanwhile, she always lay there, pretending to be asleep, listening to them sounding like two wet seals fighting over a fish, beside her.

And, once, when she peeked at him (skinny, thick gold chain dangling against smooth olive skin, with what Carmine called his Mexican wipe, or scruffy goatee, and quick dark eyes), he saw her and asked Carmine about getting him some of that—meaning *her*—now rolled up into a tight ball beside them.

"She just a kid," she heard Carmine say. "She don't know up from down."

"That's what I'm *talkin'* about," he said. "That's when it's *good.*"

"Here's what's good, baby," Carmine said then.

Her eyes squeezed shut, she soon heard the seals barking and flapping their flippers again over another fish. And the very next day, she called Lillian, her new cassie, or caseworker, and was out of there by the weekend.

17 ♀ LILLIAN

After a while she knew all the hot drops in the city. Some were decent, and the wife would heat her a TV dinner, while the husband was busy putting together his crossword puzzle at the other end of the table, and then they would just sit there and talk with her, telling her how sorry they were she had to go through this. They were trying to do their little part. Sometimes there was even a clean bed for her. And the scent of warm toast in the morning.

Some were not so decent. She could always tell before she even got there, because Lillian would be extra nice, or distracted, saying things like: "You know, this was all I could find at the last minute, sweetie.", or, "Gosh, babes, we were even lucky to find you *this* one!" Then bitching about her caseloads, and no place to put them, and she didn't know how much longer she could deal with this shit, she really didn't, what they were paying her. And maybe she would go do something else. Then sometimes she would start crying, holding the steering wheel with one hand and blowing her nose with the other, saying, she *was* trying to do the best she could, she really was; while Connelly would sit there, trying to block her out, wondering what was waiting for her at the other end; anything, she suspected, except a microwave dinner and some pleasant conversation.

And it was at one of these not-so-decent drops one night, lying there in the dark and trying hard to go to sleep, to just shut everything out around her, she thought about herself, only different. She remembered when she first thought there was some sort of grand plan or design for her. That was at the Cardswells (so long ago it seemed, but not really), and there was a grand design, with her in the very center, and all she had to do was follow it along, be a good girl and do what she was told, and everything would work itself out. She had really thought that then.

But now, lying there at that moment, she wasn't sure. She realized there probably wasn't any design for her after all; or, if there was, it certainly wasn't a very good one; or it was too deeply hidden to matter. So now what? She didn't know. She only thought how everything that had happened to her just happened. It didn't seem to have anything to do with her personally, it just happened; it was happening everywhere, to everyone; and it didn't really matter if it *was* a design or chance or whatever. It was happening. And something else would happen in that next instant. And the instant after that. And the important thing was to somehow know that. Be aware of that. Because the one thing she did know right then was, if there was something else there, with the day by days passing, it didn't have a whole lot to do with *her* world at that very moment. Or the next.

And finally she slept.

*

Lillian, of course, was determined to change all that, in spite of what she called her own "particular challenges," which, like so many things about her, she was never that clear about. As during one of their first talks, she told her that being a caseworker was sometimes like being a miner, mining for those two hidden golden nuggets: the perfect parents, just for her.

"They're out there, sweetie," Lillian repeatedly told her. "And they're looking just for you. And it's my job to bring you together. That's my deep purpose in life now."

At other times, Connelly saw, there was no deep purpose, or any other kind of purpose, she could tell, when they would be out driving somewhere, or nowhere, and Lillian would be all to pieces about something.

It didn't take her long to realize, as far as cassies went, Lillian wasn't that good. And after a while she realized she was most likely absolutely horrible, and might eventually cause her some kind of harm, although unintentional. But then, slowly, she began to see her differently; that she might, in fact, be the best kind of guide and protector she could ask for, if she could just keep herself from falling all to pieces, which happened, right in front of her, more than she cared to witness.

The first time she saw Lillian she knew she was different from every other caseworker she'd had or seen or, most likely, *would* see. She came into the horribly cramped welfare office looking and smelling delicious, dressed in red satin, pearls, and white-strapped heels, with a long fuchsia boa about her neck, smoking her Gitanes Blondes ("Sorry, sweetie, my last real vice.") and putting them out in the mother-in-law tongue pot in the corner, until the director came in and told her smoking wasn't allowed. That's when Lillian apologized profusely and told him she had no idea, absolutely no idea at all, and turned and told Connelly they could go for a drive instead, "So we girls can get to know each other a little better. Sound like a plan?" Fondly crinkling up her nose at her and gathering up her blue-leather organizer and pretty little cigarette box with the silhouette of a Spanish gypsy woman flaunting a tambourine.

This all occurred in a five-minute flip and flur that made Connelly dizzy with the sheer unrehearsed orchestration of it.

Lillian drove a little red sports car, and they went down the coast, with the car-top down, where Connelly told her everything she could think of about herself; coming back, Lillian said it was her turn, then proceeded to tell her how she had once been an actress in Los Angeles, but gave it up after being unwilling to "cross over all those bridges certain someones wanted me to."

She'd had a few bit parts in movies, and she told her the titles, none of which, Connelly admitted, she'd ever heard of. Then she told her about the commercials she'd made, singing and waving her hand back and forth, with the cigarette between her fingers: *"Got that right—look! Got that great—style! Got that way about you!"*

Connelly admitted she hadn't heard them either, which obviously disappointed her. "But you know, Lillian," she said, "I hardly ever watch TV. I usually read or something. But that one about laundry soap sounds familiar."

"Really?—*Wouldn't life be wonderful if we all used Agree? Wouldn't life be fabulous if we could all agree, to use—A-gree!*"

"Yeah, I think I've heard that one."

"That's great, sweetie. I always thought that was one of my better ones."

Going round a curve, shifting gears, she lit up another Blonde, smoking, satisfied.

When they stopped at a drivin along the coast highway for hamburgers, Lillian told her how she'd finally made up her mind one day, and went home to Nebraska where she'd eventually got her degree. "One thing I learned real good, sweetie," she said, taking a big bite out of her burger, "is that the world has lots of nice people, including kids, and lots of predators out to get them. I know because they got to me a few times, but we won't go into *that* now."

They sat there chewing and looking through the windshield at the girl skate past them with another order.

Lillian wiped her mouth with a paper napkin. "But what I will tell you is, at one point, I decided to go after them—the predators—any way I could. I knew who they were and I was going after them. At first I was gonna be a lawyer, but that wasn't close enough. I wanted to be at ground zero, you know? I wanted to be right there where those fucking animals pulled kids into bedrooms—sorry, sweetie—but that's where I wanted to be." And she took another bite, chewing, her eyes flaring like two struck matches.

Connelly, nibbling at her food, watched her for a while. "Is that your real name, Lillian Barkley?"

She shook her head. "Nah, Patricia Brown, actually. Everyone at home still calls me Patty. But after I left Hollywood and got into all this, I just kept Lillian. It seemed to fit better what I was trying to accomplish, don't you think?"

Connelly told her she thought it did.

*

Those bridges, crossed and uncrossed, Connelly saw, seemed to have been a very important part of Lillian's life. "It's choices, you know, sweetie," she told her on one of their drives, not really to anywhere in particular. She preferred doing that when they met and reviewed her case. She hated being indoors, and especially those gloom-and-doom government office buildings, as she called them. "They're all so fucking depressing—sorry, sweetie," she said. "Who can be original in someplace like that? Who can think what to do next? Not me."

One day they went north, across the Golden Gate, into vineyard country, when she made the comment about choices. "God knows I've made some lulus," she said, shaking her head and lighting up her first Blonde. The top was down, and Connelly watched the wind whipping her colorful scarf and cigarette smoke, when Lillian's head fell back and she screamed. She looked over, excited: "Scream with me, sweetie! Scream with me!"

Connelly did, letting her head fall back and screaming as loud as she could. They were both screaming now, screaming and then laughing, crossing over the bridge, the orange massiveness of it rising high above them, surrounding them.

"Okay, that's enough," Lillian said when they were over it. "I don't want you hurting your lungs or anything."

They drove along the winding road, and Lillian told her how she ran away from home when she was fourteen. "That's when I first went to California, jeeze."

"Why'd you leave?"

Lillian glanced at her, curiously. "You know, sweetie, not everyone has great parents like you did. My old man was an alcoholic. He never abused us bad or anything, but he never helped us much either, which, I guess, is the same thing. So, as soon as I could, I left and tried to figure it out on my own. That's those choices I was telling you about."

Then Connelly noticed she grew quiet and, after a while, she saw she was crying. She could see the tears rolling down from under her sunglasses, and she leaned back and stared the opposite direction.

Suddenly Lillian said, "He had a heart attack the same year I decided to quit the business, go back to school." Connelly looked back and saw her wiping her eyes. "I guess I figured it was safe to go home."

"What about your mother?"

Lillian shook her head. "She did what she could." She hesitated, lighting a cigarette with the little dashboard lighter. "She's dying now," she said, leaning back.

That was also the day—them first buying sandwiches from a roadside deli; then pulling into that shady spot beside the hillock vineyard—Lillian told her how she really felt about her.

"You know, we're not supposed to say things," she said, chewing her sandwich and sipping her drink through a straw. "It gets real complicated real quick."

"About what, Lillian?"

She shook her head. "I just think you're a great kid, that's all. And I think I can trust you, otherwise I'd never say a word."

Now they both sat there in silence, except for the rustling paper from the sandwiches.

Lillian said, "I just wanted you to know, if I didn't have so much baggage, so much working against it, I'd take you in a heartbeat." She waited and then looked over. "So…would you let me?"

Connelly sat there. "You know, Lillian, unless that moment ever came, I don't know what I'd say. I really don't."

Lillian nodded, and they both sat there then, both looking ahead, neither saying another word about it.

18 ♀ THE HOT DROP

Finally, there was the other kind of drop that was not hot in the same sense as the first two. This one had its own special kind of heat, an evil heat, Lillian warned her, where she could get burned real bad, real quick.

Of course, she'd already heard things, she knew things, and told her, "Lillian, don't ever leave me someplace like that, okay?"

"Like those things are planned," Lillian scoffed. "All the planets have to be in awful alignment for that to happen, and fate fucking the laws of nature from an unnatural position or something—sorry, sweetie."

Then Lillian's mother died and she had to return home, to Nebraska, for a week.

"When I get back we may have some good news," she said before she left. "I've met this couple—he's a teacher, and she's a magazine editor, and they can't have kids. And I told them about you, showed them your file. They're real interested, kiddo."

She told her what date she would pick her up for the interview.

Then she left.

The second night, a fire started in the group home Lillian had placed her the previous month. The smoke alarms began to ring, and everyone woke up in a panic. Connelly grabbed her shoes and backpack and ran outside, into the rain, with everyone else. They were all standing there when the fire trucks came, and then the police, and finally the caseworker on call, who sorted everyone out;

and soon everyone was being loaded into different vehicles, taken to different hotdrop locations.

She was put into one of the police cars and driven south, through an industrial park that looked unreal to her, in the deep night, with towers of glowing lights jutting up into the ceaseless rain. She wondered what they made there. That's when she realized, as large as it was, spreading out on both sides of her, she could not see a single soul. It was an empty world. And she settled back against the seat and listened to the two policemen talk about fishing and their wives.

Beyond the park was darkness; then an ugly one-block commercial strip; then more darkness. Finally they came to an isolated suburb where there was a cluster of small houses and, beyond, a trailer park they pulled into. They drove down a muddy driveway, between two rows of trailers, to the back of the park where there was a yellow and brown doublewide unit against the fence. In the headlights through the rain she saw a sign on the trailer that read: Manager.

The policeman that wasn't driving got out and went over to the trailer and up the wooden steps to the front door. The door opened and she saw a woman there. She thought she could hear some kind of music playing inside. Then the policeman came back and opened her door. "All right, miss," he said.

She got out, dragging her knapsack behind her, and the policeman shut the rear door. The police car was backing up and turning around before she even got to the wooden steps.

"Hurry up," the woman said. "I don't feel like dealing with no sick kid on a night like this."

She went up the steps and past the woman, without even looking at her, into the trailer.

The woman shut the door behind her.

Now she was standing there, soaked in her pajamas and tennis shoes, fumbling with her backpack. There was a small living room where three people were sitting, surrounded by twangy guitar music and blue smoke, holding drinks and watching her.

"My name's Lorelei," the woman said, matter-of-factly. She was barefoot and wore tight black nylon slacks and a half-unbuttoned pink blouse. Her face was tiredly pretty and wrinkled around her eyes and mouth, and she was smoking a cigarette. She pointed.

"That handsome dark-haired one's Gene, my husband—you keep your hands off him."

Everyone laughed in front of her.

"That there's Walter, or Walt, we call him, and that's Samantha—"

"Or Sam," said the other woman.

They all laughed again.

She stood there, dripping.

"You're getting my carpet all wet," Lorelei said. "They don't pay me enough to take you kids in and have you ruin my carpet, c'mon."

Lorelei herded her the other way through the trailer. They went through the kitchen and Lorelei asked, "You hungry?"

She shook her head.

"Just tired, I bet. They said there was a fire over at the Oxford home."

"Yes ma'am."

"Well, you'll sleep with my daughter, Ester. She's quiet and don't wet the bed or nothing. You don't wet the bed, do you? I told them, no bed-wetters."

"No ma'am."

They were standing in a narrow hallway, and the woman stood there, looking at her. "What's your name?"

"Connelly."

Lorelei shook her head and took a drag of her cigarette. Her free hand reached up and arranged a wet curl, Connelly could feel, across her forehead. "Well, you're pretty as a Georgia peach. That's where I'm from, halfway between Sharpsburg and Peachtree City. Eugene too. Then they laid him off at the upholstery factory, so we came out here. He works at the chemical factory now, making bug spray and stuff." She stood there, smoking.

Connelly said, "Is there somewhere I can change?"

Lorelei smiled and winked at her. "Sure is." She reached behind herself and twisted a doorknob, shoving open a narrow door. "Bathroom's right here."

Connelly nodded. "And the bedroom?"

Lorelei pointed over her shoulder. "Second door on the right. You can come out and sit with us if you want. You're big enough."

"I'm real tired, ma'am."

"Suit yourself. I feed Gene breakfast at six, before his shift, and you kids at seven. I only want one set of dishes to wash."

She left her then, sauntering down the hallway, smoking.

Connelly stood there and listened. After a moment she heard the burst of laughter from the front room, and the twangy guitar grew louder. She slipped into the bathroom, shutting and locking the door behind her. She looked around. Everything seemed neat and in place. There were fluffy orange terrycloth covers on the toilet lid and seat, and a jar of some sort of scent—jasmine, she smelled—sitting in the middle of the tank lid. There was a wicker basket with magazines beside the toilet. She pulled back the shower curtain and saw the tub was mostly clean and there was shampoo and fresh soap there, and she felt the little stab of relief from that. She hated having to ask for things. Next, feeling better about it, she kicked off her shoes and removed her pajamas and underwear. She looked around and there was a coat hanger on the back of the door. She hung her wet clothes carefully on the hanger, and rehung everything back on the door hook.

From her backpack she took out dry underwear and slipped them on, feeling the soft cotton, warm against her cold skin. She only had one set of pajamas, so she took out her khaki shorts and her Nine-Inch-Nails Capital-G T-shirt and put that on instead. She felt better in the dry clothes. Then, remembering she had to pee ever since she stood there watching the fire, she did that, sitting there, thinking about Lillian, wondering if she should call her. She'd given her her cell number in the beginning, just in case; but she finally decided no, not with her dead mother and all. Maybe later.

Afterward, she re-shouldered her pack, picked up her wet shoes and hanger of wet clothes and slowly opened the door. She looked out and didn't see anyone. Then she made her way down to the second door on the right, and stood there. She looked up and down the hall, and then turned the handle and went inside the room.

She stood there, her back against the door, letting her eyes adjust to the dark. The room wasn't big. There was a double bed in the center, and a dresser and mirror on one side. A ceiling fan squeaked slowly above the bed. She noticed the lights on the fan were glowing dimly above. She searched around the room and discovered the closet, and hung her wet clothes on the doorknob, setting her shoes and backpack to the side. She looked at the bed.

She saw the girl sleeping on one side, her back to her. She went to the other side, pulling back the covers—and there was someone there as well. It was a small boy, curled into a ball and sleeping.

She stepped to the edge of the front room, and everyone looked up at her again.

Lorelei said, "You change your mind about joinin' us?"

Connelly said, "There's a boy sleeping in the bed."

"That's *your* son," Lorelei said to her husband. She looked back, explaining, "That's just little Ronnie, honey. He always crawls in bed with us or his sister if there's a storm outside."

The husband Gene stood up and walked past her down the hall. When he passed her, he looked down at her, and she looked away.

She followed him down the hallway and waited outside, while he gathered up the boy and carried him out and down the hall. Then, quickly, she went inside the bedroom and shut the door. Lying in the bed she felt the heat from the boy's body, and she snuggled deeper down, pulling the covers around her, remembering the cold rain, and being even colder in the air-conditioned police car. Now she felt the warmth tingling inside her, and the warmer feeling of being safe, after everything that had happened that night. She looked around the room and wondered, yet again, what would it be like to have your own bedroom, your own family, knowing that when you woke up you would still have that?

Then she thought about how she was eleven now, and her parents had been dead for nearly five years; and she found that there was so much she was forgetting about them, about their lives then, in order to concentrate on what she had to do now. That bothered her a lot. But she didn't know any other way to do it. She had to do for herself, didn't she? There really was no one else for that, was there? Well, there was Lillian and a few like her that had cared, at least a little, for her; but she thought how most people just got on with their lives, and didn't wait for them—their lives—to just happen or something. They just got on with them. Like she was trying to do. She *had* to do. *Oh, Moggie,* she remembered that little green book for the first time in a while, closing her eyes, hearing the squeaking fan above her.

*

She opened her eyes. She had been asleep, but it was still dark, and the fan was still turning, squeaking, above her. She lay there a full minute before she realized how thirsty she was. She was so thirsty, she guessed, because she was so warm now. That's what woke her up, the burning thirst inside her.

She got out of bed and crept over to the door, opening it, and listened...Silence. She went out into the dark hallway and began to walk down it, toward the front rooms, still listening. When she got to the edge of the hall, she stopped. She looked out into the open area and saw, dimly, the kitchen to her left, set apart by the preparation and breakfast counters, and heard the automatic coffee maker hissing and gurgling coffee down into its glass pot; and the larger living room beyond, now empty and silent, the party over.

She felt along the wall and found light switches. The first one she flipped turned on the ceiling florescent lighting in the kitchen. She walked into the kitchen and saw the noisy coffee maker beside the sink, and the dirty glasses on the counter beside the empty gin and whiskey bottles. She peeked into one cabinet and then another, until she found drinking glasses. She took one down and half-filled it at the sink.

She leaned her stomach against the sink, sipping the tepid water and staring through the small dark window, wondering what was there, beyond, wondering when the light would come, as all she could see was her own reflection, looking back. And she was leaned there, taking tiny sips, not thinking of anything else, when she saw the figure appear in the window beside her own reflection, beyond the counter behind her, standing.

She froze.

He said sleepily, "Coffee's ready. Thought I heard something else. Knew it wasn't Lorelei—she's snoring like Cooter Brown in bed."

She set down the glass in the sink. "I was thirsty," she said, explaining, half-turned.

"Hey, take all you want," he said. "We pay flat rate."

She swallowed, standing there, listening to the coffee maker's final spit-and-hiss, as she also heard him come around the counter, into the kitchen. She glanced and saw he was dressed only in his red underwear. And she swallowed again.

Now he stood there, between her and the opening, yawning and stretching his arms, then he rubbed his thick dark hair and face, working his hands down his body, until he was scratching himself below, watching her.

He asked, "Want some coffee?"

"I think I'll go back to bed," she said. She stood there, unsure.

"You're sure a fidgety thing." He was slumped to one side, leaning against the edge of the counter, with one hand still slipped half in his underwear. "Lorelei said you was eleven. You look older, them legs; you look, shit, older'n twelve."

She knew men better now, little things, things she'd heard or seen. How quickly they could change from one moment to the next. How they looked at her one way around people, and a different way when they were alone. How, no matter what they were saying or doing, they seemed taken, possessed, *deeply*, by only one thing. And how they always seemed disappointed, just a little, by whatever else they were doing instead. They all seemed somehow crudely simple to her, seeing them from a distance, and often more complex—a little more dangerous and even strange—close up. She wasn't sure.

She looked at him and said, "Can I please go to bed?"

He was just standing there, looking back at her, smiling in a way that made her uncomfortable, as if her skin was starting to rise up atop her flesh and crawl along.

He said, "You ever played around with boys? Bet you have."

She started to walk around him, when he reached out his hand, as to touch her, and she pulled back.

"Now what the hell," he said. "I ain't gonna hurt you none, girl."

"Can I go to bed? *Please?*"

He pointed a finger at her. "We took you in. Don't you forget that."

"Don't they pay you for that?"

He looked surprised. "And don't get sassy with me. I don't like sassy girls none—especially ones ain't got nowhere else to go. Ones ought to be grateful for what comes to'em."

"I just want to go back to bed. I don't want any trouble."

Now he was grinning, shaking his head. "Shit, you ain't causin' no trouble. And I ain't gonna bother you none. Now go on back to bed, so's I can have my coffee in peace, all right?"

She lowered her head and started to move past him, when he grabbed her and pulled her against him. She struggled now, trying to pull away, and he jerked her hair, pulling her head back, and was kissing her. She could feel his tongue inside her mouth and along the side of her face, and his hand wriggling beneath her shirt, squeezing her breasts.

"Got titties like butter scoops," he whispered, stale-breathed, against her ear.

After a moment she made herself relax. She was remembering something...something Yolanda had taught her about dirty boys...finding him with her hand below, touching him...hearing him moan and feeling him relax in response...when she gathered herself and jerked up her right knee, as hard as she could, at that exact spot her hand had been—hard against the pressing bulge of his underwear.

He made a noise, like the high-pitched squawk of a lone bird, and shoved her away from him, bending over and holding himself below.

"*I be goddamned,*" he squeaked, holding his breath.

Next, he raised up and stumbled toward her, as she backed into the corner where the two counters met. She saw his hand and felt the jarring sting, knocking her backwards over the counter.

Her head throbbing and swirling like it would fall off, she grabbed at the glass container of hot coffee and slung it behind her, splashing him, as he batted it away, and it smashing it to the floor.

"Now—stop, damnit!" he yelled, first giving off a little hop on one foot, while trying to wipe away the burning coffee; then overcome and charging toward her instead. She felt his full body slam against her again from behind, feeling his hands grabbing beneath her shirt, and then feeling her shorts being yanked down toward her knees, his frenzied hands grabbing her below. She was still half stretched over the counter, her mind in pieces, when her gaze skittered about before her, and she saw the enameled wooden block, with the knife handles protruding. She wasn't thinking at all. Not at all. But, vaguely, she saw her hand reaching out, jerking back on one of the knives, as he jerked her around to face him.

She only heard the scream as a wounded animal, surprised, snarling in her face. She swung her arm again.

"You bitch!" He fell back, one arm holding another. "You goddamn little bitch!" he said again, glaring at her, his eyes squeezing shut and open. "What the hell you do that for?"

Seeing the sudden streams of blood surprised her, and she dropped the knife and began pulling up her panties and khaki shorts.

"You conniving little—" he said, quieter now, taking time to look at the cuts on his arm and side, making little gasping sounds as he did so. "You little *whore*."

Then she heard the other voice, calling.

So did he and cried out: "She *stabbed* me, Lorelei! She fucking *stabbed* me! And she *burned* me too!"

"Oh my Lord!" Lorelei said from somewhere off.

When she saw him lunge forward again, she fell to the side. But he wasn't after her. She saw him open up one of the cabinets and reach, one-handed, inside, taking out a porcelain jar there—a pink pig covered in red roses with green stems. Then he turned around and threw it down against the floor, smashing it, scattering coins and dollar bills over the floor.

Then he went back to pathetically holding himself together again, as if he would otherwise fall apart, as Lorelei rushed into the room, saying, "Gene, Gene, what in the world?"

"She stabbed me, Lorelei," he moaned. "I caught her in here stealing your grocery money, and she stabbed me. Then she threw the coffee pot on me."

"That's not true," Connelly said, shaking her head. "That's not what happened."

"You *shut up!*" he turned on her, screaming. "You done enough here—now you just *shut up!*"

"Look at this mess," Lorelei said, looking around.

"Lorelei, that's not what happened," she said.

Now they both told her to shut up. And she understood then, looking at them both.

Lorelei made her go sit in the living room, telling her not to say another word. Not one. From there, she watched them both swearing, both stumbling barefoot about the broken glass, until Lorelei got a broom and swept everything into one corner. Then Lorelei called 911, yelling at the operator that her husband had been attacked, and they needed an ambulance *and* the police. After she hung up, she wrapped towels around Gene's bleeding arms and head; finally placing an ice bag on the burn spots, one after the other; all the while he moaned and held himself.

"Get me a beer, Lorelei," he whined. "I really need a beer."

"All right, baby," Lorelei said, getting it.

Sipping it, he looked over at her and said, "I knew she was trouble the minute she came wagging ass in here like some half-drowned damn *cat*."

"Don't talk, baby," Lorelei said, lighting herself a cigarette. "Save your strength."

Meanwhile, both of them continued to glare occasionally toward her, as if she were the cause of everything.

When the police came, Connelly saw it was the same two that had dropped her off, hours prior. First they talked to Gene and Lorelei, and then they took her into the police car and talked with her. She told them exactly what happened, including the part where Gene threw the pink pig on the floor, and lied after. While she was talking, the ambulance arrived, and she saw Gene being carried out of the house on a stretcher and loaded in the back.

"Will he be all right?" she asked the two policemen.

"Most likely," one of them said. Neither of them seemed that concerned.

"We've been out here a few times," the other one said.

She sat there, listening to the two of them decide what to do with her. Because of her age, they talked about bringing her down to the juvenile detention center. Then they decided that was too much paperwork, when one of them said, "Let's just let the city sort it out."

The other one laughed and picked up the radio handset, clicking it and saying, "502."

She heard a lady's voice say back, "502."

He clicked again. "502. We have a 5150, one-time juvenile female, transporting to Gen H."

"10-4," said the lady.

He replaced the handset.

She realized they were taking her somewhere, and she asked one of the policemen if he could get her backpack from the house, and he did. The last thing she saw was Lorelei standing alone at the door, dressed in a nightgown the same carrot-orange color as her bathroom treatments, smoking and watching them drive away.

19 ♀ ER

She wasn't sure, but everything now seemed to be coming together inside her head. She could feel it there, rushing together, from every direction, and she leaned her head against the police car window to calm herself. There was one moment—staring out at the ugly gray dawn rising over the skyline she had seen so often riding with her parents, but now looked like a different place altogether—she felt as if she were different from every other person alive. But different in a bad way, cut off somehow, shoved into some dark corner of living, where everyone was now turned and looking at her, threateningly, accusingly, just like Lorelei and Gene had looked at her. And she tried to make sense of that. She tried to tell herself it wasn't real, she wasn't like that, she shouldn't feel that way; as the ugly gray dawn rose up and washed down over her like some hideous poison ocean, descending, dragging her down into its depths and not letting her go. And she held her head gently against the window, her eyes closed shut now, and wondered what was happening to her.

Click: "502."

"502," the lady repeated.

"We're 10-97."

"10-4."

She opened her eyes and looked around. It was the city hospital: huge, brick—they'd brought her father there once when he broke his finger, trying to open a window. But she wasn't hurt, except where Gene had grabbed her and hit her; she certainly didn't think she needed a hospital. A warm bed, for sure. Maybe a cup of hot tea with lemon and honey. But she knew, too well, for too long now, to just do what she was told, and not make trouble, and it would go easier for her. She told herself that, and then she shut her eyes and felt the coming together inside her head again—the great, dizzy, shifting movement there—until she knew for sure she would pass out.

The policeman opened her door and she got out.

There was madness here. There were ambulances about her, and other police cars, and people everywhere. She heard something about a riot somewhere in the city, and another gang shooting, and one of the policemen was saying, "It's still Friday night and the Injuns are still inside the fort. We're turning you over to a hospital deputy. You'll be okay."

In the mad wash about her, standing there on the filthy sidewalk, she took Priscilla out of her backpack and held her to her. That made her feel a little better, her spinning head. When the fat deputy came waddling up to her, holding out the report the policemen had given him, she nodded and followed him inside.

The emergency room was packed, and it was an hour before they could talk to the lady at the admissions desk. During that time, the deputy left her mostly alone, going and doing other things. She thought about just leaving, walking out, but she didn't know where else she would go, or what she would do. So she stood there, pressed into one corner, and looked out into the madness: people lying about on stretchers; people crying and moaning; children and babies crying and moaning; policemen leading about shackled men in orange jumpsuits (that somehow reminded her of Lorelei); people sitting down and holding their heads, or standing and holding their heads; and everyone seeming to talk a different language, or talking the same language of pain, she wasn't sure. Because everyone there seemed to be hurting or maybe confused about what was actually happening to them. Then on one of the stretchers she saw Gene, half raised on one elbow and, it seemed, telling two homeless men about what had happened to him, showing them his wounds, as she moved farther along the wall where he wouldn't see her.

Once, when the deputy passed by, she asked him, "What will they do with me?"

He looked at her and shook his head. "They just want to hold you in psych emergency for a while. Make sure you're okay. It's all routine."

"But I feel fine."

He nodded. "They'll contact the Child Crisis people and let them know you're here."

He wandered off again.

Finally he came back and led her over to the admissions window.

The older lady sitting there and chewing gum looked out at her. "What's *she* here for?"

"5150," the deputy told her. "She's on psych-hold. Assaulting her guardian."

The lady looked back at her. "Which one, Harry, the girl or the doll?"

He sighed. "They don't have nowhere else to put her, Lucy."

"We're on ambulance divert, Harry. We're turning away everything but last will and testaments; they're laying people on bamboo mats in the psych hallways; besides, this ain't no nursery."

"It was a dump and run, Lucy—what else was I supposed to do?"

She stood there listening to them arguing, wondering what they would do with her. Then the lady said she would do what she could, but they would have to wait their turn.

She went back and stood in her corner. After a while the space about her began to clear out a little. There was even a chair nearby that she sat in, rocking Priscilla. Then she grew tired of that, and put her back in her backpack, searching there until she discovered a packet of crushed crackers at the bottom; and now she leaned back, opening the wrapper, eating the broken pieces, one by one, letting them dissolve in her mouth, looking about her...until she saw—him.

She wasn't sure exactly when she recognized him. Her eyes had passed over him once or twice, when she realized, in some far corner of her mind, he was looking at her. And she took another crumb of cracker into her mouth, when she looked back at him again—standing slumped against the wall, across the room—and she looked and looked, and suddenly she knew, as the cracker packet slipped from between her fingers.

Trembling, unaware of anything else, she shouldered her pack and slowly stood. All the while, he had continued to watch her, slumped so, looking out at her beneath shaggy brown hair, almost covering his eyes. But not enough she couldn't see them, his eyes, knowing them so well, knowing everything about them, in every instance, every mood, now again looking at her, knowing her back, she saw.

She slowly made her way across the floor, moving unaware through the people milling there, to where he stood. Now she stood before him, thinking how tall he looked. How different. Then, so slowly, gently, neither of them might have been aware, her hand rose to touch the side of his face. And when her fingers touched his skin, as to prove to herself, she heard him say, "Hello, Con."

She was crying now. She threw herself against him, her arms forcing their way around him, holding him tightly and knowing, this time, she wouldn't let him go. Barely feeling his hand on her shoulder, she said, "Oh, Eric. *Eric.*"

She held him, not letting go.

He said quietly, "What are you doing here?"

She raised her head, wiping her tears on his shirt. "It's nothing. Something stupid."

He half-smiled.

She said, "What about you? What are *you* doing here?"

"They're moving me again," he said, still half-smiling. "I was here and now they're moving me."

"Moving you where?"

"Atascadero."

"What's that?"

"State mental."

She looked at him. "Why would they put you there, Eric?"

"More observation, I was told." He half-smiled again. "Said I did something, hit someone, I think." He shook his head. "I don't remember, Con. That's the truth."

Then she looked at him closer, the odd bright and dull of his eyes. "They've got you medded up, haven't they?"

He didn't answer. He looked around again, staring off.

"We should sit down," she said.

"They told me to stay here?"

"Who?"

"Those two watching us."
"Where?"
"By the window."

She didn't care. She made him sit down. She found a bench and they sat there, and she held his hands in hers. "What about that family, Eric? The ones that were adopting you—the Kelemans?"

He shook his head, looking away. "They had problems. First, little ones. Then big. She caught him with someone—his secretary, I think. Now they're divorcing, which apparently puts adoption way down the priority list." He looked back at her, then away. "So, who hit you?"

She shook her head. "It doesn't matter."

He looked back, his gaze meeting hers, and now when he looked away, she could see the difference there, she could feel it, the understanding between them. When he looked back, his eyes were shining. "You're so beautiful, you know that? My little sister. All grown up."

"Hardly." She leaned against him, smiling, pressing him. "And you look so mature. So handsome and serious."

His laugh was dry as it was empty, as someone would laugh at an improper joke.

Now they sat there, leaning together, telling each other the things they remembered, what they could remember. Where, before, she had hated the waiting, now she wished they could wait there forever; they could remain just so together, never parting. She told him about the time, during parents' night, how he stood by his science display, "You remember—the one where you were comparing electric circuits, and you gave that little speech when you won."

"Parallel and series. You remember that?" he said, amazed.

"Oh yes," she said softly.

Then he recalled the camping trip they made, when a storm had blown in, blowing over the tent; and the four of them scrambled about, gathering everything up, seeking shelter at that nearby motel.

"Remember that night, Con, that awful room, and we were all soaked, and the shower didn't work right, and we put the beds together and played rummy? Remember?" He stopped now, smiling.

She looked at him then, knowing she couldn't let him go this time, she just *couldn't*. She said, "They lied to us, didn't they, Eric? It was all a lie from the beginning. And they're still lying, aren't they?" He looked over at her. "I'm sorry, Con. I—" He shook his head.

"But, don't you see, it's not us, it's them. It was never about us."

He sat there, unmoving.

Meanwhile, she again had the feeling inside her head of everything going apart—stretching out far, far, inside her—and then coming back together, making her dizzy. She pulled his hands against her forehead.

"Are you all right?" she heard him say.

She looked up and saw the two men there, before them. "No," she said, and fell against him, holding him.

He whispered, "Don't you see? We were supposed to meet here. Don't you see?"

She was crying again. "What are you talking about, Eric."

"I'm talking about things we can do. And things that help us. Don't you see—something made us meet here. Something's telling us."

"I don't understand," she said, pushing her face against him, into him, as if she could be part of him, and they couldn't separate them again.

"Our van's here," one of the men said. "Time to go, chief."

"*No*," she said, looking up at them, hating them.

"Here," Eric said quickly.

She watched him, shaky-handed, remove his plastic hospital name bracelet and hand it to her. She threw her arms around him again, but he undid them, and held her away from him. She looked into his eyes, but now there was nothing else there. Nothing he could tell her.

He may have kissed her after that, she wasn't sure. She thought he did, lean forward and kiss her forehead, the corner of her mouth, his hand brushing her bruised cheek. But then they were gone, and she sat there, staring down at the plastic bracelet, reading his name and date of birth and the doctor's name: Milson. Finally she lowered her head, wrapping her hands and arms around herself; and she must have been crying, because she heard people around her, talking to her; but she didn't know at all what she was doing; only that she didn't want to move anywhere, ever again; she wanted to stay right there and not move, because she was tired of moving; she was tired of not knowing, and not having, and she was tired of the moving; and she was tired of the lies—especially that—telling her it would be better, telling her it would work out. That was it. She was tired of everything.

"Y'all need to work something out here." The voice rough, distant. "This is bullshit."

After a while, she felt herself lifting up; surprised, in fact, that it was Moggie lifting her up, along with Freddie, and they were going to a place where they would be safe. It was a place no one could find them and harm them, and they wouldn't make any noise, and they would just stay there, until the danger was past.

"Oh, Moggie," Freddie whispered beside her, "what ever could happen next?"

"Shhh," said Moggie, "don't make a sound or Benadarne's soldiers might find us. They're very near, I'm sure. My wizard's twitch can *feel* them near, and my nose is itching awful."

"That's certainly a lot to itch, Moggie," Freddie said.

"*Quiet* now."

So they stayed there, hidden away; and she didn't make a sound after that, none of them did; except that they could still hear the crying, from somewhere far away: a quiet, relentless sobbing that seemed to last the night long, and made them uncomfortable, wondering who in the world it could be. But they said nothing else, not a word. Not even when the others came with a rolling gurney, pushing themselves right there between them, and put her on it, wrapping her up tightly.

"Remember," she heard Moggie whisper behind her as they rolled her away, "don't tell them a *thing*. Not a *thing*."

20 ♀ GEN H PSYCH

After a week they let her sit in a chair in the hallway and watch the things going on around her. The odd parade, passing. She didn't look at them in the beginning, but she knew they were there. She knew everything she wanted to know. And when they gave her medicine, she swallowed it. And when they placed her in the dining room, she ate a little, and then stopped, sitting there, waiting to be brought back to her chair.

They were all together there: the men, the women, and her. She finally realized she was the youngest there. There was a boy, she thought, in one of the other quiet rooms. When the door to the room was open she could hear him screaming: "They're coming inside me! Get them out of me! Get them out!"

It was a boy's voice. But she never saw him.

Another woman reminded her of Agnes, from the women's shelter, calling for her Margie; except, this one called for someone named Tom.

"Tom? Tom?" she said quietly, with a rising and dropping intensity, wandering back and forth before her along the hallway. "Tom? Tom?"

The woman was tall and hideously thin, with streaks of gray in her dark hair, and sores covering her arms and legs. Connelly stared at her face once as she passed, and she looked like she might have once been very smart, very different. She still had that glimmer of fond intelligence in her eyes; and she stopped before her now and looked down at her.

"Have you seen Tom?" she asked.

Connelly shook her head.

"Tom fell out of a tree, like Humpty-Dumpty," a man said, passing. "He had a great fall."

"He fell off the *wall,* you moron," said another man going the other way. He was a tall, slender black man, wearing a sort of shiny green turban; and he winked and smiled at her as he went sashaying by, saying, "Queen LaSheen knows all."

She and the woman exchanged glances, when the woman turned and began to follow the man in the turban. "Tom? Tom?"

"Oh, Lord!" said the man, stopping and stamping his feet, his hands like honey-colored flames, flickering up on either side of his head. "Now she thinks *I'm* Tom." He turned to the woman. "Mrs. Leon, Tom is not in the building at the moment. My name is Rupert, not Tom, Rupert Bates; otherwise known as Queen LaSheen, in those more discriminating venues of entertainment, in parts of the city that shall remain anonymous at the moment."

The lady stood there, unmoving. "Tom?"

Connelly watched him reach up with both his hands, gently embracing the woman's arms. He said softly, "Sweetheart, Tom is not here. Now it's time for General Hospital in the day room. Would you like to go watch General Hospital with me?"

The woman gave no reply, and he began to lead her toward the day room. Then he gave off a high-pitched squeal. "What kind of shit is this? We're all *in* General Hospital, Mrs. Leon. Gen H Psych, to be exact." And he gave off another high shrill laugh, as they disappeared around the corner.

*

One day she saw a man grab a nurse's writing pen from her hands and stab her in the face. The nurse screamed and pushed him away, the pen still sticking from her cheek; and attendants came from everywhere, grabbing him, dragging him to the ground and holding him there. People were running away everywhere, screaming, hiding their heads and faces in their hands, in corners, wherever they could find. She sat there, watching everything happening around her, until someone was there, grabbing her arm. It was Rupert, now without his turban, but with a chic cinnamon-and-avocado-colored scarf wrapped tightly about his head. He escorted her into the day room, chastising her.

"You can't just sit there like Sad Sadie, little beauty. Around here, violence begets violence. It feeds on it. Some of these crazies see something, and it gives them ideas, and, of course, they always go for the weakest among us; the least able to defend themselves, like you and me, for instance.

He found them seats in the corner where they watched everyone catching their breath and calming down. Rupert adjusted her hospital gown, which was open behind her. He re-tied the string around her neck, tucking everything neatly about her green pajama bottoms. Then he picked up a movie magazine and began flipping the pages, making occasional little gasps and squeals of disapproval.

"Taste is certainly not a God-given right among the rich and famous. Just *look* at the cheese and boloney on *that* sandwich!"

He showed her the picture.

They sat there.

After a while he leaned toward her and said in a confidential tone, "Little beauty, if you ever wish to talk to me about anything, I am, indeed, widely recognized as one of the world's foremost listeners—so you go right ahead, any time, any topic you desire."

They sat there, and finally she said, "Are you a dancer? I heard someone call you that."

Rupert gasped, dropping the magazine in his lap. "She speaks."

Connelly lowered her head, and Rupert reached over, taking her hands in his. "Yes, little beauty, I am a dancer, of sorts; although I prefer the term female illusionist. That is, I seek, in the grand forum, to defy the very precepts of biology itself. To denaturalize all notions of gender and femininity. To ultimately destroy those accepted beliefs concerning not only the boundaries of sexual provocation, but the very essence of the species' protoplasmic effect." He stopped and sighed, as she continued only to sit there, staring at him. "Actually, I am most known for my strip and lip to J.Lo's 'Si Yo Se Acabo' that borders on the more indiscriminate edges of egregiousness."

She sat there, looking at him. "So why are you here?"

He again squeezed her hands and fell back in his chair, seemingly exhausted, picking up the movie magazine and fanning himself. "Better living through chemistry, sweetheart. I'm bipolar.

That is, one moment I'm riding the manic wave of omnipotence—I truly believe I am capable of any feat I set my mind to, and, even more, people will admire and applaud the exhibition—and the next moment I have sunk to those depths of despair, I shall not even attempt to describe. Ironically, the mania is Queen LaSheen's engine she uses to drive the entire reeking manifestation. But eventually the engine runs out of gas, or collapses in on itself, or whatever engines do, and I come here. You see, dear, I'm what's known as a Frequent Flier; except, instead of points or miles or bags of peanuts, these good people give me Clozaril to shave the waves, and Prozac to fill in the valleys, and Zoloft to send me down that happy highway again."

He sat there smiling, again flipping magazine pages. He glanced at her. "Now it's your turn, little beauty. Tell LaSheen all, or at least wet her wick with a little gossip. Hopefully those tranquilizers I've seen them give you haven't turned that pretty head into a soggy sponge, or robbed your identity, or maybe there's some awful Jack Nicholson-Nurse Ratched mind-fuck thing going on. Oh Lord!" Now Rupert leaned toward her again, taking up her hands again, a little urgently. "Tell me, baby. Can you remember and tell me anything that happened? I mean, how can someone like you, end up at this place? Do you even *remember*?"

Connelly sat there, and for the first time realized she actually *didn't* remember, or not very much. In the first place, it was so hard to concentrate now. In fact, she couldn't concentrate on very much at all; mostly, what was happening right in front of her at that moment, and even then it was hard to exactly understand things. She thought and thought and remembered fighting with someone—he was in his underwear, and she was fighting with him. And she remembered it was raining and ugly. And there were policemen. And then…there was Eric. Or was there? Was that all a dream? Had she dreamed everything, especially the part about Eric? She wasn't sure, because, right then, it all seemed like it had happened to someone else, not her. And besides, it bothered her to think about it, any of it. It bothered her in a way, a bad way, she had never felt before. She looked down. "I think, when I was little, my parents died…I think, since then, it hasn't been the same…I think—" She stopped now and shook her head. She looked up. "Can you help me back to bed, Rupert?"

"Of course, little darling," he said, squeezing her hands.

*

When Lillian finally arrived, she was like a too-hot, too-bright whirlwind, circling about her protectively, and scattering everyone away. That was the feeling Connelly had, first hearing the entrance-door buzzer and seeing her enter the ward, and the effect she seemed to have on everyone, patients and staff included, until they were alone in her room.

"I can't *believe* this," she said, pacing back and forth. "I can't believe they would put you someplace like that—those trailer-trash bumpkins—and then compound the disaster by, somehow, someway, dumping you here. Those fucking idiots!" And she slammed down her organizer on the tile floor. Connelly flinched, startled, sitting on the bed. Lillian looked over. "Sorry, sweetie, but they should have called me. They're always supposed to call me, and they know that. Besides, since I buried my mother, I'm trying to quit smoking, and I'm all to fucking pieces again. Sorry, sweetie." She picked up her organizer and came and sat down beside her on the bed. She unzipped the case and took out a packet of gum from inside. She pulled out two pieces and handed her one of them. They both sat there now, chewing gum. Connelly knew Lillian was thinking hard, like when she would smoke and think, except now she was chewing gum and thinking.

Her gum snapping, Lillian said, "They've got complex posttraumatic stress all over your chart and file—do you have any idea how that complicates things?"

Connelly shook her head.

"First place, they put you in a nuthouse, and there's all the stigma and bullshit baggage that goes with that. Then they diagnose you PTSD, and now you're stamped and certified as well." She stared at Lillian, uncomprehending. "Sweetie, as a rule, foster parents tend to shy away from bringing, shall we say, the more unknown elements into their midst. Someone, they think, who might wake up in the middle of the night and cut everyone's throat while they're sleeping."

"I would never do that, Lillian."

Lillian heaved a sigh and reached over and pulled her to her, hugging her. "I know, sweetie, I know. I just have to work harder, making sure everyone else knows that."

They sat there for a while, just talking. Connelly wanted to tell her about Eric. She really did, because absolutely no one else knew about it, except her; and she thought she should tell someone, for whatever reason.

But when she opened her mouth to try and do that, she stopped. In the first place, she still couldn't decide if it was real or not. She thought it was, but she couldn't be sure. And she remembered the plastic hospital bracelet, just like the one she was wearing, that Eric had given her. But they had taken away all her things, so she didn't know. The bracelet *could* be in her backpack, or maybe it wasn't.

Then there was that awful feeling again that nothing that was happening to her, or even what she was thinking, was real. Or, if it was real, it was someone else's real, not hers. And, sitting there beside Lillian, even as she felt her warmth, and smelled her delicious mingling smells of fruits and flowers, she felt sure she was someone else, or she was watching someone else be her. She was both inside and outside of herself, or someone, and she wasn't sure about any of it. The thing was she had the amazing horrible feeling of not knowing where she should be right then, or who she should be, or what she should be doing; only that something was happening, or no, and she didn't know, even if she could figure out *who* she was supposed to be.

So she sat there, saying nothing, and Lillian pulled her tightly against her once again.

*

They decided to move her "upstairs," to the seventh floor, where Rupert was going. There was a meeting with her and Lillian and the doctors, when Rupert burst into the room—his green turban askew, his gown flung open and flowing out behind him, his too-big house-slippers flopping noisily against the tile floor—pleading with everyone not to separate them. Breathlessly, he told Lillian, "Believe me, gracious lady, this precious child will never again be as safe as she would be there, with me and my friends to look after her."

"Friends—as in all men?" Lillian was leaned forward, looking around the table.

Rupert sniffed and looked imploringly at one of the doctors.

The doctor said, "It's our Gay Focus Unit."

"Oh," said Lillian, leaning back.

Rupert looked over at her. "Love the tangerine boa, by the way."

*

Connelly liked it there much better. There was a wonderful patio they were allowed to go and sit in the sun, the breeze blowing her hair; and there were actual *birds* that flew into the trees, looking down at her with their little cocked heads, and airplanes high in the sky, going—she wondered where?

She got the impression most of them there, in the ward, were Frequent Fliers like Rupert. They all seemed to know each other very well, and she enjoyed sitting there, listening to them catch up with each other's lives. Her two favorites, besides Rupert, were Victor, who told her he had been schizophrenic since childhood, and also had an obsessive-compulsive disorder he was trying desperately to manage, and Manuel, who was an autistic savant, and became severely depressed when he couldn't figure out, as he said, "solutions" to the problems that kept forming themselves inside his head.

And the first time she sat with them on the patio she observed the fingers of Manuel's right hand flaying the air beside his head, as if he were tickling some invisible spot there. Then he raised his left hand, slightly lower, and those fingers began to flay and flicker up and down, tickling the air, as well. First one hand, then the other, then the other again. It almost looked to her as if the two hands were talking to each other, back and forth.

"Enough with the damn *counting*, already!" Victor finally burst out, crumpling the newspaper he had been trying to read, into his lap.

"The damn counting!" Manuel repeated, equally frustrated. "Damnit, Victor, you almost had it."

"Had what?" Victor said.

"Had what?" Manuel repeated again. "The solution. You almost had the solution, and then I stopped me."

"Figure it out when you're alone," Victor told him. "I just want a little peace and quiet—is that too much to ask?" He crossed and re-crossed his legs three times and cleared his throat.

"Too much to ask," Manuel said. "Then I have my fucking peace and quiet."

"Thank you!"

"Thank you!"

Victor straightened out his newspaper and began to read again, when one of Manuel's hands again offered a flicker of dissent, with

three fingers rising and exhibiting a quick series snare-drum-like rolls; and Victor lowered his newspaper and glowered at him; and Manuel turned away, miffed and whispering, "I go to hell, Victor, and don't ask you for rubbing my shoulders again."
"I won't."
"I won't."
Victor sighed, the calm resuming.

*

Another day they were sitting there, there was a trembling and a movement, as if they were all sitting on a large floating raft on the ocean, rising up and settling back down. The trees swayed, and the birds flushed from the limbs as if they'd been shot out.

Connelly gripped her chair arm until the swaying stopped. She looked around the patio and saw staff members running haphazardly this way and that, while everyone else—the patients—seemed unaware anything had occurred. They were all sitting, reading, staring, faces with eyes closed pointed toward the placid sky.

Rupert looked up at her and said, "What's the matter, dear?"
"Aren't you afraid of them?"
"Afraid of what?"
"Earthquakes. Didn't you *feel* that?"
"*Earth*quakes!" said Victor. "Sweetheart, I have *mind*-quakes doing triple-backwards somersaults off the fucking Richter scale. Earthquakes ain't shit." Then he crossed and re-crossed his legs three times and cleared his throat.

That was also the day she asked one of the aides for a few sheets of copy paper and a pencil, and sat there, doodling and sketching each of them: Rupert, sleek and flamboyantly scarved, and leaned back in his sophisticated slouch; Victor, sitting straight-backed and distinguished, his eyes askew for something, anything, out of place; and Manuel, thin and bent, a fluttering hand aloft, as if testing the changing winds. Sitting there, she realized, for the first time she could remember, she didn't have to worry about things. That is, locked away there, high in the sky (like the prisoner-princess Zaureen, kept in Benadarne's Castle of Oblivion, whose kingdom and family had been laid to ruin, and that refused Freddie and Moggie's attempts to rescue her and give her back her memory), she didn't want to be rescued then either. And maybe never. Instead, she could stay there, surrounded by her sweet, odd friends, and forget everything that had happened, or might happen, and have her own fragile and empty peace of mind, like Zaureen—like Victor, like all of them—desired.

So she sat there, making her sketches, until Rupert happened to look over her shoulder and squeal with astonishment. "Little beauty—where on earth!—they're like *photographs!*"

Everyone, from all over the patio, gathered around her now, and she fiddled with her pencil nub instead. But Victor, who seemed oldest to her, or at least was best at organizing and arranging everything around them, clapped his hands and said, "All right, everyone back to their seats. We're obviously interrupting our pretty baby's creative process, flocking about her like mynah birds at a seed convention. Everyone!" He clapped again.

When they were seated and asked her about it, she sat there a moment; then, suddenly, she told them how she would sit and watch her father paint; and, after he was gone, she had always drawn things, at first, mostly as a way of remembering him; and then just because she liked doing it. That surprised her. Remembering that, was the first real, clear thought she had had, since…she could remember. And she closed her eyes and let more of that scene come inside her head; and she saw him working—his hand and brush applying the paint—and she could see him talking to her, laughing and joking—and then it shut out. It was gone.

She got up, the sheets of paper tumbling and scattering across the breezy patio, with everyone running about, trying to catch them, as she ran inside to her room, closing her door shut behind her.

*

One day they brought her to another floor. There was a large room there that did not look like the other hospital rooms. It was more like an artist's studio: there was a long crafts table there, with assorted crafts things on it; and there were scattered easels, and behind one of them a lady was painting. Connelly knew immediately she was a therapist. She could *smell* the oily-roily air about her, could see the all-knowing inquisitive glance that pretended to not really look. She was barefoot in her smock, and had long gray hair tied loosely behind her, and she pretended mostly to ignore her, offering her a smile and saying: "My name's Jeanne. Would you care to paint with me?"

She didn't answer her. Instead, she made her way slowly around the room, looking at the things others had done. Artwork of the insane. She stopped before one piece and stared. It was a girl's tormented face in acrylic, stretching agonizingly down the canvas to some near breaking point.

"You're right," Jeanne said. "It's the best thing here."

She looked back at her, but she was just painting of course, as if she'd been talking to herself.

She continued her wandering and poking about, until Jeanne said, "Those drawings you did of some of the men in your ward—they have sort of an illusionist aspect to them, like little penciled photographs. Can you paint me something more from your impressions, your feelings about something? I'll bet you can."

Connelly stared at her. "I don't have any money."

"What?"

"You said bet. You said I'll bet you can. But I don't have any money to bet you."

The therapist smiled. "I'll tell you what, you paint me something from your mind, something you just have an impression about, and you're just painting it how you see it—in your mind. Then I've got something special I'll show you."

Connelly continued staring at her, when the older woman looked away, becoming immersed in her own painting. She looked around and walked over to one of the easels displaying a fresh canvas. She found a broken stick of charcoal and first made a few quick lines, sketching in the cross and the barest outline of the figure upon it; then she dropped the smudgy nub and chose a flat, one-inch brush and began to lay down thick rough strokes of bitter rust and ocher yellow and jagged stabbing shards of absolute black and crimson. It didn't take her long, and when she finished, she realized Jeanne was standing behind her. She cleaned her brush.

Jeanne said, "I've never seen the crucifix presented quite like that. Those are angry strokes, Connelly—but for whom? Are you a wayward Christian, perhaps?"

"Yes, but that's not Jesus."

"Oh? Who is it then?"

She put away the brush and looked up at her. "The last man that tried to rape me." She sniffed. "So what were you going to show me?"

The therapist stared back at her, then blinked and said quietly, "I'll get you a smock to wear."

*

She took her down to the main lobby of the hospital. In one out-of-the-way corner was a seating area, with several paintings on the wall. They sat there, side by side, and Jeanne said, "That's Diego Rivera's *Tortilla Maker*. Hardly anyone knows it's here. Your mother has cancer, or your son has leukemia, and here's a lady and a girl making tortillas." She shook her head. "Art can only assert itself when real life stands aside a moment. But those moments can be very important when we let them be." She pointed at the other painting. "Frida Kahlo's *Doctorcito querido,* her beloved Doctor Eloesser, who once worked here and treated the artist for her back pain."

They sat there, looking at the paintings.

Connelly finally said, "So if I come every day and paint for you, will you give me back my mother and father? My brother?"

The therapist shook her head. "We're not deities here, Connelly, no matter what some of us may think. Sometimes I don't even think we're very good shaman. But we do, on occasion, help people. And I'd like to try and help you, if you'd let me."

Connelly looked back at the lady and the girl, making tortillas. She looked at the way he used shadow and light to reveal and hide, or diminish, what was there. She said, "Can we come down here sometimes and just sit? I like to look at the people passing by. I like to see their faces."

"If you like."

She looked at the therapist, and then looked back at Kahlo's dignified doctor, standing funnily beside the little sailboat on the table. "All right then," she said.

21 ♀ THE LETTERS

Each day with Jeanne, she began to see her life like layers of paint—one piled haphazardly, carelessly, atop the other, and all spread out over some rough, unyielding surface. And she wished she could rise up in the air for a better perspective, see herself better, and what it was all doing with itself, with her, she said. It was all piling up and piling up, and she had no perspective about it, any of it, and she didn't know where she was going with it, or anything about it, and it was nearly overwhelming her, she told her. And she didn't know what to do with it. It was all out of control, and she just didn't know.

Meanwhile, Jeanne told her she didn't know anything about all that, but she was certainly a good artist, and maybe she should think about that instead.

"Think about what *does* make sense for you," she said. "What you're doing with those colors and designs make perfect sense to me. Why don't you follow that instead? Don't worry about the rest of it. You can't see it anyway. You said so yourself. So just leave it alone and follow what's right there in front of you. Follow what you can follow, and tell the rest of it to go to hell."

*

The first day of September they threw her her first real birthday party, she'd had, since her parents had died. Rupert made her put on a blindfold and escorted her along the ward hallway; and when he pulled the blindfold from over her eyes—they were all standing there in the dayroom, singing Happy Birthday and clapping. There was a big cake with her name, surrounded by twelve pink candles one of the attendants was lighting.

"Make a wish! Make a wish!" they shouted.

She shut her eyes and blew.

Everyone cheered and clapped again.

"Twelve years old," said Rupert, "and never been—well, anyway, she's twelve years old."

"I organized everything!" Victor said, beaming.

"I did not," Manuel argued. "You helped just as much."

"Yes, yes, you blew up some balloons," Victor said with a dismissive wave of his hand. "You achieved World Peace, we salute you."

"I go to hell, Victor."

"Well, let's all have our cake and ice cream first," Rupert said.

It was a wonderful party. There were presents—sketch pads and good drawing pencils and pastels—and Victor's carefully orchestrated games, producing a melee of confusion; and, for a grand finale, Rupert secretly changed his clothes, darkened the room lights, and got through most of 'Si Yo Se Acabo,' amid much tumult and cheering, before the staff was able to regain control, and the head nurse announced p.m. meds would come early that afternoon.

Lillian also came, giving her some new underwear, which she badly needed, and, once they were finally alone, a manila envelope she had noticed her holding.

"I guess these have been following you around," she told her. "They've probably been sitting in someone's out-box forever."

She carefully opened the envelope flap and peeked inside.

There were two letters from her Uncle Boyd, sent, about a month apart, the previous year. The first was from Dili in East Timor; the second, from Port Moresby in New Guinea.

"That guy gets around," Lillian said.

When she was able that evening, she went out alone on the patio to read them. The mailing address on them was the Cardswell's, and she saw both envelopes had been opened and taped back shut.

She opened the first one, from Dili, and read:

Dearest Niece,

JAMES SNYDER

I hope this letter finds you somehow. I only found out about Sister's death last year when we made port in San Francisco, and I went to visit everyone and found someone else living in your apartment. I talked with an old woman there who said she used to baby sit you and your brother, and she told me what happened. I only had time to visit Sister and Michael's graves before we sailed. I don't know what to say about it to you that you probably haven't already said yourself, except she was a fine, beautiful woman that I loved very much, and I shall miss. And Michael was a fine, good husband and, I know, father. I know you and Eric must miss them both terribly, and that is all this merchant marine can think of to say about it. I am sorry, Niece.

Anyway, I sent out many queries from many different places and finally got this address. I hope you are still there or, if not, someone will be kind enough to forward it on to you. Apparently, as best I can tell, you and Eric have been separated, and I am also trying to get a note to him. If you talk to him, or know of his whereabouts, please let him know I am trying to contact him.

Niece, I hope you are making some kind of life for yourself, but from the confusing mishmash I am getting from different agencies, I am beginning to wonder. It is certainly unfortunate, in this instance, our side of the family was never very fruitful, and now you and Eric are left to deal with that fact. Such is fate, huh? I have thought more than a little about quitting the roving business and maybe trying to raise you two, but I finally realized that would be a mistake. I am no kind of parent, and, as well, my personal manners of life would not go so well with the interests of children like you and Eric. So I can only pray to God you are finding a way with it. I have thought and thought was there anything else I could do, and I have only one idea that is most likely worthless, but I am as unknowing about that as everything else, so I thought I would mention it to you.

I'm not sure if your mother ever told you about our Texas branch of the family, as we were never very close to them, but they certainly exist, and I once paid them a visit when we ported in Corpus Christi for a week. John Walker was the family patriarch, and he went down to Texas from Tennessee in 1843, or so I was told by Elizabeth Walker (or Liz, as she prefers you call her), your cousin there, who was engaged at the time to a Jack McCullough. Your great-great grandfather, Samuel Walker, left Texas for Chicago around the beginning of the century. I remember Liz joked with me how Sam met a Swedish girl (your Great-Great Grandma Inga) and they ran off to get married, which no one there cared about; but, apparently, he did it just before fall roundup, and he's never been forgiven for that injustice. Anyway, I recall I had a wonderful visit, and learned a lot about our family; and I remember Liz said she was going to write your mother and grandmother a letter. We also talked about a family reunion, but I took off again for parts unknown, and I think Em was in college then, and nothing ever came of it. And now your mother's dead, and you and Eric are the last of our side of it.

Of course, I'm not sure if you would even be interested in making contact with Liz, but I thought I would tell you. I thought about writing her and telling her what happened, but I decided to leave that decision to you, depending, naturally, on your current circumstances, which I know nothing about. Think about it, Niece. I'm sure Liz would love to hear from you, and she would most likely ask you and Eric to come there to stay. In fact, I'm sure of it, knowing that pretty Texas girl I got to know at the time. Also, by now, I'm also sure everyone has forgotten how Sam left them hanging in a clench. Ha!

Well, I have just looked for Liz's address and realize it's probably in a shore-locker I keep at Port Moresby. I've decided to send this on, so you can be thinking about it, and I will send her address on when we arrive there in a few weeks.

I close this with my love and prayers everything is fine with you, or at least tolerable.

Your Uncle Boyd Walker

She quickly folded the letter and slipped it back inside its envelope and, without pausing, tore the tape from the other envelope and took out the single sheet inside, opening it and reading,

Dearest Niece,

As promised, enclosed is Liz and Jack's mailing address in Texas. I can't remember if I told you in my first letter, but they still live on John Walker's original ranch, or spread, as they refer to it there. I recall much heat, a rattlesnake under the porch, and how I kept expecting John Wayne to come riding down out of those surrounding hills. Also recall the best peach cobbler I've ever tasted.

Well, nothing else to say now, as we ship out tomorrow, so here you go.

Take care of yourself (and I hope you decide to contact your cousin Liz, I think you would like her),

Uncle Boyd
(Here's their address.)
Mr. and Mrs. Jack McCullough
Circle-W Ranch
FM 121
Comanche Falls, Texas 78885

She was still sitting there when Rupert came and sat beside her. He asked her if he could comb out her hair, which, he observed, resembled an abandoned beehive. Doing so, he asked her about the letters, and she told him they were from her uncle, but didn't tell him anything else.

That night she went to bed early and lay there, going over everything in her mind, everything her Uncle Boyd had said, and what it could possibly mean.

The most amazing thing to her was that she had a *family* somewhere. She had a real family, even though they were, more or less, a distant one, and they had no idea she was even alive. But just the thought of that, of some kind of family, gave her such a feeling, she thought she would float up from the bed and right out of the hospital. Thinking that, she cried a little, very quietly in the dark, holding the letters against her chest. They were *her* family, she thought, over and over, until she fell roughly into sleep.

By morning she'd made up her mind and sat in a corner of the dayroom, writing to her cousin. *Dear Cousin Liz,* she began the letter, and then decided that was too familiar and crumpled the sheet. *Dear Mrs. McCullough,* she wrote and threw that away as well. Too formal. She sat there, thinking a moment, and then wrote: *Dear Elizabeth.* She stopped, looking down at it. Yes, familiar but not too. So she wrote:

You don't know me at all, but I'm Emily's daughter. That's Emily Pierce, or Walker, as you would know her. Well, she and my father were both killed in a car accident when I was six. I'm twelve now, and I've been pretty much on my own since then. That would be me and my brother Eric, who is fifteen. As things happened, they separated us a while back, but I think I know where he's at. Anyway, I found out about you through my Uncle Boyd, who I know you know, and he said maybe I should write you and—

She stopped again. And what? Ask her to take me in—me and my brother, just like that? Of course she would have to tell her where she was at. And Eric. What would she say then? What *could* she say? *Oh, dear sweet Cousin Connelly, it was sooo nice hearing from you. And you say you're currently being kept in a city psychiatric ward, while your brother's locked up, snug as a bug, inside a state mental hospital? How perfectly charming! How absolutely delightful! You both must come see us sometime, someday, when you're feeling better...Much, much better. But for now—see ya, don't wanna be ya!*

What then? And she realized if that happened, she didn't know what she would do. To lose one family, and then have another; and they don't want you, or they're afraid to want you—she didn't know.

Now she sat there, doing nothing, until it was time to go paint with Jeanne.

While she was there painting, she almost told her about it. She wanted to ask her what she should do, but she knew Jeanne would tell her she should write the letter. And then she would have to write it, and then she would know the truth, and that would be it. So she said nothing about it. She painted and said nothing.

Then when she met with Lillian alone in the conference room that afternoon she almost told her as well. Of course, Lillian asked her about the letters, and she told her her uncle was doing fine and wished her well. But she knew if Lillian knew everything, there would be no holding her back. She would sit right down with her and help her write the letter to Liz. And then she would mail it for her. Or maybe she would do a computer search on her little pink laptop and find Liz's phone number and actually call her. That was Lillian, and she knew that, so once again she said nothing. She listened to her say instead, "So do you remember that couple?"

"Couple?"

"That couple before you got yourself thrown in the nuthouse. That professor and the magazine editor. The ones that can't have kids and they wanted to meet you."

"What about them?"

Lillian smiled. "They called me. They said they talked about it, and they still want to meet you. They want to get to know you better."

When she just sat there, glum-faced, Lillian said, "Kiddo, let's not forget what we talked about before. You're not exactly princess with a dowry at the moment. You got some baggage here, you know. Besides, I've met them, and they're the real thing. And they're interested in you. They say, if it works out, they want to adopt you. Do you understand that? Do you know what that could mean for you?"

She did, she thought. She understood very well. But she also understood she had a family now, her own real family, with blood ties to her own mother, and to her; and she wanted to go live with them instead. She appreciated this other couple's interest, she really did, but she was so tired of it all. She was tired of strangers taking over her life and doing what they wanted with it.

"Lillian," she said.

"What, sweetie?"

Then she realized she didn't know what was worse: to know the truth and maybe regret that forever, or, perhaps, to always have that possibility, no matter how remote, inside you, where you could keep it and protect it forever. Maybe that was better than having nothing.

Maybe.

She finally leaned back and said, "So when do I meet them?"

"Tomorrow if you'd like."

She nodded, feeling as if some dark covenant had been signed between them, just like the one Moggie made Freddie sign—with a bloody X—at that critical moment the most wretched, perilous part of their adventures began.

*

But when she met them the next day, it wasn't at all like she expected. In the first place, when they were bringing her down on the elevator to the cafeteria where they could be alone, the woman, who said her name was Clair, looked at her, then pulled her to her, hugging her, and said, "I've been *so* wanting to do that."

Her husband Richard said, "You can't even imagine. She's been like a kid waiting for Christmas. She even lifted one of your file photos and has it tucked away on her car visor."

"Oh, stop, Richard," Clair said. "You're embarrassing the poor thing."

"Anyway," he said, "we know everything about you we've been allowed to know."

"But we want to know more," Clair said, hugging her again.

Then, when they were sitting in a corner of the cafeteria, eating their sandwiches, Richard said, "I know I'm jumping the gun on this, but, if everything works out, we've been talking about adopting your brother as well."

Connelly stopped eating. Now she could barely hear Clair say, "When we read your profile sheet, we saw what you'd written about what you most wanted—to be with your brother again."

Then she heard him say, far away, "Connelly, we've both wanted children since we were married, and can't have them. Then Clair saw your photograph and read your bio and that was it."

"You were absolutely perfect," Clair said. "We feel so fortunate to have found you."

"You do still want that, don't you?" he asked her. "I mean, to be with your brother? Because if you don't—"

Clair said, "Oh, now look what you've done, you big oaf. You've upset her."

"No," she said, wiping her eyes. "I'm not upset at all." She looked at them. "And, yes, I still want him. To be with him, that is."

"Good," he said, smiling at her. "Because I've always wanted a son."

"I promise you," Clair said, setting aside her sandwich, and taking up Connelly's hands in her own, "your life is about to change in ways you can't even imagine."

"She means that," Richard said, winking at her, and taking a bite of his sandwich.

When she was alone in her room again, she carefully placed Uncle Boyd's letters, as well as the letter she had started to Cousin Liz, back inside the manila envelope and put them away.

That night, in a strange fitful sleep, she again dreamed she was running in through Benadarne's fearful Out Door, when Vladiscone attacked her—rising up and raging onward, scorching the barren earth about her, his great blooded paws clawing the air—as she sprang aside and swung hard her sword, fighting him off, and at last made it through, breaking the evil spell.

Then (though she knew she couldn't go home again) such a feeling of hope, of peace, overcame her. Finally, taking Moggie's hand, and walking out of the Forest of the Night for the last time, she did wonder if her life, her brother's, was finally about to change in ways "unimaginably wonderful," as the Grand Wizard had announced to Freddie; though she could hardly imagine, saying, "Oh, Moggie, what *ever* could happen next?"

And as he was about to formulate yet another of his ever-curious opinions of things to come, tweaking his nose, his wise eyes narrowing, she felt the unseen hands of consciousness shaking her, shaking her, as all about her dissolved into the obscure light of morning, of…next.

22 ♀ THE HOUSE ON THE OCEAN

For some reason she remembered him standing there the day they brought her there. Though she had been heavily sedated, she remembered that, and wondered why. And she thought and thought and finally realized he reminded her, in some vague, receding manner, of her father. Not so much the way he looked or acted, but his fatherly presence reminded her. And then one day he came into her room and stood beside her bed, and she knew it was him, even with her eyes closed.

"Connelly?"

She held her breath.

"I know something's happened to you that, for whatever reason, you don't want to talk about now. I just want you to know, should you decide you want to talk with someone, I would listen."

She waited, unmoving.

"I saw you when they brought you here. I was standing in Admissions. And for some reason you reminded me of my own daughters. I have two, younger than you. Anyway, you reminded me of them. And I couldn't stop thinking that if you were my daughter, and for whatever reason I wasn't there for you, I would want someone to talk with you. To try and help you. That's what I was thinking, Connelly."

What could she say? What could she absolutely say that would matter or change a thing? Instead, she opened her eyes and looked at him. And although he looked perfectly normal, perfectly caring and concerned, it was as if she were looking at an alien, of sorts. A creature certainly not of her world, her experiences, but something entirely from another world, another universe, even.

And she turned away, shutting back her eyes again…letting her mind go back—not far now. Not so long ago. When she knew this time was different. This time would be different. This time…

They lived in a part of the city she had never been, called Sea Cliff, in a large, lovely Spanish-style home, setting in the middle of a one-acre garden, overlooking the Pacific Ocean. From her little curving bedroom balcony, on the second floor, she could see the ocean disappearing into the horizon one direction; then, turning, the Golden Gate Bridge and Marin headlands, cloaked in their mysterious misty mornings, or splashed against sun-bright afternoons, the other.

The first time Clair had brought her there, and they both went out on the balcony, she grew dizzy with the sweeping immensity of the prospect.

Clair said, "It you'd like, Wilma can bring your morning tea out here. Wouldn't that be a fun way to start your day?"

She managed a nod.

It was perhaps minutes, or even seconds, that same morning they had first driven her there, she was overcome with the enormity of what had actually happened to her. Perhaps the very instant they had left the curving avenue and driven windingly back among the high-shading, shaggy-barked eucalyptus and twisted-trunk, glossy-leaved red madroña, and came out onto the circular drive, and she saw the house, first thinking it a painting—unreal, an artist's fancy, with the bruised-peach rays of sunlight dappling down through the trees, against the rising and falling line of red-tile roof, and the washed shades of pink and ivory stucco: A little lost castle in the woods.

And by the time they brought her inside, and she found herself ensconced in the hushed and comforting, yet somehow threatening, world of polished granites and beveled glass and rich dark woods, she felt overcome, and only wanted to turn and run back out, back into the festering arms of that other more familiar life of endless stinking, retching hovels; of fighting for scraps and crumbs and the shredded sanity of her own sheer existence, still lingering raw and pungent in her mind.

It was too much. Just too much. She felt like a starving dog trapped inside a meat factory. And there were the familiar mixed feelings coursing through her, as she'd felt every time she had entered that latest abode of charity: humiliation, fear, shame, disgust, mixing with the tiniest pangs of curiosity and even superiority (knowing she wouldn't be there that long).

"Why don't you girls just hang out awhile," Richard said. "Connelly, Clair can show you around, show you your bedroom she's been decorating for weeks, and I'll go see what Wilma's digging us up for lunch."

But additionally this time, shaking her head to clear it and looking around, she suddenly wanted to scream, like when she screamed with Lillian crossing over Golden Gate Bridge, but now she didn't know why. And she didn't want them to think her any crazier than they probably already did. So she followed with feigned complacency behind Clair and said nothing. But all the while, inside herself, she was screaming.

*

In the beginning, when she wasn't hiding in her bedroom, pretending to do something, she would go down to China Beach, at the foot of the cliffs. They were both so sweet about it, leaving her alone, giving her time to adjust in her own way.

Clair said, "Just remember, this is all new for us as well. We have no idea. We need your help too."

Sweet.

The beach wasn't very big, there was a much larger one, Baker Beach, toward the bridge; but it was her place, her little world apart, she did not feel so surrounded and overwhelmed. Richard showed her how to get down to it, and after that she went every day, walking along barefoot in the sand, staring across the water. Usually she took Spitz along with her, throwing pieces of driftwood for him to fetch. She asked them what kind of dog he was, but they didn't know; they'd gotten him from the pound. Then Richard said he thought he had some wire fox terrier in him, but mostly mongrel.

"We're just alike, aren't we, Spitz?" she said to him one day, walking. "We're both mongrels they got from the pound."

Spitz dropped the piece of surf-beaten wood at her feet and sat there, panting, watching her with dark shining hopeful eyes. She picked it up and threw, and Spitz ran off in a bouncing frenzy.

Afterward, she would walk back up the road from the beach, touching the little lone palm tree, at the road's bend, for good luck; then up the steep stairs, passing under the evergreen canopy, to the top.

THE BEAUTIFUL-UGLY

At the house she would let herself and Spitz back in, then go quietly up the curving, too-solemn cherry-wood stairs to her bedroom, which she always felt funny, in the beginning, entering. Feeling like she was breaking into someone else's most magical and private space; and they would find her there—trespassing—and they would take her away again.

Usually she sat on one of the stuffed French chairs and looked around the room, which was very large and wonderfully decorated and filled with every sort of thing (she tried to imagine) a girl's bedroom could possibly have—an enormous fluffy bed with a canopy over it, and miles of soft, rich fabrics sweeping away in every direction; and a grand carved desk with tiger paws for feet; and a small glass table, and Hollywood chairs for tea; and a pretty dressing table and mirror; and a huge television (flat as a pancake and mounted on one wall); and real artwork (bright, startling abstracts and deliciously fresh water-color landscapes); and bronze and painted porcelain statuettes of fat little men in military coats and pretty ladies with parasols; and more dolls than Suzy Cardswell could ever imagine; and an entire zoo of stuffed animals; and two computers (one on the desk and a notebook to carry about); and a custom sound system built into the wall; and a gym set in one corner; and...a vase with fresh flowers that Wilma, she saw, changed every afternoon, around three.

"Let me know if you need anything," Clair said when she first showed her the room. "I had to ask friends with daughters what to do. Honestly, I didn't have a clue."

Neither did she, but she said nothing then, except thank you, it was all very nice.

The attached bathroom, they wandered about after, looked like a display she'd once seen in an abandoned Neiman Marcus catalogue, while the walk-in closet (big as an elephant's den) was mostly empty.

"I wanted to have you here first," said Clair. "Girl, we are so going shopping."

She could only imagine.

Then came the usual tug-of-war over her old dirty-green Mercy backpack.

"You can't want to keep that filthy thing?" Clair said, finally letting go of the strap.

"It's just something I need, Clair," she told her. "It's like my security blanket, okay?"

"Okay," Clair replied softly, an eyebrow arching. "But if you ever want it gone, just let Wilma know." She was turning away, when she stopped and turned back again. "Would you like me to have it dry cleaned, at least?"

"No thanks."

She nodded, obviously disappointed, but she let it be. And after she was gone, Connelly found a corner, at the far back of the closet behind the shoe cabinet, and hid the pack there. She wanted to take Priscilla out and put her on the dresser, but she was afraid Clair or Wilma would snatch her up—seeing her there so mottled and ravaged among their row of pristine beauties—and throw her out; so she covered everything with one of the afghans off the bed and left it alone, turning out the light.

Now, each day coming back from the beach, she sat there quietly, looking about the room, trying to understand. It was nearly a week before she finally got the nerve to slowly stand and walk over to her desk. She pushed the button on the desk computer and after a moment of grinding and wheezing a screen appeared; a scrolling pink calligraphy on an aqua sea: WELCOME HOME, CONNELLY! WE LOVE YOU! CLAIR AND RICHARD

Music played through the speakers. It was Beethoven's *Für Elise*, she could now hardly recall, her mother had loved.

*

Almost too quickly, she realized, her life was changing. Before she could even grab onto something, anything, familiar, suddenly nothing was as it had been. And nothing from before could compare to those things happening around her, *to* her. Nothing.

There were moments in the beginning, feeling overcome, she would sneak into her closet and sit cross-legged on the floor, rummaging through her raggedy, duct-taped pack, taking things out and staring at them. Of course, there was Priscilla, now beaten and bald, as well as her few scrimps and scraps of ever-changing, ill-fitting, hand-me-down clothes; but there were other things: a Polaroid snapshot of her and Yolanda and Beatrice at Pilgrims Mercy, hugging together and making silly faces at the camera; the small white zippered Bible from the Cardswells'; the tiny pink doll's brush Agnes had given her at the women's shelter; one of Lillian's empty Gitanes Blondes cigarette boxes ("Sweetie, what you want *that* for?" Lillian asked her when she picked it out of the trashcan, but she only shook her head.), with the gypsy woman and her tambourine; another snapshot, this of Rupert dressed as Queen LaSheen that always made her smile; her uncle's letters and her unfinished letter to Cousin Liz; and her most precious things— Eric's letters, as well as the plastic hospital name bracelet he'd given her in the emergency waiting room, before disappearing from her life again.

Because, as it happened, she pressed Richard, as soon as she had dared, to bring her brother there, to her, like he'd promised. And he had, indeed, called Atascadero with her sitting there in his office, anxiously listening to him talk to one person, then another. But they wouldn't tell him anything. So he drove down there with his lawyer, and that's when they told him Eric had been living in a halfway house when he ran away.

Of course she didn't believe him when he told her that and called Lillian. The next day she called her back. "It looks like he ran off with that other boy, sweetie," she corroborated his story. "It doesn't look good. Apparently they beat up the res and stole some money. I'll let you know if I hear anything else."

But she never did hear anything else. Lillian.

Then Richard hired an investigator to look into it. And he was able to follow them, through the other boy's family, all the way to New York City, where he lost them again.

"We still have opportunities," Guthrie told them. Guthrie was the investigator, an ex-cop, Richard had told her. And when he said that, she was looking into his eyes, and they seemed like eyes filled with confidence and hope, she wanted to believe. He said, "Anyway, maybe we'll get lucky and he'll get himself picked up or something. I've got the word out. I'll be in touch."

Then Richard gave him his check and he drove away. And watching him leave felt as if the last part of her past life was leaving with him. It was just gone. There had been one tiny chance for them, for her and Eric, and now that was gone as well.

Afterward, she went back to her closet and read his few letters over and over, trying to cry as quietly as she could, so no one would hear her; and then finally closing her eyes and holding her breath (with one hand squeezing the heart-shaped locket, with its tiny hidden key to her parents' hearts, tucked beneath her blouse), trying to remember what it was, like something scratching at her mind from the outside, trying to enter there, trying to tell her something, to warn her, or maybe only trying to calm the heaving there, which, she feared, might break it apart again at any moment. Until finally she heard Wilma calling for her, telling her she had fresh-squeezed her some orange juice and warmed her a brownie. And she threw the afghan over everything and went out, turning out the light.

*

It was Wilma, in fact, that was the key to her new life. To comprehending (to even the smallest degree) what that life was, and how she could possibly fit in to it. She had seen that almost immediately, first arriving there, when the three of them were standing there, a little stiff and unsure, when a rather corpulent black woman, dressed in a flowered moo-moo, came waddling into the room, her shiny shaking-back-and-forth face near bursting with emotion, and wiping her hands with a dishtowel, exclaiming, "Oh, praise *Jesus*, my baby's home at last!"

And before Connelly knew a thing—in fact, instinctively drawing back a little, before freezing in place—she felt herself swept like a windblown wisp into the air by arms powerful and soft, her face covered with wet smooching kisses, and squeezed till she hurt. As quickly, Wilma dropped her back down and issued as assured proclamations the same next steps already decided: "Ms. Clair—you take this child and show her her new home—but don't y'all be gone too long, 'cause I got salmon melt, cream cucumbers, and chilled raspberry parfait waiting for her. Mr. Richard—I need you to trim the bread crust off just like I showed you, but don't go near cutting off your finger this time, and we got to stop everything and go looking for a Band-Aid." Then she laughed, clasping her hands together, before grabbing up Connelly again, giving her one last squeeze.

As both Clair and Richard, with an evident long-acquired air of privacy, seemed mildly lost at what to do with her now that they finally had her, Wilma held no such airs, and knew exactly.

"Child, you come help me in the kitchen, and I'll show you some things."

And Connelly was immediately pulled into a lush and dizzying world of trans-family-and-generational history and gossip, until she felt herself hardly more than cut and primed and deep-soaking in one of Wilma's rich, saucy marinades: "You see, sweetheart, my

THE BEAUTIFUL-UGLY

daddy worked for Ms. Clair's daddy—that be Mr. Brace (Oh, he such a fine, decent man, baby!)—all the way down in South Carolina, where I grew up. Now daddy was a gardener, you see, he took care of the Brace grounds—they all owned a summer home, you see, down near Charleston—and daddy, he cut the grasses and planted the color, as he always called it, and pruned all them trees and bushes and such. Then, when Ms. Clair was born, Mr. Brace (Oh, he such a fine man, darlin'!), he asked daddy if I could come out here to San Francisco and help out. And daddy said he thought that would be all right, and he asked me, and I said I thought that would be all right, and so I came out here and been here ever since, raising up Miss Clair from her poopy drawers, to Paris perfume, to marrying Mr. Richard. Then when she asked me to come over here and help out, I came. And I'm still here, God willing."

She worked now, smiling.

Connelly said, "Don't you ever go home?"

"Oh—yes, indeed, baby!—every year at Christmastime." She shook her head and sighed. "And every year I go back, there's less folk to hug than the year before. My own mama died year last. Now my daddy still hanging on, and every year Mr. Brace (Oh, he such a *fine* man!), he still send him that thousand dollars. But daddy don't spend it on nothing. He fishes for catfish out behind the house, and once a month goes into the city for the wrestling matches. You see, he a gentle man, baby, always was, but he loves to holler and stomp his feet at all them dirty wrestlers!"

Wilma chuckled again, and, after a moment, Connelly saw her eyeing her aside. "Both your folks dead, I reckon, sweetheart?"

"Yes ma'am."

Wilma nodded. "Well, sugar, all I can tell you is, I ain't never seen that woman excited about anything like you. You see, when she was just a little bitty girl she had a bad fever almost killed her; and I believe it did something to her woman parts, and she can't have no young'uns now. And she always tell me: 'Wilma, I want my own precious daughter more than anything.' And now she gone and got you, and she contented like I ain't never seen. God bless you, child!"

Connelly hardly flinched now as Wilma, wiping away a tear, put her big arm around her and gave her a little squeeze this time.

23 ♀ BEAUTIFUL-UGLY

With Wilma's seemingly endless and provocative insights, and calming, steadfast presence, along with long walks with Spitz on the beach, she began to understand, and to accept, what was really, finally happening to her: a family. For the first time, in so long a time, she felt part of an actual family that accepted her and wanted her, and (most important) she wanted back.

It was certainly not the family she would have imagined. How *could* she? Or maybe even the family, given the choice, she would have chosen. But the more she thought about it, she decided families really had nothing to do with everything being perfect and exactly as you wanted. A family in the best sense, she finally decided, was more an opportunity, a challenge even, to see herself and everything around her in a different way. To be pulled in different ways that, alone, she might not have ever gone, always becoming something different, sometimes scarily so, and knowing you had someone there to watch out for you, even as it happened, and to comfort you, after it did.

Clair, in fact, saw it more as a total makeover that, she informed her (once Wilma had her at least halfway settled in), she needed badly.

"You don't have to bother," Connelly let her know.

Clair looked at her seriously. "You start school in one week, and I've cancelled all my appointments."

"Really, Clair, I'm fine."

THE BEAUTIFUL-UGLY

"What you are is a beautiful mess," she said. "You don't know makeup. You don't know hair. You don't know style. You don't even take baths. You know, darling, you have your own bathroom now, with a forty-thousand dollar Dino De Laurent's shower—it's yours, no one else's—and you can use it anytime you wish."

She sighed. "Well then, maybe some new jeans?"

"Uh-huh," Clair said.

What made matters worse was that Clair was not the magazine editor Lillian said she was. She had been once. A fashion editor, in fact, just after her modeling career had declined "imperceptibly," as she put it, "then suddenly." Now she was something else called an independent fashion stylist.

"What's that?" she asked her.

"Oh, I'll show you," said Clair.

It helped that she could now envision Clair having gone from poopy drawers to perfume, as she seemed so overwhelmingly capable in everything else she did.

"That woman got more things hanging in the air than a stringbean bush," Wilma whispered deliciously in her ear when they were alone in the kitchen, cutting vegetables. "Her little baby telephone playing that same damn song over and over in her purse, always going here and then going there, carrying clothes in, then carrying them out, meeting all sorts of fancy, important people and going to parties and whatnot—I don't see how she even know which way is up—and I'm hoping, now that you're here, she might just slow down some, even though it be near the same as slowing down some wild, crazy wind, coming down the mountainside."

Wilma shook her head.

Then she and Clair began their makeover week together, which she finally decided wouldn't be that bad, even though she had no idea what to expect, or what was expected of her; because this seemed like a different sort of relationship than she'd had since she was on her own. She was too young when her mother was alive to know and do the things, she thought, Clair had in mind. And she wondered about it, even as they drove north out of the city, all the way up to a day spa in Calistoga, called The Rack. There, Connelly was amazed to find herself, as well as Clair, stripped naked and covered in a sort of oozy mud from head to toe; afterward, they showered, then were laid out on tables (she thought, like Wilma would lay out two pork loins, side by side) and rubbed and scrubbed—again, from head to toe—with hot, oily lava rocks, until she knew she would crumble to pieces. Then they ate a little lunch, with both their bodies still throbbing and glowing red from the rubbing, wrapped in towels, as Clair told her how her parents (whom she hadn't yet seen, as, according to Clair, they were still vacationing in Europe) had given her and Richard their house as a wedding present. "We certainly couldn't have afforded it," she said. "As hard as I work, and I'm still in the low sixes, and Richard, for heaven's sake, is a literature professor at a teeny-tiny liberal arts college in Berkeley—an all-girls' school, nonetheless. I think he pays *them* to sit around all day and ferment in recherché postmodernist angst with that giggling gaggle of nubile neophytes he calls students."

Clair had a martini to pamper herself, and gave Connelly the olive to suck and chew.

They spent the afternoon having their faces and hair and nails done, and then went shopping at a few of the local boutiques, where Clair began her style training—what was currently in fashion that "worked"; what was more "vintage"; how you could endlessly mix and match things to create fabulously different "effects"; and how there were some things she should never, ever attempt, "no matter how daring you feel, darling." And by the time they were finished, it was late, and Clair suggested they spend the night up-valley, rather than making the long drive back to the city.

"Oh—yes!" said Connelly, who felt oddly drained and relaxed, and didn't feel like driving anywhere too remote.

Clair called Richard to let him know and then made some inquiries, and they found a bed-and-breakfast in the hills above town. Before they drove there, Connelly asked her if they could do a girls' night together.

"And your definition of that is?"

"Nothing really. We just buy some munchies and hang out and talk about things."

Clair seemed amused. "All right, but I'll leave the menu to you," she said.

At the grocery store Connelly threw various cheeses and three kinds of crackers and tins of boiled oysters and salmon and a sausage and some strawberry soda and a quart of raspberry sherbet into the cart. Then she grabbed a bag of chocolate chip cookies as well.

"Well, there goes our day of abjuration and fasting," Clair said, following behind her.

They left the town below and drove up along the narrow, snaking road, disappearing into a cleft wooded valley; whereupon, a curving banked rise gave way onto a drop-off to their right, the hillside suddenly tumbling out of sight below into a tangled nadir of stunted, twisted live oak and mossy rock and brown-dried grasses, flattened here and there by unseen wildlife.

Connelly stared down into this lovely, threatening abysm and tried to think about how she felt now; and she thought she felt wonderful and warm and more at peace than she'd felt since…before. But she also felt full of expectation and a little anxious, and she decided that was because of Clair, who always seemed filled with little bursts of anxious expectations, always bubbling to the surface of her pretty, tawny skin; her gray-green eyes, flashing.

*

There was a little cluster of cottages, six or so, scattered back up the gentle hillside, mostly hiding among the forest. When Clair had called about letting one for the night, the lady told her they were being renovated and wouldn't be available until the following month. That's when Connelly observed what Richard had called Clair's "more persuasive side." And Wilma had told her, "That woman can make ducks cluck and the sun go backwards, she a mind to it."

"I see," Clair said, holding her cell phone to her ear and winking at her. "Are any of them finished?" She waited, listening to the reply. "One then—well that's wonderful. Can we have *that* one for the night?" She listened. "Oh, we wouldn't mind that. It's just my daughter and myself, and it's been such a long day for us. We'd love to stay with you. I can give you another hundred dollars for your trouble." She listened. "No, it would be absolutely no problem. And of course I'd like *you* to give me some of your cards to pass out. I do know some people." Listening. "Wonderful. We'll be there around fourish. Thanks *so* much."

She clicked her phone shut. "Cabernet Cottage Number 1 and the one tucked farthest back into the woods. And, by the way, we've been forewarned—the boy deer are in rut."

Dusk was already descending by the time they got settled, and they went out on the back porch, sitting side by side in rockers, and watched the deepening twilight. There was a small meadow between them and the darkening-green forest wall, and they watched little movements in the grass, trying to see what was there.

"I never do this," said Clair. "I never just do nothing. I feel like I've forgotten something."

Connelly sat there. "Well I'm used to it. I've done this a lot."

Clair reached over and touched her hand. "Do you feel all right?"

"Very."

They were surprised when the porch lights came on by themselves.

"They must be on some sort of sensor," Clair said.

"Or maybe a ghost. I'll bet there're ghosts around here. They probably live in the woods and come out at night."

"You're probably right."

They could hear the insects' song, rising and falling through the darkness.

Connelly looked over at her, wondering what she was thinking. "Are you hungry yet?"

"I'm starving—I never thought you'd ask. That wasn't much of a salad at lunch."

"I was too sore to eat, but I'm better now."

"Me too."

Inside, they spread everything out on the table and began eating. She saw that Clair didn't eat much. Before long, she was making notes in her little notebook she carried everywhere.

"That's not allowed," Connelly finally told her.

"What, darling?"

"When you have girls' night, you can't do that. You can't work. That's one of the rules."

"I see," Clair said, smiling. She put away her notebook and picked up a cracker, forking a piece of salmon on top and eating it.

"Do you like it?"

"Absolutely delicious."

"And we still have the cookies and sherbet."

"Yum."

After they brushed their teeth and hair, they put on pajamas Clair had bought for each of them that afternoon and lay in bed, in the semi-darkness, with the pale light shining in from the front and back porches.

"I could live here," Connelly said.

"You could?"

She nodded.

"Then you've got more grit than I have," Clair said. "It's nice, but it'll be even nicer to get back to the city tomorrow. I've got the whole week planned for us."

Connelly lay there, staring at the ceiling. "I could just stay here and paint. I could do that."

She knew Clair was looking at her. "Do you miss your parents much now?"

"Not really. Not like before. It's funny, but after a while it's like they have something they're doing, and I have my thing. I've just gotten used to that."

She heard Clair sigh and say, "Your father was an artist?"

She nodded. "I can remember one time he painted my mother holding me against her, and we were both naked, but the way he painted us you couldn't really see anything, you know?"

Clair nodded.

"I can still remember he called that *A Study in Blues,* and he sold it to someone for five thousand dollars. Isn't it funny how you remember things?"

They lay there.

Clair said, "I remember when I was, oh, about eight, I guess, and we were vacationing in Charleston, and my father hired this carpenter to do some work for him. And when he arrived to do the work, he brought his son with him, and he was maybe a year or two older than me. Thomas. That was his name. Thomas Reilly. And it took me about an hour to fall head-over-heels in love with him. My first crush. And by the time my father brought us back home, to San Francisco, little Tommy and I had taught each other all about kissing. Gosh, I'd never imagined there were so many ways to do it. However, when we went back the following summer, I found out he'd died that winter. He had cancer, and his father told my father he'd known it even the previous year, and he never said a word to me. And I remember I went out to the barn where he and I used to go, and I cried and cried. 'He never told me,' I kept saying over and over. 'He never told me.'"

After a moment Clair looked over at her. "May I just hold you?"

Connelly slid over against her, feeling her arms go around her. "That feels good, Clair."

"I'm glad," she said, "because you're going to feel a lot more of it."

*

Sometime during the night, Clair's phone rang. A female singer's chirpy little voice, that Connelly thought sounded like a chipmunk with a cold, filled the little cottage: "*I like the way you make me feel, you make me feel so good, baaaby...*"

She heard Clair fumbling in the dark. "Hello."

She could hear a man's faint voice, talking.

"Derrick?" Clair said. "What's the matter? What time is it?"

The man said something, and Clair said, "Yes, I know you don't wear watches. That's why you're always late."

The man talked.

"No, Derrick, I can't do that. I'm spending the week with my daughter."

He talked.

"No, I didn't give birth since the last time you saw me. I'm adopting someone, Derrick. Now why are you calling me in the middle of the night?"

He talked.

"Well, that's too bad, but I told you I'm busy this week. What happened to *your* stylist?"

He talked for a longer time, she could hear the tone of his voice, rising and falling like the insects in the grass and woods.

"Well, I'm sorry to hear that. Maybe if you weren't such an asshole, people wouldn't always walk out on you. What?"

He talked.

"Yes, Derrick, you're an artist. All those snapshots of pouty, underfed girls, wearing clothes no one else will, are absolutely changing the world."

He talked.

"I can't believe you're asking me to do this. You could go bowling with your balls, do you know that?"

He talked.

Clair sighed deeply. "What are you shooting?"

He talked.

"Uh-huh," said Clair. "Who's the model?"

He told her.

THE BEAUTIFUL-UGLY

"Shala Marr. Little Miss Beautiful-Ugly that just got out of rehab. Wonderful. Just another lark in the park, right, Derrick?"

He said something.

"Yes, I'll be there. And, Derrick, you so fucking owe me."

Connelly heard her phone click shut.

She heard Clair sigh again.

"Is everything all right?"

"Yes, darling," said Clair. "Just one of my more high-maintenance friends that needs a helping hand—again. He's doing this women's magazine spread about breaking up—as in a man and a woman—and isn't it ironic they hired *him* for that; anyway, his stylist ran off on him."

"Now you have to help him."

"Oh," Clair said. She slid over to her and held her. "Derrick works very quickly. And he *is* a genius, although I'd never tell him that. Besides, now you can see a little of what I do."

"I don't mind."

"You're so sweet."

They lay there and she could hear Clair's breathing grow quiet and even.

She whispered, "Why did you call her that?"

"Hmmm?" said Clair.

"You called her beautiful-ugly. How can she be both?"

"Oh, that's just an expression we use in the business. It's a very rare quality, actually. I mean, it's not really so unique being attractive and able to walk upright down a runway—*I* did that; but every so often you'll see a girl, trying so hard to break through, and you just know it's not going to work out for them. I mean, everything's working against them, and you feel sorry for them, really—like Shala Marr with her crooked nose and offset eyes and skewed mouth and her body, my God, her body, and you just know, there's no way. Then something happens. Somehow she's able to pull it all together, and keep going, and make it happen. The cameras start clicking, and, if they're very, very lucky, it works; and it's amazing when it does."

"But not all the time."

"Usually, no. Usually it doesn't work. And sometimes it works for someone, and then it stops working. It just stops, and then it's over. And most photographers hate working with someone like that. It's too big a risk. Derrick, of course, loves it. He loves pushing it all the time, pushing it till it breaks, in fact."

Connelly was looking into her eyes and said, "You loved him once, didn't you."

"Derrick? Everyone loves Derrick, until they start hating him." She leaned over and kissed her. "Now let's try and salvage what's left of our sleep, shall we?"

But, instead, Connelly lay there, thinking about what Clair had said about Shala Marr being beautiful-ugly, and why; and how, maybe, her own life was like that. Things had happened to her, around her, that were so ugly she couldn't stand to think of them now; and how a far fewer things had been so beautiful she could hardly stand to think of them either. How they both hurt, but in different ways. Both sides were extremes, and it was easier just to stay in the middle and try and deal with things, with life, that way. Because the beautiful and the ugly parts were so painful and so dangerous, like Clair said—it just stops, and then it's over. Dangerous.

And finally she rolled on her side, away from Clair, and tried to go back to sleep.

*

In the morning they drove back to the city, to the commercial park where Clair had her office. There, Connelly watched while Clair and her assistant chose some pieces (vintage, as she knew now) from several clothing racks in a back room, and they carried them out and hung them on the rack in the back of Clair's SUV. Then they drove over to Golden Gate Park, to a pretty spot near the Japanese Tea Garden, where she saw a group of people were gathered near two white vans, being unloaded.

She shut her eyes that moment…and there was the time the four of them had come there to picnic, she recalled. It was windy that day, and she and her father had tried to fly a kite, but the string broke, and the kite was carried over the trees. *Those* trees, she thought, opening her eyes now and looking.

When she walked over to the group of people with Clair, she saw some men setting up lighting on poles, and another man, very handsome and unshaven and dressed in rumpled jeans over sneakers and a black T-shirt, was coming toward them, shaking his head. "I know, I know," he said. Then he saw her and stopped.

"Well now, what have we here?" And he held out his hands in front of him, framing her face.

"Derrick," Clair said pleasantly, "you try so much as taking a Polaroid of her *shadow*, and my lawyers will be having that ambulance chaser you have on retainer for lunch, literally."

"My, my," he said, smiling and lighting a cigarette, "motherhood makes you feisty, don't it."

Then he turned to her, smiling, holding out his hand. "Derrick Jacobs," he said.

She shook hands with him. "Connelly Pierce."

"Clair's the hired gun that keeps me straight," he said, his dark eyes twinkling, looking into her eyes. "You know I could make you famous, Connelly Pierce."

"So could robbing banks," Clair said. Then she put her arm around her. "Darling, why don't you go over by the grownups." She pointed. "And remember—no matter what anyone asks you—tell them no."

She heard Derrick laughing behind her, when the two of them began talking about other things. She went over to where the fold-up chairs were placed and sat down. It was interesting, watching everyone get everything ready. There was certainly a lot to do, just to take a few pictures.

That's when she saw the girl getting her face done, sitting at a small fold-up table with another woman. After that, she saw the girl, who was tall and angular and moved like a wobbly beautiful gazelle, go with Derrick and Clair over to the SUV. They were there for half an hour, trying on different clothes, until she came back, wearing a pretty black-and-white print dress, and heels. She sat down beside her, nervously shifting about. She took a pack of cigarettes from her bag and lit one. She continued shifting nervously beside her.

The girl finally looked over at her, fingering an earring, and said, "Are you someone's kid?"

"Clair's," she told her, feeling good saying that.

"She's nice," said the girl, smiling. "But Derrick's a dick, isn't he?"

She didn't answer her, and they sat there, as the girl smoked.

The girl said, "I was supposed to do this golf opening thing down in Carmel, but Derrick said his thing couldn't wait. He's such a dick, but he pays good. My name's Shala, by the way."

"Connelly."

"Fab name."

"Thanks. So's yours."

"Thanks."

They shook hands, and Connelly couldn't help but remember what Clair had said about her crooked nose, her offset eyes, her skewed mouth, and her body, my God, her body. But she tried not to stare.

"Have you ever modeled?" Shala asked her.

She shook her head.

"You could, you have classic features and great hair and your eyes are fucking amazing, not a fucked-up crossword puzzle like I got." She smoked. "Actually, I was in a car accident, and they didn't think I would live. One leg's shorter than the other now, so I can't do runways. Fact is, no way I should be doing *any* of this shit, but here I am. Dicks like Derrick keep calling me back when they want just that right sort of freaky effect, you know?"

"I think you're very pretty."

She smiled, crooked-mouthed. "Pretty, no; persistent, yes. But you're sweet for saying that. And if you ever decide to do anything—modeling, I mean—let me know, and I'll hook you up with my agent. That is, if you can deal with all the dicks."

She flicked away her cigarette and got up, taking her bag, and went back to the fold-up table, where a man arranged and sprayed her hair, and the woman touched up her makeup again.

Finally Clair came over and sat down beside her. "So what did you think of Shala Marr?"

"She's nice."

Clair looked at her, smiling. "Having you is so different than I thought it would be."

"Are you disappointed?"

"No," she said softly, with a bare shake of her head.

The shoot went quickly, as Clair promised. Derrick seemed to know exactly what he wanted, and people were busy around him, helping him achieve it. But in the end, she saw, there was just the photographer and the model. She was fascinated, watching the way Shala moved before him, around him, improvising and responding to his words: walk this way, walk that, eyes up more, look down; then standing tall and still, having one of Derrick's cigarettes, as

THE BEAUTIFUL-UGLY

Clair took some double-stick tape from her bag and did something to the dress. Then shooting again.

There was finally one shot Derrick seemed to need. She heard him tell her, "Need some ugly now, Shala. Some closeout. You're supposed to be telling him good-by, not you just saw some sad shitty chick flick or whatever. Need some real ugly here, baby. You can do that now, can't you? Just one. Squeeze one out for the fucking history books and your portfolio, and we can all go home. You can go back to that shitty little apartment of yours, with that shitty little boyfriend of yours, and both of you shove some more silver sugar up your noses and have another lousy mid-day fuck. What you say, girl?"

"Fuck you, Derrick," said Shala, obviously upset.

He clicked. "That's better, but the fat bitch still ain't singin'." He moved around her, clicking the camera, like some stealthy animal moving in on its prey, closer and closer, clicking, clicking.

Then he leaned toward her and whispered something, Connelly could not hear.

She saw Shala shaking her head, pinching her mouth tightly.

He leaned forward again, whispering, lingering there, before moving back.

The moment seemed to hang between them, when her face suddenly appeared to melt, then freeze, her features contorted, as she leaned savagely toward him, arms stiff as steel rods at her sides, fists clenched like pistons, and screamed: "*You fucking bastard!*"

He clicked as she turned, breaking into tears, and stumbled away.

He clicked her fleeing and said, "Houston, we have liftoff."

No one else said anything.

Then he stood there, looking into the camera screen, and smiled.

He came over and sat down on the other side of Clair. He lit a cigarette, looking off, and said softly, "Bacon's on the table, mama."

He smoked, relaxed now.

They were breaking down the equipment. Everyone was moving around quietly, preparing to leave.

"Don't you ever grow even a little weary of yourself, Derrick?" Clair asked.

He ignored her, smoking.

24 ♀ THE ART SCHOOL

The school they placed her was called Greystone Academy of the Arts, and was the premiere fine-arts preparatory school in the city. In addition to all the math and history and science and language classes, which her personal counselor kept referring to as "supplementary needs," the focus was obvious. "We're most serious about art," said the counselor. "The almost infinite verisimilitude of the aesthetic experience, no matter what your medium of choice."

Connelly wasn't sure exactly what she meant, but she was sure now about the midnight-blue, silk-chiffon bolero with charmeuse detailing the counselor was wearing, accented by a soft-glowing string of pearls. But then, beyond Clair's brand of select and edgy fashion tutelage, she wasn't sure about most of what she had seen or heard since arriving for her initial interview, which hadn't gone well.

The questions they asked her about her art, and art in general, she didn't really know how to answer. "I don't know *why* I paint," she told them finally. "My father was a painter but…I don't know. All I know is, when I stop painting, I feel a little lost. For a while, I don't know what to do with myself."

The three faces, staring back at her across the table, reminded her of the three goldfish (Minnie, Moochie, and Moolah) she and Wilma kept in a corner of the jade-granite kitchen counter, staring up at her from their liquid world, pursing their soft open lips when they wanted to be fed. And she had the overwhelming urge to sprinkle some sort of salty flakes into the air between them, and satisfy the hungry, disappointed gazes she was seeing.

Clair had assured her it was all a formality, regardless. "Father's on the board of directors," she told her. "Brace money has bought a lot of mortar for the brick there. Dad'll make the phone call."

In any event, after showing them the pieces she'd hurriedly completed for her portfolio review, and which they only commented were "interesting," she received a letter of admission the following week.

*

That feeling of being overwhelmed she felt in varying degrees since arriving in her new life, only continued, or grew worse, arriving at that school the first day for classes.

She was late to begin with—the official school year begun weeks prior—and, she saw, everything was already well in motion there: the lessons, of course, but also the patterns, the intricate rhythms of school, were already established, and now she had to catch up. Her teachers drew her up long lists of makeup homework, which again threatened to overwhelm her; but Clair soon had everyone's email addresses and took charge. She divided up the assignments, day by day, and, each day after work and school, she came to her bedroom to check on her progress. She brought her cups of tea and sat with her, helping her; which Connelly secretly found unnervingly wonderful, such attention.

"You don't have to do this," she told her, knowing how tired she must be from working all day.

"Oh yes I do," Clair replied. "I've waited too long to do this, and you're not going to stop me now."

She and Clair were growing ever closer, she realized, and in so short a time. It was as if the older woman was trying to catch up with something in her own life, even as she herself was catching up with *her* schoolwork. Whatever the reasoning, she found herself evermore curious about what was happening between them, the delicate give-and-take she felt occurring, and the feeling of trust, and of something deeper than that, a sort of almost concrete bonding, she felt. Even more, it was something growing, like a living thing, only invisible and warm and richly felt, making her feel stronger and more alive. And Clair as well, she hoped.

Which was a good thing, especially with what was happening around her at school. As even after she had begun to catch up with her classes, there were those patterns, those intricate rhythms, to deal with.

Of course, she knew it was going to be different from the other schools she had attended. The kind and degree of her new life around her warned her about that. These had been mostly poor or common schools, some simply horrible, and some struggling to be better than was their due. But each had been different, in their way, and much alike in others. There was a dreary sameness about them, but also a manner of eccentricity about them, she liked. There were many ways to be poor and common, she found, while struggling to escape that condition; but what pretensions there were, were usually hard fought for and displayed like so many raggedy badges, impressing few if any in the shared struggle.

Meanwhile, within Greystone, a sort of rarified omnipresent mindset seemed to pervade. And that place—it also seemed to her, passing through the doors and wandering in a twilight state along the hallways, until she found herself sitting down in her first class, Drawing I—did not seem to inhabit the same universe as those other places she had been. There was a *specialness* that seemed to drift and linger along the hallway with her, and into the room. Then she noticed the way the instructor seemed to be teaching, while trying not to appear so occupied, and the students listened, pretending not to. There was an affected casualness about everything, an air of indifference, and even boredom, as if all necks were clasped with the same gold broach, holding and covering over everything a grand red-velvet cloak of shared self-importance.

She hated it there almost immediately.

Luckily, she met Zack her first week, whose locker was right above hers, and who hated it there as much as she did, and who helped her along. Zack, who lived in Millbrae with his sheet-metal-working father and waitress mother and three brothers and sisters, was there on what he called a "squat pass," or scholarship. He drew wonderful cartoons, lampooning the teachers and particular students, and told her he wanted to eventually move into multi-media, specifically film.

"I'm gonna direct," he told her at lunch. "All Indies stuff. Hollywood's crap. Digital's blown everything wide open. Computers. Visual effects. Although, I'm more into character studies. Anyway, the studios are done for. Junk-food factories for the mindless masses. Fuck'em."

They both sat scrunched into a corner, looking out. Zack was small and pale skinned, with fierce dark eyes, and long wavy dark hair that flowed over his collar, tumbling down his thin back. He dressed in what he referred to as "Salvation-Army black," and pretended that he wasn't hungry. "I'll just have a smoke later," he told her the first day when she asked him why he wasn't eating.

She wondered if the squat passes they gave didn't also include a lunch, but was afraid of asking him and hurting his feelings. Instead, she began to take a bite or two of her own food, and then feign fullness. "I guess I'll just toss this," she said, pausing, "unless you want a bite or something."

He hesitated. "Well, maybe a bite," he said, shrugging one of his pointy shoulders, before attacking her tray. "You sure you don't want any of this?" he asked her, shoveling in the food.

She shook her head. "Wilma brings a little tray every morning to my room, and she always has me milk and a big cookie when I come home."

"That your mom?"

"No, she told me she was my sweet aunt. She runs things there."

He nodded, chewing, his feverish eyes glancing about the tray. "My mom runs our house. My old man's a Vietnam vet. He can't walk too good now and works part-time on the night shift." He smiled. "Of course, rich girl like you wouldn't know 'bout things like that."

She looked away, saying nothing.

*

Each day at lunch she liked watching him eat; and she began to ask him beforehand what *she* felt like. "The chicken looks good," he'd say. "The green pudding."

She noticed his mind worked better once he'd eaten. She found him very funny, doing impressions of some of the teachers and the students—all the stuffy, artsy mannerisms abounding—and he also began telling her how things really worked at Greystone, especially with the Artsirati.

"The what?"

He wiped his mouth with his sleeve and leaned toward her. "A guy told me it's like this secret society that's been here since not long after they opened the place, right after the Civil War."

"Do you think it's real?"

"Sure it's real. The guy that told me's in it. I helped him with some of his drawings one day, and he told me then. He said he wanted me to stay out of trouble, and it was better if I knew about it so I could; and he told me if I breathed a word about it, and they found out, I'd get my ass kicked, first, and ran out of school, second. I believe him. He said it's like this military thing, with soldiers and captains in each class, and some mysterious guy they call the Major that runs things." He stopped, glancing around, and said, "See that guy over there with the red sweater, surrounded by those retro-beatnik bitches in shades? Careful now."

After a moment she turned and looked casually around, seeing the group of them, then looked back.

"That's Dullen Prentiss, the soph class captain. I know a few others, all money and family, influence and connections. Anyway, that same guy told me they absolutely hate the squat-pass kids. Call it muddying the water. He told me just to keep my head down, and stay out of the way, and maybe I'd make it through here; or maybe not." He smiled his baby-face smile at her. "But what am I telling you for. You're rich and beautiful like them. They'll probably be tapping you before long, and I'll have to find a new lunch buddy."

"No you won't," she said, looking away.

"Why not?"

She looked back. "Because I'm not one of them. I'm fostered, Zack. Both my parents died when I was six, and I've been passed around ever since. I just happen to be here right now."

It was the first time she'd seen him speechless about anything.

"Wow," he finally said. "An actual fucking orphan." He seemed to mull that over. "Well, don't let them find out. In their eyes, that's probably worse than being a squatter."

"Well I don't care about them," she said. "That's not why I'm here."

"No?" he said. The smile. "You've been on your own since six and still don't know how the world runs, huh?"

She didn't answer him. The warning bell rang then, and they separated, each going a different way down the hallway to their next class.

*

In fact, months passing, how her world was running was almost always on her mind.

In the beginning she kept waiting for them—Clair and Richard—to change their minds about her. She knew they would. And each day she came home, she expected to be pulled into his or her office and told: "We're sorry, Connelly, we really are, but we've decided this isn't working out.", or "Somehow we've made an awful mistake about this and you have to go back. In fact, we called Lillian a short while ago and she's on her way over, right now, to pick you up."

Each day she thought that, until each night she was tucked safe and sound between Wilma's tight-pulled silk sheets, and she sighed, staring out.

Then after so many weeks had gone by, and she was still there, she wondered what else could be happening. What else was wrong that she was missing? She didn't know, and she couldn't figure it out, but she kept looking and waiting, until finally, one night, Clair came to her room, knocking lightly as she always did, and then entering to kiss her good-night, and then going away. And, for some reason at that moment, she knew. They weren't going to let her go. They weren't going to throw her back, as everyone else had done. And when they told her how much they loved her (which they both did every day), she realized they weren't lying to her.

Now, for the very first time in her life since she was alone, she stopped worrying. It was almost like a terrible fever she'd had for ever and ever, and finally it just broke. And she knew: She belonged to someone again. She had a family. That was everything.

*

After that, she began to look at them differently. More closely. Their bad and good habits, and the curious little familial things about them, they probably didn't notice at all, but she saw clearly now, and that endeared them to her even more.

For instance, she was surprised to learn neither of them had hardly ever been down to the beach. Her beach that she loved. They told her their lives were so busy, they rarely had time. She thought it funny how they'd bought a house right next to it, the beach, and then didn't use it.

Instead, she saw they would sit out on their stone patio, evenings, sipping martinis and watching the sun die beautifully over the ocean's horizon.

"We really bought the place for the view," Richard admitted.

So one Saturday afternoon in the late fall she made them go down there. She told them she wanted them all to have a family picnic, a barbeque, just like her family used to have. After they realized she was serious, it seemed to throw everything into minor turmoil.

Clair said, "Darling, I take it this is sort of like girls' night out, but for the whole family."

She nodded.

"Well, we'll have to tell Wilma," said Richard, as if it were an approaching event of dire consequence.

When he did, Wilma came out of the kitchen and into the living room they were sitting.

"Sweetheart," she said, "how we gonna go cook our food down there on that dirt?"

"It's sand, Wilma. And I found an old hibachi in the garage. People do it all the time. We sit on the deck and watch them."

"Ain't they *bugs* down there?"

"A few."

"Oh my Lord."

She turned and went waddling hurryingly back into the kitchen to prepare.

It took them over an hour; then each of them carried or pulled something—a picnic basket or box or rolling cooler. She walked ahead with Spitz and Richard who, drink in hand, and with the brisk afternoon breeze blowing off the water, called out, rich-voiced:

"*O wild West Wind, thou breath of Autumn's being,*
Thou, from whose unseen presence the leaves dead
Are driven, like ghosts from an enchanter fleeing—"

He stopped, setting down his basket to light a cigarette; then, when they were walking again, he told her how as an undergraduate he'd done some repertory acting.

She looked behind and saw Clair and Wilma following: Clair, with her usual expression of amused indifference; and Wilma, swatting at something and talking nonstop, looking around herself.

THE BEAUTIFUL-UGLY

On the beach, Richard started the briquettes in the hibachi, and Connelly helped Wilma with the food, while Clair lounged on a blanket, sipping sparkling wine and looking out at the approaching, breaking waves.

"I got us some nice dollah shrimp," Wilma whispered. "Them damn Viet-neeze fishermen tried to sell me them fifty-cent shrimp out of one basket, and I told them I wanted them *dollah* shrimp out that other basket." She chuckled. "They just laughed once they knowed I was on to them." She turned and waved her arms. "Go way, ducks. Y'all go on now."

Connelly looked back. "Those are seagulls, Wilma."

"They all ducks to me, sweetheart. They all walk funny and stare at you with them little beady eyes. Y'all go on now." She waved her arms again.

They had a wonderful time. They ate the barbeque, then went for a walk along the beach, and afterward watched the sun go down, sitting there.

"It looks different from down here," Richard commented. "More elemental or something."

"I think they's chiggers biting," said Wilma, slapping at her legs.

"It's nice," Clair said, pulling her into her lap and softly running a hand over her forehead and through her hair. She began to feel sleepy, hearing Clair say, "We should make it our family routine, at least once a month."

"Oh my Lord!" Wilma laughed. "Then I better go find me some long pants somewheres, or these bugs gonna make a barbeque out of me!"

And she laughed again, swatting.

*

Other things.

Not having to worry now where she would sleep that night, or if she would even have something to eat, she began to remember things again. Things she'd forgotten, or that maybe she'd pushed somewhere, in the far back corner of her mind where they'd be safe. Out shopping the boutiques at Cow Hollow one day with Clair, and, going around a corner—there it was—the little park they went on Sunday afternoons.

She stopped and said, "Our apartment's nearby."

"What, dear?" Clair said, stopping with her.

"The apartment we lived in when they were killed. It's right over there."

"Would you like to go there?"

She thought, and then shook her head. "No, there's no there now."

The places they went when they lived in that apartment (very poor and very happy) began to spring up all around her, as if pieces of her mind were on turnstiles, turning creakily about and locking back into place. And the two of them *were* sweet about it when she told them things, either of them insisting they all revisit them: dinner in Chinatown, fish and chips at the wharf, this or that little art museum or gallery they had taken her. They were patient and gentle and sweet.

And it was her that finally stopped it, not them.

She just stopped mentioning things, because she realized, for all of it, there *was* no there now. There never was. And when you die, all the there's go with you. Everything goes with you, or at least the real life of those things, which are all that matter.

Anyway, they didn't notice, living such busy, complicated lives themselves. They didn't notice a thing.

*

She liked Clair's parents, who lived in a big, pretty house on Russian Hill, and told her she could call them Grandma and Grandpa, if she wanted to. She called them Ralph and Mary instead, and they were fine with that. The first time she went there, Ralph showed her his antique toy-soldier collection, and Mary gave her a silver necklace with a tiny blue stone.

"She won't wear it, Mom," Clair said. "I've tried, and all she'll wear is that little gold heart."

"Then it must be very important to her," said Mary. "But she can still keep this necklace, and think about me when she looks at it. Will you do that, dear?"

She nodded and hugged and kissed her, and the old woman began to cry.

"There she goes," said Ralph. "Dependable as the Fountains of Rome."

"And don't give her any money," Clair said, "because she'll only give it away to street people. We've stopped giving her an allowance because of that. She gives it all away."

"Well, we're just happy you're part of the family now," said Mary, wiping her eyes.

She loved spending nights there, which she did sometimes when Clair and Richard were going out. Then they would order in pizza, which Harold, their live-in butler, would serve to them in his slow, dignified manner, going around the dining table and saying: "Would you prefer cheese or sausage, ma'am?", placing a slice on each of their plates. She couldn't help but giggle, seeing the two of them, dressed to the hilt, carefully cutting their pizza slice and chewing.

"I've never eaten pizza served by a butler," she told them the first time.

"Is there any other way?" Ralph replied.

Afterward, she and he would play backgammon or chess, while Mary read one of her cozies, and Harold served each of them a small glass of sherry, and some chilled juice for her. Or sometimes they just sat there, staring at the fire burning in the fireplace, and talking. She asked them questions about places they'd been, and they loved talking about them.

"What's most amazing," said Ralph, "are the similarities, not the differences. In the end, I like to believe humanity has a shared heart. It makes things easier, doesn't it, dear?"

"Yes, it does," said Mary.

Sometimes they asked her about herself, how she was getting along, and was there anything they could do for her? They never asked her about her past; they seemed to somehow already know about that, but were too polite and sweet to pry.

Ralph only said once, "You know, Connelly, it's very hard to understand why some things happen. Actually, I don't really think we're meant to understand them, or it wouldn't matter if we did. They would still be there. But what I believe is important is to try and understand what we want to do with ourselves—what we're looking for, if you will—and then to try and do it well. There really isn't much more to it than that, is there, dear?"

"I can't think what it would be," Mary said.

When she turned thirteen they bought her a beautiful chestnut mare that she called Penelope, and they boarded her with Clair's white gelding, Amadeus, at a private stable along the coast, south of the city. Not long after, they left for a yearlong Aegean cruise, and she missed them terribly for weeks.

25 ♀ GIRL OF A CERTAIN AGE

Being thirteen seemed to make a difference, she saw. She was different, or becoming so. The soft plump of her tummy was hardening and tightening and moving slowly up her chest. Her hips were starting to flare into noticeable curves, and the silkiness of her skin developed a glow that made her eyes shine like two black pools against sun-reddened snow.

As well, she saw things differently, or more clearly. Things she didn't notice before, or perhaps didn't care to.

For instance, she saw how Clair stole things. Little things. Silly things. But she stole them.

Because in the beginning she seemed to be with her almost constantly, as Clair seemed to always be shopping, stopping and poking her nose into this boutique or that thrift shop or flea market—it didn't matter where.

"I find some of my best stuff in the unlikeliest places," she said over and over as an apology. "You always have to be out there, because there're things there, undiscovered, that could make the difference, and you have to be there and find them. You can't be lazy about it. Lazy girls don't work. I work."

So they shopped a lot, and Clair seemed to enjoy having her along like one of her clothing accessories, or some pretty piece of jewelry she always wore, and she saw things even then. At first she didn't believe she saw it and put it out of her mind. But then she would see her again, and finally made herself realize, and she watched her.

She was very selective about it. She never stole anything from the nicer places. It was always the poorer shops and markets, the cluttered stalls; and it was always things she could have paid pennies for: costume jewelry or a scarf or wallet. Once, she took a tarnished little picture frame she apparently needed for a shoot or something, or maybe didn't.

When they were driving away, she asked her, "Why do you take things, Clair?"

"What, darling?"

Connelly sat there, looking out her window. "You take things and don't pay for them. I've seen you." She turned toward her. "Like that picture frame just now. That old woman wanted a dollar for it, but you took it instead."

Clair sat there a moment. She was half-smiling, seeming to gather herself, her thoughts. "I'm not sure. It's just a feeling that comes over me. I'm standing there, minding my own business, and something comes over me, telling me the time's right, everything's right at that moment, and just do it. And so I do."

They drove for a while. Connelly was turned away, looking out her window again, but not seeing anything.

Clair said, "I don't take anything of value—"

"It doesn't matter."

Later, stopped at a stoplight, she heard her say, "I've thought about seeing a doctor or someone. What do you think?"

Then the light changed and they drove on, not talking about it anymore.

*

Even more important, being thirteen, was how *she* was fitting in. How *she* was doing, among them. She wasn't sure. And there was that terrible insecure gnawing that began to return, like the worst sort of hunger, or being lost in some woods, that she had felt the very first night Melissa left her and Eric at her office, and she felt, in varying degrees, every day and night since then. Yolanda had called it "that nasty old foster fear," and told her to get used to it, "'cause it ain't going nowhere." But it did go somewhere for a while. When Clair and Richard had first taken her, and they told her those things over and over, and finally she believed them. And the feeling disappeared.

But now that she was thirteen it seemed to be coming back again, nasty and fearful, and she wondered.

Curiously, after she asked Clair about the stealing, she noticed she didn't take her along with her as much; and then it was usually for a specific purpose: to buy school clothes for her, or if she was picking up something for a job; but she stopped taking her on the casual shops, when, Connelly knew, she was probably still stealing things.

She'd also stopped asking her about when she and Richard were going to proceed with the adoption, because that seemed to bother her as well. It seemed to frustrate her if she brought it up. Of course, in the beginning it was Clair that had talked about it; how, more than anything, they wanted to make her legally, positively, theirs, so no one could ever take her from them. And there were meetings with Lillian and the lawyers and the family services people, in the beginning. Then, after a while, Clair seemed to become busy with other things—she took on more work and had to make trips to New York and Paris—and she told her, when everything settled down, they would go on with it.

But things never did settle down.

She thought about it, and thought about it, and decided Clair was actually afraid of going through with it. She was afraid of the commitment. And she was afraid of losing control. Because, as everyone knew, you could dump a foster brat any time you wanted. But when you adopted someone, the freedom to choose was gone. You belonged to each other then, and no one could run away. Or at least you weren't supposed to. And if there was one thing she knew about Clair, it was that she enjoyed her freedom to choose things, to have control of things, not to take on commitments she couldn't discard, like a bad dress, at a moment's notice. That, and just the way she looked at things. Like fashion. Which was always new. Always changing. And maybe, in Clair's mind, she wasn't new anymore. She was sooo last year, and her attention was elsewhere now. Whatever. So she stopped asking her about being adopted.

And Clair certainly didn't mention it anymore.

*

The last part of being thirteen seemed complicated at first, but the more she thought about that as well, the simpler it seemed. She was sure there was a mathematical equation or scientific principle that covered it, but since she was never very good with either of those, she could only think of it as a simple fact of her ever-changing environment. This is, when Clair began to move away from her, move out of her life, Richard began to move in. Simple.

*

Once, when she was twelve and had not been there that long, she came up from the beach a little earlier than normal, and discovered Clair in one of the living rooms, making love with a much younger man, one of the models, she thought, from one of her jobs.

She knew Wilma and Richard were both out, running errands, and she should have still been down on the beach; and now she saw them, through the partially open living room door, thrashing about on the couch. Clair was moaning like she did when she had one of her migraines, only louder, and saying nonsensically, "You fucker, fucking, *fucking* me!"

And the young man's exhausted, tortured face, his eyes squeezed shut, seemed to her the epitome of valiant failure, not fucker, fucking, *fucking* me like Clair wanted.

So she slipped past the door and up the stairs to her bedroom, where she sat in a corner, flushed and reading a book, and tried to pretend she was the only person left alive in her whole wide world.

There were other occasions. Being so organized and practical minded, she saw Clair preferred those young, beautiful, readily available people she worked with—both boys and girls. She didn't seem to have a preference, rather more a quick need or sudden itch that needed tending or scratching, as quickly and efficiently as possible, so she could move on, get back to business. Always business. Meeting deadlines. Checking off her endless checklists: There, that was the fuck, and now I have the lunch with…

Oddly, Connelly noticed she didn't really try to hide it; she didn't seem to be even vaguely ashamed of it, like she was about the stealing. More shocking was when she realized Richard most likely not only knew about it, but wasn't that bothered about it as well. She even overheard them joke about it, occasionally making sly little comments about this or that person, how they compared with this or that other person, and giggling like silly children.

The only exception to Clair's convenience rule, that she knew about, was Ron, who ran the stables they boarded their horses. She seemed to go out of her way to go down there and be with him; because, as Connelly decided, Clair didn't really care that much about riding hot wet horses until she was hot and wet herself.

When they went there, they would usually start down the beach, with the waves playing about the horses' legs, when Clair would rein in.

"I think I'll just hang around here today," she would say. "Why don't you ride down to the bay and back (which they both knew was an hour's journey, at least). Be careful. And keep your phone on."

Then she would turn her white horse around and soft gallop back toward the stables.

Ron was about Clair's age, good looking, in a hand-tooled, leather-saddle sort of way, and had a chipped tooth that made him look like an over-aged little boy. But somehow, Connelly felt, he was very different from those startled, annoying models Clair would bed as casually as she refreshed her lipstick. It was the way she acted around him. As he was the only person she had ever seen Clair defer to, asking his opinion about things with that helpless, oh-my-goodness voice, that was not the Clair she knew at all.

Ron had a little attached apartment behind the stables, and after they'd gone there a few times together, she no longer even made a pretense about it.

"You go," she would tell her, and simply turn and disappear through the apartment door, as if it were the most natural act in her world.

Then driving home she always seemed to be in a sort of dreamy daze about everything, commenting on the beautiful scenery, which, at any other time, she could care less about; and how she was simply starving and could they stop somewhere for a burger?, even though she survived on tiny salads and fruit cups, and always complained of being bloated.

*

Richard, on the other hand, was quite different about it. She had noticed that the first time they interviewed her in the hospital cafeteria, with Clair all over her, all over everything, as if she veritably wanted to *consume* everything around her. While he sat there, being merely pleasant and interesting, smiling and (at least, according to Rupert) looking ravishingly handsome.

"Sweetheart," Rupert told her when they brought her back to the seventh floor, "if *you* don't want to go with them—I will. OMG, did you see those broken-glass bedroom eyes on that man?"

"Broken glass?"

THE BEAUTIFUL-UGLY

"Mmmm, as in *I* would crawl over broken glass, just to be there, bleeding, looking up into them."

"Oh."

In the beginning he usually left them to themselves, her and Clair, and did whatever it was he did. And she never tired of noticing the contrast between them: Clair, a whirlwind, chewing up bits and pieces of life, and spitting back out the pithy leftovers she didn't want; Richard, a study in slow motion, thinking rather than acting (Clair constantly acted without consulting her consequences first), forever in moody meditation with those vague drifting airs about him.

She couldn't help herself, and asked Clair as soon as she dared how they met.

"In school. He was actually a grad-student teaching assistant, giving a class called 'Sex and Shelley,' and there was always standing room only. And it was really quite disgusting, the way the girls would throw themselves at his feet, every chance they had. I never did that, which I think he noticed; I, rather, merely collapsed at his feet, now and then. When we began dating, I actually received death threats, which, of course, he immensely enjoyed hearing about; laughing out at all us fevered ninnies. And he was always so damn self-effacing about it, which only made him even *more* attractive, until we were like a swarm of bothered bees, dripping tiny drops of honey behind him wherever he went. *Disgusting.*"

She saw it even then, in fact. Richard was forty-five, gray-locked at his temples, and bought his white dress shirts sizes large to cover his developing paunch. But the girls were still there: his Nubile Neophytes Club, as Clair called them. And Connelly, coming home from school, wondered at first why it took so many assistants to sort papers, and look things up for him, and bring him cups of tea or a drink.

They were also very protective of him, especially Veronica, who Clair called the lead Nube. She said, "She's a political science major, with a minor in Eastern philosophy, and she's so much as told me I wasn't fulfilling Richard's needs."

"What did you tell her?"

"To fulfill to her little heart's content, of course. I also told her Richard was sprinkling sweet tarts like her on his morning cereal, while she was still trying to figure out how to stop shitting herself. She actually took offense."

But, she noticed, where Clair was so brazen about it, the awful infidelities between them, Richard never left a clue. She watched him, and he more often than not seemed annoyed by them, hovering about him in twos and threes, and would often send them packing, usually when he'd had a few drinks.

"Bitches be gone!" he would bellow from the patio, and, knowingly, they would gather their things and flee. Then he would sit out there, staring at the ocean and fuming. 'They offer me hamburger out,' quoth the golden-haired Apollo, 'whilst I have steak in.'" And he would laugh and then sit there, shaggy head drooping, taking a snoring nap before dinner.

Clair wasn't impressed. "Don't let him fool you," she said. "He's well-fucking them all and not batting an eye."

"I've never seen a thing."

"You won't either. He's an absolute master. He had my undies off before I could say, 'Please hurry!' And I never once saw his hands move."

Still, that was the hardest part about being thirteen: of course, how she fit into all of it; and why did two people who seemed to genuinely, honestly, love each other, seem to lead such complicated lives, both together and apart. How could they say they loved each other and then do the things they did? And she tried to think how her parents would have reacted, involved so, complicated so, and she couldn't make it fit. None of it. That was not how they were, individually or put together; that was not how their love was, which only complicated it even more for her.

When she finally couldn't help herself anymore, she asked Wilma about it, who immediately raised up both her hands, saying she didn't want to talk about it, she didn't want to touch any of that with a ten-foot bean pole; then she quickly pulled her into the kitchen to flower some radishes and said, "All I can say is, it's a damn shame how some people carry on. And they both like two little lovebirds in the beginning, and couldn't keep their pawing hands off each other; and now, Lord knows, them pawing hands is going in every direction at once, it seem sometime."

"Do you think they still love each other?"

"Like the sun rises over the green earth and sets down on the blue ocean, child."

"Then why do they hurt each other like that? They pretend they don't, but I can see their eyes. It's like they're lost from each other, and act like they don't care, but they want to find the way back. Or that's how it seems anyway."

"They always seem to work it out some ways," said Wilma, sighing one of her heavy, done-talking-about-it sighs. "I don't know how, but they do. It's like they know, no matter what happens—and, sugar, they's a lot of what, happening here!—they better not lose each other. 'Cause God don't give us too many chances to find someone. Or maybe one or two, if we especially deserving. And sometimes no chance at all, if we ain't, or just can't see. And when we do, and we spite that, God knows. He knows what we done. And how, now, we got to live with that, brokenhearted and all. And then he does the worst thing in the world he can do with someone who's spited him."

She stopped talking.

"What, Wilma? What does he do?"

"Nothing, baby. He don't do nothing at all."

*

Being thirteen, she finally decided, was being allowed to see, to begin to know, things that, earlier, would not have made any sense. Because they barely made any sense now. Barely. And she wondered if getting older was just being allowed to see the complications better. She hoped not. She hoped it was more. Besides, deep in her heart she thought people, more often than not, made their own complications. Like Clair and Richard. And maybe, if we were lucky, there was a God to help us sort them out, or we did the best we could, if there wasn't.

She didn't know. Just like she thought she'd finally found herself a new life, and now she didn't know about that either. That was complicated too. And she thought how, given the opportunity, she would have crawled over Rupert's broken glass, with bleeding knees and hands, to find an answer to something. To anything. Anything at all.

And then, almost too preoccupied to even notice, she turned fourteen.

*

Maybe if she had not been so distracted, she would have noticed. Maybe she could have even prevented it, or slowed it down. But when she finally realized what was going on, it was too late. For some reason (and she never, ever would find out why) Clair stopped caring about her the way she once did. And what made it worse was that she still felt the same old way about Clair. In spite of all those bad little things about her, she now knew, she still cared for her, and probably even loved her. And when she tried to talk to her about it, Clair was cross with her for the first time.

"You need to do for yourself a little," she said. "I mean, we've given you everything on a silver spoon, and you need to do your part."

"I *am* doing my part, Clair."

"No, because if you were, you wouldn't be bothering me with such nonsense."

"I'm talking about how you're acting around me now. How you're treating me."

"How am I treating you? I'm not treating you any way."

"That's what I mean. You're almost totally ignoring me, and I don't know what I've done to deserve that, and I don't like that."

Then she was crying, and Clair was late for an appointment, and that was that.

She went walking on the beach with Spitz until after dark.

Returning, Wilma met her coming up the stairs, flashlight in hand, and chastising and hugging her tight all the way home.

Clair was still out when they got there, but Richard was sitting out on the patio, having a drink; and she went and sat with him. She just felt so lonely and confused then, she was sick to her stomach. They sat there looking at the headland lights and the bridge, and then Richard started talking about someone named Spengler, and his ideas on civilizations—flourishing, and then decaying and collapsing, and then new civilizations rising up—she had no idea what, and then he was silent.

Fifteen seconds, maybe thirty, and then he said, "Did I ever tell you what a beautiful young woman you've become?"

Not thinking about it, she said, "Well, I don't feel like that at all."

"No?" She vaguely heard him shift in his chair. "You may be the most beautiful girl I've ever seen. And I've seen a few."

Now she began to sense something...different. And the sick, lonely feeling inside her began to flutter and jerk and change into something else she knew equally well. There was suddenly the old apprehension, the tiny red warning light flashing inside her mind, and her other, sharper senses began to come alive again.

She felt his hand touch her hand, and she looked at him.

"Clair shouldn't treat you the way she's doing," he said.
She didn't say anything. She couldn't.
He said, "Girls of a certain age have special needs, and she knows that as well as anyone, damn her."
Slowly, she pulled her hand from his and tucked her arms around herself, staring out.
He was still sipping his drink, having his cigarette, when she rose and went inside.

*

Like Clair said. He was very good.
Nothing really seemed changed, out of the ordinary. The three of them were still living there (she didn't even like thinking of Wilma within their same nauseous, poisoning little circle), at the beautiful Sea Cliff house, overlooking the ocean, the entire world, it often felt. But she knew everything was different, or would soon be.

With Clair having, in her way, abandoned her, she was alone a lot. She still did things with Wilma, and sometimes Zack came over to hang out; but Clair had been, for so long, more of her life than she realized. Until she wasn't there much.

Now there were spaces, empty time to be filled, especially weekends. And more often than before, she was around *him*. She saw how he always made it seem unintentional, meeting in the hallway, bumping noses rounding a corner; if she went out on the patio, he would usually be there shortly, bringing out something to read with his splashing glass of single malt, ignoring her. Then, after a bit, they would chat.

The thing was she had decided she wasn't really worried about it. She knew she could control him, she could control anything about him, she knew. After all, he wasn't pushy, he was still the same old Richard, sweet and funny and not demanding at all. Except for the fact there was one other little thing he wanted from her, he hadn't much changed at all.

Actually, the biggest difference she noticed was that his girls didn't come around anymore. His Nubes were nowhere to be seen.

Clair noticed it too, and a few times made snide remarks aside to him, and then let it go.

Connelly thought it had something to do with a confrontation she'd had with Veronica, who, at best, had always preferred to ignore her as if she didn't exist, or, at worst, gave her those odd combo icy-melting stares when, apparently she felt, they were forced to inhabit the same planet together.

Then, once, Veronica came out on the patio, and found Richard telling her one of his awful but funny jokes, and both of them laughing, and she looked at her differently after that.

One day she met her on the stairs, coming back up from the beach, and blocked her, saying, "Look, Richard has his work he needs to finish. He's trying to finish his novel and other things you wouldn't understand. So you need to stop bothering him so much, do you understand me?"

"I'm sorry," she told her, "I thought *I* lived here."

Veronica was looking down at her, standing on the steps below her, and shaking her head. "You're a *foster* child. They felt sorry for you and took you in. Get over it, and leave him alone."

Then she turned and walked in a huff back up the stairs.

That's when Connelly looked up, higher, and saw Richard, standing on a point of the bluff above, looking down like some character from one of those Grand Guignol stories they were discussing in English.

She never said a word to him. She didn't have to. They were gone after that. Just gone. As if he'd wiped them off his personal blackboard with a clean eraser.

After that, it was mostly just the two of them.

26 ♀ A PSYCHOSOMATIC DIVERSION

As he drew closer and closer to her (she could actually watch him doing that, reminding her of how Derrick had circled around Shala Marr, drawing closer), she had mixed feelings. One part of her was absolutely *sick* about it, thinking about it; and she began to throw up as a routine in her ten-thousand dollar Dino De Laurent's granite and aged-porcelain toilet, thinking about it, about him, with his frumpy-smug, middle-aged swagger about her; as if she could possibly find anything attractive toward him, like stupid moths toward a burning flame.

But, at the same time, another part of her liked being around him. As she'd previously admitted to herself, he was mostly harmless; and she had no doubt, at any moment she would resist him, or tell him to leave her alone, he would have done so without comment or retribution. After all, girls of a certain age were never a problem for him. And thinking on that alone, she understood the danger about him: a little closer, always a little closer, because there was no harm, was there?

Too, he *was* fun to be around, with his little-boy's zest for knowledge and life and everything else she saw about him. More fun than any of the other men or boys she knew, including Zack. He never took himself seriously, and put himself, his impressive abilities, down as a routine, including his chances of ever being anything more than he was right then.

"A fucking writer," he told her one afternoon, sitting there, belting them down. "Yes, a real fucking writer, indeed. You've read bits of my novel. What is it about intelligent, well-turned academics that, when they try to put down a bit of fucking prose, it transmogrifies into the most hideously astute mess imaginable? Do we think we're too smart for the jist of it, or for the readers? Are we not common enough? What is it about the elite mind and the muse that just don't *mesh? God,* if I knew the answer to that, I would be the envy of every Tom, Dick and swinging Harry walking those hallowed halls, wouldn't I?"

She knew he didn't really want her to answer, and just sat there, listening, enjoying the sound of his voice, the turn of his mind.

Now when he touched her, she didn't pull her hand away so quickly. Naughty boy, she was thinking. He really was just a naughty boy. His Nubes had called him that, and Clair, and even Wilma. So he must be that, mustn't he? Just that. A naughty, harmless boy; his big, warm hand reaching over and covering hers, massaging it a little, before pulling it away, and telling her another funny story. With Clair gone, his attention felt like a warm, glowing light upon her.

One day, sitting there, he held out something to her. "Ever seen one of these?"

She looked, and looked away. "Of course—I go to art school, don't I?"

He laughed. "So you've smoked before?"

She shook her head. "Not really. Some girls made me take a puff one time—at this home they put me—but I didn't like it."

"Probably alfalfa leaf mixed with parsley." He lit it and sucked, holding in the smoke as he held out the joint, gasping, "Here."

"No thank you."

He released. "We're both sitting at home, for God's sake. What—you think we're going to get high and commit our double-suicide off the cliff? I have tests tomorrow."

She laughed. He had a way of making everything seem so harmless, so all right.

She took the joint and tried to puff it like a cigarette.

"No, like this," he said, showing her how to hold it between her thumb and first finger. "Now suck in slowly and deeply and hold it."

She did. It wasn't so bad. It wasn't anything, really. She breathed out.

They passed the joint back and forth, until he produced a little clip from his shirt pocket to hold the end. "The roach," he called it, which they smoked as well. Afterward, they both sat there. He smoked a cigarette, while she stared across the ocean, dividing up the colors of the water. She suddenly realized she could do that. She could take the colors and stack them, one on top of the other, like blocks, or she could separate them, and move them around. She was actually moving parts of the ocean around, as if it was a giant canvas, and she was painting it, and painting it over. It was such fun! She was smiling.

"You like it?" he asked.

She nodded.

He suddenly disappeared. She looked, and he was gone, and she was alone, but she didn't mind. Spitz came out and hopped comically around her, looking up at her, and she laughed.

Then Richard suddenly returned. He had sodas and potato chips.

"Wow," she said.

She ate a chip and it felt like it was growing inside her mouth, the salty-fried flavor of it growing.

They both ate half the bag of chips before they stopped.

"My God," Richard said, belching, "I'm starting to think Idaho, or is it Idahoan?"

She laughed again, not even knowing why.

They sat there, unhurried.

"We could watch a movie," he said.

She looked at him and was surprised: He did look like a little boy now, sitting there, mischievous, watching her back. "Movie?"

"One of those movies we bought you. We could watch one."

She didn't care. A movie was fine. She didn't care.

Somehow they both got to her bedroom. They were on the patio, and then they were there, with Richard fumbling with things—her DVDs, her TV remote. She collapsed in a chair, looking about her room, which now seemed like a princess's room. Colors suddenly burst out on the flat wall-screen: *Shrek*. Oh, she loved *Shrek*. She sat there, amazed, seeing it all different now. Everything was different.

Richard came and sat at her feet. She barely noticed, watching the story unfolding, new and crazy-wonderful, before her.

At one point she felt him massaging her feet, her bare legs.

"Don't, Richard," she said, trying to pull away.

"I thought that might feel good."

"It does, but don't."

"All right."

He stopped, watching the movie, laughing with her.

Then he was doing it again, his big hand massaging her legs, looking up at her naughty-boy-faced. She shook her head, looking back.

"What—do you want me to stop?"

"I already told you."

"All right," he said, grinning. But he didn't stop. And now she closed her eyes, leaning back in the chair. It did feel good. She didn't move, letting him.

"Oh, I know something better," he said.

"What?" She opened her eyes.

"Here." He was pulling her off the chair, onto the carpet.

"What are you doing?"

"Something better," he said. "Much better."

"I can't."

"You can."

She felt limp as one of Wilma's dishrags, her head spinning, being draped out, full-length, on her stomach. She laid there, cheek against hand, feeling him massage her backside. Feeling wonderful. Feeling somewhere she'd never been before.

His hands slid between her legs.

"No," she said, trying to roll over. He stopped her, feeling his fingers below.

He whispered, "Do you know how beautiful you are? Do you have any idea?"

She tried to rise up and he held her down, easily, his body covering over hers like a lumpy blanket. He was kissing her, deeply. At one point she saw white and pink-flowered spaceships go sailing through the air; then she realized they were her shorts and undies. His hands were doing things below, and she felt great trembling waves rising up inside her, and rolling through her. It felt so right then. Everything that was happening, she was feeling, felt so right. She lay there and let him have his way. She couldn't think. And everything felt so good. She lay there, her princess room spinning in circles about her.

She felt the sharp stab below. "Ahhh!" she cried out, trying to rise up, but unable.

He was all heavy and smothering, and she tried not to move, as he moved against her. She rolled her head to one side, seeing her shorts and underwear where he'd tossed them; then watching the movie, the donkey and Shrek walking side by side, talking. She waited for him to be done.

Finally, he was standing up slowly, puffing and wheezing. She didn't look at him. She stared at the television. But she could feel him standing there, looking down at her.

He said, still puffing, "I'll be damned, I'd have wagered one of those sweaty schoolboys had gotten to you by now."

For some reason, she thought that was the cruelest thing anyone had ever said to her.

She heard him leave, and she lay there, staring out.

Then he returned. He was holding a spray bottle of something and a rag. "You need to move, sweetmeat."

She moved aside and looked and there was a spot of blood on the carpet. She watched him cleaning the spot. Then he looked at her, smiling his old familiar smile. "Grilling steaks. Hungry?"

She didn't answer him.

"Well, I'll be out on the patio," he said, and left.

Lying there, she was thinking about what happened, when the thought came to her: *What did it really matter?* Beyond the one thing he wanted from her, what? Because, she knew, no matter where they put her or who she was with, it would be the same thing. She knew that. Now, at least, if she gave him what he wanted, she controlled it somewhat. She decided who would have it and where, so she controlled it, didn't she? Because if she didn't let him have it, or she told Clair about it, then she wouldn't control it anymore. They would give her back and that would be it. Then it would be someone else's turn. So what did it matter, really?

After a while she got up, feeling the stiffness and soreness below, and put her underwear and shorts back on. She turned off the movie and went out on the patio, where he was grilling steaks.

"Hungry now?" he said pleasantly.

She didn't answer him. She sat down in her chair and looked out over the water, watching the rolling waves below, crashing and subsiding against the shore.

*

He took her to his doctor for the pills. He told her to damn well keep them hidden, but it didn't matter because Clair never came to her bedroom anymore. But Wilma did. So she kept them hidden in her backpack in the closet and took one each day.

Then they waited for Wilma to go shopping or a movie with a friend or to church. She went to church a lot, praying for this or that to happen. And, of course, Clair was…Clair. She was never there. The house for her had become merely a re-freshening post between appointments. Richard was sure she'd found a steady. He found a man's sock in her purse and wondered aloud what the effort had been to put it there. Then he hung it on the front doorknob, and, leaving, Clair took it down without comment and stuffed it back into her bag.

Usually when they made love, they smoked a joint first. She told him she preferred that. What she didn't tell him was that, if she didn't take something, he was just an old man, fucking her. But if she was high, it was better, a little. He looked better, with that naughty, little-boy's expression, but not so much now. So they smoked and fucked, and then he would grill them something. She could give or take the grilling, but she liked being outside afterward. She liked the fresh air. The ocean breeze, making her feel clean again.

Then one day, before they did it, he showed her something else. He took her to his office and took the small zippered bag out of a locked desk drawer. On the glass top of his desk, he cut the powder into four straight lines.

She watched him and said, "Is that cocaine?"

"Bolivian marching powder at its finest, darling."

He did it first, sucking one line through the straw into one nostril. Then the other.

Then she did it: one, two.

"How do you feel?" he asked.

She couldn't answer him then. She was just feeling it coming in to her, coming in to her, like the waves breaking onto the shore, and everything so cool and clear, watching him wipe off his desk with a Kleenex.

That day, for the first time making love, she didn't want him to stop. "Keep going," she whispered urgently. "*Please.*"

"You're going to fucking kill me," he said, gasping for air.

After that, at her insistence, they did the coke for the fucking, and the weed for the grilling.

It became a routine she, more and more, looked forward to.

*

As the days passed, she thought about it a great deal. She decided it was like his Spengler and his rising and falling of civilizations. Being in the system was like that, being fostered: there was the rising and falling to it, and finally there was the collapse. Usually it all happened very quickly. Sometimes, like with Clair and Richard, it just took longer.

But she was in no hurry. She knew, more than she knew each of the pieces of her own broken-up life, only more of the same was waiting for her. It might look different at first. It might smell and taste and feel different. But it was the same. And it would be again. So she was in no hurry.

At the same time, she was seeing it differently now. It was the same, but it was always different, but this was really so. Being fourteen, she thought. Being fourteen made it different. And she could see it all there and didn't care anymore. That was probably the biggest difference. She was fourteen now and she didn't care anymore. And a frightening thrill went up her backside, thinking that. Then, passing, it was still just more of the same.

*

One day she took the streetcar to the salon and had them cut her hair and color it.

She brought them the picture of the punker band, the girl singer, and said, "Like that, only angle it here."

The girl at the salon looked at her. "Are you sure? You have such beautiful hair."

She had color samples from her painting class: industrial metallic red and green.

"And these for highlighting—there and there. Exactly."

"Interesting," said the stylist. "Different."

"Nouveau roboto," she said, and the girl laughed.

Afterward, she went to the thrift shop and found the black jeans, still decomposing, and the black laced boots, and the ratty mocha one-sleeve top, bearing her left shoulder with its tiny mole, the same as her mother. She changed there and left her designer clothes behind. Clair had paid a fortune for them. The Chloé shoes alone were a mint.

When she got home, Clair was standing there. All she said was, "I'm not sure I understand."

She went past her, ignoring her, to her bedroom, and looked in the mirror. She didn't recognize herself. Good. Then she went out on the patio and sat beside Richard. Spitz barked at her at first, then approached her, tail curled between his legs.

Richard, smoke and drink in hand, said, "You look like young Cleopatra on acid."

She took his cigarette and began smoking it. "Are you going to fuck me tonight? She's away, and I need it. Bad. And coke."

"Careful," he said, taking back his cigarette.

She sat there, but not feeling nearly as different as she thought she would.

*

Several times Wilma tried to question her, knowing something was wrong, and asking if there was anything she wanted to talk about. She told her no thank you. She was fine. She was having a little boy troubles, but she was fine.

"Well, I'm always here, sugar," Wilma said.

"I know that."

"I'll say a little prayer for you," she said, giving her a hug.

So when he wasn't there, she tried not to be also. She spent more time out, usually with Zack, wandering about the city.

One day they were at an open-air book stall on Geary, near Union Square, going through the discount books, when she found something and gasped.

"What's the matter?" said Zack.

She said quietly, "It's one of my mother's college books. See." She showed him the inscription on the inside cover: *Emily Walker, Medieval Literature 401, Tolsen Breck.*

"I thought your name was Pierce."

"Walker's her maiden name. This is before she married my father, Zack."

"Maybe it's a different Emily Walker."

She shook her head. "I know her handwriting. Let's see if there's more."

They looked at all the books on the tables, but that was the only one. She felt disappointed, but happy she'd found what she had. She held it tightly against her.

"They sold everything in our apartment to pay bills," she told him. "And I'm sure everything is scattered everywhere, like this book."

"Maybe it's a sign," Zack said. "Maybe she's trying to contact you or something."

She looked at him. "Maybe you should give me two dollars, because I'm broke."

She couldn't wait to get home. She had decided she wanted to be alone when she looked at it, and told Zack she would see him at school tomorrow. Then she took the bus, and ran from the stop to the house, and ran up the stairs to her bedroom, shutting the door.

She lay on her bed, holding it gently in her fingers, as if it were some fragile treasure, looking at it, amazed. Then slowly, carefully, she began to read.

It was an odd little book called *Revelations of Divine Love*, apparently written in the fourteenth century by the first woman, or so identified, ever to write in English, or Middle English, as was this case. And she struggled for several pages before she finally began to understand the nature of the words, even words that had no comparison to anything she knew began, after a time, to make sense. Plus her mother she saw had also struggled, and, in her tiny, delicate hand, made copious notes and translations in the margins, which she followed with more interest than the text itself. And it was as if she and her mother were reading it together now, the past and the present combined, to seek out what was there, to try and understand its meaning together. She felt that deeply, and felt as calmed and fulfilled as the young author whose presence and insight they were sharing.

She fell asleep at one point, until Wilma was there, full of bustling concern and bringing her a cup of soup; and she told her that maybe she wasn't feeling well, and maybe she wouldn't feel well tomorrow either, and could she call the school for her? And, by the way, not say anything to Clair?

Wilma stood there, hand on hip, looking down at her, shaking her cocked head and saying, "I just don't know what's happening round here anymore. I swear I don't."

"I just need some downtime, Wilma."

"*Downtime?* Then you better downtime yourself into some clean pajamas, and wipe all that cake and frosting off your pretty face, or you'll get some downtime all right."

Wilma stayed right there with her while she changed and peed and washed her face and hands; then she tucked her in bed and sat on the bedside, feeding her the soup.

"What's that you're reading, child?"

"It's about this young woman who almost dies having a vision of Christ's Passion."

"Lord have mercy, and why you reading something like that?"

"It was my mother's book. I found it today in a bookstall downtown."

"Well Lord have mercy." She fed her a spoon of soup and wiped her chin.

"She says we're filled with God's will, and no one's really damned, and sinful things are just as important as goodly things to help us understand Jesus' love."

"She do? Well I never."

"And we have to go through the evil to reach the good, to understand it, and to create our own self-nurturing souls."

"Ain't the soul God gave us good enough?"

"I don't know. I haven't gotten that far yet."

She fed her the last spoon, and wiped her mouth again, and then kissed it. "Well, don't you stray too far from the Lord's pastures, child, and I'll call the school in the morning—you being so sick and all."

Wilma stood up to leave.

"And, remember, don't tell Clair."

"Lord have mercy," Wilma said again, going out and shutting the door behind her.

*

She was called Julian of Norwich, which apparently wasn't even her real name, which was never known. And the short preface said she was born into an age of calamity: the Hundred Years War raging about her; along with the Black Death, which freed an entire third of the population from the necessity of living; and famines and general chaos scourging the countryside, entire lands, about her. And her mother had written in the margin: *Who wouldn't desire to have a psychosomatic diversion under those conditions?*

THE BEAUTIFUL-UGLY

She called the visions *Shewings*, and they came one after another over several days, during which time she was surrounded by family and friends, and received the last rites. And it was while the priest held the crucifix before her that she saw Jesus' hot, red blood flowing, and she entered the entire ordeal of the Passion and the agony of Christ, including the mortification of his body. Then Connelly remembered what she had seen, albeit only once and for only minutes, sitting exhausted in the Cardswell's garage. She wondered if that meant anything, and decided it didn't, in comparison to Lady Julian's ordeal.

By the next afternoon, when she had finished the book, and reading, over and over, her mother's notes, she lay there, staring out. She thought about how, after the visions, Julian had spent the rest of her long life trying to understand what they meant, and writing these understandings down. She had become an anchoress at the church, which meant that she lived in almost total contemplative seclusion, in an attached bungalow, answering the fervent questions of those seeking answers through a tiny grille built into some part of the anchorhold. And (she liked to think) she had apparently died in joy and peace, perhaps alone, or with her maid at her side, her life fulfilled.

She randomly opened the book again and read one of her mother's notes: *When you are finally purged, brought to nothing, at ground zero, all is exposed, all is laid bare, nothing hidden—then do you know yourself. Self-knowledge as purpose for this ordeal, this journey, we call existence.*

On the opposite page, she had written with angled lacy delicacy into one corner: *Me to M.P. is my sin to his soul, my chaos to his order, my confusion to his understanding, my self-induced paradox to his sweet love, my yin to his yang. Amen.* And Connelly wondered how long she had known Michael Piece then. Long enough, she decided, to be appropriately turned inside out, fallen so in love with him.

Then she closed the book, and closed her eyes, and thought about the similarities of the two—Lady Julian and her mother. How both were seeking understanding, to know, and found love instead. And whether it was some kind of spiritual love or the crazy wonderful love of another—was there really any difference? In the end, did it really matter? And was it that simple? As simple as seeking and finding love, in whatever guise? She wondered. And she decided, if there was a God, and if he or she was not about everything to do with love and forgiveness, then what did it or they matter? What else remained that mattered so much? Nothing she could think of.

Only then did she think about her own journey, and what she was seeking, and where she was now. And the confusion, that for a time these two women had dissolved inside her so wonderfully and completely, returned. What was her purpose, after all? To merely survive? To be fed and clothed and, in turn, ignored and abused? Is that where she had arrived after so long? Lady Julian found a universe from her bed, and it was all about love. What had *she* found? She didn't know. It was a paradox, like her mother had written, but without the sweet love she sought, the need for which all of a sudden returned. It swept inside her now, filling her up with its lush, ominous presence and purpose; and she lay there, breathing a little hard, pressing the book against her stomach, trying to decide, but unable.

27 ♀ THE OFFER

Her painting instructor, Mr. Gladdens, told her during one of their private student-teacher talks that any artist worth his salt needed a sense of place, of belongingness, to succeed.

"I have San Francisco," she told him. "That's a place, isn't it?"

"Well, for you it's more complicated than that," he snapped.

He was a bitchy old gay man who broke the school rules by smoking his short black Turkish cigarettes in his office, standing askew at his tiny window, blowing out the smoke.

"Does this bother you, Connelly? I can stop."

Everyone knew he was even bitchier when he wasn't smoking.

"No," she said. "It smells like fresh asphalt. You know, like when they're spreading it, and you're driving by with the window down."

He seemed to consider that. She knew it was easy to distract him, which everyone did; otherwise, he might go into one of his art rants: its obscene commercialization, its utter lack of moral purpose, of individual character, for nearly a century now; which, of course, he always pointed out, he didn't necessarily mean in the more confining Biblical sense; rather, its usurpation by the specialists, the cultural relativists.

She waited, biting her lip.

"I mean, of course it's a place," he said gloomily. "But it's grown so stereotypical, don't you think? Its identity's cracked and eroded like the earth beneath it. I don't trust it anymore. I'd move, but I don't know where I'd go. Can old queens move to Des Moines?"

She sat there, unsure.

He sighed. "What I'm trying to say is, somehow I feel something's missing from you, from your work. Something important that relates to you and what I know about you. And I think it's something larger, like your vision. I can feel it, I can even see flashes of it, occasionally—like the way you're trying to open up that street scene, against the buildings holding it in. I just don't quite understand it. I don't know where to go with it. Where *you're* going. But I'm sure you'll find out."

Then he again began studying her painting he'd mentioned: an impressionistic street scene near one of the shelters she'd once stayed. It sat on the easel he had in one corner of his little office. He took a last drag from his cigarette and stubbed it out in one of his disposable tin-foil ashtrays he fashioned from the roll he kept in his cupboard; then he went and stood before the easel.

"I'm actually talking in more of a spiritual context, rather than concrete streets filled with broken syringes and smelling like wino piss." He looked over at her. "You're the best natural painter I've seen…for quite some time, Connelly. You don't listen to a damn thing I tell you and, somehow, you make it work. So I say fine. Do that. But you haven't cracked into yourself yet. If you're going to be a know-it-all about it, then you need to find a way in, really in; and then, perhaps, you've the will, beyond that, where only the best of the best can go."

She shook her head, not understanding.

He said, "All I'm saying is, stop painting by the numbers, stop relying on your talent to get you through, your painless intuition, if you will. Do you want to end up painting advertising murals on the sides of chowder houses? Or teach art history to a bunch of self-satisfied poseurs that could care less about the vicissitudes of a damned thing? I'm saying you need to go off by yourself, lose yourself, and then really find yourself. You have to go off the deep end and somehow survive. Now I don't know how you would do that—I certainly tried and failed—but you have to find a way and then do it. There's no other way. And you're too good not to, Connelly Pierce." He looked at the painting again and sighed. "Anyway, I'm forced to give you another A, even though we both know you're still working Comme Il Faut Street, telling me to go fuck myself." He looked at her. "Now get out of here. I've got a parents' conference in twenty minutes, and I need to spray the air."

*

One night she dreamed of Eric, briefly, vibrantly. He was standing in the shadows before her, holding out his clenched hand, saying, "It's everything, Con. Everything's there—but you have to find it. Go find it." And then he opened his hand, revealing the tiny glowing hazelnut there.

She woke with a start in darkness, afraid, panting. And she knew then, it was almost over. It was almost time.

*

At school the next morning, someone left an engraved note in her locker. *If you pose for us, your nomination will be rendered.*

She showed it to Zack at lunch.

"It's them," he said. "The Artsirati."

"What are they saying?"

"That they want you. That if you disrobe for them, they'll consider letting you in their little club."

"Oh really."

On the note she wrote: *No thanks.* Then, on the way to her next class, she pinned it to the public-announcements bulletin board in the main hall.

After school, she was standing at the bus stop when Dullen Prentiss pulled up in his orange-sherbet Porsche convertible, Foo-Fighters blaring. "Wanna ride?"

"No thanks."

"I really think you should."

She knew Dullen a little. Even though he was a senior, they'd worked together once on a decoration committee. And twice she'd danced with him at the goofy, Friday-afternoon sock-hops they held at school.

She got in the car. "Do you know where I live?"

He smiled at her and peeled away from the curb.

Leaving the city, driving back into the hills, he said, "A few of us put our necks out for you."

"What, so you can see me naked?"

He shook his head. "I just think you should be a little more appreciative."

"Yeah?"

"Yeah. Some people would think it's quite an honor to be asked in."

"Well I'm not some people."

"I know that." He reached over, running a finger below her skirt hem, along her bare thigh.

She pushed away his hand, and he laughed.

He asked, "So—are you allowed to date yet?"

"Not really."

"What does that mean?"

She shook her head, looking out her window.

"You don't think I've noticed you?"

"I have no idea."

"Well I have."

"Good for you."

"Yeah?"

He slammed the shifter forward, the engine screaming, the car bucking and shuddering, going around the curb. He didn't say anything else until he pulled into the driveway. He stopped the car with a jerk and said, "You really need to think about what you're doing."

"What do you mean?"

He looked away. Then he looked back hard at her. "You have yourself a nice day, awright?"

She knew then that if she got out of the car that would be it. She said, "We're from two different worlds, Dullen. Even more than you know."

He nodded. "You don't know what I know, Connelly. You don't know a damn thing. Now get out."

She got out then, and he peeled away, leaving her behind. She turned and walked slowly up the driveway.

*

In art she began to paint a series of geometrical mud-colored sucking vortexes, each more turbulent, more uncontrolled, than the previous. She had no idea.

The first one, Gladdens left a note pinned to it: *I'm not saying a word, but follow this.*

She did, although she couldn't tell him, anybody, where it was leading.

The Saturday after she'd finished the third in the series, Clair returned from a Los Angeles business trip a day early, and came into the master bedroom she was sleeping with Richard. She woke up, and Richard was smoking a cigarette. Clair was standing there, looking bemused.

"Touché," Clair said softly, and left.

After a moment Richard looked over at her. "Well, I certainly don't feel like grilling today."

*

She put herself in the fourth one, near the center, ready to be sucked down forever within the dark hole.

Gladdens told her to come see him that afternoon. When she went there, he asked her, "Is everything all right?"

She was sitting in the chair beside his desk. She lowered her head. "I may not be around much longer, Mr. Gladdens."

"You're not thinking of doing something foolish?"

"No, nothing like that. I may just have to leave soon."

"Is there anything I can do?"

She looked up and shook her head. "I just want you to know, you've made a difference for me. Thank you."

He looked at her a moment, then he stood up and went over to his little window. He lit a cigarette, blowing out the smoke. "That's the trouble with teaching. We give you just enough to become dangerous to yourselves; then we have to stand aside."

*

It finally happened that Friday. She got to school and walked inside the main entrance, and she saw it: Her face. Everywhere. There was one giant poster hanging completely across the hallway, and there were other posters—hundreds, maybe thousands—all of her face, and all stuck along the wall, covering the lockers. Everywhere. And every single one of them said: *Won't you do your part? Be a foster parent! Deserving girls like this need your help!*

Everyone was standing there, watching her. Every single one of them.

From somewhere, there was Zack, pulling her arm. "Let's get the fuck out of here."

Taking the bus downtown, she told him, "I'm not going back there. Ever."

"That's what those fuckers want, Con," said Zack. "They want to chase you out."

"They did."

At Fisherman's Wharf Zack bought them fries and cherry sodas. They sat there the rest of the morning, looking at everyone. She said, "I'll be leaving soon."

He looked at her. "Because of that Artsirati bullshit?"

"No, it's more than that. But that certainly doesn't help. I've got to find my brother, Zack. I've got to go find Eric. That's all that matters to me now."

"Can I go with you?"

"No. You've got to stay here and show them—for me."

He lit a cigarette. "Will I ever see you again?"

She leaned forward, kissing his brow.

They sat there awhile longer but, since she'd told him what she did, it wasn't the same. They'd said goodbye already, and it wasn't the same. So they walked to the bus stop and separated, each getting on their bus, going a different direction.

*

When she got home, Wilma was in the kitchen, sobbing her eyes out, trying to prepare dinner. "Ms. Clair say you got to go back. She say we can't keep you no more."

She grabbed her, hugging her and weeping.

"Where are they at now?"

Wilma wiped her eyes with her handkerchief. "They both went down to the government offices to sign the papers. Ms. Clair say she want you out of here by tomorrow. Oh— my baby!"

"It'll be all right, Wilma."

"Girl, how you say it's gonna be all right and everything falling slap apart? *How?*"

"It just is, that's all." She hugged her again. "I love you, Wilma. I'll always love you."

Wilma fell into one of the kitchen chairs, shaking her head, before bursting into tears again.

Connelly went to her bedroom and pulled her knapsack from the closet. She slipped a few things inside it from her dresser and bathroom; then she took one more look around her room and went out.

She made her way quietly through the house to Richard's office. She knew where he kept his key and unlocked the drawer. Inside was the small roll of cash he used to pay his dealer, and she put this into one of the side pockets on her backpack. Next, she took out the zippered bag and opened it and cut herself two thin lines of

THE BEAUTIFUL-UGLY

coke on top of the desk. She did the lines: one, two, and wiped her nose. Then she put the bag into the pocket with the money and zipped it closed. She lifted the backpack onto her shoulders and made her way out of the house, stopping only once to bend down and hug Spitz, before leaving.

She watched for Clair's car as she walked down the driveway. She decided if she saw them coming she would hide in the bushes until they were past. But they never came. At the bus stop the express was just pulling up, and she got on, with the doors closing shut behind her. She thought how all her life she had done it their way—all of it their ways—and it didn't work. Now she was going to do it her way. She was going to find Eric. She was going to find her brother and take care of him. And no one in the world was going to stop her this time. No one.

The bus lurched, pressing her into the corner of the seat and window, before moving down the pretty, shaded boulevard, and through the quiet neighborhood, disappearing quickly behind her.

28 ♀ CROSSING AMERICA

*H*e *came again the next afternoon and said, "I've taken you off the meds. I don't think you need them. Do you?"*
    She continued gazing off at some unfixed point above her.
    She heard him sigh. "Connelly, I didn't want to have to tell you. I was hoping we could work through this, you and I, without the need for this. But that's not happening, and probably won't happen, so I'll tell you. They're transferring you to the state mental hospital at Imola where, unless something happens to change that, you could very well live out the rest of your life." *He paused, and then said,* "Is that what you want?"
    Is that what she wanted? He was asking her if that's what she wanted.
    "Of course it is," *he said.* "You tried taking your life, and that failed, and now you're letting the system that failed you do it for you—right? Talk to me, Connelly. I want you to goddamn talk to me right now, or there's nothing more I can do for you. Do you understand what that means? Do you?"
    One beat. Two. When she swallowed and looked over at him. "All I understand," *she said,* "is that I want you to leave me alone. Please."
    "I can't do that."
    And she looked away, finally letting it all go…
    There was a game she played, crossing America. She would pick out a house in the distance, passing by, and she would fill it with the different people she had known. She would imagine what the house looked like inside and who the people were living there, and what they were doing at that very moment. Each house was different, but she and Eric were in every one of them. However,

she didn't include her parents now. They were far enough away, it no longer seemed necessary. They no longer mattered like that. They were like statues you saw in a museum, that maybe were real people once, but now were only memories carved in wood or stone. Anyway, she liked the game, and it helped her pass the endless hours it took to get across the country. It was a big country, she realized after a while.

*

Some parts of America did not seem real to her. The high empty plains of Nevada and abruptly seeing the Great Salt Lake appear out of the desert did not seem real to her. The Rocky Mountains in Wyoming, melting down into the endless swaying seas of Nebraska grass did not seem real. Chicago did not seem real. Against the blue sky and the blue ocean of water behind it, it was a shining, sun-gilded city, like Oz, but bigger, seeming friendly and menacing at the same time. Leaving behind the terrible turnpikes and entering the cool silent woods of Pennsylvania did not seem real. There were springtime flowers everywhere, and she saw deer: a doe and her two fawns beside the highway, looking frightened and bewildered by all of it. Then night came, and by early morning, going over a little rise, she suddenly saw New York City—black-glowing against the red dawn—and that seemed most unreal of all.

*

Actually, what seemed real were the little things, in between, she saw and did. All of the bus stops seemed real, and they all seemed the same after a while: get out, get in, go potty, buy a sandwich, see the people, smell the different smells, drink the bottled water—it was all tired faces and odors of unwashed flesh and stale urine after a while, and quite often she stayed sleeping on the bus, until they were moving again, and she could look for another house to put herself in.

The little towns seemed real: Winnemucca, Elko, Rawlins, Laramie, Kearney, Iowa City, Princeton, Mishawaka, Barkeyville, Stroudsburg, Allamuchy, Parsippany. But they blended too, after a while; and she slept, and would wake up in some tiny place she had never heard of, or would again. And she closed her eyes.

Little scenes, played out, seemed real. Snippets of muffled conversation. Images—sudden, and then gone. A bus trip across America, she decided, was an endless exhausting hum, broken up by tiny impromptu soap operas, performed quickly and cheaply for her benefit, before dissolving again into that constant highway hum, only to reappear in a spit and snarl and sob and whine a hundred or five hundred miles beyond. Crazy, ever-changing, ever-the-same.

She met Diane like that. She got on in Chicago after she smiled at her, standing in front of the women's-room vanity, saying, "You got any more blow?"

"Beg your pardon?"

The girl raised her hand, and a finger gently wiped the dusting of white powder from her right nostril. "Eyes like big pretty black-violet Spanish olives," she said softly, lazily, before smiling again.

They went into one of the stalls, locking the door behind them, and Connelly sat on the toilet lid, carefully cutting out the lines on her makeup mirror. The girl took the straw she was handed and kneeled down, quickly and perfunctorily sniffing the glass clean, before handing the straw back and wiping her nose.

"Thanks," she said.

Then Connelly carefully put everything away, zipping closed the backpack pocket. When she stood up, the girl pushed her back against the stall wall, kissing her deeply on the mouth, whispering, "My name's Diane."

"Connelly."

"You with anybody?"

Connelly shook her head no, and the girl kissed her again.

*

Going east into the dwindling twilight, Connelly felt the tiny spoonful of snow-white powder mixing and dissolving into her bloodstream, and lining up everything clearly and reasonably inside her head and throughout her body. She was staring out the bus window, busily peopling this house and that; she was listening with great interest to the story of repeated abuse and abandonment Diane was recounting of her own life; she was thinking how suddenly nice and enjoyable it was to be safe and snug on the bus, talking with her new friend, and heading toward New York City to find Eric. For the first time, she thought then, she was really in control of her own life and destiny. Everything was clear and reasonable at that moment, and Diane was telling her about getting married at sixteen to a nineteen-year-old truck driver named Bruce Whitlock that nearly beat her to death—that, in fact, caused the miscarriage of her little Ella all across their kitchen floor, saying, "It looked just like someone threw down a bowl of spaghetti and meatballs."—before she ran to the neighbors' house, who called an ambulance and the police to help her, and she finally made her escape from the hospital to the downtown Chicago bus station.

"My family lives in the Bronx," Diane said. "My grandfather moved there from Puerto Rico thirty years ago, and my father's still running the same grocery store he started back then. There's a lot of us Perezes there, so if that asshole wants to come looking for me, he's welcome to, 'cause my brothers and uncles'll kill his ass once and for all. Of course, he knows that, so I don't think he's even gonna try."

She stopped talking then, and Connelly turned from the window and looked at her. Diane was sitting there with her head back against the seat and her eyes closed, and said, "So what about you? What's your story?"

Connelly turned back to the window, as if vaguely looking for something—a certain house, a face—anything. "I don't have one," she said.

*

When it was dark, Diane said: "Let's see if we can stay awake all the way into the city. You know, like ride this high all the way down through the Lincoln Tunnel, into midtown and the Port. Then I'll call one of my uncles to pick us up and take us home. Then we'll eat something good and go to bed for like three days. How about it?"

Diane also told her she didn't have a cent on her. "When I ran, I ran. I don't have my bag, my phone, my makeup, anything."

"How'd you pay for your bus ticket?" Connelly asked her.

"If you really want to know, I had to suck this sailor off. I begged the prick just to give me the money, but he said he really needed a BJ bad, so I did it. But it wasn't so bad. From that angle, he was kinda cute."

Connelly bought her cigarettes and them both something to eat. Diane said, "When we get home, I'll pay you back."

"Don't worry about it."

"No fucking way—I always pay my own. Anyway, thanks for the smokes and the blow and the chow. You're a real lifesaver."

Their bus broke down outside of Cleveland, and it was morning before another bus arrived to take everyone back to the downtown terminal. By noon when they had, according to Diane, "got it right" once again in the bathroom stall, Connelly's hands were shaking, and she couldn't make them stop.

"Here," Diane said, taking something from her pocket. It was a small tan pill. "I use these sometimes to calm my nerves."

"You sure?" she said, wondering how she had the pill, after running away without anything.

Diane leaned over and kissed both corners of her lips, whispering, "Scout's honor."

When they were on the highway again, she felt better. Her hands were still, and that was the afternoon she saw the deer and the wildflowers, and she smiled. She leaned her head against the window and thought about how she would look for Eric. Actually, she didn't know how she would, but she was sure she would think of something. She would find a way. She felt so calm then. So peaceful. It only made sense that, somehow, there would be a way…somehow…looking out the window, with her forehead pressed softly against it, at the wide-eyed doe and her two skittish fawns, standing on the green hillside amid the blue and yellow flowers, as she slept.

*

It was dark again when she woke up and, for a moment, had no idea what was happening. In fact, she'd forgotten she was on the bus. Then she remembered and looked around. Next she thought they'd broken down again, but she saw the bus was stopped in front of some tiny bus station, and people were milling around outside, smoking and talking, going in and out of the station and the little attached restaurant, and she started to relax.

She looked around for Diane. She wasn't on the bus, and she couldn't see her anywhere outside. She waited, watching.

When the bus started to load again, preparing to depart, she wondered if maybe she should get off and go find her. Maybe something had happened to her. Maybe—when suddenly she felt down below her legs, where her knapsack had been tucked away, to find nothing there.

She jumped up and ran down the aisle, pushing past the people there, down the bus steps and into the station. In one of the bathroom stalls, tucked behind the toilet, was her open knapsack. She grabbed it up and carried it out to the sink, looking at it, all the open pockets. Of course the coke was gone, all her money, but everything else seemed to be there. She took Priscilla out and held her for a long moment against her chest; then she put her away, zipping up all the pockets, and walked slowly back to the bus.

She stayed awake the rest of the night, leaning against her window, staring out into whatever darkness or light was passing. She wondered if anything Diane had told her was the truth; then she realized it didn't matter at all. She was sure the world was filled with people like Diane, and she was sure it didn't matter if they ever told the truth or not. Being good some of the time, or telling the truth some of the time, didn't matter at all if you took advantage of others. No one could be a little bad if you did things like that on purpose. You were just bad, and you had to answer for that, and there was no excuse for it. She looked out the window, angry and fuming for a while, mad at herself for being so trusting; then she began to think about what she would do now. She had no money. She didn't know a soul in New York, except, of course, Eric. But she didn't think she would be lucky enough to find him right away; so she thought about what she could do instead, but could think of nothing. She would have to wait and see. After all, she had no idea what to expect, so how could she plan anything? She couldn't, that was all. She would just have to wait.

At one stop in New Jersey she got out to use the restroom and could smell the sausage and eggs cooking on the grill, the warm breads from the oven. People were having breakfast, and, for the first time, she felt hungry; and she stood there a moment, watching everyone eat; then she went on, trying not to think about it.

Back on the bus she found a stick of gum in her knapsack and unwrapped that and chewed it, looking out. But the gum only seemed to make her hungrier, and she put it back in its wrapper and, again, tried not to think about it. She realized, knowing she didn't have any money only made it worse, because there was nothing she could do about it. It was easy being hungry and having money in your pocket, or having someone like Wilma bringing you cookies and milk. That was easy. But when you had no choice— that was different. That was scary.

She was still thinking about being broke and hungry and afraid when the bus went over the short hill and, absolutely out of nowhere, New York City appeared in the distance before her. She had seen pictures of it, but now she realized it wasn't the same. She saw the black, lighted city against the sheer red sky, and there was nothing familiar about it. It looked like something entirely apart, entirely unto itself, and not like any city or any place she had ever seen. She swallowed, staring at it there, disappearing and appearing again, ever closer. Too big, she thought after a while. It was just too big. Nothing should be that big, wondering, watching its approach, as it grew and grew, until finally the bus was going swiftly down into the lighted tunnel below the river and coming out the other side. And then she was there. She was finally in New York, and she had no idea what she was going to do now. She sat there, looking out.

*

Things came to her—at her—the moment she stepped off the bus: There were the harsh lights, and the awful mixing odors of hot exhausts, and scorched grease, and burnt rubber. And there were the people, everywhere around her, overflowing, going in every direction at once, jostling and pushing and shoving and trying with all their might to get—there—wherever *there* was.

A man stood in front of her, short and dark-skinned, and dressed in a shabby blue coat and dark frayed tie. He was sucking hard the damp bent stub of a cigarette. "You have friends?" he inquired.

"Pardon?"

"Place where sleep." His smile was tight and yellow. "I have friends. We go there. Now."

He reached toward her.

She turned the other way, and the man came after her, hesitantly grabbing her arm, which she pulled away; and he left her, she saw glancing back, idly wandering off the opposite direction, lighting a fresh cigarette.

On the street it was the same, only more. Then she stood there and felt something different than she had ever felt. There was the encompassing, pressing feeling of enormous energy about her, seeming to fill her and drain her in turn. She listened, hearing the constant hum, as if she suddenly existed inside some giant invisible turning turbine; and there was the omnipresent hum, and the feeling of raw energy, surrounding her, as if simultaneously releasing itself and seeking some primal source of renewal. It was a feeling both exhausting and exhilarating; and she stood there, momentarily closing her eyes…listening…feeling the vibration against her skin, thinking: *So this is it. This is New York.*

THE BEAUTIFUL-UGLY

She began to walk slowly down the sidewalk, and was immediately bumped from one side, then the other, before her, behind her—realizing she was suddenly in everyone's way, and they were apparently all joining quickly together to run her to the ground, without a thought—and she made her way to the side, pressing against the stone wall there, looking out. Everyone seemed to have the same fixed, determined faces, and seemed to know exactly where they were going, and the shortest, quickest way to get there. They didn't seem so unfriendly; rather, more full of various critical and elevated intentions, and some kind of shared, steely purpose to achieve them.

When she stepped back among them again, she tried to match their pace, their hard and common resolve, even though she had no idea where they were all going, or what they would do once they got there.

*

She spent most of the day walking. That's what everyone else seemed to be doing. Everyone walked in New York, it seemed; or at least half the people did that, while the other half wildly drove their cars and buses and trucks and bicycles—all apparently trying to run the walkers down. It was great fun, she saw, how the walkers would gather at a street corner stoplight, waiting for the moment when they would storm the street, taking it back from the drivers; when, usually, the yellow taxis and rattling delivery trucks would form a line and charge ahead, pushing the walkers back onto the sidewalks. No one seemed to pay attention to anything else but the game they were playing, and it seemed a wonderful way to pass the morning in the towering brash city about them.

Finally she grew tired of the excitement of walking in New York and looked for quieter lanes to move along. She found a park with quaint old townhouses facing it; and there were women pushing strollers and boys on skates and barking dogs and vendors selling food. For some reason, she had never thought of New York having such things. She had always imagined it filled skyscrapers and clamorous streets, which of course it had in abundance, but she saw there were other things.

Then for a while she tried sitting in the park, trying not to think about being hungry, but she couldn't help it, as everyone else seemed to be eating something. It was lunchtime and everyone was eating, everyone else in New York was eating, except her.

So she got up and began walking again. She was still tired from walking all morning; exhausted, in fact, from the entire journey across America; but she decided it was better to be tired and walking, than to be still and hungry. So she began walking straight up one street, which she saw was Fifth Avenue, and which seemed to go on for ever and ever, until evening began to arrive, and the towering lights above her began to come on, and the street still kept rolling out before her, never-ending, just like America.

*

By nighttime she found a place to sleep. She had left Fifth Avenue some time back and found a 24-hour deli along one street that looked fairly safe. It was mostly residential, and there were ordinary-looking people moving up and down the street, going into the old brownstone buildings that lined the street, turning on their lights and preparing for the evening.

She stood outside the deli for a while, watching the people eating inside, before she turned away.

Behind the deli was a brick alleyway with a dumpster tucked back into one corner. And the way the dumpster was sitting created a hidden pocket there no one could see. No one would bother her there. She peeked behind the dumpster and saw the space and then squeezed herself through. There, she sat down in the corner, placing her knapsack against the wall as a pillow and stretching out. It wasn't so bad, except for the smells coming from the dumpster, which she tried not to think about, and the hard, rough ground.

She lay there and thought about her bedroom back in Sea Cliff and the wonderful way her bed would swallow her up each night within its deep softness. She wondered what Richard and Clair and Wilma were doing right then; then she remembered it didn't matter, because Clair was through with her, and once someone was through with you that was it. There wasn't anything else to do about it, except leave, find something else, which is what she was doing.

Then she thought about all the people she had seen that day. New York *had* some people. And she wondered how she would ever find Eric among all those faces. She didn't know. She didn't see how she would do it, but she would. You move on when you have to move on, and you just do whatever comes next. Those were the rules she understood better than anything. She didn't particularly like them, but that was all there was to it.

She nestled her head deeper into the knapsack, feeling Priscilla inside, pushing back, and she slept hard and deep, dreaming taunt, vivid little dreams that were forgotten long before she woke up.

*

It was a roaring that woke her. Her eyes came open, and she heard the terrible groaning and roaring, and saw the dumpster rising off the ground before her, trembling and shaking and screaming as it went; and she pushed back against the wall, waiting for it to clear the space. Then she jumped up, grabbing her knapsack, and ran out, past the dumpster and garbage truck, entwined in each other's steel embrace, as if in mortal combat. She glanced up at the driver's surprised face and continued on, out to the front of the deli, where she stood off to one side, catching her breath.

It was still dark, but she could feel the already morning air about her. She looked inside the deli and saw the few people still sitting there, eating their hot breakfasts and drinking coffee. She wondered what would happen if she went inside and asked for something to eat. But she decided they would probably hold her and call the police, and she stood there, unsure.

Next, a man came out of the deli and, right before her, threw the remainder of whatever he was eating into a trashcan along the curb. She stood there, looking at the man walking away, then back to the trashcan. Without a thought, she walked over and reached down into the can, grabbing the brown wrapper up and backing away.

"Hey!" someone called out.

She turned around, and there was another man there, shuffling out of the shadows toward her.

"What the hell you think you're doing?" The man's scrawny, pinched red face came into the circle of light from the lamppost behind her. He looked ill.

She stood there.

"This is my spot," he said. "What'd you get there?"

"I'm hungry," she said.

"So am I." He stood there looking at her. "You're just a damn kid. What you doing out here rummaging garbage cans?"

"I told you I was hungry." She could smell the scrambled egg from the sandwich.

He seemed to think about it. "Well, get the hell on then, and don't come back here," he said, turning away. "Damned tourists."

She walked down the street, unwrapping what was left of the sandwich, with her hands shaking from hunger, and began taking bites, hardly chewing. It was egg and bacon, and tasted so delicious she ate the whole sandwich before she realized it.

Now she walked on, feeling a little better than before. She had slept a little, and now she had eaten a little, as well. She thought about that and suddenly realized maybe there was another way after all. That is, if she didn't have money or a place to stay—maybe there was another way of doing it. It wasn't at all how she thought it would be, but it was a way, wasn't it?

So she spent the morning searching out street-side breakfast eateries; and by the time the day's light seemed as full as it would get in those deep glass-and-steel canyons she wandered, she had scrounged and eaten nearly an entire syrup-soaked pancake, half a green apple, most of a salsa-covered chicken burrito, several gulps of a melted cherry slush, and a handful of fried potatoes from an almost untouched box that read: *Tater Tots* in big red letters, which she passed over to an old woman she met, digging about in the same trashcan.

"Sweetie, you didn't find any catsup packs with those, did you?" the woman asked.

They both dug deeper, until they discovered several packs inside a separate wadded paper bag.

"Good—that gives me my red vegetable," said the old woman, with satisfied primness, before scurrying over to a bench where she could sit and spread everything out upon her lap.

Afterward, walking aimlessly about, Connelly couldn't stop thinking about it. Above all, New York seemed a city of mere survival, of finding a way to hang on—foremost—with whatever else you intended, coming along only after, if possible.

She realized, before she could even think about looking for Eric (and she could *feel* him there, she knew, at that very moment, somewhere among all those faces), she would have to first survive, day by day, even hour by hour, or nothing else mattered. As she also felt it a place, should she find herself reaching that point, with nowhere to turn, that would not be so forgiving.

She thought about all that, walking and looking.

Of course, she had been surviving all her life. Her life was mostly that: an ordeal of survival; so, thinking of it so, it didn't seem like such a big deal; except that it was. It was a much bigger deal than she'd ever imagined possible.

Now, looking about her, above her, craning back, back her head and still unable to see the tops of the sheer sleek sheets of stone and glass and polished metal rising, somehow incomprehensible, untouchable in any common, everyday sense, she knew there was a difference, although she couldn't understand it then.

Anyway, she was too busy searching out sources of food, drink, a place to potty, a place to sit and rest when she was so tired she couldn't think anymore. These seemed most important then and, she figured, would be for some time. Survival first, and all else would come after, if possible.

*

With evening approaching, she was sitting on a bench at the edge of Central Park when she overheard a boy and girl having a conversation about their plans for the night; and when they rose and wandered off, she followed them, eventually descending the subway stairs. There she watched how they waited until just the last moment, when the policeman's back was turned, when they both suddenly jumped the turnstile and entered the A train.

She quickly followed, entering the same middle car, and finding an empty seat.

That night she slept on the train, which seemed to wander forever through the outer city boroughs; and she thought it was much better than the stinking cramped nook behind the dumpster. There was something almost comforting about the ongoing lighted rumble of the subway, at three a.m., with the odd, pale trickle of faces, entering and departing into their whatever, wherever lives, while she slept in spurts and fits. And it seemed, in her mingled, twilight state of sleep and consciousness, as if New Yorkers had found yet another oddly human way of living together, in the most unusual of circumstances.

29 ♀ ROXY

In the morning she got off in midtown, near Times Square, and began making her rounds. She had decided she liked these trash bins best, because there were so many people, mostly tourists, it seemed, throwing away food by the bagful. She could be more selective here; and that morning she found a nice half-bagel, thickly smeared with strawberry cream cheese, and a nearly full Espresso House latte, still steaming.

She was sitting there, watching the incredible flashing-and-streaming advertisements surrounding her, the crush of people, when she noticed the pretty, perky-eyed, fresh-faced girl, standing in her raggedy blue jeans and sneakers across the sidewalk, watching her. She had her dark-red ponytail shoved through the back opening of a black-and-yellow CAT ball cap, a brown leather handbag slung over her shoulder, and beneath her black leather jacket she was wearing a black-and-red-lettered "Pisskats Rule" T-shirt, showing a feline lady-of-the-evening, leaning against a lamppost and smoking, as was the girl watching her. She was half smiling, shaking her head.

"*What?*" Connelly confronted her brusquely, meeting her gaze, as she was quickly learning to do.

The girl didn't move.

"I mean—is this your territory or *what?*"

Now the girl flicked away her cigarette. "What fucking woodwork you crawl out of?"

"What?"

"People got diseases, you know. Anyway, how can you eat that crap?"

"Because I'm hungry. And I'm broke."

"Really?" The girl feigned surprise, then shook her head. "Let me clue you something, little sister. This is New York. And if there's *one* thing you don't have to worry about in this overblown, over-hyped shithole, it's going hungry. Everything else is negotiable, but finding food ain't one of'em."

Connelly stared at her.

The girl finally shrugged and said, "Why don't you throw that crap away and we'll go get some real breakfast."

Connelly searched her eyes. "I told you, I don't have any money, and I don't have any drugs either. So if that's what you're looking for—"

"It ain't," the girl said quickly. "And if it was, I sure wouldn't be tagging onto some little West-Coast twit, digging round in garbage cans."

"How you know I'm from the West Coast?"

"You kidding me?"

Connelly stood up and threw away the food, following her.

The girl looked back. "So what's your name?"

"Connelly."

"Yeah, well I'm Roxy. Charmed, I'm sure."

But before Connelly could say another word, she saw her already moving away—melding into the madding crowd, as if the most normal act imaginable; and she had to almost run to keep up with her.

*

They got their orange juice from the Coalition for the Homeless food van.

"They got better juice than the church," Roxy explained. "But St. Michael beats 'em on scrambled eggs—with the melted jack cheese and all. So we get our juice from Co-Ho and our eggs from Jesus."

Connelly wasn't sure if she was joking or if that was just her manner. She seemed to do everything in a seamless blur: talking, smoking, walking, eating, even relaxing after she'd finished her four bites of scrambled eggs and nibble of toast and jam. She was always in motion, her dark green eyes taking in everything around them, as if gauging, processing what they saw, for whatever reason.

But Connelly was hungry and ate all her food, watching Roxy watch her eat. The church dining room wasn't big, about twenty seats at half a dozen or so tables tucked away in a corner basement room; one you entered from an alley, going down some rickety wooden stairs; and one which emptied quickly once the motley group of people there were finished eating. There was a small boxy TV in the corner with the morning news on, but no one seemed to be watching it. Connelly watched the story of last night's murder unfolding on the screen, an unnamed female college student from Morningside Heights, while smearing marmalade on her last bite of toast. Eating it, she asked Roxy, "So why you being nice to me?"

"I need a reason?"

"Yes."

Roxy stared at her a moment, then shook her head. "Let's get outta here. What I need's a smoke, and these fucking priests are getting on my nerves."

*

They spent the day wandering the city, which Roxy obviously knew intimately.

Still, she said more than once during the day, "God, I hate this fucking place."

"Then why don't you leave?" Connelly asked once.

"You kidding me?"

Sitting in Battery Park Connelly first told her about coming there to find Eric, describing him to her, and asking her if she'd seen anyone like that, which, of course, she hadn't; or, if she had, there were, like, a million other guys like that, saying, "So good luck with that one, baby."

Then she listened to Roxy, or, "at least according to the birth certificate my mama keeps locked in that little red fireproof safe: Roxanne Ostarello, from Piscataway, New Jersey."

She smiled her pretty, fresh-faced smile, which seemed so at odds against her tough manner.

"That far from here?"

"'Bout a million light years, to be exact."

Then Roxy told her own story of an overbearing father, who wouldn't let her date Joey Shertzer, her high school sweetheart. So when Joey came to the city to work for his cousin's auto body shop, Roxy followed, breaking ties with her family in the process. A year later, Roxy became pregnant with Joey's baby, about the same time the cops raided the cousin's shop; which, by then, had branched off into, according to Roxy, "the much more profitable arena of specialized parts procurement."

"Joey could chop a Jap JIT down to the axle and lugs, and the engine still be hot as one of his old man's pastrami sandwiches," Roxy said proudly. "He was smooth, you know? I mean, real elegant with a rip-saw and cutting torch. God, I love that fucking guy."

She smoked, looking out over the choppy water.

"Where's he at now?"

"Doing three to five at Attica."

Roxy had half a reefer they smoked, crossing Bowling Green, staring up the high-walled canyon of Broadway, receding into the distance; then got sandwiches and milk from a Co-Ho food van, and ate their lunch strolling down Wall Street.

Connelly couldn't help feeling amazed by everything she saw there: moving, churning, rising about and above her; the feeling of elevated importance of everything there. Meanwhile, Roxy seemed barely to notice a thing and, when they were done eating, told her, "Listen now, little sister, you go stand over there and look, you know, like helpless."

"Like what?"

"Just do it. Hurry."

Connelly moved quickly over to the side and stood at the foot of the granite steps, rising into the rigid forest of white and gray marble columns above. She watched Roxy scanning the milling crowd about her; finally zeroing in on a lone, young, well-dressed businessman, coming quickly up the steps, talking on his cell phone. Without hesitation, she stepped in front of him, blocking his path. The man appeared momentarily startled, looking back at her, as she leaned toward him, eyes imploring. "Mister, could you please spare a dollar or anything, so I can feed my little sister? She ain't eat since yesterday."

Connelly saw her point toward her, standing there.

She stiffened as the man looked over at her, staring her up and down; then, grimacing, still talking into his cell, he grappled with his wallet tucked inside his suit coat, before handing over to Roxy a crisp, new five-dollar bill.

"Oh, thank you, sir," Roxy said, as he brushed past her, continuing his conversation.

Roxy sauntered over to her, shaking her head. "Hey, didn't I tell you to look a little hungry or something?"

"You said helpless."

"Yeah, well somehow you managed to look both guilty *and* constipated, if that's even possible."

"So I'll do better next time."

"I hope so. That is, if you wanna be, like, partners or whatever."

"Is that what this is about then—being partners? Like ripping people off and stuff?"

"Yeah—stuff. You know, I been looking for someone like you for a while. Sort of cute and clueless—but in a nice way."

Connelly thought about it. "But isn't all that against the law?"

Roxy smiled, shaking her head. "Look around you, sweetie. This whole fucking place is against the law. All these suits you see running round just ain't got caught yet."

Connelly shook her head. "I don't know, Roxy. Like I told you, I just came here to find my brother. I'm not exactly looking for a career in crime or anything."

"Hey, you still gotta live, don't you? Anyway, I got my preferences, I pay my way rather than take handouts, even if I do gotta riff the public; but it's better than sucking strange dick, or taking candy from whoever, if you know what I mean."

Connelly stood there, still unsure.

Roxy shrugged and lit a smoke. "So you wanna keep digging round fucking garbage cans, fighting off the rats, picking up on everyone else's regurgitated shit, that's fine with me. Knock your socks and join the club, baby. World's filled with volunteer victims and leftover losers like that, huh?"

When they both finally stood there, face to face, eyes filled with tormented guile, but unblinking and even brave in their momentary posture.

*

That afternoon they made forty-seven dollars in thirty minutes before a cop that Roxy knew came along and told them to go "shake their marks" somewhere else for a while.

"This is fuckin' *Wall Street,* Roxy," the cop said. "You got balls like my Uncle Harry."

"How's the wife doin', Frankie?" Roxy asked him.

"She went up to Saratoga with her mama to play the horses. How's the kid doin'?"

"Doin'. See ya."

"See ya."

Late afternoon, sharing a pizza at a Chelsea sidewalk parlor, Roxy told her she may as well come stay with her. "It's just Ruby and Maudie there, so there's plenty of room."

"Who're they?"

"Ruby's my little girl, and Maudie's an old woman that watches her while I'm out, you know, doing my thing."

Connelly nodded. "Well, like I said, I can stay until I find Eric. Then we're gonna get a house together."

"Whatever," she said, waving her hand, lighting up a smoke. "Anyway, while you're around, I'll give you a third the take."

"Why just a third?"

"Cause it's my operation, that's why. And cause I got expenses you don't. I got the kid, and I gotta take care of the old woman, you know."

"All right then."

They ate the pizza, then went back out on the streets, making another thirty bucks by evening, when Roxy brought her over to a nearby grocery where she bought a few things, including some Gerber and diapers for Ruby, and a roast beef and Swiss for Maudie.

Then they headed home.

*

Which, Connelly discovered, was in East Village, or, more precisely, under it. Off Second Avenue was a short dark alley, at the very end of which was an old battered metal door with white-flaking enamel lettering which read: *IRT Emergency Exit. Authorized Personnel Only.*

Roxy dug through her bag, producing a pink rabbit's foot and chrome chain, with a heavy-looking tarnished key dangling from it. She held it up and winked. "MTA maintenance master. Don't ever leave home without it, huh?"

"Where'd you get that?"

"From Ace fucking Hardware—where you think?"

Once inside and the door shut back was absolute darkness.

"Don't move," Roxy told her.

Connelly could feel herself standing on some sort of squeaking metal grating; then a row of dim yellow lights, in cobwebbed porcelain fixtures, flashed on, and she could barely make out the rusted metal landing and curving stairs descending.

She followed Roxy down the narrow stairs, holding tight to the railing.

"Watch out for those pipes and hangers over your head," Roxy warned her. "You'll feel 'em before you see 'em."

"Ouch," said Connelly, hitting her head almost immediately.

"You tall as me, girl," Roxy said. "And only fourteen too? Must be the fucking milk hormones or something."

The concrete landing below opened into a larger room, which appeared to have once been some sort of repair shop, now long abandoned, with wood-plank benches and piles of scrap metal everywhere and old metal lockers, doors hanging askew, and various debris piles: old newspapers and burlap bags and paint cans and wooden spools of wire and cable. Connelly noticed a large plump rat crawling out of one of the spool openings; then she saw the Flatiron Machine Shop calendar, hanging over one of the benches, dated December, 1947, with a picture of a smiling brunette, hands on hips, leaning back in a one-piece bathing suit and high heels, a Santa Claus hat on her head, saying: *"Remember, boys, when you think metal—think Flatiron!"*

There was a brick tunnel beyond the repair shop, perhaps a hundred feet in length; then another set of metal stairs, leading to a boiler room, with a single boxy Rite Mfg. Co. boiler sitting cold and still in its center. Beyond this was a wider, brown-tiled hallway. Halfway along it, Roxy opened a door and there was an old bathroom, with toilet stalls and sinks and a pull-chain shower at one end.

"Once upon a time, I figure, this was for the workers down here," Roxy said.

"Does it still work?"

"Cold water does. But, hey, who's complaining? Me and Maudie scrubbed this thing for days when we first moved down here. It was a fucking mess."

Connelly looked at her. "How long you been here?"

"Year or so. Ever since Joey was locked up and I decided I didn't want to kiss another welfare worker's ass."

At the end of the hall was a door to the left and, to the right, another set of stairs. Roxy pointed down the stairs, saying, "That leads down to the tracks and more tunnels. It goes on for, like, fucking ever. And you can come in that way too. But it's more dangerous, so we usually come and go by Second Avenue. Anyway, little sister, welcome home."

Beyond the door was a narrow, low-ceilinged barracks-like room. There was a blanket hanging over a strung rope, dividing the space in two; and to the right Connelly saw the old woman and the child, sitting on the floor before an old black-and-white television. They were watching *Wheel of Fortune*, and the audience was applauding. Neither the old woman nor the child paid any attention to their arrival.

Connelly watched Roxy set down her handbag and the grocery bags, and go over and pick up the child, who did her best—craning her neck away—to continue watching television.

"How's my precious little red Ruby?" Roxy cooed, bright-voiced. "Did my baby miss mommy today? Did she?"

Ruby stared at the television and Roxy kissed her forehead and set her back down on the floor. She said, "Maudie, I got you a roast beef and Swiss, and a Dr. Pepper. It's on the counter."

Maudie stared at the television, saying nonsensically, "We didn't believe it would ever go that far."

"Maudie, we got company. This is Connelly. Her and I are gonna work together now. We're gonna be partners."

"It went the other way for so long and never came back," said Maudie, as if talking to the television. "For so long we had no idea."

Roxy lit a cigarette and said, "Bellevue dumped Maudie back on the streets, I guess, even before I was born; at least, according to people who knew her back then. But don't worry—she's harmless. She's just sort of out there, somewhere else, who knows."

"Milford said it would take that long, and no one believed him," said Maudie.

"I think Milford was her husband or something," Roxy explained. "Sometimes, when she talks about him, she starts crying like a baby."

"Did we ever know?" said Maudie. "Did we ever realize?"

Roxy brought her the sandwich and drink, and she sat there, quiet now, eating and watching television.

While Roxy fed Ruby a jar of peas and carrots, Connelly looked about the room. There wasn't much to see: a battered vinyl counter, upon which sat a hot plate and several cardboard boxes. There was a mattress with rumpled blankets and a few bare, stained pillows on the floor, in the corner before the counter, and another mattress to the left of the television. There were also several wooden spools, scattered about, she figured, that were used to sit on.

She sat down on one of the spools, waiting. Sitting there, she felt the rumble, and remembered the tremors she would feel in San Francisco. "What's that?" she asked.

"Trains, silly," Roxy said. "You'll get used to'em."

When she was finished with the feeding, Roxy released Ruby, who stumbled back across the floor toward Maudie and the television like a tiny drunken sailor. Then she searched through one of the cardboard boxes on the counter, producing a small square red and yellow can with some sort of Chinese illustrations: long-legged birds, standing in a sinewy lotus-covered river; willow trees lining the banks. Roxy rolled the joint from the fixings inside the can, and they both lay down on the mattress, passing it back and forth.

Roxy watched her, asking, "So how old's your brother?"

"Seventeen."

"Same age as me," she said, almost pensively. "And your parents died?"

"When I was six."

"Fucking bummer."

"Yeah," said Connelly. "Bummer."

They lay there, perfectly still, after the joint, staring into each other's eyes.

Connelly said, "So where do I sleep then?"

"Here," said Roxy. "Right here. Ruby likes sleeping with Maudie. They go to sleep every single night watching *I Love Lucy*."

Connelly nodded.

Roxy watched her closely. "So you gotta problem with that?"

"No," she said, barely shaking her head. "No problem. I was just wondering."

"Okay then," said Roxy.

Next she pulled off her ball cap, tossing it aside, and moved over against her, slipping her arm beneath her, and pulling her

THE BEAUTIFUL-UGLY

against her, kissing her full on the mouth. Connelly felt her hot, slick tongue, and tasted her peach lip gloss, and smelled the mixture of jasmine and cigarette smoke in her hair.

She nestled against her, sighing, when Roxy whispered in her ear, "I'm glad I found you first, Connelly Pierce."

"Milford said it would take that long," Maudie said from across the room. "But no one ever believed him. No one ever knew."

And the audience laughed and applauded.

30 ♀ JESSING

Roxy called it jessing. That was her catchall word for what they did out on the streets, usually among the tourists, as in, "Let's jess that motherfucker."

"You sure?"

"Look at him. I mean what a fucking gumba."

A gumba was someone who, according to Roxy, was just *begging* to be jessed.

"Like they should have this sign around their fucking necks, saying, *Gumba from Toledo. Come and get me.*"

Awful, Connelly thought. Roxy was absolutely *awful*—the way she looked at people and then used them. But, deeply, she also found it fascinating, the things she taught her, then actually doing them and finding out that they actually *worked.* People actually believed them and gave them money. Fascinating. Even though Roxy was quite blasé about the whole thing.

"Actually, it's simple psychology, sweetheart," she said, lighting a smoke. "Nothing—and I do mean not a fucking thing—is more alluring to some swinging dick than two pretty, defenseless, tight little tails like us in trouble: I'm sick or you're hungry; mom's dying up in Poughkeepsie and we ain't got the bus money; the car's outta gas and daddy's funeral's tomorrow; those mean old pickpockets just pinched our last penny; yadda, yadda, yadda. Important thing is, they gotta get it quick, and if they don't—then you get the fuck out, and fast. 'Cause there ain't no in-betweens. And you need to remember that, Connelly Pierce."

She nodded.

"No, I mean it, Con. Remember, even swinging dicks got egos."

"I said I get it, Roxy." Which she did, even though she still thought it awful and that, most likely, they should be doing something else instead; although, she couldn't think what that might be at the moment.

Because on good mornings they could take in one, two hundred bucks, seemingly without effort. The sun was shining. The tourists were smiling and milling about like ants at a picnic, staring up at those same silly sights, taking the same stupid pictures, almost stumbling over each other to help them out. Then, they never jessed in the afternoon when, according to Roxy, the gumbas usually got bitchy and tired.

"Always get'em fresh and fed," she said. "Nine to noon's peak time. After that, the kids start whining, the feet start barking, no one gives a fuck you got problems. They just wanna get back to the hotel, take a crap, grab a nap or order some room service."

Meanwhile on bad mornings you could feel it pressing gloomily down upon you like a hot wet hand; and they had to work hard for their ten dollars in change. That's when they got the boloney on white and carton of milk from Co-Ho's, and hung out with some of Roxy's friends; or maybe spent the day in Central Park, smoking weed, watching Maudie and Ruby toss stale breadcrumbs to the ducks in the pond; or simply crawled, more than a little exhausted and defeated, back inside their tunnel, and onto their long-fouled mattress, snuggling together beneath the filthy rumpled blankets, where Roxy whispered her the importance of establishing street cred, without which you were no better off than any other gumba tourist; who, as she now well knew, were like the feeder mice in the pet stores they would take Ruby to play with the puppies—kept, albeit, alive, but without any real individual value or other purpose; kept around, in fact, only to keep the pythons fat and happy. And that snake-pit city (Roxy said to her in her husky, wet-night voice, unbuttoning her blouse, peeling her jeans down her long lanky legs like fresh tight banana skins, then kissing her everywhere softly, slowly, with an almost wrenching tenderness) was filled to the brim with writhing, slit-eyed pythons; smoothly, slyly shedding one skin for another, while waiting to be fed.

When finally everyone slept; the entire room intermittently shaking with the ceaseless passing trains, day unto night.

*

From the fall (when she turned fifteen, although, as was her habit, telling not a soul around her) into the winter, Connelly came to understand there were two central constants driving her life now.

She made a sketch of Eric, trying to capture how she thought he would look then, with a printed message at the bottom: *To Eric, or anyone who's seen him, or knows his whereabouts: Please leave a message at Lacy's Bar, Con.* Lacy being a friend of Roxy's in the Village, who told them they could use her place as a point of contact.

Then she made copies, and she and Roxy spent an entire weekend placing them about the city; afterward, backing away and waiting to see what would happen. As the weeks passed, and the winter grew harsh, and the copies of Eric's face and her message to him slowly faded and dissolved beneath the elements like all the other desperately hopeful face-and-message postings she saw there. Until they were no longer recognizable. Until there was nothing left but the cold silence and her gradual acceptance that, in all probability, the chances of finding her brother in that city of eight million and counting, and starting life anew with him, were almost nil.

After all, the last time she had seen him was in that hospital emergency room in San Francisco—how many years ago? And just look what had happened to her since then. And what must have happened to him as well? What else must his life have become? Did she really think that none of that mattered, that they would, one day, merely meet again—brother and sister, with hugs and kisses, and dusting each other off—and just start over? Did she really, really think that?

While all the time trying not to think of anything at all, with her mind starting to oddly twitch and blur as she stood out on the street, jessing that dwindling trickle of winter tourists who, she discovered, could be absolute assholes, with an icy, forty-mile-per-hour wind blowing down their backs, as she blocked their path, and tried her best to convince them to stand still for just *one-simple-fucking-minute—huh?*, and remove their fur-lined gloves, and give her their hard-earned money, for whatever bullshit excuse she was offering up at the moment.

*

Meanwhile, the other constant in her life *was* real and *was* there for her to hold and love and share everything, bad and good, that was happening to her. And she began to more and more count on the very presence of Roxanne Ostarello, from Piscataway, New Jersey, even though Roxy made it perfectly clear from the get-go what was really coming down.

"Like don't get the idea I'm some fucking lesbo or something, and I'm tossing Joey over for *your* tight little tail, cause that ain't gonna happen—you understand me, Con? Do you? Now I want you to look at me and tell me you understand me."

She looked at her. "Yes, Roxy, I understand you. Why are you making such a big deal out of it, anyway?"

"'Cause *you* seem to be making a bigger deal out of it, that's why."

"I ain't making shit."

"You telling me you love me ain't making a big deal out of it?"

"Well you told me you loved me."

"Like a little sister I love you. Like a jess-the-fucking-gumba partner I love you. Not like some fucking lesbo lifetime-commitment I love you. I love Joey like that, and that's it, and you need to understand that. So tell me you understand that, Con. Tell me now."

"Of course I do, Roxy. *Fuck*."

"And when Joey gets out, for all practical purposes, our partnership is probably over."

"Yes—I understand that too. So stop making such a big fucking deal out of it."

"Besides, you're still just a kid. You need to get yourself somewhere and get back to school. You gonna be jessing when you're forty or what?"

"What about you—you never finished high school either."

"Don't fucking worry about me. I'll probably do something with Joey anyway, so don't fucking worry."

"I ain't fucking worried, and don't you be worried about me either."

"I ain't fucking worried. I'm just offering you some advice, that's all."

"Yeah, well fuck your advice. I got plans too, you know."

"Yeah? Well what plans you got?"

"Just go to hell, Roxy. Just go to fucking hell, all right?"

Roxy lit a smoke and smiled. "One day at a time, sweetheart, just like every other swinging dick on this fucking island."

But always after they fought they would end up in bed, making new love again, angrily hot and madly urgent, each time like it was the first time; only whispering their heartfelt apologies as an afterthought, when they held each other and Roxy said, "Just remember, sugar lips—"

"I *know*," Connelly said. "I fucking know already, all right? So just shut up about it, would you?"

*

In January Roxy took a bus up to Attica for Joey's first parole hearing. Connelly stayed behind, taking care of Maudie and Ruby, and waiting to hear the outcome. Part of her knew how much Roxy wanted him back, and hoped for the best, for both their sakes. But the larger part of her hoped otherwise. She was crazy in love with Roxy, and she knew it. And she didn't see it as a boy or girl thing. It was just a love thing. She told Roxy that. And even though she'd been told back often enough that things would never work out that way, she still hoped they would. She prayed they would. Even though she knew, eventually, they probably wouldn't.

The thing was, for better or worse, she now saw Roxy and Maudie and Ruby as her family, like one of those countless families she'd pieced and re-pieced together, crossing over America. But she was living in New York now, and they were her New York family, and she felt fine about that. She felt perfectly normal about it. And the fact that she found Roxy so fascinating, and everything she did and said, and every way she looked, always caught her by surprise, and always took away her breath just a little, only made it better, or worse, as it was. So, on the third day after she'd left, when Roxy called her crying at Lacy's (as they'd previously arranged), telling her Joey's parole was denied, she cried too.

"I'm sorry, Roxy," she wept into the phone, even though she was happily crying from relief, knowing she had her for at least another year. "So when are you coming home?"

"Today—right now," Roxy said, sounding overwhelmed. "This place is a fucking nightmare, Con. And my poor Joey being here."

She hung up, still bitterly weeping.

Meanwhile, Connelly was walking on air. She bought a pot of rainbow pansies and food for their snug little home. There, she gave Ruby a bath and fed her, and then danced with her about the room, singing: *"Mama's coming home! Mama's coming home, Ruby!"*

Both Ruby and Maudie stared at her with those same stupefied expressions, before clustering back together, watching their TV game shows, and Maudie saying, "It doesn't change anything, you know. Milford said everything was the same, and no one believed him."

"I believe him, Maudie," Connelly said happily now across the room. "I believe everything Milford says."

"Well, I don't know why you would," Maudie said doubtfully. And then fell silent.

Still, nothing could destroy her mood. She snuggled into bed that night, smoking a reefer, thinking only of the following night, when Roxy would be back in her arms, and the night after that, and after that, contented, slipping into her sweetest dreams she could remember.

*

But the next afternoon it was different. As soon as Roxy got off the bus, and taking her home, where she only lay down on the mattress, saying nothing, doing nothing—she knew something was different.

She's just depressed, Connelly thought. She'll get over it.

She crept around the room, trying to take care of everything else, so not to bother her; waiting for her mood to change; waiting to get the old Roxy back.

That night they slept apart on the mattress, Roxy not wanting to hold her or be held.

"Just leave me alone," she said. "Just take care of the fucking kid and the old woman, and leave me alone, and we'll get along just fine."

*

In the morning when Connelly awoke, Roxy was not there.

She came home in the afternoon, and Connelly was relieved to see she was smiling now, moving animated about the room.

"Where you been?"

"Uptown."

Now Connelly stared at her, seeing her smile differently, feeling uneasy about it.

"Uptown?" she said, knowing the only reason they ever went uptown was to buy weed. "You mean the Barrio?"

"Yeah the fucking Barrio—what choo fucking think?"

"But we still have half a bag, Roxy."

Roxy glanced at her. "Yeah, well I decided I needed something besides fucking grass, sweetheart."

She took a paper bag out of her coat pocket and pulled out a small bottle of blackberry brandy. She twisted open the cap and took a swallow, then she held it out. "You want some?"

"No thanks."

Roxy shrugged and took another swallow. Then, with her other hand she pulled another bag from her other coat pocket. This was a clear plastic sandwich bag she threw down on the counter and turned away.

Connelly looked down at it, seeing the bundle of crack vials and the glass stem inside. She looked over at Roxy, walking about the room in a sort of aimless, jerky fashion, taking tiny sips of the brandy. She said, "Well."

Roxy turned and looked at her. "Well what?"

"So you're smoking rock now?"

"So what? You smoked it, didn't you?"

"You know I didn't."

"But you snorted."

"A little."

"Then don't try and play Little Miss Goody Two Shoes with me, I wanna smoke a little rock."

"I ain't playing nothing, Roxy."

"Good."

"Anyway, I thought you told me you only did weed, 'cause that's what Joey wanted. Joey said only weed—nothing else."

"Yeah, well Joey ain't fucking here now, is he."

Connelly didn't say anything. She could sense Roxy had her mood on—her bad street mood, not her good one—and she knew better than to say a word. She became occupied, preparing Maudie a sandwich; opening a jar of Gerber for Ruby.

It was while she was feeding Ruby the peas and carrots that Roxy said, "Anyway, it's just for a little while. Just now and then till Joey gets out. Otherwise, you know, I don't think I could fucking stand it."

When Connelly was done with Ruby, she gave her back to Maudie and began to straighten things around the room. Meanwhile, Roxy was standing at the counter, firing up her butane lighter beneath the stem. Connelly could hear her sucking in. She glanced over and saw her standing there, head down, weaving a little back and forth.

"That's the one," she was saying, gasping, holding her breath in. "Oh yeah—that's the fucking one."

After a while Roxy turned on their brown radio with the broken case, they'd found one day, sitting atop some discarded furniture along a Greene Street curb in SoHo. It was Vanilla Ice and "Ice Ice Baby," and Roxy gave off one of her little pleasure squeals, and began dancing around the room. She was a good dancer, and twisted and bobbed around Connelly, who was trying her best to ignore her, still pretending to do things.

Finally Roxy grabbed her arm and pulled her to her.

"No, Roxy," she said, trying to pull away.

"No, Roxy," Roxy mimicked her and kissed her hard on the mouth. "You fucking cunt, you always taste like licorice, you know that?" She kissed her hard again. "You're just like a fucking piece of candy, a little candy cunt, you know that?"

Both their bodies, together, swaying to the music.

"Well, at least your attitude's improving," Connelly said, trying to catch her breath.

"Yeah, well that's not all that's improving. My libido's improving too."

"Is that right?"

Roxy suddenly held her at arm's length, her green eyes shining like wet emeralds. "Look, why don't cha, like, take a blast too, so you can feel what I'm feeling. Then, when I do to you what I'm fixing to do to you, you'll know what it's all about."

"I don't think so, Roxy."

Roxy looked into her eyes. "I thought you said you loved me."

"You know I do."

"No, cause if you did, you'd blast with me."

"Don't fuck with me like that, Roxy."

"I ain't fucking with you. I just want to share something special with someone special."

"Uh-huh. And if I don't?"

Roxy shrugged. "Then I'll just go find someone else special who will."

"You mean that?"

She swallowed and smiled her twisted, hard little smile, her eyes still glistening. "Whatta *you* think? Joey's still up in fucking Attica, trying to keep some nigger's dick out his ass. Meanwhile, I'm living down here in this fucking hole, with a kid I don't want, and a nutjob I can't get rid of, and a candy-cunt girlfriend, looking for her long lost brother. So whatta you think? I got anything to lose or what? Huh?"

Connelly finally nodded. "But only because I love you."

"And I love you," said Roxy. "And we'll keep loving each other, and jessing fucking gumbas, till I get Joey back, or you get back your brother—deal?"

"Sure, deal."

"Good," Roxy said, seeming oddly excited or agitated, Connelly wasn't sure. "So we gotta plan. It's good to have a plan. Now let's blast this fucking rock, before I crawl right outta my motherfucking skin, awright?"

"All right," she said.

*

Late one winter night the subway police broke into their little underground hideaway, shining flashlights and shouting, and making Maudie and Ruby cling crying to each other, and told them they had a week to get out, or they would be arrested for trespassing.

Roxy knew that meant they would take Ruby away, and, instead, went to, as she called it, "the enemy," asking for help.

By the end of the week they were moved into a converted welfare complex in the Bronx, near Tremont and the Cross Bronx Expressway, called Hotel Cascade. Over the columned entrance there was a frieze, between the rotted, peeling architrave and cornice, showing a snow-capped mountain range, that Connelly thought must have once been quite lovely; though she wondered why they would build a hotel by that name in that place. The caseworker that helped get them into their little furnished apartment, told them she would try and find them someplace better, but they would have to go on a waiting list, which, she said, could take a while.

Still, in spite of the abundance of roaches and rats, and the derelict neighborhood, surrounding them, they were grateful they'd found anything at all, and with its own bathroom and tiny kitchenette, which excited them both. They also noted the complex was only a couple of blocks from the D train station, so they could move easily back and forth, in and out of the city, which, they knew, was important for their jessing, and for their drugs. Anyway, Roxy said, she wanted to keep Rico as her dealer, because she said she could trust him, and he'd even given her a credit line. She told Connelly she didn't trust these Tremont dealers. She'd heard things about the way they did business, and thought it best to avoid them. Overall, she decided, they hadn't done so badly, and she wondered if all this was a sign things were looking up for them.

"Maybe this'll be our year," she said to Connelly their first night there. "Maybe this year something'll happen with Joey, or maybe you'll find your brother or something—huh? What choo think?"

"Sure," said Connelly, "why not."

They were sitting at the pink-and-black plastic laminate kitchen table, and Roxy was using a stout wire with a tiny bent hook she'd made at the end to scrape the crack resin from several of their glass stems into gooey little balls they could smoke. The resin, or res, was very concentrated, and the blast was always good. Roxy packed two stems, and they lit them up together, sucking in and bowing forward their heads, as if in mutual prayer. Then, afterward, they made Maudie a peanut butter-and-jelly sandwich, and fed Ruby some applesauce, before heading out, taking the D train down to Rockefeller Plaza, to jess tourists for an hour or so; then heading up to El Barrio to meet Rico, as was their routine.

31 ♀ THINGS SHE NEVER TOLD HERSELF

Early one icy-dark spring morning Connelly rose before everyone else and made herself a cup of instant coffee; then sat there, trying to decide about something. She drank the coffee, trying to clear her head, and decide.

The thing was, she was no longer sure about it, about any of it, and she was trying to decide what to do. But she knew, whatever was happening, things were not working out like she'd planned. Nothing was working out, and things seemed to be getting worse in fact. Then she thought about what she *had* actually expected to happen, and she wasn't sure about that either. Of course there was the hope she would find Eric, and she still had that (like she still occasionally looked at the faces, although with far less enthusiasm and expectation than she had in the beginning), but she wasn't sure about anything else she'd expected, and maybe there was nothing else, in which case she wasn't disappointed.

Then she thought about Roxy, asleep in their tiny, stuffy bedroom. She still loved her, or thought she did, but that was becoming different too. Somehow her feelings, their relationship, seemed more...fragmented than in the beginning. In fact, everything seemed more complicated and fragile and desperate than before, and she wondered why? But then she knew why, didn't she? All she had to do was look in the mirror, at the dark hollowing around her eyes; at the tiny red spots appearing on her skin; at her dull, listless hair. At her whole face, her entire self, gaunt and seeming wound up like a spring, in the bathroom mirror, in fact. She knew. And she knew it was becoming the same with Roxy, and maybe more so. As sometime in February Roxy had announced she was through blasting, because she was just plain fucking tired of being so wired all the time.

"I need to get some fucking sleep," she said, agitated and jerky, as she always was then. "And I can't sleep blasting through biscuits like boxes of Good and fucking Plenty. I need to fucking *sleep*, Con. Fuck this shit."

So they'd gone over and met Rico beside a weed-choked soccer field in Jefferson Park. Connelly stared at the two teams playing, with some of the players wearing the yellow and black gang bandannas around their foreheads, while Roxy told Rico she wanted a Z of the best stuff he had.

"All my shit's best, you know that," Rico said, acting put out. "Anyway, what happened to my little cracker queen?"

"Yeah, well that shit's got me on twenty-four, seven, Rico," Roxy told him. "I need to get myself straight, you know? I mean, *look* at my fucking face. I can't even fucking *dream* no more. You know what it's like not having no dreams?"

Rico laughed and sold her the ounce of heroin.

Then, on the train back to the apartment, Roxy told her, "By the way, sweetheart, I don't wanna ever see you strawing down on this shit—you understand? It's strictly off-limits."

Connelly looked out the window at the dismal passing landscape. "What are you now, my fucking mother?"

"You know snorting dope ain't like blasting a little ice, Con. You know that."

Connelly looked at her. "And you can handle it any better?"

"Yeah, matter of fact I can. Besides—" she laughed her dry hoarse laugh, "we need a designated driver, don't we?"

"You're not funny, Roxy."

Roxy fell back against the seat, seemingly exhausted, closing her eyes. "I just wanna sleep forever, or at least a week. I'm so fucking tired, Con. I can *feel* the tiredness in my bones, you understand me?"

She had, in fact, closed herself and her Z-bag up in the bedroom and slept for a week; coming, stumbling, out in a daze only long enough to shove a wad of bills into Connelly's hands, and tell her to go hook with Rico for her, because she just couldn't pull herself together. Then she stumbled back into the bedroom and closed the door.

Later, after Connelly had made the buy and was coming home, she did decide to straw down (just a quick one; then, minutes later when she still felt nothing, two long pulls) on the fresh bag, a little curious, but mostly because she was tired as well, exhausted to her bones, in fact, just like Roxy had been; then, getting off at the Tremont station, she suddenly became nauseous and stumbled into a corner, vomiting and holding herself, wondering what was happening to her.

But once she was back on the street she could feel herself starting to settle down, and a wonderful lightness and feeling of being entirely at ease with everything, with herself, overcame her; and she stayed out awhile, walking aimlessly about the neighborhood, now like she was walking about on clouds, or walking straight through the middle of a really delicious dream.

When she finally did return to the apartment, she crawled into bed with Roxy, who only looked back into her eyes, and saw what was there, what she'd done. Then they held each other, both their heads nodding together now, before sleeping, deep and dreamless.

Now she made herself a second cup of coffee; then she crept into the bedroom, past Roxy motionless on the bed, and retrieved her backpack from the closet.

Back at the kitchen table she rifled through the bag, retrieving Uncle Boyd's letters, as well as the letter she had begun to her Cousin Liz; and she sat there, reading everything again, thinking about everything.

What was she going to do? What could she do? With the way she was now, with the way everything had turned out for her—what *could* she do? *What?* And she lowered her head down against the table and the letters and cried, without understanding at all why she was doing that, right at that moment. Because, she realized, it had been so long since she had cried about anything at all.

After a while she got up and washed her face at the sink, and began to look around, until she found some half-decent paper and a rat-chewed pencil nub in the corner behind the couch.

Then she sat at the table, staring down at the address Uncle Boyd had provided, and that seemed, somehow (sitting there in that stark, awful place and coming down off her latest high), not quite of any world she was familiar:

THE BEAUTIFUL-UGLY

Mr. and Mrs. Jack McCullough
Circle-W Ranch
FM 121
Comanche Falls, Texas 78885

She sniffed and wiped her nose, and next scratched the end of the pencil nub with her fingernail, exposing the dull point of lead. She hesitated only a moment, no longer having any doubts or expectations to distract her, and began to write:

Dear Cousin Liz,

I have no idea if what I'm about to say makes any sense at all. But I'm going to say it, and then I'm going to put it into an envelope and send it to you. And then I'll be done with it, once and for all.

As I've already said, I guess we are cousins. My name is Connelly Pierce, and I'm the daughter of Emily Pierce, or Walker, as you knew her. She and my father Michael were both killed in a car accident, well, a long time ago, leaving me and my brother Eric, as the saying goes, to our own devices. Anyway, I'm fifteen now, and Eric is eighteen, although I have no idea where he's at. But that's another story, a longer one, and I don't have much pencil left.

She stopped and scraped her fingernail against the pencil nub again, and went on.

I guess, what I want to say is—I'm curious about you. Who you are. What you're like. And the fact that you're really my family, and that you really knew my mother, is, of course, a big part of it. The truth is, dear Cousin, I have not been doing so well with myself lately, and I thought, just maybe, knowing someone, talking with them—even by letter—might help me a little. But, really, I have no idea.

Of course, I am not asking you for anything. Please understand I don't need money or anything. But, as I said, I am mainly curious if you are even real or not. I've been told you are. And I have this address (I mean, my God—do you really live on an actual ranch? And in Texas? Which, like a friend of mine said, seems like a million light years from where I'm at now.). But I don't know for sure. And I keep getting this crazy notion that you're something made up; you don't really exist, like so many other things I've encountered lately.

Anyway, if you do exist, I've already taken up far too much of your time. So I'll just say, if you have any inclination to drop me a note and say hello, it would mean a great deal to me. That is, knowing there is someone out there with my family's blood running through their veins, for some reason, seems very *important to me right now. Don't ask me why, because I don't really understand it. Any of it. I just feel it, that's all.*

Either way, it was nice talking with you, Cousin.
And here's to (hopefully) future conversations,
Connelly (Walker) Pierce

When the post office opened she got dressed and walked down and stood in the line, and when it was her turn she purchased a stamped envelope. She went over to a table and wrote Liz's address on the front of the envelope, along with her return address, and then slipped her letter inside and licked and sealed it shut.

At the letter drop, she stood there for a full minute, undecided; then she finally reached up and dropped the letter through the opening, and it was gone. She had finally done it. But then after, walking back to the apartment, she had the overwhelming feeling of having just made a terrible mistake; and she wondered if, somehow, she could get the letter back. But she decided that was impossible, and what was done was done.

So she went back to the apartment, making Maudie her instant oatmeal, feeding Ruby her prunes, and waiting for Roxy to eventually wake up.

*

Some afternoons, after she and Roxy were done for the day, she would slip away and go wandering through one of the art museums—the Modern Art or the Guggenheim or the Whitney—or sometimes go gallery-hopping deep into this or that neighborhood. She had learned how to control her high, just so, so she felt, standing there, just like she was descending, deeper and deeper, into the composition and texture of whatever she was seeing. Like she was actually inside the work, able to stand right beside the layered intricacies of it (the subtle techniques and particular styles and secret little tricks of it), unfolding; or oftentimes she enjoyed pretending she was right there as the artist created it, looking over Rembrandt's ruffled shoulder, or Jackson Pollock's burly, paint-splattered T-shirt; watching the blunt fingers and detailing brush moving in intricate feathered strokes over a tiny corner of canvas; or the calloused hands and wide house-painter's brush dribbling and slinging paint across it like an exploding universe, thinking: *No limits, there were no limits after all, were there.*

She often thought of Mr. Gladdens and what he had told her: that she must first lose herself, go off the deep end, before she could really find herself. And she wondered if what she was feeling was what he had meant by that. But she finally doubted that. She doubted her obfuscating heroin high was what he really meant. Or was it?

Still, looking with a slow-fermenting wonder at those works, she was hazily perplexed how she could ever lose herself so well as to even come close to any of what she saw; which, she understood (even in her dopiest of states), had often only been achieved by the greatest of sacrifices. And more often than not had nothing to do with any form or school of art, but was an expression of something beyond the act of creation: rather, some kind of life-hardened existence at its most primitive and pure. But which she still did not know, did not understand, and doubted (standing there, hour by hour, her floating, nodding mind contemplative and mystified by all she saw) she ever would.

*

Meanwhile, there was something else her addled mind had perceived, ongoing, with a dimness of concern that changed with an awful suddenness, late one morning, as Roxy held her naked in bed and whispered in her ear how it really was a simple matter of economics, of supply and demand versus value for services rendered; that is, the dope they were consuming could no longer be supported by mere panhandling for gas money or a bus ticket home; and how they had to, as she said with a kiss and sigh, elevate their game.

Connelly pulled away from her, brows furrowed. "Elevate what? What are you saying, Roxy?"

"I'm saying our expenses are going up, and we gotta come up with new ways to pay for'em—that's what I'm saying."

"Like what kind of ways?"

"Like how the fuck should I know. Like I need to think about it, okay?"

Connelly thought about it and said, "Well I won't be a prostitute."

"Like Joey wouldn't kill me if I started peddling my ass."

"Or give blowjobs or anything like that."

"Hey, I ain't sucking dirty dicks for a living either," Roxy agreed.

They lay there, still and entwined, until Roxy said, "Anyway, Rico cut off our line till we pay it down, so we gotta do something pretty quick."

"What line?"

"What choo mean what line? Our fucking credit line. The way you been burning straws like a fucking choo-choo train and you're asking me—what line?"

"How much, Roxy? How much are we into him?"

"Five large or so, last time I checked."

She felt sick, absolutely sick, about all of it. "Why didn't you *tell* me?"

"I been telling you. But your mind's been somewhere else lately, on art museums and shit, so you ain't been listening. Now you got no choice, that's all."

Connelly lay there, trying to understand what she was hearing.

She felt Roxy caressing her. "Look, girl, stop making such a big deal out of it, okay? I mean, it's not like we're strapping on, hanging out in shooting galleries, spiking a whack, or anything stupid like that. So stop blowing things outta proportion, would you?"

After a while Connelly said, "Why don't we just stop, Roxy?"

"Stop what?"

"You know—stop everything. Why don't we just get clean and go somewhere and start over?"

She heard Roxy giggle, and felt her snuggle against her, and say, "Sure, we'll both just give up doping—just like that—and get ourselves a couple of cush jobs over at some Burger fucking King—that it? That what you want to do?"

"We could do anything," Connelly said, disappointed. "We could do anything we wanted to."

"Sure we could, baby," said Roxy, squeezing her. "People do it every day."

They lay there then, holding each other and not talking, not moving at all.

*

Finally Roxy put it together. She came up with the idea when, one afternoon cleaning out her handbag, she found the pink rabbit's foot and MTA maintenance master key they'd used to access their underground dwelling in East Village.

"Hey, I got an idea," she said, staring at the key. Then she looked over at her, sitting curled up in the stuffed chair across the room. "You know how sometimes when we're waiting for the subway, minding our own, those fucking creeps sometimes hit on us? Even creeps in suits, packing those thousand-dollar, alligator-skin computer bags? You know?"

Connelly did. She also remembered how much Roxy hated all that, usually coming back on them: "Limp dick motherfuckers!" she would curse them to their face, jabbing her finger at them, surprising them. "You know we ain't fucking legal!"

When the man would get this horribly pleasant smile on his face and say something like, "All right, all right, I'm sorry. I didn't mean anything by it." Then go scurrying away.

While Roxy yelled after him: "You got a daughter, motherfucker? You got a little girl at home like me? You sick *fuck!*"

Connelly nodded.

"Okay," Roxy said, becoming more excited. "Now you also know how all the subway stations got those ventilation and equipment rooms at the end?"

She did as well. In fact, Roxy had taken her on tours of more than a few of them, usually when they needed to use a bathroom, or, for whatever reason, needed an alternate route back to the street. All of them were different, she remembered; some just block rooms, containing pieces of humming, roaring equipment; and some with stairs leading down into tunnels or up to street exits on entirely different blocks. She knew Roxy felt special, knowing about them and having access to them; and she told her more than once never to mention "the key," as she referred to it, secretively.

"What if we put those two together?" Roxy said. "I mean, work out a sort of push-and-pull thing—you know like that big sister-little sister thing we used to do."

Connelly said, "I guess that means I'm the push."

"You the cutest and youngest. Anyway, I do better on the pull, you know that."

"I guess."

"Hey look, it'll be like any other jess. Just another gumba-and-gas-money thing. We just got to be a little more selective, that's all. First off, we got to make sure the mark's right. Make sure it fits our profile. And then we got to get the timing down. That's real important."

"I don't know, Roxy. I got a feeling in my stomach about this one."

"What kind of feeling?"

"Like maybe we're pushing it too far this time."

"But didn't I tell you we got to elevate our game? That's what we're doing, we're elevating."

She sat there, considering it. "I guess."

After that, they spent the afternoon working through it—deciding which stations would work and wouldn't, which ones were most private, where they had access to stairs, just in case. Then it was a matter of blocking it out like any other jess, like actors blocking out moves and dialogue on stage, which they did right there in the living room: who did what, who said what, until Roxy thought they were ready.

*

On Monday morning, still in bed and sharing coffee, Roxy told her they needed something "a little special" for what was coming. Then she leaned over and pulled that something out of the drawer of her nightstand.

Connelly looked at it. "It's just a reefer."

"Naw," Roxy said. "Rico calls'em wet sticks. Weed laced with angel dust. It's a dis-associative, baby. That means it helps you cope with things, shall we say, out of the ordinary." And she laughed her dry-hoarse heroin laugh and lit it up, sucking in the smoke and handing it over.

By the time Connelly was getting dressed, putting on her halter top and short-shorts and heels, she saw herself in the mirror, being drawn backwards, as if she was being pulled down a long narrow corridor, looking back at herself in the distant mirror. And it was hard to put her makeup on, because her face felt like it was a mile away, staring back at her.

Meanwhile, out on the street was even worse. Everything was coming at her very quickly, toward her, and then flashing past her—from there and there and there—and then, in the next instant, pulling, stretching, slowly away from her, like the elastic bands of a slingshot being drawn backwards to a point of loaded momentum, ready to unleash itself.

It was unnerving.

"Are you seeing this?" she asked Roxy, getting, wobbly legged, on the subway.

"Uh huh," Roxy said. "Like Alice in fucking Wonderland."

"I don't know, Rox."

"We'll be okay—just take the ride, enjoy the sights, awright?"

But by the time they reached their destination station, she was feeling more in control. That is, everything was still coming at her in rushing starts and sudden stops, but she was not so confused by it. She was handling it now. In fact, she did feel the dissociative effects of it helping her: feeling as if it was not really her there, doing what she was doing; seeing the people about her as if they were behind a sort of glass wall, separate from herself, and she was merely observing them there, not a part of them. That felt better. Not being a part of them felt better. And she wandered back and forth along the train platform for nearly an hour, in her shorts and flimsy top and heels, before she saw her first decent mark.

He was standing off to the side, holding on for dear life to his laptop bag: a fat little forty-something, unsure about what to do next, like they usually were. But the suit looked good, and the way he was staring at her left no doubts in her mind; so she went over to him and said, "Hi."

It was perfect. She was not really there, doing that, and neither was he. Perfect.

"Hi." She saw him smile and swallow. "Isn't it a little cold to be dressed like that?"

"Oh, I know where it's warmer," she said.

"Yeah?"

She nodded, people rushing past, then slowing to a crawl. "Yeah. And it's right over there. Nice and warm and private."

He was looking around, probably seeing who was watching them.

"No one cares about us," she said. "Anyway, here comes the train."

"That's my train," he said.

"Yeah, and there's another one right behind it."

"Yeah?"

"I promise," she said. "So you want to come with me where it's warm and private."

"How much?" he said. His eyes had that bright, panicked look men got.

She saw him perspiring. Then she saw the train rushing toward her. She shifted on her heels.

"I'll do a hand for fifty, mouth a hundred."

"You must have a nice mouth."

She wrinkled her nose at him, she thought, like a bunny rabbit would. "Yeah, well I make sure I brush my teeth every morning before school."

The train pulled up, and people—moving fast, and then slow—were getting on and off.

They were just standing there when she realized she had to move. She had to draw him in.

"Just follow me," she said.

She turned and walked slowly down to the end of the platform. She didn't know if he was behind her or not, but when she got to the door and looked back—he was right there, shifting from one foot to the other, looking entirely uncomfortable and out of place with everything.

She took the key out of her pocket and opened the door. She looked at him. "Hurry, before someone sees us."

He went inside the room, and she followed him, closing the door. It was a big room, with different kinds of machinery, making their strange noises. You couldn't see the back of the room where, she knew, Roxy was hiding.

Standing there, she saw the way he was looking at her and said, "What?"

He looked embarrassed. "Can I kiss you? I mean, I'll give you another hundred."

She laughed. "What—you think this is like a date or something?"

"No, I just—"

"I need my money up front, mister."

Awkwardly, he set down his case and took out his wallet. He handed her two fifties.

"All right," she said after a moment. "But just a little peck."

He smiled, handing her two more fifties.

She folded the bills and slipped them into her pocket. Then she went over to him and let him kiss her on the mouth, closing her eyes, letting her mind go wherever it desperately willed, but still feeling his insistent, disgusting tongue.

"Okay that's enough," she said, pushing him away. She smiled. "Time to take care of the real business."

He stood there, his face flushed red and dumbly waiting.

She squatted down before him and, taking her time, undid his belt and opened his pants, unzipping them, and pulling them down his legs. Next she pulled down his boxer shorts, slowly, watching his half-limp member trying to rise up before her. She took it in her hands, slowly massaging it back and forth, as it grew harder.

"Suck me," he said gasping. "Suck me now."

"Oh, I'll suck you, mister."

She hesitated, continuing to massage him, trying to hold off.

"*Hurry,*" he said. "Before I—"

Where was she? Where was she fucking at?

Finally, when she thought she couldn't wait any longer, there was a movement behind her. She looked up and saw the man looking over her head, staring at what was there.

Next she heard Roxy's loud, urgent voice exclaiming: "Sister! Oh my little sister! There you are—I been looking for you!"

As on cue, the man's cock went limp as a wet noodle in her hands. She released it and stood up. As they'd planned, she broke into tears, standing there between them.

"What the fuck's going on here?" Roxy demanded. "What choo doing to my little sister?"

"What is this?" she heard the man say, astonished, standing there with his pants and striped shorts bagged around his ankles, looking back and forth between the two of them.

"She's *retarded,* you motherfucker," Roxy said. Then she added, "And she's got a *birth* defect."

"I didn't know," he said.

"You didn't *know.* Can't you see she's just a kid?"

"She solicited *me.*"

Connelly moaned and wept even harder.

"She's fucking retarded, you asshole. She don't even know what she's doing, okay?"

"Well, how was *I* supposed to know that?"

"'Cause you ain't supposed to be hitting on little girls to begin with, that's how. Oh boy, wait till her daddy finds out."

"No—" he said, panic sweeping his face. The next instant he was grabbing at his shorts and pants, pulling them up.

"He's a fucking cop too," Roxy added. "A train cop. And he's probably right outside, with his gun, looking for his retarded daughter."

Connelly stood there sniffling and wiping her eyes.

Meanwhile, the man was a contorted blur of zipping and buckling—trying to pull himself back together, trying to get out of there. "I'm going," he said breathlessly. "I'm going now."

"Well I'm telling daddy."

"No!" he shouted, snatching up his computer case. "I'm leaving now."

He began walking quickly toward the door.

"Mister, oh mister," Roxy called out to him.

He stopped and looked back. "What?"

"I need a hundred too."

"*What?*"

"I said give me a hundred, or I'm gonna go out there and start screaming for daddy."

He stared at her. "I don't have a hundred. *She's* got it all." Connelly saw him point accusingly at her.

She broke down crying again.

"What cha got then?"

"A few twenties—just small bills."

"*Ohhh*," Roxy then moaned as if in pain, and her head fell back, screaming, "*Daddy!*"

"My God," said the man. He pulled out his wallet, snatching out the remaining bills there and throwing them on the floor. "There! That's all I have!"

"*Daddy!*"

The man turned and ran out the door, slamming it behind him.

Connelly fell forward into Roxy's arms. They were both laughing, holding onto each other; as well, Connelly felt like she wanted to start crying for real this time.

"Oh my God!" she said, feeling suddenly overcome with the moment. "Oh—"

"Fucking gumba," said Roxy.

After a moment Connelly looked at her. "*Birth* defect?"

"It just came to me at the last second. Brilliant, huh?"

Connelly shook her head, still feeling overcome.

"C'mon," said Roxy.

Together they grabbed up the money off the concrete floor. Then they turned and ran back into the machine room, exiting through a rear door, and following the concrete corridor to an emergency stairwell, which brought them right back to 42nd Street, and away.

32 ♀ BOBBY

Days passing, Connelly more and more had the sensation of being trapped inside the same horrible dream, playing itself out over and over, with little or no variation, regardless of any outcomes. However, she was vaguely aware of some things: they had paid off Rico, according to Roxy; for the first time they had extra money to buy things—new clothes, a real kid's bed for Ruby, plenty of liquor and cigarettes, and a nightstand filled with whatever they needed, to feel however they wanted. Most often, she only wanted to go from morning until night, feeling as little as possible; in fact, only enough to function, to do what was absolutely necessary, until evening, when she could escape back into the dull but gripping fingers of forgetful sleep.

*

One day Roxy handed her something: a small satiny envelope, a letter that most likely had lain in their mailbox for days, maybe weeks, as they rarely checked inside it. She stared at the delicate, lacy handwriting, recognizing her own name, and then looking with unfixed suspicion at the name of the sender: *Mrs. Elizabeth McCullough;* when she remembered that dark cold morning, sitting at the kitchen table and writing her cousin the letter—then going out and mailing it. Now she made herself understand, her cousin had answered her. She had actually answered her back, and what did that mean? Not much, she decided after a moment. Considering how she *was* now, and how everything had turned out, not much at all. And for the first time she felt ashamed of herself. She felt sick and ashamed, and only wanted to hide herself away. She certainly didn't want to expose herself now to some unknown, opinionated relative, probably leading some grand, normal life, or to anyone for that matter, ever again. She stood there, holding the envelope in her hands, staring down at it, undecided.

"You got a letter, sweetheart," Roxy said, as if having to explain that fact to her. "You gonna read it or what?"

Instead, she went to the closet and shoved the letter into the bottom of her knapsack, relieved to be done with it.

"People get letters, they usually read'em," she heard Roxy going on.

"Yeah, well I ain't fucking people."

She watched Roxy set the mirror on the bed and lay out their dope lines, which they did; then they took off their clothes and crawled together beneath the blankets, passing the cigarette and apricot brandy bottle back and forth, and listening to the television in the next room, as Maudie said, "When it finally came, we didn't know what to expect, so we just let it go. We never did understand what it meant."

Then they slept.

*

Some days were smooth as glass. The element of surprise. The look. The grab the money and run.

Others, not so well. The mark would balk, realizing it was a setup, when negotiations would ensue. Of course, they always wanted the blowjob, and Roxy would ask them, "Would *you* suck your dick?"

Then they'd have to jerk the creep off, until he came, groaning and releasing himself in jerking convulsive spurts across the machine room floor; after which, they would take their fifty and run away.

Either way, Connelly always felt the same about it; and she began to need more and more help just to get going each morning. She would start with her crack blast; then do the blow of horse; then, when she felt leveled out, she would get out of bed, stumbling about, wet stick dangling between her lips as she got ready.

She actually felt the vaguest semblance of relief when, one day, Rico told them about someone he knew from the neighborhood, an elderly Puerto Rican gentleman named Mr. Ortiz, who would give the two of them a hundred bucks each just to make out in front of him.

"You sure?" Roxy said. "Sounds like a willy-wacko to me."

"He ain't no willy-wacko," said Rico. "He's just a nice old guy that owns a few cuchifrito shops and likes watching girls make out, 'specially white girls."

Rico arranged for them to meet with Mr. Ortiz at a coffee shop located in the rear of a little bodega on 116th Street.

When they went there, he proved to be the perfect gentleman. He was a small, olive-skinned man, using a polished black cane to get around. He had a neatly trimmed goatee, and wore a dark pinstriped three-piece suit, and hat with a purple-silk band. He bought them coffee and small pastries, and sat there smiling and clutching his cane between his legs, watching them eat. Connelly nibbled on a tiny white-and-pink cake and watched the Spanish women buying meat from a lady behind a glass counter across the room. The women were all busily, fervently, talking together, and pointing at the particular cuts they were interested, while their children laughed and played about their legs; and the lady behind the counter wrapped pork chops and loin and sausages in brown paper, and passed them across. Connelly smiled, watching the scene, and heard Roxy telling Mr. Ortiz about Joey, and how they planned on getting married when he got out of prison.

"Talking about him makes you happy," said Mr. Ortiz. "I can tell."

"I'm nuts about him," Roxy said.

Mr. Ortiz smiled and nodded.

He owned an entire brownstone, just off 125th Street, and his driver drove the three of them there in his yellow Lincoln.

"You own this whole place?" Roxy asked incredulously when they pulled to the curb.

"Yes, my dear, I do," he said.

"And you live there all alone?" she pressed him.

"I have a woman who cooks for me, and another woman who cleans. Then there's Melio who drives me around and waters the plants; otherwise, yes, it's just me."

"That's something," Roxy said, impressed.

Inside, wandering through the rooms, Connelly imagined they were wandering through a private museum, which, in effect, it was:

the 19th Century furnishings, the forest of polished wood, the fine original finishes and tapestries and sagging draperies, the portrait paintings that Mr. Ortiz said he had no idea who they were. "I purchased everything intact from the last heir of the family that had built it in the 1880's," he said. "The neighborhood was in descent at the time, and I got it for a good price."

A little Spanish lady, quiet as a mouse, brought a tea set to the master bedroom they ended up in. They sat at a table and chairs, in a small offset parlor, sipping tea, while Mr. Ortiz told them about his childhood in San Juan. Connelly watched Roxy yawning, bored; and Mr. Ortiz stopped talking and smiled.

Roxy, scratching at her chipped fingernail polish, asked him, "So what choo want us to do, anyway?"

"Whatever you would normally do. You'll find I'm very easy to please."

"Yeah?" she said.

She and Roxy exchanged glances, when they both nervously giggled, and Roxy asked Mr. Ortiz, "Okay if we smoke a joint? You know, just to get us in the mood and all."

Mr. Ortiz chuckled and lightly coughed. "Well, I definitely want you both in the mood." Then he nodded toward the bed. "Why don't you make yourself comfortable, and just forget that I'm here."

"Sure, why not," said Roxy.

They went and lay on the bed, passing the joint back and forth, and talking about tomorrow's jess—what station they would hit, because they were afraid of repeating themselves too often. Until finally Roxy lay the roach clip on a saucer on the nightstand beside the bed and looked at her, smiling and winking. "Guess it's showtime, girl."

At first Connelly decided the joint didn't help much. There was still the old man, sitting there quietly, sipping his tea and observing them. But the way Roxy looked at her, into her eyes, as if to say: *Don't worry about him. It's just you and me like always, okay?* Finally she did forget about him, and was only aware of her fingers, and Roxy's fingers, slowly making each other naked, and then lying naked in each other's arms. Roxy was kissing her, whispering, "You taste just like fucking licorice, huh?" Then working her way down her body, giving her those little sucking kisses, until she felt her tongue below, and she was arching her back, gasping and grabbing the thick red hair between her fingers, and pushing and pulling her at the same time; and when she came at last like she was riding the wildly undulating ocean wave onto the far, gentle shore, her face fell slack and wet to the side, and she saw, as through a filmy veil, the polite, nodding head in the distance, and the small hand holding limply the silver spoon, stirring sugar into the finely painted porcelain cup.

*

After that, they came every Thursday, because, as Mr. Ortiz told them, his doctor appointment was on Wednesday, and he wanted something to look forward to the next day.

Before long, the weekly trips to Spanish Harlem became something the two of them looked forward to. The old man, as Rico had said, was harmless as a fly, never trying to touch them, or wanting a thing from them beyond his original request. He was always the epitome of politeness and charm, serving them tea first in the bedroom, during which they began smoking the joint to give it more time to kick in, and going over to the bed afterwards.

After they were finished, Mr. Ortiz would pay them: always the two crisp one-hundred-dollar bills, he placed beside them on the tea table. Roxy would swoop them up with her hand, and stuff them away; then they would both thank him, each giving him a little hug, which he accepted in good grace with a chuckle, his cheeks flushing.

Before they left, he always insisted they have some lunch. And the cook, a dignified, sadly smiling woman named Serafina (who made sure she proudly told them the first time she met them she was Cuban, not Puerto Rican), would prepare them big hot plates of sliced pork loin, black beans and rice, fried plantains, and boiled yucca covered with crispy-fried cuchifritos that—always to Serafina's dismay—Roxy smothered with ketchup before eating. But they always ate everything, cleaning their plates, as it was usually the only hot meal they'd have all week; and, besides, the joint they'd smoked, and the sex they'd had after, gave them awful munchies, as Roxy always reminded her.

*

It was on one of these weekly forays into El Barrio, and while they were eating lunch, that they first met Bobby Ortiz, the old man's grandson; who, after he said "Hi you's," and left the room, Roxy leaned toward her across the table and identified immediately as "a made guy."

"A what?"

"You know—a pimp or dealer or whatever, working the streets," Roxy said, pouring ketchup all over her cuchifritos. "A made guy."

"How do you know that?"

"You kidding me?"

Oddly, they saw that Mr. Ortiz did not seem to care a great deal for Bobby's presence there, which, at best, he seemed to merely put up with. And the first time they were together was also the first time they'd seen the old guy act as anything other than the perfect gentleman.

"*¿Qué quiere usted?*" he snapped, his delicate old olive hands gripping the head of his cane, his face darkening.

"Nothing, Grandpa," Bobby said in a mildly innocuous whine. "I'm just dropping by. Can't your favorite grandson drop by and see you? Make sure you're doing okay?"

The old man, dark-faced, turned away, saying nothing more; as Bobby made himself a plate of pork and yucca, and went wandering out of the room, lips smacking noisily.

After the second encounter, Roxy told her, "You know, I think he's kinda cute."

"Whatever."

"C'mon, he looks like a cute little Latin teddy bear, cuddly and sweet."

"Didn't you say he was a made guy or something?"

"Yeah? Just like we jess gumbas and things for a living. So what?"

"So nothing, Roxy."

Connelly finally had to admit to herself he *was* good looking. And he didn't look or act anything like she'd imagined a made guy would look or act. In the first place, he was only nineteen, which, when he told them, they didn't believe, in spite of his cute baby face. Then when the old man reluctantly corroborated it, for some reason, they were amazed. Also, he wasn't very big, only an inch or so taller than she or Roxy was. And he didn't dress sleazy or anything. He usually just wore jeans, sneakers, and T-shirt, but usually with a nice blazer; and when he did wear a suit, it was always dark and conservative and well-tailored. She noticed he spent a lot of time on his cell phone—always talking in that same calm, quiet, though vaguely minacious voice—and he drove a BMW: a big metallic gunmetal-gray one, with a sunroof and chrome wheels.

But mostly it was the way he talked to them, to her and Roxy, as if he were like any other guy their age, making little jokes that made them laugh, and teasing them, saying, "You girls are gonna give my grandpa a heart attack, doing your little strip and dip in front of him like that. Won't cha feel bad then?" And then (when Roxy told him: "Well, at least he'll die happy.") laughing his quiet teddy-bear laugh, before wandering off to take another call.

*

Still, there was something about him, something darkly instinctual and familiar, Connelly could feel and didn't like. He was obviously coming around so often because he knew they would be there.

The old man warned them: "Don't let my grandson influence either of you girls. You're both nice girls."

Then for two weeks they didn't see him at all; but he appeared suddenly on the third week, just as they were finishing lunch, and offered them a ride home. Of course, Roxy agreed.

When they told him their address, Connelly could see the look in his eyes, but he didn't say anything until they were driving over the Third Avenue Bridge, when he said, "Look, I know how things get sometimes. I mean, it gets tough out there sometimes. I just want you to know, if you ever need anything—anything at all—you call me, okay?"

Connelly, sitting in the backseat, saw Bobby give something to Roxy, who was sitting in the front passenger seat beside him. Then Roxy turned around and passed something back to her: a business card containing only Bobby's name: *Roberto Ortiz,* and his cell phone number. Next, she saw the way Roxy looked over at him, and heard the way she said, "Sure, Bobby. Thanks." And she knew what that meant. But she also knew she didn't dare say anything to Roxy. So she sat there, holding the gold-embossed card between her fingers, and looking out the dark-tinted window.

The next week, Bobby invited them over to his place for dinner. Then she and Roxy argued when she told her she didn't want to go. But she finally went anyway, knowing that was the easiest thing to do, and, she felt, having neither the strength nor desire to resist.

A black Cadillac Escalade picked them up. The dark-suited driver was a short squat man, with a big black-haired head and powerful-looking chest that Connelly thought looked like some kind of Indian. He wore dark wraparound glasses and didn't say a word driving them over to Park Avenue, where Bobby had a luxury suite in a brand new building.

When they got there, he met them smiling beneath the high-ceiling entrance and crystal chandelier. He said, "So, did Salvo take good care of you?"

"Sure, Bobby," said Roxy, her shining eyes reflecting the elegant overhead lighting.

Before dinner, he gave them a tour of everything, including the sunken media room, with the huge flat-paneled television, hanging above the fireplace; and the master bedroom, with the enormous round bed beneath the mirrored ceiling. Connelly saw the way Bobby and Roxy held hands throughout, and kept shyly looking at each other. She saw that Roxy was just beside herself to let Bobby know how nice everything was. Meanwhile, Bobby seemed nervous and excited as a little boy showing off his toys. And she was afraid she would actually get sick to her stomach; especially, once, when Bobby stopped and looked back at her, saying, "You're awfully quiet, Con."

But she only shrugged and said, "It's nice, Bobby. It's real nice."

"Well," he said, "I hope you girls are hungry."

"We're fucking starving," Roxy said.

She saw them both laughing together now, staring with their own private, shared understanding into each other's eyes.

Regardless, Connelly decided dinner was not so bad. They sat at a long candlelit glass table in the dining room, where a tall, thin, mute, Spanish butler named Juan kept their wine glasses full, and a small, nervous, mulatto chef named Raymond personally served them thick steaks and stuffed baked potatoes, and kept asking if everything was all right. For desert they had layered berry parfait, garnished with fresh mint sprigs. Roxy, to Bobby and the chef's delight, had a second.

As they ate, they noticed, besides Salvo, another barrel-chested Indian lurking about.

"That's Domenico," Bobby told them, smacking his lips as he licked the sticky-sweet parfait off his spoon. "Friend of mine brought him and his brother Salvo up from the Chiapas

Highlands—straight out of the jungle—and I got them from him and taught them everything. I mean, they didn't know to use toilet paper when they got here. Kept using my good linen to wipe their ass."

"Whatta they do?" Roxy asked, staring down into her second empty parfait glass.

He looked at both of them, smiling impishly. "Any fucking thing I want'em to."

*

Much later, going home that night, Connelly sat alone in the back seat of the Escalade, while both Salvo and Domenico sat in the front, talking quietly in some strange tongue she only knew for sure was not Spanish. For some reason they drove with the interior light on, and Domenico kept turning and looking back at her with that same odd expression she'd noticed at Bobby's. He was a little cross-eyed and always seemed about ready to smile. And now he was looking back at her like that—cross-eyed and almost smiling—she saw reflected in the window she was pretending to look out. But it didn't bother her much. Bobby had sent them out on some "mission," as he called it, and told them to make sure she got safely home first; and they had both stood there, barrel-chested and ready, nodding like obedient canines. That, of course, was just after she and Roxy had argued about spending the night there like Bobby wanted.

"What about Ruby?" she asked her.

"She fucking sleeping," Roxy replied, emptying her wine glass, and then waving it in the air toward Juan, already moving swiftly toward her, bottle in hand. "And when she gets up in the fucking morning, Maudie can give her some fucking juice. You know I got a life besides my fucking kid."

"Oh really?" was all Connelly could think of to say.

"Yeah, really."

That's when she told Bobby she wanted to leave; and now she sat in the back of the Escalade, wondering what it all meant. She thought some line had been crossed between her and Roxy, but she wasn't sure what. But she realized Bobby and Roxy probably had a thing now, or maybe Bobby was only pretending to have a thing, and had other ideas. She didn't know. Once again, she wasn't sure about a single thing in her life, except when those two Indians dropped her off in the middle of the silent Bronx at four a.m., and

Domenico held open the door for her, she was sure she saw the biggest gun butt she'd ever seen, sticking up from inside his dark suit jacket, as he stared back at her, a little cross-eyed and almost smiling.

33 ♀ THE LAST JESS

Late the next day, when Roxy finally came home, the first thing she said was, "Bobby wants me to stop jessing gumbas, and he wants me to stop showing my ass to his grandpa."

Connelly didn't say a word. She had just finished feeding Ruby her peas and carrots, and making Maudie the grilled cheese and Dr. Pepper she wanted, and was cleaning up the mess. Meanwhile, Roxy was walking around the room, sucking on a reefer she'd dug out of her bag, kicking off her high heels, and unzipping and dropping her miniskirt to the floor. She flopped down on the chair in the living room in her red polka-dot thong underwear and said, "You want some of this?" Meaning the reefer.

"I don't think so," said Connelly.

"You wanna blast then?"

"No."

"Then what you wanna do?"

"What the fuck do you care, Roxy?"

"What the fuck you got an attitude for?"

"What the fuck you care?"

"Didn't say I did."

"Then stop asking me."

"Fucking cunt."

"Yeah, well I know you got yours fucked."

"Yeah, and he's got something you ain't—he's got a dick like a party-size Bryan sausage."

"Like I care."

"Like you should."

They ended up blasting and doing some lines, then going to bed for the afternoon, making love until dark, when Roxy told her that nothing had changed between them, while she knew that everything had.

Holding each other in the dark, Connelly said, "Are you gonna go live with him?"

"I don't know."

She hesitated and said, "Did he ask you?"

"Yeah, he said he wants to take care of me; you too if you want; even though he thinks you're too damn morose for being so young and cute."

"I'll bet. So how many girls does he have working for him?"

"Didn't ask."

"No? So I guess, you go live with him, it'll be different for you. I mean, different than all those other girls."

"He said I'm different," said Roxy. "He said he's been looking for someone like me."

"And you believe him?"

"Sure, why not?"

"Because...I don't think he cares anything about girls, Roxy. Any girls. And I think he'll tell you whatever he thinks you want to hear. Then I think he'll use you, just like he's using them."

"Oh, is that what you think?"

"Yes."

They lay there, silent.

Connelly finally said, "Anyway, what about Joey?"

"What about him?"

Connelly sighed. "All I'm saying, Roxy, is maybe you should take your time. Don't jump into anything. That's all I'm saying."

Roxy said she didn't want to talk about it anymore, and they didn't. They both fell asleep, and the next thing Connelly knew it was morning, and she could hear Ruby and Maudie watching television; and, for a moment, it was almost the same again.

*

However, the following week, Roxy and Bobby had a fight about something (Connelly thought it was about Ruby, but Roxy wouldn't say), and she came home crying and throwing things around the apartment and slamming doors. Then she suddenly went out again, and came home after two hours, carrying a plastic grocery bag, which Connelly watched her tuck surreptitiously back into one of the kitchen cabinets.

Then she walked around the house as if in a daze. "I don't know what I was fucking thinking of," she said, finally sitting down in the living room. She sat there, slowly shaking her head back and forth. "I love Joey, not Bobby—don't I?"

"Roxy, are you all right?" Connelly asked her.

She looked over at her, her green eyes like hot quivering pools. "I'm per-fet-ly fine. I'm per-fet-ly okay."

The four of them sat there, watching television.

Later that evening, when Roxy finally stumbled off to bed, Connelly went to the kitchen cabinet and took down the plastic bag and looked inside. There was a box of individually sealed syringes and a box of cotton balls and a robin-egg-blue rubber strap and two Z-bags of black-tar dope. She stared at everything for a moment. Then she put it back on the shelf and closed the door.

The next morning when she made her way out to the kitchen she found Roxy already there, sitting head down and slumped at the table. She went over to her and saw the rubber strap still tied around her upper arm, and the syringe sticking, dangling, from the inside crook of her elbow. On the table in front of her were the spoon and the soggy cotton ball and the pink butane lighter. Connelly now carefully pulled the needle from her arm and set it on the table, then removed the rubber strap.

While she was making herself a cup of coffee, Roxy suddenly came awake, annoyingly chatty-voiced, behind her. "You know, Rico was right."

"I don't want to talk about it, Roxy. Anyway, you're an idiot for shooting up like that."

"Yeah?"

"We always said that was the one thing we wouldn't do. And now you've done it."

She heard her laugh quietly behind her and say, "Yeah, I guess I have, huh?"

*

Connelly was surprised how quickly things did seem to return to normal. As usual, there was no money, and they went back on the streets again. But now they didn't even have Mr. Ortiz to depend on, because Roxy didn't want to go anywhere near Bobby. And it grew more depressing each morning, waking and having to go out; then coming home in the evenings and watching Roxy shoot up, hearing her say, "You really need to try this. Because it makes it all worthwhile."

"Sure, Roxy."

"But you need to be where I'm at, baby. You were always where I'm at, and you're not now."

Until finally, one rainy afternoon—when she could no longer think of any reason *not* to be there (for anyone or anything in her life), but there seemed to be every reason, remaining, why she should—she did agree to go there; and watching Roxy excitedly, carefully, lay everything out. Next, she scrubbed her arm down with the alcohol, strapped on the thick rubber band, and prepared the spoon. After the pea-sized chunk of black tar heroin and water began mixing, she used a toothpick to stir the solution. Then she dropped in the cotton ball, and they both watched it swell like a dirty-white, blood-gorged leech. Roxy shoved the needle of the syringe into the center of the ball, pulling back on the plunger, filling the shaft with the murky solution.

"You got nice fucking veins," she said, pinching up her pale skin into a red welt.

Connelly watched the needle slipping smoothly into her arm and the plunger descending. As she raised her head, looking into Roxy's smiling face, a spreading warmth emanated out from somewhere deep inside her, filling her quickly up like hot sticky syrup filling a bottle. And she was soon only vaguely aware of falling back against the chair; her slow, heavy breathing.

"Oh my," came a voice.

"Told you," came another.

She was caught there now, unmoving, only feeling its tingling wondrous rapture, swelling and shrinking, rising and dropping, inside her. "Oh my."

And Roxy's soft, pleasured giggle, mixing with the rich warm niceness of everything.

*

Of course, they both knew there was a difference. In the first place, Roxy still had Bobby on her mind. She admitted it and said she couldn't fucking help it. Then there were the afternoons, after they came off those hot awful streets, they began to look forward to more and more, when everything unpleasant would dissolve like magic "spiking a whack," as Roxy called it. Still, there was a difference. They just weren't as focused as before. They seemed preoccupied, in fact, routinely messing up easy jesses that, before, never would have happened. One or the other asking: "You okay?" And the inevitable: "Course I'm fucking okay." When they knew otherwise. Although, after a while they stopped mentioning it, as it all got embarrassingly sloppier and sloppier, and only looking forward to getting home and simultaneously spiking their whack, leaning comfortingly together, cheek to cheek, at the kitchen table...as the night drew on...and the summer deepened.

*

In particular, the late-July day they saw *him*—watching them back—had not been a good one. It had been a long hot muggy morning and no one wanted to be bothered, no one was buying their bullshit, no matter how desperate and helpless they tried to appear. And they were standing there, waiting for the train to take them home...when they saw him there, leaning against the column beside the tracks, bobbing his head to the music coming through his earphones, watching them.

Then, for some reason, Roxy got into one of her old anxious moods and said, "Let's jess that motherfucker."

"You sure?"

"Look at him. I mean what a fucking gumba."

Connelly looked at him again: a short scrawny white guy with butched, bleached hair, wearing baggy khaki pants and a baggy Hawaiian shirt, bobbing his head to his music and staring at them. "He ain't our profile, Roxy."

"I know he ain't our fucking profile, but let's just do it for the fun of it. Nothing else, we'll shake his jake for a deucer and go get some pizza and beer, huh?"

"I'm tired," Connelly told her. "Real tired. I just wanna go home and get whacked."

"We'll get whacked later," Roxy said, grabbing her hand, pulling her toward him.

He stiffened a little, seeing them coming, but remained leaning at the column, his head still bobbing.

"What cha doing?" Roxy said, coming up to him. She didn't wait for him to answer, but said, "Me and my friend saw you looking at us. Thought you might like some company."

Connelly saw how he appeared a little taken back by what he was hearing. He looked like he was trying to grow a beard, but couldn't. Next, she saw the single gold earring in his left ear. It was a diamond stud with a little gold hoop dangling at the end. It was then, seeing him up close—his vacant, colorless eyes, and that dangling earring—she felt it: Something not right. Something wrong. She touched Roxy's arm and said, "Let's go, okay?"

Roxy laughed anxiously, ignoring her. "What cha say? You want some company or what?"

After a moment his face appeared to relax and he smiled, his lips pressing razor-edged, and saying quietly, "How much?"

"Ah, we'll do a hand for twenty," said Roxy.

"Yeah? A hand for twenty? Wow, that's a deal."

"Yeah, well it's late, and we just saw you standing here."

He frowned. "Imagine that."

"Let's go, Roxy."

"But today only," Roxy said, fidgeting, ignoring her. "So you buying?"

"Sure, I'm buying." he said. "But—where?"

"Just follow us."

"Roxy," Connelly said.

"How many times I gotta tell you—no fucking names," Roxy said, grabbing her hand and pulling her down the station pier to the maintenance door at the end. There she looked around to make sure no one was watching; then used her master key to unlock the door, and the three of them entered, shutting back the door. Roxy turned on the lights.

"This is pretty cool," he said, standing there, looking around at the dim, flickering, overhead fluorescent lighting, and the big metal blocks of whirring equipment, moving the heavy, wet air down dirty plenums. His earphones were hanging around his neck as he walked deeper into the room, looking around. "I'm impressed."

"That's nice," Roxy said, coming up behind him. "Now why don't you give up the deucer, and we'll get you taken care of, okay?"

"Sure," he said, turning, facing her at an angle.

Connelly, standing by the door, saw him slip a hand behind himself, slipping beneath his shirt. The next thing she knew, the hand was coming out, swinging around, and Roxy was knocked backwards to the floor. As she cried out—emitting a sort of strangled, helpless sound—blood spurted from her face, from her nose and somewhere around her eyes, blood pouring down, dripping in thick crimson splotches onto the filthy, grease-splattered concrete floor.

Next, Connelly saw him pointing the large semiautomatic revolver toward her, grinning and calmly telling her, "Get away from the door or I'll blow your fucking face off. Now."

She moved away from the door.

"There," he said, swinging the revolver toward a corner of the room.

She went there.

Meanwhile, he reached down, grabbing Roxy by the hair, jerking her up.

She cried out again and he said, "Shut up, you fucking skank."

Roxy was crying, clutching at his hands, and he again swung the gun, cracking it against the side of her head. He hit her again and blood poured faucet-like from her ear.

Connelly cried out, her hands covering her mouth, as she saw Roxy slacken, falling backward to the floor.

"You shut up!" he screamed at her, jerking the gun momentarily back toward her. "And you, you fucking cunt, I don't do hand jobs—got it? And I never, ever, fucking pay—got it?"

He jerked Roxy off the floor again, into a more or less sitting position; but now she only groaned, her blood-matted head falling sideways, while he tried to hold her upright. He shifted his hands, now holding her up by the hair with his gun hand, while his other hand fumbled with himself, his zipper, taking his member out and tilting back her head—her smeary blood glistening beneath the light like splotches of bright red paint against her face and her darker red hair.

Connelly, her tear-wet hands covering her mouth, pushing herself into the corner, listened to Roxy gagging and choking, as he forced himself against her. He'll kill her, she thought. He'll kill her now.

"No—me," she said, stepping from the corner.

"You get the fuck back there!" he screamed again, pointing the bloody gun at her.

"Please. Let me. *Please.*"

He stared at her, seeming confused about what she was saying. But finally he blinked, as if understanding something else then, and said, "How old?"

"Fifteen."

"That right?"

After a moment she saw him let go of Roxy, letting her slump back to the floor, and nod. She walked slowly over and knelt down in front of him. She saw, oddly, he didn't try to touch her. He just stood there, looking down at her, expressionless. Then she looked down and saw Roxy's smeared blood on his pants and stomach and stiff member, and she shuddered.

Kneeling there, she thought how she only wanted to get to the other side. She was there, right now, and she only wanted to get to the other side. That was all. There was nothing else. She leaned toward him, taking him into her mouth—tasting the sweaty sourness of him—and began looking for only that…For the other side.

34 ♀ LATIN KINGS

When it was finally over, she called Bobby. She didn't know what else to do. Listening to him, she thought how his voice now seemed calmest when things were the worst.

"Where did the ambulance take her?" he asked quietly.

She was crying, trying to talk. "I don't know. When the police came, I moved back into the crowd. Oh Bobby—he hit her so hard."

"Don't worry about that. I'll take care of that. Where are you now?"

"Still downtown."

"The Village?"

"Yeah."

"Okay, you go home and wait. I'll be in touch."

"All right."

"Wait—listen," he said. "She's still a juvenile, and she's in the fucking system. As soon as the cops run her name, they'll probably call the welfare people on her. They do, they'll be dropping by to pick up the kid and the old woman."

"What do I do?"

"Nothing you can. Tell'em you're the next door neighbor. Tell'em you were just helping out. Have a name ready."

"Okay, Bobby."

"I'll be in touch."

She heard his cell phone click shut.

*

He was right. Two days later the police knocked at the door, accompanied by a man and woman from child protection. They took one look around, and listened to Maudie babbling incoherently about "They were the ones coming, but we didn't know. We thought it would be something else. Then they came for us anyway.", and took the two of them away.

The day after, Salvo showed up in the Escalade and said to her, "Bobby wants you there."

She pulled her backpack from the closet, stopping only to slip inside the plastic works bag from the kitchen cabinet, and followed him out.

When she got there she shrieked with joy, seeing Roxy in Bobby's bed. She was lying there—her face swollen and stitched, her head wrapped with a wide gauze bandage—and Connelly fell against her, both of them holding each other and crying together.

"That motherfucker," Roxy said after they were settled down. "I wasn't out. I saw him holding that fucking gun to your head, pretending he'd shoot you after."

"It doesn't matter," Connelly said. "Besides, at that moment I didn't really care anymore. At least he let us alone after that."

"Motherfucker."

Regardless, it was all brought doubtlessly to closure by week's end. That's when she and Roxy were out on the wraparound balcony, having just spiked a whack in her bedroom, and were sitting there now, nodding and enjoying the warm morning sun, when Bobby sauntered out and placed a small silver serving dish on the table between them, and left without a word.

It was Roxy that raised the dish's lid, setting it aside, to reveal the curled-up, maw-shaped slab of reddish-purplish flesh, studded diamond and tiny gold hoop still attached.

They both sat there, staring numbly down at it.

"You know," Roxy said after a moment, replacing the lid and lighting up a smoke, "I got a feeling our lives are gonna really start changing now. What choo think?"

*

But almost before she could decide one way or the other, their lives did change. And that change was sudden and complete and without much fanfare. Bobby, she observed, was like that. He liked things quiet. In fact, they learned that was his sobriquet on the street: *El Tranquilo*, The Quiet One.

With Roxy in his bedroom, and Connelly in one of the large, airy guestrooms down the hall, it soon seemed like it had always been that way. Bobby made sure they had everything they wanted or needed, and all they had to do in return was behave themselves. That is, don't make a fuss or cause a scene or draw unnecessary attention to themselves. Be quiet.

"Otherwise, you understand, it's bad for business," Bobby joked with them at dinner.

And for Bobby, they were beginning to understand, business was everything.

For her part, Roxy decided the first thing she needed to do was to let Ruby go. Bobby had never said a word, but Roxy realized that there was nothing quiet about having another man's kid in your house. Besides, when Joey got out of prison, she knew the first thing he'd want to do is see his kid. So she made up her mind, and Bobby seemed pleased with her decision.

"Who knows," he said. "Maybe one day we'll have our own kids."

"Sure, Bobby," said Roxy. "Whatever you say."

In the morning Salvo drove them down to the family services office, and Connelly watched her sign a release so her mother could take Ruby back to New Jersey, to Piscataway, and raise her there.

"That's the best thing for her, don't you think?" Roxy asked her, driving back. "I wasn't no kind of mother. I couldn't do shit for her. Now at least she's got a chance, don't you think?"

Connelly sat at the opposite end of the back seat from her, tight against the door, mystified, remembering the release that had slowly taken place between her and Eric and their parents over the years. Something not of their doing. Not of their control. That was Death's cruelly idle release over time; its disconnection with the living. Now Roxy had accomplished the same thing, in minutes, by signing a paper. She wondered then, what else was life about but bonds that—any heedful way possible should never be broken, rather nurtured—what else? It was meaningless otherwise, she knew very well, because she had felt that for so long, in so many ways. And the pang she felt then, hollow and deep, inside her, as she leaned her head against the dark-tinted window, looking out and whispering, "*Oh, Eric.*"

"What?" Roxy said.

"Nothing," she said, straightening herself. "I said sure, Roxy. Sure. Now she's got a chance."

*

The second thing Roxy decided to do was make sure everything was perfect for Bobby at home, so he could concentrate on the business outside.

"You don't have to do anything, Rox," he told her. "I got people to handle everything."

"I know," she said. "And they do a good job. I just want to make sure it goes okay for you, take care of the details. Didn't you tell me once the details are the difference between the winners and the losers?"

"Yeah?" said Bobby.

Roxy nodded, spreading out her arms before her. "Well, do you see any fucking losers here?"

Bobby laughed, but then called his immediate staff together and told them, "Okay, Rox runs things around here now when I'm not here. Just let me know if she goes willy-wacko or anything."

"Yeah, I'll go willy-fucking-wacko," Roxy said, hugging him and kissing him affectionately on the cheek, then deeply on the mouth.

Late the next morning, when Bobby had left for the day and the two of them were eating breakfast, Roxy announced she was cleaning up. "I promised Bobby last night—no more drugs and *definitely* no more shooting up. What the fuck, Con, Bobby told me Rico works for *him,* and Bobby doesn't touch any of that shit. So I'm officially off it, starting now."

Connelly stared at her. "So what does that mean? I gotta get whacked alone now?"

"If you wanna get whacked it does. I'm gonna be clean like Bobby."

"That's bullshit, Roxy. We always jess and whack together. *Always.*"

"Don't you understand? My jess and whack days are over. All of a sudden I got a future for myself. Bobby told me his old man kicked his ass outta the house when he was fourteen, and he ain't never had any sort of real home. Now he says he wants one with me, maybe start a family or some shit—and I ain't fucking that up. No way."

"So what am I supposed to do meanwhile?"

"Bobby says, you behave yourself, everything's fine. You wanna spike a little spoonful now and then and stay quiet about it, he's fine with that. He can get you all the prime you need. But if you start causing problems, unsettling the balance of things, then you gotta go, that's all. So, you okay with that? You understand how it has to be?"

She sat there, staring down in a pout at her untouched eggs.

Roxy fidgeted in her chair and said, "You need to tell me, Con. You need to let me know, 'cause Bobby wants to know, and 'cause I ain't fucking kidding here."

She finally looked up at her, trying to smile. "Sure, Rox, sure. I'll behave myself. You won't even know I'm around."

"That's good. That's what Bobby wanted to hear."

"Anyway, what else *can* I do? Act the fool and get thrown back on the streets again?"

"You see," Roxy said, smiling, "it all makes perfect sense now, don't it?"

*

After that, Connelly observed, an odd domesticity settled over their lives.

Waking usually around noon, she'd slowly and carefully lay out her works on the nightstand, then strap and shoot and lie there, floating on her sea of tranquility for an hour or more; usually until Roxy came in to drag her out to the breakfast table, saying, "C'mon, we got shit to do."

There, Juan poured their coffee and uncovered the marmalade tin, and she sat there, nibbling at a piece of toast, and watching Roxy smoking and talking to Bobby on her cell, asking him what he felt like for dinner, telling him she loved him, telling him to be careful.

Then, after Roxy finished her to-do list for the day, they'd shower and get dressed together, with Roxy bitching at her the whole time about being so whacked and not "half-dosing" like she told her to do.

Each afternoon, Raymond drove them down to the farmer' market where they made their purchases for the day—everything fresh, including cut flowers. There was also a kiosk there where

Roxy bought Bobby his favorite magazines: *Playboy, National Geographic*—"Anything with lots of pictures," she whispered to her the first time they went there. "He ain't much for reading. Fact is, I think he's fucking dysleptic or something—he told me he dropped outta the ninth grade—but he loves looking at the pictures, huh?"

Usually in the afternoon, while Roxy was busy getting everything ready for Bobby, she would take her nap; and this was usually her best sleep of the day, deep and restorative, when Juan would wake her around six or seven, leaving her tea set and muffin, and a white or red carnation in a thin-necked vase.

There was a small flat-screen television on her bedroom wall she turned on each afternoon, while she sipped her tea. She never really watched anything—it all seemed to be people arguing with each other: people standing in front of a judge and arguing, or people arguing on the news programs—and she usually ended up turning it to the Weather Channel and staring at the temperatures, listening to the bouncy music. She thought, maybe one day, how she might like to be a weather person. Just stand there and smile and point at the map. She enjoyed thinking about that, imagining herself saying: "Good news for you folks in Middle America—we now have a low moving in, which means the possibility of some much-needed rain for all those thirsty crops. But I'm afraid our friends up in the Northeast are still in for some hot weather, with that mean old heat wave just hanging on. Meanwhile, for y'all down in Dixie, we still see some summertime Gulf influence, bringing those pesky and persistent afternoon thunderstorms. While moving into the Southwest, we have an entirely different story to tell…"

Evenings, she would wake up enough to understand (again and again) how meaningless her life had become. And she would lay there, frustrated and confused and lethargic as a molting bug.

Usually Bobby was late, and Roxy would come into her bedroom to talk. One evening, both of them lying stretched out on the bed, she asked her, "Rox, doesn't all this seem a little strange somehow?"

"Strange how?"

She shrugged. "Just everything around us. Don't you see what I see?"

"Sure I see it," she said. "And I also see my family that doesn't give a shit about me, like Bobby's family about him; and I see what you and I went through out on the streets—streets still out there, by the way; and I'm thinking: well, it may be strange, but it ain't any stranger than the shit I've already been through."

"Maybe," she said.

"Ain't no fucking maybe, sweetheart. You know, in bed at night, Bobby tells me—if he had his druthers—he'd rather be doing something legit, something with some class to it; but he tells me life don't work like that. Life ain't there to be your friend, he says. It's just there and you got to deal with it, or it'll deal with you. And maybe it ain't pretty. And maybe it ain't nice. And maybe, like you say, it's a little strange. But what is, is. And what a girl like me has to decide is: who's she gonna end up with?—someone who life's kicking in the ass, or someone who's kicking back? That's Bobby to me, baby. He's kicking back, awright?"

"Sure, Roxy," she said, knowing it was best to drop the whole thing then.

When Bobby finally did come home the three of them would sit down to dinner, and Connelly always watched the two of them, Bobby and Roxy, pretending they were having the most ordinary dinner you could imagine, just like any other ordinary family having dinner, at four a.m. Roxy would sit there, telling Bobby about her day. Then Bobby would tell her about his. Then they would both look over at her, as if she were supposed to talk about her day; but she always ignored them, picking at her food, until they started talking about something else.

Usually, after they finished telling each other about their day, Bobby would start bitching about the business—how he was going to change things soon, and how he was working on some things. How the girls, that is, the black and Latino prostitutes he pimped, were nothing but "high fucking maintenance." And how the drug business was "too fucking wacko." That's when he would take Roxy's hands in his and talk about doing something else, something where he wouldn't have to be gone all the time, night and day, and could spend more time at home with her, "just like everyone else."

And Roxy's eyes would shine.

Late one night Connelly watched him surprise Roxy at the dinner table by giving her an engagement ring. It was a big diamond and Roxy started crying and hugging Bobby, and then hugging her and showing her the diamond, as if that was the answer to all of her problems.

"Great, Roxy," she managed to say. "Congratulations."

Bobby was effusive, having Juan bring him a big black cigar, which he lit up and leaned back, puffing, even though she knew they made him sick.

"I'm doing some business with Sal Cordero now," Bobby said then. "We got this little merchandise exchange thing going, and if it works out, I'm dropping everything else."

"That's great, Bobby," Roxy said, holding her hand up in front of her, staring at the ring. "I always told you Sal's got a good head for business. I always told you that."

Bobby said, "Yeah, well, Sal's working through some things too. He's got some old partners he's letting go. Says he wants new blood in the operation. We been talking awhile."

He hooked a thumb inside his silver vest, leaning back, puffing the cigar.

"That's great," Roxy said, moving her ring hand back and forth in front of her. "I think this may be the start of something good, you know?"

"Yeah," Bobby agreed, smoking the cigar.

Connelly had seen Sal Cordero a few times around the house. She knew he and Bobby were good friends; Bobby had worked for him in the beginning, before, as he put it, "I knew aces from assholes." And apparently Sal had helped Bobby get started in his own operation, which, she could tell, meant a great deal to him.

"I owe Sal my fucking life, that's all," he said once at the dinner table, after Sal had left.

Meanwhile, she thought he was the creepiest human she'd ever seen. The first time she met him, Bobby had a few friends over for drinks, and she was helping Juan in the kitchen with the hors d´oeuvres, when a large, hulking, bearded man, wearing a black eye patch, lumbered silently through the doorway, to the refrigerator, where he refilled his glass with ice, apparently not wanting to use the ice from the common bin in the living room. Juan (she figured, who knew him) smiled and gave him a little bow, as he stood there, weaving a little, looking back only at her through his good eye. Then he turned and went out, and she felt a tiny shudder go through her, before she went back to what she was doing.

Later, when she brought out the food tray, Bobby introduced her to him; and again he only stood there, looking down at her, moments passing, before he said: "Yeah, we met."

As if voices had fleshly bodies, she envisioned a growling brown bear, also with an eye patch.

"Oh really?" Bobby said. He looked at her. "You be nice to Sal, Con. He can do things for you, hear?"

"Oh really?" she said back, and immediately saw her mistake on both their still faces. So she stuck out her hand. "Nice to meet you, Mr. Sal."

"Just Sal," he said, his damp, heavy paw covering her thin fingers and palm, squeezing. "Like Bobby says, you ever need anything."

"Sure, Sal."

She knew, in her life thus far, she'd never met anyone like him, nor wanted to; and she probably wouldn't have given him a second thought, if it hadn't been for Roxy, who, for some reason, was fascinated by him and wouldn't stop pumping Bobby for information about him, and then passing it on to her, even though she begged her not to.

"He's the real deal, sweetheart," she said when they were alone. "A real fucking gangster."

"I don't care, Roxy."

"You should. Someone like that, place like this—he can do a lot for you."

"Yeah, I know. Bobby already told me."

Sal, as Roxy told her, was Italian and Puerto Rican and "into a lot of things."

According to Bobby, she said, the Italian side of the family became potato and onion farmers not long after they began arriving at Ellis Island. The Puerto Rican side owned a few small delivery trucks that serviced Manhattan and the Bronx before and after World War II, when the two families began doing business together—the trucks bringing the produce to market—and merging: Braulio Cordero marrying Achiropita Rossi. Carlos Cordero was the fifth of their ten children, who married Maria Vincent when they were both seventeen, and started C. Cordero Trucking, a food and beverage distribution company that eventually covered the five boroughs and Eastern New Jersey. Salvador Cordero was the third of their five children, and, before he was twelve, the unanimously proclaimed Black Sheep of, not only the Cordero clan, but the Vincent and Rossi clans as well.

"Sal was in and out of prison, messing with the gangs," Roxy explained. "I guess he was a real pistol, growing up."

Connelly knew, or felt she did. Actually, it wasn't so much the way he looked that bothered her, or even the way he looked *at* her, as what she felt just being near him. She'd been in and around danger enough to know the rising or sudden, sickening feeling of its approach. And that was the feeling he gave her. As if he was not someone who avoided things bad or dangerous or violent, but relished them, preferred them, and didn't care much, or at all, about things ordinary and nice. And he seemed like someone who was always ready to stop whatever he was doing in order to, in a blink, strike out at whatever was nearest him.

Roxy told her how, as the story went, everyone close to him had shunned him, until the family business got into trouble—first with the competition, then with some of the local criminal elements that were vying with each other to take it over. That's when the family finally went to Sal, who was running with the Latin Kings then, and asked for help.

"According to Bobby, Sal took over the business and started kicking ass," Roxy told her one night when they were sitting there, waiting for Bobby. "Pretty soon everything was back to normal, and, as a joke, Sal renamed the company Crown Corporation, you know, like the crown in Latin Kings. Bobby says now he uses the business for cover for his more, shall we say, profitable enterprises."

"Uh-huh," Connelly said, flipping through one of Bobby's *National Geographics*.

"Well, I think it's interesting anyway," Roxy said. "Bobby says he and Sal are moving merchandise around the city with those food trucks—Velveeta and flat screens, pickles and iPads. Who'd a fucking thought?"

"Yeah, who?"

"Hey, you fucking cunt, at least it's keeping a roof over our heads, awright?"

"Sure, Roxy. Whatever you say."

The door burst open then, and Salvo and Domenico came in, looking menacingly around as they always did, followed by Bobby.

"Speaking of the devil," Roxy said, her green eyes twinkling, pulling down her miniskirt as she jumped up off the couch to go greet him.

THE BEAUTIFUL-UGLY

*

Then early one Sunday morning there was gunfire.

It was around three a.m., and she and Roxy were sitting there, waiting for Bobby, when they heard the popping noises in the distance and the squealing tires.

"Goddamnit," Roxy said, jumping off the couch and running to the balcony to see.

Connelly followed her, and they looked down on the street below, seeing the mingle of people and cars below.

"What happened?"

"I don't know. Don't say nothing, okay?"

They waited by the entrance door, hearing the elevator doors open and the muffled rush of footsteps down the hallway. Then Roxy threw open the door and cried out: "*Bobby!*"

Salvo and Domenico were helping him down the hallway, surrounded by the others, and Roxy ran to him. She pushed Domenico aside and put Bobby's arm around her neck, helping him inside the apartment and over to the couch where he lay down.

"*¿Qué pasó?—shit!*" Bobby said. His face was white and he stared out—startled—before him.

Salvo produced a switchblade, the thin long blade springing out, and cut away Bobby's shirt, revealing the gunshot wound in his side. He raised him slightly, looking for an exit wound.

"Bullet's still inside him," he said.

He was bleeding all over the couch, the blood dripping down on the carpet.

Roxy, sitting beside Bobby and holding his hands, glanced at Salvo. "Go call that doctor Bobby knows. That Argentine motherfucker."

"Colbert," Bobby panted.

"Yeah, Dr. Colbert," said Roxy. "You got the number?"

"Yeah," Salvo said and went to make the call.

"Domenico," said Roxy, "go get the first-aid and we'll try and stop the bleeding."

"Those *bastards*," Bobby said in a gush of breath.

"Don't talk, baby," Roxy said. She touched his forehead with her hand. "You're hot like a frying pan."

Meanwhile, Connelly stood there in a daze, surrounded, she was vaguely aware, by some of Sal's men—menacing figures she'd seen around before, dressed in their black and yellow gang attire, with their tattoos of lions and tigers and five-pointed crowns and stars showing. She heard the bald swarthy one beside her say, "Sal's on his way."

Roxy looked up and said, "Why don't you guys go down and watch the street, before they come back and torch the fucking place."

As they were leaving, Domenico brought the first-aid kit.

Roxy looked up at her and said, "Sweetie, you come help me with this. Domenico's like a bull in a fucking china shop."

When the doctor removed the bullet from Bobby's side, Roxy grabbed it off the tray he'd placed it and pressed it to her lips, whispering, blood-lipped, "This one's going round my fucking neck."

After the doctor left, Bobby, resting in his bed, told Sal, "I want the girls to go down to your place on Long Island for a few days, until things settle down."

"Good idea," said Sal.

"No fucking way," Roxy argued. She was sitting on the bed beside Bobby. "You know I ain't leaving you here."

Bobby shook his head. "I need you out of the way right now. Sal and I need to take care of some things."

Sal said, "I'll take good care of him for you. You two go out to the country and lay on the beach awhile. Go ride the horses."

"I don't wanna ride no fucking horses," said Roxy.

"Rox," Bobby said patiently.

"It ain't fucking fair, Bobby," Roxy whined. "You *know* it ain't."

"I know," he said. "But it's what fucking is."

35 ♀ WHAT SHE FOUND THERE

It was a misty gray dawn when Salvo drove them out of the city. While Roxy faintly snored, curled up in the opposite corner of the back seat, Connelly stared out the window, thinking how unusual it was to see real houses surrounded by trees again. Then she realized it was the first time she'd been out of the city, into the actual countryside, since she'd arrived. And she began to enjoy herself a little, looking again at normal things, things familiar and forgotten.

When they drove through the village of Babylon, she saw clusters of families, dressed up and holding hands, going inside a white-steeple church. She turned in her seat, looking back, as they passed by, faces and figures fading into the distance.

They drove out into the pretty country beyond the town, down a two-lane highway, with the trees pressing closely against them from either side. She had lowered her window now and smelled the cool air, sweet and salty in turns, shutting her eyes.

At a driveway entrance, she watched Salvo punch in the security-gate code—the gate opening slowly from left to right—and drive through. She reached over and touched Roxy.

"Wha—wha?" Roxy said, coming awake, a trickle of spittle running down her chin.

"We're here, Rox. We're at Sal's place. Wipe your spit."

Roxy's hand swiped her chin and then wiped her hand on her jeans, looking around. "It's a fucking fortress," she said, twisting in her seat. "I think I even seen a camera over there."

But Connelly thought it only looked very secluded and very beautiful as they drove slowly along the winding asphalt lane. She looked out at the various gardens, wandering away from the drive, back into the big trees. Soon, everything was a garden, overgrown and lush, with only tiny, mossy-stone footpaths and stone benches, here and there, breaking the verdant growth, as if it had been there forever: a Garden of Eden, right there on the edge of Babylon.

An old three-story, pale-yellow colonial house appeared, nestled in the middle of a surrounding forest on three sides, while on the fourth side was an expansive swath of dark-green hillside lawn, stretching all the way down to the blue, still water. She saw all this in a glance, coming over a little rise, and caught her breath, hearing Roxy say, "Well, this must be the place, huh?"

*

Connelly loved it there as much as Roxy hated it.

"I miss the fucking city," Roxy said every night they crawled together into bed. "I miss Bobby."

In the beginning, Roxy called Bobby several times a day to check on him. Then he told her to "stop fucking bothering me, would you?" and to only call once a day—at eight p.m.—and her entire day was spent waiting for that hour to arrive. Meanwhile, she would stay in her bedroom, once again spiking just a little whack to forget everything that was happening to her, and lying near comatose in bed, until the late afternoon. Then she would get up, haggard, raspy and groggy, and occasionally stumble down to nibble at the buffet table set up three times a day in the dining room, or, more likely, just wander out to the porch and sit, smoking one cigarette after another, waiting for the moment she could push Bobby's quick-dial button on her smartphone.

"That motherfucker better take care of himself," was normally the limit of her conversation, sitting there. "I don't know what I'd do if something would happen to him."

Curiously and ironically, Connelly now felt no desire whatsoever for any mood-altering alternatives to the already faintly mysterious and comforting feeling of emotional satiety and well-being she received, stepping from Salvo's beefy black SUV, arriving there.

It was an odd sense of closeness or belongingness she felt, following the young maid up the worn gray entrance steps, through the lovely, ornate rooms, up the staircase, and down the corridor to their bedroom.

"I feel different," she told Roxy, unpacking.

"What different? Like sick different or something?"

"No." She shook her head, looking around the room. "More of a nice different, I'd say."

"Listen here," Roxy said, pointing a finger, "don't you go willy-fucking-wacko on me now—awright? I already got too much shit to deal with, without you piling it on. Anyway, it's probably just your period or something."

"It's not time for my period. And they never made me feel like this."

"How the fuck should I know," Roxy said, missing Bobby terribly, as she threw a handful of her underwear into a dresser drawer.

So Connelly stopped talking about it, only quietly unpacking her own things. Then she went downstairs, still feeling the same.

On the wide front porch, sitting on two rockers, she met Sal's mother, Angelina, and his Aunt Waleska from Jersey City. The sisters were both widows and spending the summer there, as they had done since Sal purchased the property, five years prior.

They were a gushing fount of information about the old place.

"They call it Hollybrook, the estate," his mother said.

"Did you see the old sign at the entrance?" Aunt Waleska asked.

Leaning against the railing, she told them she hadn't.

His mother said, "The real estate agent said it's over two hundred years *old*. Can you imagine?"

She shook her head.

"Been in the same family the whole time," Aunt Waleska said.

"The Williams family from England," said his mother. "And can you imagine the generations been through here?"

"According to Sal, the last heir was a hedge funds manager in the city," Aunt Waleska added. "When they arrested him on fraud charges, he had to put the place up to pay the lawyers."

His mother said, "Sal bought it fifty cents to the dollar the second week it was on the market. What a deal!"

She finally excused herself and went for a walk down the sloping lawn to the water. There she sat inside a pale-yellow latticed gazebo, with a green cupola, and stared out over the pier and water, and then turned back toward the house and surrounding grounds.

She thought of the comment Sal's mother had made about the Williams family, and the generations of them passing through there, and wondered—was that what she was feeling now? The cumulative effects of generations of this unknown family about her and calming her so with their lingering impressions? And she imagined the nature of those generations and all, or even a fraction, of what might have occurred around them, to them: the births and deaths; the moments and times of turbulence and tranquility; the loves and the hates and the gamut of in-between emotions, spilling over the house eaves and down the long green lawn, and pouring into the deepening water their endless variety and infinite result.

Two boys suddenly appeared through the trees, near the shoreline, and came toward her. They walked along the sand, and then turned and came up the lawn toward the house, passing her and seeing her. They said nothing, and one of the boys, she thought about her age, was smoking and flicked his cigarette in her direction, staring. The other boy looked slightly older, and glanced toward her, then away. They were both slender and tanned and had long fair hair, dressed only in swim trunks. They went up the hill to the house.

She sat there awhile longer, then rose and went walking down the beach, watching sea birds flocking in ever-revolving patterns out over the water.

*

A routine quickly developed. She rose and dressed for the balmy late-summer weather. Then she went down to the dining room and had breakfast, usually sitting with Sal's mother and Aunt Waleska, or, if they hadn't yet arrived, alone. She noticed how, occasionally, people came and went from the estate—single people or families, she guessed were relatives or acquaintances of Sal (though, his mother or aunt never once acknowledged their presence), showing up for a day or weekend and then gone—but usually it was just the staff of about eight or ten, and his mother and aunt, and her and Roxy…and the two boys she had first seen coming out of the woods.

Of course, Roxy already knew about them and told her in private, "Don't say a fucking word to the old ladies about'em. Just pretend they ain't here, like those two do, huh?"

"Who are they?"

"Bobby warned me Sal usually keeps a couple of his boy-toys stashed out here, out of public view, so to speak."

"Sal's *gay?*"

"Well, he ain't no hermaphrodite, sweetheart. And Bobby says, other than making the occasional adjustment to his liability portfolio, that's his most degenerative asset. Plus Sal knows he's got a reputation to keep up, so he doesn't like to flaunt things, you understand?"

"Uh, sure, Roxy."

She always ate a good breakfast, because at first she went walking, and then, after one of the staff showed her the stables down the dirt service road behind the house, horseback riding. There was a gray-spotted gelding named Gillette that she liked, and they always saddled for her.

Then she would take the equestrian trail back through the woods to the beaver pond. There was a meadow there she let Gillette graze, while she walked around the pond, or sometimes sat beside it and read a book from Sal's library. Sometimes, after breakfast, she made herself a scrambled-egg-and-muffin to bring with her and eat, reading. But usually she ate nothing at all until evening, after her shower, when she would usually find Roxy sitting with the two old ladies and talking, and she would join them.

The library, meanwhile, had been a find for her. Snooping about the house, she discovered it the end of the first week. Later, Aunt Waleska told her how no one ever went there that she could remember, and the door to it was always closed. But that day she opened it to peek inside, and was pleasantly surprised.

It was a big room with a big bay window overlooking the grassy approach to the water—gray-green and choppy under swooping gray clouds in the distance—as she went in, looking around, lingering there for an hour. There was a map table and reading couches before the fireplace, and the collection, mostly histories and travel stories and biographies of people she'd never heard of, with many old French and Italian texts, along with a large shelf of cookbooks and books on farming and ship-building and the making of wine. Then she found the fiction section, and looked and looked until she found *Pride and Prejudice,* which she kept with her.

Oddly, there was a naked lady mannequin, standing in the far opposite corner from the entrance, she'd first seen, peeking inside.

It was an old mannequin, posed in the stylish slouch, she guessed, of the forties or fifties; and she wore a lady's brown-felt hat with a peacock feather stuck in the band, and humorously had a variety of costume necklaces and colorful party beads hanging around her neck.

"Are you the librarian?" she inquired when she first went in.

But the naked lady only stood there, posing and staring out before her with ethereal indifference.

Then, leaving with the book, she sensed something, and turned in time to catch that remnant gaze of unremitting ambiguity, saying, "Oh, don't worry, I'll bring it back."

She went out, still smiling; closing shut the door behind her again.

*

Sal came down the third weekend, and Roxy was relentless, pursuing him with questions about Bobby, and when they could return to the city.

"He's still recovering," Sal told her, soon trying to escape into his estate office. "You need to hang for the time being. We'll let you know."

"Fuck hang," Roxy said. "You motherfuckers ain't telling me what's going on here, and I need to know. I'm a part of this now, just like you, Sal."

"Bobby's okay, Roxy," Sal said with some desperation, trying to shut his office door, her foot was blocking.

"Then why ain't he coming out here with you then?"

"Because he's got a bullet hole through his fucking gut, that's why. And because he's taking care of things there."

Roxy stood there, leaning into the door. "When can we go back, Sal?"

Sal sighed and wiped the perspiration from under his eye patch. "Soon—next week then, if it's okay with Bobby. Now—does that satisfy you?"

"Like a piece of ass on Sunday morning," she said, smiling, pulling away her foot.

That night Roxy made Bobby commit to a particular day—"All right then, Friday. You can come back Friday, for God's sake. You sure Sal's okay with this?"

"I love you, you fucking gimp," Roxy told him, quickly punching the disconnect button on her cell.

After that, Connelly saw, it was all about the return. About going home. The next morning Roxy was out of bed before her, already packing.

"Rox, it's only Sunday," she said, watching her from under the sheets dance about the room. "We still have five days."

"It ain't never too soon to start for paradise, sweetie," Roxy said, rearranging her suitcase for the third time. "Ain't you excited?"

"Hardly."

"Well I'm busting a gut to get outta here. What's your problem?"

Connelly lay there, peeking out from under the sheets.

Roxy glanced at her. "C'mon, don't you miss the city?"

"A little, maybe. But, you know, Rox, I'll be sixteen in a week or so, and that means I've had six years of bliss, and ten of…I guess, whatever's the opposite of that. And now I'm just tired. I've been tired for so long, and the city doesn't help me with that. I mean, to deal with that. It never did."

"Boring bitch."

Then she snuggled her head under the sheets and listened to her packing and repacking, complaining happily the while.

To make matters worse, that morning a gushing tempest moved in off the ocean, bending big trees into positions of kneeling prayer, and sending lawn furniture airborne. From the porch, Connelly watched Sal and his two boy-toys, Tony and Robin (as she'd heard him call them), frantically rushing about in the wind and rain, securing things. She was curious about the way Sal acted around them, and discovered it wasn't much different from the way he acted around everyone else—pointing his finger and barking out orders and otherwise ignoring as one more nuisance in his life. But she did see them again, later during the quietest part of the afternoon when the rains were gentle and steady. The three of them were gathered around the remains of the lunch buffet, making sandwiches. She had passed by and glanced in, seeing Sal dressed in an odd sort of purple and gold oriental gown and slippers, and the boys in accompanying gowns of green and blue with silver trim. And the boys were giggling and jostling each other, while Sal piled meat and cheese on his French loaf. Afterward, the three of them disappeared back into the bowels of the old house, toward Sal's bedroom, while the kitchen staff pulled the buffet and began immediately laying out the evening repast.

That was the last time she saw Sal, who left sometime during the night. And the next morning she saw the two boys, fluttering about, as usual, like anxious birds around the pancake chafing dish.

*

The quiet rains continued through the week. Old Ray at the stables told her the trail was too slippery and muddy to take Gillette out; but he did let her comb and feed the animal, and she went there every morning after breakfast. Afterward, she went walking in her yellow slicker along the edge of the water, usually thinking about returning to the city, which always left her pensive and anxious.

Roxy, meanwhile, had all of her bags packed and setting along the wall beside the bed; then she had taken up her daily position on the porch, where she smoked and counted down the days and hours.

But that depressed Connelly too much, watching that, and each afternoon she fled back into her library sanctuary, stretching out her lean body across the huge, timeworn, nautical maps of Long Island Sound and Gardiners Bay and the oceans beyond, studying their fathom marks and intricate coastlines and shelter islands, wishing she could visit them all.

Afterward, she always ended up sitting in the old stuffed armchair nearest the naked lady, trying to read something, but usually only sitting there, catnapping off and on, and letting her mind drift where it willed.

She was there on their last afternoon, having just come awake for, perhaps, the third time. She turned and saw the heavy, filtered light through the bay window, the tops of the dark-green trees fluffing in the wet wind, when she turned back toward the mannequin and saw *it* for the first time, mingled unobtrusively within the cluttered mix of costume jewelry and colored beads. She sat there, looking at it, not understanding it, but still something registering minutely inside her—distantly familiar and vaguely warming and so long forgot.

She was not even aware standing up, the book sliding from her lap to the floor, and going there. But she was suddenly standing there, before the mannequin's unnoticed, oblique gaze, her hand reaching slowly out and taking it up as some long-sought boon, at last recovered.

Next, she carefully, gently removed it from around the mannequin's neck (first, brushing aside the feathered hat from atop her bald head), and then held it in both her hands, her unblinking gaze taking in the small, concaved shape of it, attached to the blue ribbon, and reading the engraved script on the medal: *First Place, Hawthorn-Regent Elementary School Science Fair.* And the date.

Tears ran in silent paths down her cheeks, one or two dropping and hitting near the center of the medal's indenture, as she pulled it to her chest, breaking into sobs.

After a few minutes, she turned and made her way slowly out of the room, through the house, to the front porch.

Roxy was still there, smoking and gazing out. She looked over. "What's the matter with you?"

Connelly held out the medal and ribbon. "It was Eric's. He won it at school when he was nine. It was the only thing he kept from our apartment when they took us away."

"You *sure?*"

She nodded.

"So where'd you get it?"

"Sal's library. It was hanging around the mannequin's neck, and I've been looking at it every day and never seeing it. Oh, Roxy, he was *here*. Eric was right here, and he left this behind."

She stood there quietly crying, holding the discovered treasure from her past tightly against her. Then she felt Roxy there, holding her in her arms.

"It'll be all right, baby" she whispered, kissing her forehead. "It'll be okay, I promise. That guinea-spic motherfucker."

Roxy made her sit down on one of the rockers, and then she took out her handkerchief and wiped away her tears. Now she sat there, watching Roxy light up a smoke and lean casually against the railing. After a moment Roxy turned on her cell with her thumb and hit a call button, listening and smiling, and said, "Hey Sal, it's Rox. What—caught you napping? Sorry 'bout that. But listen, there's something I need to ask you, and I don't wanna hear nothing coming outta your fat fucking mouth but the honest-to-God truth, awright? What? Well, give me answers I can use and then you can go back to sleep. Now sometime in your illustrious past you had a visitor out here by the name of Eric Pierce. Good-looking kid: brown hair, brown eyes, with a little beauty mole on his left cheek, near the corner of his cute teardrop eye—just like his little sister has. Am I ringing any bells yet, Sal? No? Then, gee, maybe I better drop a dime on the local do-rights and lay it all out to them and see if it rings any of *their* bells—you understanding me, Sal? Is the picture getting any clearer for you? What's that? Listen to me, cocksucker, don't start talking about pushing any buttons on me, 'cause I got more buttons on you than a Jew fucking tailor on Bar Mitzvah eve, you scumbag asshole. What's that? No, that ain't the way it is, Sal. I love you like yesterday's toothache, you big one-eyed lummox motherfucker. Anyway, I don't wanna have to do anything like that, Sal, 'cause we're family and all. Right? What? You think that's funny, dick-wad? Look—I just need you to be up front with me and everything's copasetic, awright? What's that? Oh, you had a brain fart, huh? You think you remember the kid now? You think he was around here, but you don't know where he went? He just took off one day, and you don't know nothing else, right? What's that? Talk to your two boy-toys? Maybe they'll know more? Sure, Sal. And thanks for fucking nothing, you guinea prick."

She hard-pressed the button on her phone.

Connelly was still staring up at her in disbelief. "Now what?"

"Now nothing," Roxy said, taking a last drag of her cigarette, before flicking it out over the dripping shrubbery. "You just stay here and let me go talk to those two jamokes, awright?"

She was gone for half an hour. When she came back she had a bruised right eye and both her hands were cut and bleeding.

Connelly looked at her askance.

"Don't worry," Roxy said. "They're both sleeping like tired little babies in Sal's bed."

"Did they tell you anything?"

Roxy lit a cigarette and sat down in the rocking chair beside her. "Yeah," she said, "they told me something." She began softly rocking, looking out before her. "They told me your brother was around here about six months ago, hanging with some dude named Heath. And they told me, one day, Eric and Heath decided they wanted to go to Los Angeles and be movie stars. So they left." Roxy looked over at her. "And that's all they could tell me, baby."

Connelly sat there stunned, her face, her eyes, questioning. "Do you think they're...telling you the truth?"

Roxy stared at her, saying nothing. She turned away, and they both sat there, watching the lapping rain, the evening darkness closing in around them.

At one point, Roxy said, hush-voiced, "I guess you'll be going out there now, huh?"

Connelly looked at her, distracted, and then away. "I don't know what else to do, Rox."

"Nothing else *to* do. Anyway," she said, her voice breaking, "I already miss you like my lost bleeding heart, you hear me?"

"Yes," said Connelly, "I hear you."

36 ♀ FINDING ERIC

When they got back to the city, Roxy and Bobby gave her two thousand dollars in cash and traveler's checks, and wanted to buy her a plane ticket to LAX; but she told them she wanted to take the bus instead. She told them there was no hurry now, and she wanted time to think about things, going there. So they bought her a bus ticket, and the next morning Salvo drove her to Port Authority, and she left New York.

The journey back across America was entirely different from the first time she made it. For one thing, she felt herself preoccupied, seeing or noticing little around her, as she thought only of her brother and what must have become of him. What must his life have become? She avoided everyone around her, feeling herself momentarily exposed and vulnerable within that unavoidable stasis that was a bus trip, and pretended to read the same ladies' magazine, she'd found beneath her seat, for hour after hour, or to sleep.

For another, her sense of purpose she felt, heading to New York, was gone now. Now she no longer fondly peopled houses in the distance; she no longer considered her possibilities or outcomes of going there. She kept remembering her time in New York, and everything that happened to her, and how different it was from what she'd imagined it would be, going there.

She told herself, nothing could be certain. Nothing was assured, was it? Life, at least as Roberto Ortiz told Roxy Ostarello, wasn't there to be your friend. It was just something you had to deal with, or it would deal with you, right? And she sat there, with her face pressed against the dark window, and wondered if that was it. That it wasn't so much a question of fate or will, as a sinuous stream of tiny opportunities, given or made, that came to you, one after the other, and what you did with them. There were the causes, and the effects that followed, like a jillion jangling pinballs crashing down the field of play, and how you responded, again and again, until all the balls were silent at last. And what was her life now? And what was Eric's? And how many balls were still in play before the resounding calm, when (as she recalled Lady Julian's mincing expression of, she guessed, a little hope and more belief) all would be well...wouldn't it?

Then, passing through Memphis at just past midnight, she suddenly realized it was her sixteenth birthday; and she began remembering all the promises she and her brother had made each other, year after year, spoken or inferred, but never fulfilled; all the ordinary little wishes and dreams passed between them like so many tarnished unspent pennies, before dissolving unnoticed in their hands; and suddenly she knew—there was only one ball left, wasn't there. Only one chance. She felt that. The crucible that was New York had taught her that. The white-hot heat of horribly skewed odds and few, if any, chances. And there in the night, crossing back over the black-pungent Mississippi River and Delta, she remembered the promise she'd made, slipping furtively onto that city bus at Clair and Richard's house in San Francisco. That she would find her brother, and she would take care of him—once and forever. And now she repeated that promise as a silent prayer. She would play that last ball, and she would win. She *would*...As the bus rolled on through the night, and she tried to calm herself, quiet her mind, as she knew was necessary for such the strangely evolving sojourn she found herself.

*

However, if looking for her brother in New York was akin to finding a needle in the haystack, in Los Angeles she felt she was searching for one particular diminutive star in the stretching, reaching universe. But compared to that boisterous megalopolis, and the company of Roxy and friends, LA seemed casual and careless to the point of benignity, though as strange, but different.

She took a room at a faded pink-stucco Spanish-style inn near downtown and bought a city guide with maps of everything from Reseda to Redondo Beach, from Pasadena to the Venice Boardwalk, and sat at sidewalk cafes, sipping cups of coffee and pouring over it; as if in the endless myriad of affluent or crime-bloated neighborhoods and tangled streets and tourist attractions and information lists, she would find exactly what happened to her brother, and where he was waiting for her at that very moment.

For two weeks she walked and took buses everywhere, until she finally began to feel herself ending up at the same sun-dried, dead-end destination as before, standing there and looking out in a daze through her dark glasses, evermore unknowing and undecided; when she would get back on the bus and go back to her little bedroom at the inn, lying on her bed and making herself think: *Tomorrow. Tomorrow she would go here or there, and she would find him then. Tomorrow.* And in the morning, going there, and then returning. Until one night, near the end of the third week, she woke up in a start, sitting up in bed and realizing everything in an instant. That is, she was *not* going to find him at all. Not tomorrow. Or the day after. Or the day after that. She would never find him, and she was never meant to find him, from the moment he had left her behind at Pilgrims Mercy—*no*—even before that: From the moment, at the very beginning, their parents had left them behind, she had lost him. She had lost everything then. Because that was the moment their family had really died, wasn't it? And without their family, without that protective harbor of grace and love they'd known for, at least, a little while, how could either of them ever have ever expected to find each other, or anything that mattered for them, together, in that careless, indifferent place—How? *How?*

She broke down then, crying hard into the abysmal depths of whatever self-loathing, soul-wrenching despair she had finally wrought upon herself. So *stupid.* So crazy awful *stupid.* Then saying aloud, "Like I could just lose him, and then find him, and then live happily ever after. Like I could do that." And she bitterly wept, until she lay there in a mixing puddle of snotty tears and garish flashing images through her scorched mind, and dark remorseless dreams, until dawn, when she slept, exhausted and unhindered.

*

After several days at the inn, going nowhere now, doing nothing but staying in her room, or going out to the lobby vending machine for a cup of hot tea or noodle soup, she met a girl named Samantha, a folk singer from Beatrice, Nebraska, who was going home after failing to garner a record deal, or even a halfway decent gig.

"I've sang my last midnight love song to those same four Holiday Inn drunks," Sam said, sitting on the lobby sofa, sipping her tea. "I guess I'll spend winter at home, do some writing, and then see what I feel like come spring." She looked over. "What about you?"

Connelly sat in the armchair across from her, her legs tucked beneath her, sipping her own cup of green tea. "I don't know, Sam. I haven't really thought of anything but finding Eric." She shook her head. "You know, I had another dream about him last night. I can't help it—I keep feeling him near me. He *is* here—I *know* he is."

She sat there, unsure.

Sam was sifting through a travel magazine, half-listening to her. "You said he came out here to be an actor?"

She nodded. "Even though that doesn't sound like him at all."

"Well, if you haven't been around someone for a while, they do change, you know. Anyway, if it was me looking for someone like that, I'd hedge my bet and go hang around Hollywood Boulevard."

Connelly looked over at her. "But I've already been there a couple of times."

"No, I mean just go *sit* there," Sam said, looking up. "See, I got some actor friends here and, even though they don't like to admit it, that place is like a damn magnet to them. I mean, where else would some star-struck wannabe go hang out but over there on the good old Boulevard of Broken Dreams—standing there in the middle of Highland Center, right between those giddy Japanese picture-takers and those intolerable Babylonian elephants, and staring down at the Kodak Theater like it was their Mecca, their Stonehenge or something. Anyway, that's what I'd do."

*

She began going there every day and sitting, or sometimes walking around, poking her nose into this or that forgotten corner, but mostly just sitting and waiting and occasionally staring up at the big, white, sun-drenched Hollywood sign on the hillside above. There was an odd air being there, day after day, seeing the same weird, mixed-parade of people going by in the morning: the laid-back, pierced-and-sunglassed heads, going into their little Goth clothing shops or designer coffee shops to work, mingling with the strangely smiling, glazed-eyed tourist heads, staring down at their favorite sidewalk star, then looking, camera poised, expectantly about them, as if some Golden-Age phantasm would suddenly rise up from one of those stars—fully fleshed, gorgeously attired, and smiling again—and they, alone, would be there to witness and record it.

Then later, the now sad, mixed parade passing back by her again, with all their heads bowed a little, seeming a little deflated now, like a balloon losing air, when she would stand and join them. And she thought how they were all tourists there. No one was really *from* there, after all. It was a transient place where no one really belonged, but they all came there one day, for mostly the same reason (herself included), and then disappeared another. Until late one afternoon as she sat there, thinking how maybe she would call Roxy that night, maybe she would talk to her about going back there and doing something there (and feeling the desperation well inside her, even as she thought that), she happened to raise her head and look down the long descending line of steps to the street below, when she saw her own wan, white-haired apparition, appear out the thin air: Eric—his hair now bleached, his ears pierced, his once soft, searching eyes now staring up at her in stark disbelief—stood there, bent and huddled.

Next, he turned away and, in an odd shuffling gait, began to mingle with the milling crowd.

"Eric—no!" she called, scrambling to her feet and dashing down the stone steps to the street below, to stand there, breathless and searching faces in every direction. She pushed her way down the block in the direction she thought he'd headed, stopping at the next corner, looking around, seeing nothing.

After a minute, she turned and made her way back to the bus stop, and went back to the inn.

*

Lying on her bed that night, she thought: If he wants to see me, he will. If he wants to make contact with me, he'll do that. He knows I'm here now. He knows I'm looking for him. So it's up to him, isn't it? Whatever he's doing with himself, whoever or whatever he's become—it's really up to him now, isn't it?

THE BEAUTIFUL-UGLY

So she went there every day, sitting near the same top steps at the Highland Center, like being in the center of a giant churning movie set, and waiting. Sometimes she had the feeling he was watching her, sometimes not. And each evening, when once again he had not come to her, when he had decided that, she rose and went away.

Until the fourth evening, she was again ready to rise and leave—he came to her at last.

She sat there, watching him hobble slowly up the steps toward her. He was wearing dark glasses now, and smoking a cigarette he flicked aside as he came up to her and stood there.

"Oh, Eric," she said. She couldn't help herself. She stood up and threw her arms around him, feeling his thin backbone and his spindly arms not holding her back at all.

"Why did you come here, Con?" His colorless voice was quiet as he stood there.

With her tears smearing against his shirt, she looked up at him, shaking her head. "I've been looking for you. For months, Eric. For *years*." She felt dizzy now with his sudden presence, the understanding of that. "Can we talk?"

"We are talking."

She shook her head. "No, not like this. Let's get away from here."

Then she wrapped his arm inside hers, squeezing it, determined she would never again let it go, and led him slowly down the stairs.

*

It was called the Pig 'N Whistle, and they sat at a table at the back of the patio, having coffee, as she watched him closely, seeming ill at ease, looking away from her behind his dark glasses, even though they sat in the deep cool shadows.

"How have you been, Eric?"

He stared at her.

"I've missed you so much" she said.

He smoked and stared off. "So how'd you know where I was?"

She hesitated, thinking. "Mutual acquaintances."

He seemed to consider that, almost smiling.

They sat there.

She finally said, "May I see your eyes?"

He looked at her. "What?"

"I want to see my brother's eyes."

He stared at her again, until she felt a tiny chill on her neck, running down it, when he took off his glasses and tossed them down on the table.

"That's better," she said, but, instead, found herself looking uncomfortably into an old man's eyes, sunken and exhausted and wary, as she sipped her coffee.

He frowned. "I'm surprised you even recognized me."

"You always had a way of standing. You can't bleach or pierce that away."

He looked at her. "You don't like the way I look?"

"Of course I do. You can look however you want." She reached over and touched his hand. "What happened to your leg?"

"My what?"

"You're limping."

He shrugged. "I guess you could say I had a little problem, of sorts." His smile flickered. "A little medicinal problem. Not the taking part, the paying."

"Medicinal?"

His eyes now stared at her a little cool and hard, when his hand twisted in hers, holding her hand, while his other hand pushed up the sleeve of her red top—high, above her elbow, exposing there the still faintly bruised groupings of needle tracks. He smiled and let go of her arm, looking off again, lighting a smoke and saying, "Life's a peach, ain't it, Sis?"

She swallowed. "I didn't know where you were, Eric. I was living in New York, looking for you, and for so long I couldn't find you."

He glanced at her. "You don't have to explain yourself to me. You never did."

For some reason that bothered her, the sound of his voice, and she sat there, playing with her teaspoon, when she suddenly set it down and said, "Eric—I want to take care of you now. That's why I came here. That's why I've been looking for you. I want us to be together again, and I want to take care of you."

She stopped, feeling stupid.

But she saw it surprised him. The look in his eyes. But for only a moment, when he lowered his head, smiling, and said dully, "You take care of me."

"Oh, Eric, you know what I mean. I want us to be together again, as a family, just like mom and dad would have wanted."

He looked up at her. "I stopped doing things mom and dad would've wanted a long time ago."

"That's fine," she said. "But that doesn't mean we can't be together. We belong together."

"Is that what you think?"

"Don't you?"

He grimaced. "Actually, I hadn't thought about it much."

She shook her head. "I don't believe that, Eric."

He looked back at her. "What do you *want* from me, Con? Really. I mean, I've been watching you awhile, and you're, like, fucking obsessed by all this. So what's really going on here? Did some guy dump you, and you need a place to stay? Or maybe you're a little bored with your life. You've touched all the untouchables, and now the only thing left that excites you is, maybe, your wayward bro. A little sibling sex, just to finish things off. Huh? Is that it, Con? Is that why you're here? You know, now that we're all up close and personal, you did turn out pretty fuckin' hot, even for a sister."

She sat there unmoved, watching him. "You're not going to make me hate you, Eric. You could never do that."

"No?"

She shook her head.

He put back on his sunglasses. "I really don't give a fuck if you hate me or not."

"I don't believe that either."

He sat there hunched and disgruntled, lighting another smoke and staring off. Finally he jabbed out his cigarette, saying, "So what do *you* believe? What do *you* think? We lose mom and dad before we know which way is up or down. Then they separate us for good, because that's the way the system works. Then—and this is the part *I* like—we get to go on with our lives, or the lives those fuckers made us live. So how was your life, Con? How did it turn out for you in the end? Remember when dad would hold you and call you his little princess? Huh? Remember that? So how'd it turn out for you—" He stopped now, biting his lower lip and trying to look away, with the tears rolling down from under his dark glasses. Then he sniffled and fumbled with his cigarettes and lighter and sat there smoking and crying, saying quietly, "Why'd you come here? Why'd you have to do that? I mean, I had everything under control. *Everything.* And then you came here. And for *what*, goddamnit?"

She sat there, feeling her own stinging tears, saying, "I told you. I just wanted to be with you. That's all I've wanted for so long—to be with you again. Nothing else."

"And do *what?* Be a family? It's too late for that. Try and go back. It's too late. For us. For me, anyway. The things I've done." He shook his head.

"No, it's not too late, Eric. It's *not*. And it's not our fault what happened to us. It's not our fault what we had to do."

"But it happened," he said. "And we've done things we can't take back. Life's done things—to *us*—coming at us, and tearing little pieces off of us, till there's nothing left. Until it's through with us. Until it finally leaves us fucking alone."

He sat there now, slumped, saying nothing. She didn't know what to say then.

*

After a while, she told him she wanted to go somewhere, just get away from there, anywhere. She asked him where he lived. She wanted to go there.

"Not there.

"Why not?"

"Because it's a dump."

"That doesn't matter. How far is it?"

He sighed. "A few blocks. But it's a dump, Con. It's an old warehouse row they were trying to renovate into apartments, and, I guess, ran out of money or something. No electricity. No water. There were some others there for a while, and even *they* left. Now it's just me."

"I don't care, Eric. Let's just go there and talk. Or we could go back to my room?"

He shook his head. "No, that's all right—we'll go there. It's not far."

It was evening now, and, oddly, she noticed how once they were alone, away from the boulevard crowd and moving farther back into the dreary commercial outskirts, he seemed to relax. She was holding him now, her arm was around him, and her head was leaning against his shoulder; and she felt him relaxing, putting his arm around her as well. She felt so happy now, walking along the dimly lit sidewalk, talking. They were talking about their parents.

"Sometimes I can't remember them at all," he said. "It's crazy. They're there, somewhere in the back of my mind, but I just can't remember them."

He shook his head.

"Well, for a while I almost forgot them," she said. "But now, lately, they're coming back to me, especially since I've been out here, hanging around, looking for you. I'm remembering everything about them now, especially how much he loved her and she loved him."

Eric said nothing, but he did seem to be listening to her.

"They loved each other so much," she said.

"They did, didn't they?" His voice sounded relaxed now, almost intimate. "And they were so different—I mean, from each other. But it never seemed to bother them."

She said, "Have you ever wondered what they would've been like older? Like middle aged?"

"I used to. But just that. I could never imagine them old."

"Isn't that weird? I tried to imagine them old too, but I couldn't."

"They were just so goddamned young when they died," he said. "They had their whole lives. They were both so full of life. And then they died. I mean, isn't that just the stupidest thing you can imagine, Con? You have a wonderful life, and then all of a sudden everything gets smashed back into atoms again. Isn't that just the craziest fucking thing you can imagine? Goddamnit. Goddamn all of it."

She walked along beside him, saying nothing, only holding him tightly now.

*

In the middle of the deserted warehouse row, he showed her how the bracket for one of the door padlocks had been unscrewed, and only appeared to be secure. He opened the door and, once they were inside and the door shut back, flicked on his butane lighter, guiding them up the unfinished stairs. She looked around herself but couldn't see much—large open walls with the thick studs showing, but everything beyond hinted at in the flickering light, at being suddenly stopped and unfinished.

At the top of the stairs Eric opened another door and told her to wait there, and she stood there, watching him cross the room inside and light fat, sooty candles—one...two...three, sitting atop a sort of plywood table on sawhorses. She looked and saw a few books scattered there, an empty peanut butter jar and bread wrapper, a sheaf of papers, and a tin can with pencils in it. There were wooden fruit crates to sit on.

"Well, this is it," he said.

She stepped into the room, looking around, down at the books. One of them lay open, face down on the plywood, and she reached out, turning it around and reading: *Philosophical Milestones: An Enquiry concerning Human Understanding*. She glanced over at him.

"Just one of Hume's potboilers," he said, picking up one of the candles and standing there, seeming to consider what to do next. "I think he was trying to make us understand our limitations. That is, no matter how enlightened we thought we were, knowing our limitations versus thinking we had none. It kept us human. Grounded. I always liked that. Not believing we could do anything we wanted; opening doors we shouldn't open; knowing when enough was enough. But no one ever listens, do they? The be alls and end alls, intent on remaking the universe. Supermen marching toward Armageddon. Meanwhile, Poor David laughs and plays backgammon with his friends." He shrugged, looking around.

Suddenly, she realized, she was being allowed a peek at what her brother might have become, had things turned out differently. She said, "When you talk like that, you remind me of when you and mom would talk about things. Your science and things. Do you remember?"

He didn't answer her. "C'mon, I'll show you the master bedroom." Holding the candle before him, he hobbled past her to a rear door in the middle of the only finished wall, pushing it open.

She went over and peeked past him, seeing another half-finished room with a mattress, covered with rumpled blankets, in the center of the floor. She walked over to the mattress, kneeling down, and straightened out the blankets; then she stretched out across them and patted beside her. She watched him standing there, watching her back; then slowly he hobbled over and set down the candle and, wincing with the pain in his leg, lay down beside her, looking at her.

At that moment, she remembered when they were young, and she would go lay beside him in his bed, bothering him with questions while he tried to read. Then—her mind flashing ahead—she thought of that night at Pilgrims Mercy, and said, "Do you remember the promise we made each other when they separated us? That one day we'd be together again. And, when we were, they'd never do that to us again. Do you remember?"

He nodded.

"Well, what I think is, I think we made it, Eric. We made it to the other side, and they can't do that to us ever again. They can't do anything to us now. What do you think?"

He lay there, observing her a moment. Then he rolled over on his back, staring at the exposed ceiling. "Remember what I just said about Hume? People remaking the universe? Well, I think you may be one of those people—and there's nothing wrong with that. I think we need people like that, like you—creators and world-builders—to a degree, of course, to move things along. But I also think I'm one of those other people that are perfectly happy, for their time, finding a little piece of the world to get by. We come, we use our allotment, and then, when that's gone, we leave. No more. Do you understand me, Con? Can you?"

"Yes, Eric," she said, frustrated. "But just because we're different doesn't mean we can't help each other out."

He laughed quietly, shutting his eyes. "Classic world-builder response. Always looking beyond, to the other side, and damn the limitations."

"Never mind that. All I know is I've found you now. And I don't want to let you go."

He looked over at her. "I just think you'd be better off without me holding you back or whatever."

"But I don't see it that way. And I don't see why you would think like that."

He rolled back over, facing her. "It's just that, Sis, I've done things, I've had to do things I didn't want to. And now, you see, I have to find a way to deal with that."

"You don't think I have?"

"Maybe they've affected you less than me."

"I don't know how they've affected me, Eric. But didn't you tell me once that, as long as we're together, we've still got our family? Didn't you?"

He didn't answer her.

"Then that's it," she said. "If you tell me—for whatever reason—you want me to go away and leave you alone, I will. Is that what you want? Then tell me, and I'll go now."

She held her breath, waiting, searching his eyes as they looked back deeply into her eyes. And she wanted so much to know what he was thinking, when, at one moment, his expression appeared to change; as if, *at* that moment, he'd made a specific decision about something, and was relieved by that now, relaxing.

He finally sighed and said quietly, "No, I don't want to do that. After everything—I can't do that now."

"Then what? What about us?"

He shrugged. "I guess, if that's what you really want, we'll give it a shot then. We'll be together. But just don't say I didn't warn you."

"Oh—*Eric*," she said, throwing herself against him, trying not to cry, trying to be calm and philosophical about it, as he was, but she couldn't help herself. She *was* crying as she squeezed him in her arms, kissing his face.

Meanwhile, he was laughing, trying to hold her off, saying, "For God's sake, don't kill me with your love first."

"I *will* kill you with my love," she sobbed. "I *will*. And I'll make you breakfast every morning."

"I don't eat breakfast."

"Coffee then. We'll have coffee, and you can tell me about Hume or whoever."

"If you want."

"Oh, Eric—we're going to be so happy together." She pulled back and looked at him. "I have money. Over a thousand dollars. We'll go somewhere and find a place to stay."

He nodded, watching her. After a moment, he said, "Actually, I have some friends that have this little place up above Joshua Tree, in the San Bernardino Mountains. It's sort of a dude ranch, and they've been trying to get me to come there and dry out, and, you know, help out with things. We could go there and live for a while—at least until we get back on our feet, and you get back in school. So...whatta you think, brat?"

"Nothing," she said then, the tears still streaming down her face, listening to him, seeing his face in the candlelight. "I can't think of anything now."

They only held each other now, saying nothing.

*

The remainder of that evening came to her in an unsteadying stream of broken, moment-pieces, like shards of light-fragmenting glass that skewed her vision, her mind's eye, until she would wonder, holding onto that very last piece of jagged-edged time, what had been real and not. Was any of it real, in fact?

They talked awhile longer. Not long. She lay there, looking at him, he at her, and they talked of some of the good things they could still remember—some of the same things she had remembered so often by herself over the years, but now sweeter with the sharing—and they talked a little of the bad. It was the last stilling moment between them.

Then, the moment passing, Eric broke it off, saying it was late, saying she had to catch her bus.

"Why don't you come with me now?" she said. "This horrible place. Come back with me tonight, Eric."

He shook his head. "I have some things to do first. I'll meet you in the morning, around eight or so—over at the Center."

"All right," she said, disappointed. "But I wish you'd come with me now. I told you—if I ever found you again—I'd never let you go."

"It's just for a while," he said, smiling; then averting his eyes a little.

As they walked to the bus stop, she felt the way his hand was holding hers; she felt the way he walked beside her. And she felt the unease coming inside her, walking.

It was when they were standing there with the bus approaching that he said, "You know, Con, I don't think you'll ever know what you meant to me—"

Stopping then, his face seeming almost stricken in the street light.

She looked at him. "Eric, is everything all right?"

He seemed to gather himself now and nodded. "I just meant—you mean a lot to me, that's all."

Her head was spinning now as the bus arrived and he kissed her.

"Tomorrow," he said. "And don't you be late. You're buying breakfast, right?"

She stared at him. "You said you don't eat breakfast, remember?"

"Oh yeah, well—coffee then," he said, trying to smile. Then he turned and began walking away.

Suddenly the uneasy feeling she'd had swelled inside her, and she said, "*Eric.*"

He stopped and turned.

"Come with me now, *please.*"

He frowned at her. "Tomorrow, Miss Fidgy-Widgy."

He turned away again.

That startled her, hearing that. That's what he used to call her at the very beginning, when the four of them would drive somewhere, and she wouldn't sit still, bothering him with questions about everything beyond the car windows.

"*Eric,*" she whispered now, her voice breaking.

"Lady," said the bus driver through the open door, "you getting on or no?"

She finally turned and got on the bus, the door slamming shut behind her.

The ride back, she wondered what was happening. Why did she feel like that? Like everything was suddenly, irretrievably slipping away from her, when tomorrow was going to be the best day of her life since—since she could remember. As the bus bounced and shimmied, going down the street, things were passing through her mind she didn't understand. They were not so much images or thoughts of anything real and concrete, as (How could she say?) some sorts of feelings or emotions that were almost substantive, with a frightening texture and evil consistency that unnerved her, sitting there, seeing them rise up, fluid and red, passing away.

She shook her head, trying to stop them, looking out instead at the hot-real, liquid-aired Los Angeles night. She thought about the evening, what had been said between them, what he'd looked like when he said things. What was it? What was it he said, and was that what he really meant to say? She remembered his comment about those other people, content with finding a little piece of the world to get by. And once they'd used their allotment—nothing more. Then she remembered his face as he'd said that, and it was the same face, she recalled, when he was nine years old, trying to answer her questions about why people did certain cruel things to each other, or about animals having sex. It was *that* face, trying to explain something that couldn't be. He wanted to tell her the truth. He really did. Because that was the bent of his mind. But he couldn't. So he put on that face and told her something else, hoping she wouldn't notice. Hoping he could get past her, just long enough—

She jumped up and ran to the front of the bus.

"Please let me off," she told the driver.

"What?"

"Let me off the bus—*please*."

"Well, here's the stop coming, miss."

Once she was off the bus she ran across the divided street to the other side. Then she stood there, looking down the street, wondering if she should start running, when she saw the bus coming far down the highway. It seemed to take forever to get there, when it pulled slowly to the curb, the door swinging open.

The black driver looked down at her coming on and happily announced: "Last bus runnin'. Step easy now."

*

When she was finally back on Hollywood Boulevard, she ran. She was vaguely aware of the deep night's noisy remnant clusters of oddly coiffed and costumed people, moving up and down the sidewalk, as she ran past them, among them, finally reaching the corner she and Eric had, hardly two hours before, stood. Here she turned and ran all the way down the street to the abandoned warehouse row.

She went up the wide sidewalk to the big entrance door, opening it, as Eric had showed her, going inside. Now she stood there in the dark, listening, hearing nothing but herself, her hard breathing.

She made her way over to the wooden stairs and up them, hearing them creak, to the landing. Slowly, she crossed over the unseen floor and felt her hand against the door, the doorknob, twisting it and pushing it open.

She stood there, looking inside. Across the room she saw one of the candles still flickering on the plywood table. That's when she saw the scrap of paper, folded tent-like, beside it. A numbness moved through her—head to feet—as she walked over and picked it up, seeing the word *Sis* written in Eric's familiar sloping hand and feeling her heart now melting inside her.

She opened the paper and read: *Of course you'd come back. Of course you would. So I knew I didn't have much time. Actually, it wasn't entirely a lie. I did have some friends that had a place above Joshua Tree, and they did ask me to come there. But I told them I wasn't up to it (which also wasn't* entirely a lie). Then the place went bust and they moved up to Spokane. Anyway, daydreaming together was fun, wasn't it, Sis? But the truth is I would just end up taking you down with me. And we couldn't have that now, could we. Because, you know, dear girl, you were always the best parts of them—of mom and dad—and I was, well, you know what I was, or some of it at least. The three of us are counting on you, Con. Always have. Sorry to leave you with such a bullshit load, regardless. Please take care. Love, Eric.

P.S., No matter what, don't blame this on yourself. For quite a while I've only been looking for the moment, and I finally found it.

In a dizzying swoon, she dropped the note and made her way gingerly over to the rear bedroom door. She stood there a moment, slightly crouched, then she pushed the door open—seeing it swing open—seeing what was there: Another candle flickering beside the mattress. Something lying still on the mattress. "*Eric?*" She thought she heard the breathless inquiry. She wasn't sure. Then she heard it again, "*Eric?*"

Feeling only her beating heart, she made her way over to him, kneeling down on the mattress, only then noticing the thin arm slung to the side, the syringe still dangling awkwardly down, with the base of the plunger resting there against the too-pale skin. With a testing motion, the tips of her fingers reached out and touched him; then she placed her entire hand upon him, feeling the unnatural stillness beneath.

Distractedly, she pulled the syringe from his arm, adjusting the arm back beside him. Then she lay down upon him, holding him protectively in her arms, trying to cover him with as much of herself as she could. She held him and squeezed him gently, whispering, "Oh, Eric, why now? Why?" She held him, trying to feel something there. A little something. *Anything.* And when she did not, she merely lay there, weeping against him, her hand caressing his stubbled chin, his mute face.

Next, her mind seemingly changing about it all, she rose up, with both her fists coming down, striking his thickened chest. "Goddamn you!" she screamed in a sudden frenzy, striking him again. "Goddamn you!" When she raised up both her arms, fists clenching, arms shaking, and fell entirely across him again in a broken heap, crying, "Oh, why, why, why? Oh no, oh please, God, no, please, no, no, no…" Until she could no longer say anything, only lie there, sobbing and holding him against her, feeling nothing back.

A minute passed, and another, as she only lay there in silence, sniffling, feeling the fresh horror of his stillness beneath her, when she heard a noise. Someone was walking toward her in the open-walled adjoining room. She lay there, but with her head tilted, looking up, until she saw the face appear between the studs, staring down at her. It was an old black man, tired-eyed and suspicious-looking.

She rose up again, screaming at him, "Get away from him! Don't you *dare* touch him! Don't you *dare!*" And she stumbled about until she found a piece of lumber on the floor, and picked it up and threw it at him, as he backed off into the shadows. She stood there, her chest heaving, hearing the feet shuffling away. Then she turned around, looking about herself, unsure. She looked down at Eric again and, again, felt her heart dissolve away inside her, her mouth curling in anguish. Now she stood there, crying in broken whispers, saying, "Why, Eric, why? Did you make me a promise you couldn't keep? I don't care. Now what? You see? First mom and dad, and now *you?* Now what? You leave, and you want me to—what? Go on? Is that what you want?" She stood there, shaking her head. "You broke your promise to me, Eric. You broke your promise, and I don't owe you a thing. Not a thing. Can you even hear me? I don't think you can. You're dead now, and you lied to me. The last thing you did was lie to me, wasn't it."

She stood there, sniffling, looking around herself. Then she leaned down and picked up the candle beside the mattress and began searching the room. At last, in one of the corners, she discovered the broken beer bottle. She knelt down, examining the pieces, picking one or two or them up, and finally choosing a shard of the neck, that looked like a small brown razor, just as sharp.

She went over and sat down beside her brother, setting the candle aside, and then turned and looked down at him, thinking how the face no longer looked like Eric's face. It was true. When you die, the real you goes away somewhere, doesn't it. And she wondered where he'd gone. Of course, she didn't even know if he believed in God or an afterlife or any of that. Unfortunately, they'd never had the opportunity, the time, to discuss that. And now there was no time. But she thought he probably did; that is, believe in something. Because their mother had believed. She went to mass and she had her favorite saints. So Eric probably believed in something as well. At least she hoped he did. She hoped he wasn't alone when he left there.

And what about herself? That was harder. She was more like her father, the waffling artist, going one way, then the other; doing, saying, anything in order to paint. She was probably more like that, though there had been times, thinking about death, that the idea of falling headfirst into eternal nothingness was the most terrifying thing she could think of.

Now, curiously, it didn't bother her, thinking that. She looked at her dead brother, and she looked around at everything there, and she realized she didn't care what happened now. As long as she could leave there—now. That's all she cared. To leave there at that moment, and not have to feel anything else. Ever again. Not feel. Just that.

Unthinking, she fixed her eyes on Eric, while her left hand raked the razored glass edge across the veins of her right wrist. She faintly sucked in her breath, feeling the sickly aching sharpness there. Now she looked down and saw the red blood spouting like a tiny fountain from her skin. She *had* cut herself. And she wondered why it didn't hurt more. She thought it would hurt more. Then she put the shard of glass between the fingers of her right hand and found she could barely hold the blood-smeared sliver. Her fingers were trembling, and they felt weak, until the glass slipped away. Blood dripping, she tried to pick the piece up, clumsily pinching at it until she had it again; then she raised it and tried to draw it over her left wrist; and, indeed, she did draw a fine line of blood. But not enough, not deep enough. She tried again, and her right hand began shaking so badly, she gave up, thinking: *That'll have to do. That'll have to be enough.*

Now she lay back down across Eric's chest, folding her hot sticky left hand over his clammy hand, while her right hand gently stroked his cheek, her blood washing over his pallid face and running down his neck. She closed her eyes, and before very long saw herself and Eric crossing the big alfalfa field behind Pilgrims Mercy. It was a blinding white-sun day, and the two of them were crossing the field, when she saw the other two figures approaching, and she knew it was *them*. And she held Eric's hand tighter now, feeling happy with the moment, not wanting to let it go. She thought: *We'll go meet them. We'll just go meet them.* When she heard the noise again.

Her eyes came open, and she saw the same man she'd thrown the piece of wood at. Now he was standing inside the room, looking down at her. She heard him, deep-voiced, say, "*Why*, little missy?"

She stared up at him and was surprised how he seemed to go away from her, blurring and darkening as he went, and she blinked her eyes, trying to bring him back.

He said, "I got me a daughter somewhere, about your age." She heard the rough rasp of his feet on the wooden floor, and then, in the dimming light, she saw him swipe his forehead with a shirtsleeve. "Name's Lisa, I recall. God a-mighty."

Then, in an instant, he was gone...She came awake again, looking around, and she shivered. She felt chilled now, and started to wrap her arms about that which was beneath her; then, feeling nothing back, no warmth there, she only lay there, shivering and hearing her tiny gasping breaths: *in...out, in...out.* A minute? An hour? She lay there until finally she heard that other sound in the distance. What *was* it? A blowing horn? Like Gabriel's horn announcing Judgment Day? No, not that. She listened again. Until she finally realized—a siren. A siren in the distance, growing stronger, but then seeming to fade, as her own life was fading inside her; as if both were unsure exactly the direction they needed to take. Until finally a direction was chosen, and she heard herself—her weird breathing—and the siren fade together now...softer...softer...no more.

PART THREE

WHERE ALL THE RIVERS RUN

37 ♀ A DISTURBANCE OF ATTACHMENT

The new intern just happened to be standing in the admissions office when they brought her in. He was checking on something to do with one of his cases when the "Charity Express," as they referred to it, made the drop-off, rolling her wheelchair onto the yellow-striped holding area, and delivering her paperwork and possessions (he saw, consisting of an old green knapsack) to the receiving nurse. She wasn't there long, a minute or so, when the attendant came and wheeled her down to ACU, their acute care unit, and that was that.

Meanwhile, the new intern, still standing there, felt taken back. The image of the girl—hunched forward so in her wheelchair, with the fevered whiteness of her face and arms, her unwieldy, gauze-wrapped wrists, and her terrible expression—lingered. For some reason, at that moment he thought of his own two daughters, four and six, safely at home with his wife; when the unknown girl's image returned, and fixed itself there. He shook his head and continued his conversation with the nurse; even as the anguished, burning beauty of it—of her—remained, troubling him the while, skewing his resolute focus, which he had always considered one of his more dependable attributes.

*

Over the next several weeks he heard about her in bits and pieces, mainly during the shakedowns, the weekly staff meetings (which more often than not took on the methodical, unnerving air of an oral examination), where each of them went over their caseloads with the doctors and decisions were made. It didn't take him long to realize she—the girl he had seen arrive that day—was a special case.

In the first place, no one seemed to know much about her: the charity hospital where the jagged-edged flesh of her wrists had been stitched back together; the homicide detectives that tried talking with her there; and now Sheila, the intern assigned to her case, and the doctors there at the psychiatric hospital.

There were only the few facts from the police report, stating the girl had been picked up at some abandoned North-Hollywood warehouse where she had apparently tried and nearly succeeded in taking her own life. A motel room key had been found in the girl's pocket, leading police to an economy inn, near downtown, where they got her name from the register—Connelly Pierce (which may or may not have been real)—and belongings from her room, but not much else.

Then there was the young John Doe mentioned in the report that had, in fact, succeeded in *his* attempt.

During the initial review of the girl's case, the new intern listened to the brief titillating conversation among several of the other interns, speculating as to whether the two had been star-crossed lovers, or a romance gone bad, or just exactly *what?* That, until Dr. Mills, head of the clinical psychology department, interrupted them with a frown, telling them to please stick to the matter at hand.

By second shakedown, Sheila was confirming a diagnosis of major depressive disorder, accompanied by suicide ideation, etc., with the doctors concurring. Elevated doses of Prozac were prescribed, as well as therapy; and (as the new intern observed) those in charge of their so-called mystery girl's case seemed quite confident they would be able to do with pills and analysis, what others had been unable to do by, in their opinion, less effective means.

*

By the third and then fourth shakedowns, the new intern was detecting a problem pattern. It seemed to originate in the patient's uncooperativeness, which, according to Sheila, as well as several of the other interns and doctors that had contact with her, had reached critical levels. There was a brief discussion about alternate medications, when Dr. Mills, himself, surprised the attending circle by stating he would begin his own cognitive therapy regimen with the patient in the morning.

Now that that was settled, Dr. Wilburn turned to the new intern and requested he begin his caseload reports, and the meeting continued as normal.

*

It was not until near the end of shakedown six that Dr. Hue, almost in passing, suddenly announced that because the immediate treatments available had been unsuccessful, mainly due to the patient's continued unwillingness to cooperate to any mutually beneficial degree, case number HGS-031 was being transferred to the state mental hospital at Imola by week's end.

Then the meeting, having smoothly shifted from treatment to disposition, now shifted smoothly back, as the new intern sat there, feeling surprised and even a little stricken by the announcement, the meaning of which he knew exactly: everyone was washing their hands of her—of this Connelly Pierce, or whomever she was—and she was being placed somewhere that it didn't matter whether or not you cooperated. You would be dealt with in turn, regardless. That is, on a long, even life, term basis. And you would be forgotten. That was it. He knew very well that was what they did for those types of chronic folk. Everyone there knew that. Especially Dr. Mills, whose behavioral therapy approach apparently did not have the desired effect, and who now sat mute and erect, listening to what was being said, making occasional notes on his yellow pad.

At one point, the new intern said, "Excuse me, can we return to 031, to the girl, for a moment. If there are no objections, I'd like to review her file and, perhaps, look for some, I don't know, missing ingredient we may have overlooked."

Dr. Wilburn chuckled. "Missing ingredient? Are you a closet chef, or what?"

The new intern said, "I realize this isn't standard procedure, but then I don't think she's our standard issue patient."

Dr. Wilburn said in a huff, "This is a psychiatric hospital, not a culinary school, and there are no standard issue patients."

Sheila said, "John, that's the point. She's not talking with anyone. She's checked out."

Then Dr. Hue said, "We need the bed, son. We need to move on, for her sake and ours."

"A week," he said. "By next shakedown, if I don't have something definitive—we let her go."

Now everyone sat there, unmoving.

The new intern leaned toward Dr. Mills, saying, "I did my Life Management training at Imola before I came here." He stopped and shook his head. "Please let me try."

Finally, Dr. Mills smiled and waved his hand. "Harry" he said, speaking to Dr. Wilburn, "please do a brief case review with John this afternoon and we'll reevaluate in one week. Now, if we may proceed."

After the meeting was over, one of the other interns told him, "You realize performance reviews are two weeks away, your caseload's already full, and, by the way, you've just stepped on some very shiny shoes."

The new intern said, "I just want to take a look."

"Oh," he said, smiling. "I'll bet you do. And I guess we'll just list this one under physician's prerogatives, hmmm?"

"It's not like that."

"No?"

The new intern watched him walking away, whistling, and now he wondered.

*

When he entered the room, he saw her lying on the bed, as he had seen her often, passing by, over the past weeks. He didn't say anything for the moment. He pulled a chair beside the bed and sat there, observing her. She lay there as if sleeping, eyes closed, her face revealing nothing, her breathing imperceptible. He waited, knowing, feeling, she was aware of every single little thing about her.

She *was* quite beautiful, he thought, and then chided himself. It wasn't like that. That wasn't how or why he was attracted to her—was it? No, he knew it wasn't. But there had been something more than vaguely familiar about her the moment she was wheeled before him and sat there—how could he say?—severed from everything about her to a degree it almost seemed a willed thing. Sheila had said she had checked out, and he thought he knew what she meant by that. Something had happened to her, or things had happened, and she had finally checked out. She was through with it. With living. And now she had to put up with all these so-called experts, these mental fiddlers, about her, trying to keep her alive. Trying to make her normal again, however that was defined.

He looked at her face, scrubbed clean by the aides; her features; the almost translucent texture of her skin; the curve of her pale neck against the white curving pillow. He wondered what her natural hair color had been. As now it was a mishmash of highlights, like some beauty salon experiment gone bad. He smiled, remembering how his oldest daughter had begged her mother to highlight her hair like someone she'd seen on television. He wondered what the attraction was. He looked back at the girl and said, "Connelly?"

Of course, not a muscle moved. Not an eyelid flicker.

He said, "I know something's happened to you that, for whatever reason, you don't want to talk about now. I just want you to know, should you decide you want to talk with someone, I would listen." He sat there and then said, "I saw you when they brought you here. I was standing in admissions. And for some reason you reminded me of my own daughters, I have two, younger than you. Anyway, you reminded me of them. And I couldn't stop thinking that if you *were* my daughter, and for whatever reason I wasn't there for you, I would want someone to talk with you. To try and help you. That's what I was thinking, Connelly."

He felt his heart skip a beat as she opened her eyes and looked at him. He sat there, scarcely breathing, as those eyes seemed to examine him in some peculiar, incisive fashion for a moment or two. Then her face turned away, facing the ceiling, and the eyes closed shut again.

Well, that was a start.

He stood up and left the room.

*

That evening he was still thinking about it as he played with his daughters, while his wife put dinner on the table.

At one moment, his oldest daughter said, "Daddy, why are you sad?"

He looked at her. "Daddy's not sad, sweetheart. He's just thinking about work."

"What about it?"

"Oh, someone daddy's working with. A girl they brought there."

"Is she sick?"

"Yes, a little, or maybe a lot."

"And you're going to help her get better?"

"I'd like to do that, if she'd let me."

Then his younger daughter reached over and impolitely pulled a toy from her sister's hand.

"Daddy, she took it!" his oldest daughter complained, her eyes imploring.

"Bryony," he said with a quiet remonstrative love, "give your sister back her Nintendo."

And the *look* the little devil gave her older sister, handing it back, which he saw, and suddenly felt befuddled. Then through dinner and later, lying in bed, he thought about that look; until he realized it was the same look the girl had given him, opening her eyes. And it was a look that said nothing about any sort of innate weakness or a lack of will. It was a look of sheer determination and resolve. Or perhaps a look of warning. Even threat. Whatever it was, he realized it was not a look of someone suffering from depression. Not at all. That was the one thing he was sure of.

*

In the morning, at the hospital, he went down to Lost and Found where the patients' possessions were also kept in a separate locked area.

"What's up, Doc," said the black housekeeping attendant at the window.

"Not anointed yet," he said. "But I would like to see what was brought in with S-031. It's an old green knapsack, if I recall."

The attendant went into the back and came out after a minute, carrying the pack, and dropped it down on the counter.

"Can I take it with me?"

"Doc, you sign on the dotted line, and you and Yogi can take it all the way to *Jelly*stone."

Back in his office, he opened the flap on the pack and began taking out, one by one, what was inside, spreading everything over his desk. By the time he was finished he felt as if he had just completed a sort of abbreviated archeological dig. These were the meager possessions, he realized, of someone who had gathered them over a brief, though apparently tumultuous life. The letters, especially, were intriguing, written by Connelly's (and that *was* her name) Uncle Boyd, and, even more interesting, by her brother, Eric.

After he had read them he sat there, trying to understand everything. What he knew now was that she and her brother had been orphaned at a young age, and were separated at some time after that, and had tried, unsuccessfully it seemed, to reunite. It wasn't much, and it created more questions than it answered. He looked at the old bag, the name faded almost invisible on the front: Pilgrims Mercy. It sounded familiar, and he did a quick search on his computer—finding the state children's home website.

In an hour he had the transcripts of Connelly and Eric Pierce faxed into his office, and sat there reading them over carefully. Finally, he was only left to sit and mull over what he had, which wasn't much; but, he realized, it was probably more than anyone else had had before him. And he wondered if anyone else had even taken the time to look inside her old pack, which she had obviously lugged with her from place to place over the years. Had anyone read those letters? He doubted they had.

And it wasn't until he was, with slow deliberation and great care, placing those accumulated bits and pieces of her life back inside the pack that he thought of it, and he sat there, wondering.

*

That afternoon he sat beside her bed, watching her staring at the ceiling, and said, "I've taken you off the meds. I don't think you need them. Do you?"

He watched her there, staring out, unflinching, resolved.

He sighed. "Connelly, I didn't want to have to tell you. I was hoping we could work through this, you and I, without the need for this. But that's not happening, and probably won't happen, so I'll tell you. They're transferring you to the state mental hospital at Imola where, unless something happens to change that, you could very well live out the rest of your life." He paused, giving her a moment to understand, and then said, "Is that what you want?"

Nothing. Nothing at all.

"Of course it is," he said. "You tried taking your life, and that failed, and now you're letting the system that failed you do it for you—right? Talk to me, Connelly. I want you to goddamn talk to me right now, or there's nothing more I can do for you. Do you understand what that means? Do you?"

One beat. Two. When she swallowed and looked over at him.

"All I understand," she said, "is that I want you to leave me alone. *Please.*"

"I can't do that."

She looked away.

He felt his jaw clench. He didn't want to become frustrated with her. He didn't. But he said, "It was him, wasn't it? In the police report. At the warehouse. The boy that took his life. It was Eric, wasn't it? It was your brother. It was all the family you had left, and then he killed himself; and you wanted, more than anything, to follow him."

For a moment he thought he might have gone too far. Such a look came over her face, staring out. Such an expression, he could not imagine. Though actually not much had changed there, but her eyes. Only her eyes, opening, though without any real movement, to reveal all behind them, lurking and shrouded and hidden away from everything outside, until now.

Then the moment passed, and as any such too-young life would, with too much of that life's agony coming too fast, and too fast again, she merely rolled away from him, and began to weep.

Now he was sure about it. They had, indeed, misdiagnosed her. She wasn't suffering from a disturbance of self-regard (as one of those signposts of depression they were trained to look for), but of attachment. And there was no major depressive disorder at all, but rather a profound grief at work, a sense of utter loss, of deep and anguished mourning for the only other human being she may have so cared for. That was it, and that was all. The girl terribly missed her brother, and, as she now saw it, had nothing left to live for; just wanted to be left alone.

Then he realized it may be too late, regardless.

*

For the next several days he sat with her, trying to talk with her, to reach inside her somehow, to no avail. He finally met with Dr. Mills, reviewing his findings, and, together, they met with her, with similar results.

Afterward, however, Dr. Mills' conclusions surprised him. They sat in the doctor's office, where the new intern heard him say, "I agree she appears to be in a place where depression and grief are coexisting, creating this momentary debilitation. With the facts of her life, as you've related, there appears to be more than a few things at work here. But I see no cause for alarm."

"Even with her current state?"

The doctor shook his head. "What you're seeing is the healthy, normal process of a deeply abiding grief working through itself. As I've said, this is quite normal, and necessary. The fact is, after what she's been through, if she were *not* so grieving, would I then have cause for alarm. That is, were she not letting go and eventually moving on with her life, would that then be an unhealthy thing."

"That's what you think she's doing? Just letting go and moving on?"

"So it appears. John, these depressive symptoms, as they're associated with her bereavement, are generally non-clinical and transient in nature; and, again, this awful torment working through itself will eventually pass. I'm sure of it."

"So what can we do?"

The doctor shrugged. "Stand aside. Let nature take its course. The one thing we don't want to do now is try and treat the symptoms, which would only be further disruptive to her." He shook his head. "She lost her brother. We don't have anything to give her now. Now it's between her and all that passing; and, of course, her own understanding what she must do, once she's able."

They talked awhile longer when the doctor suggested it was probably time to transition her back into the social services system. "That's where she came from," he said. "That's where she's lived her life. And unfortunately in cases like this, there's not much else to offer her. I'm sure they can arrange some out-patient counseling; some therapy when she comes around. That's what she needs now. A group home, perhaps. Some familiar faces. At least a caseworker to talk to when she feels like it. Why don't you set that up with the admin office and we can move on."

The new intern said he would take care of it.

*

However, before beginning that process (as he was loath to do), the new intern sat in his office and tried to think of something—of anything—else; that is, other than return her to that same bureaucracy that had, in effect, dismantled her life, piece by piece, to begin with.

Sitting there, his gaze came to rest on the old green knapsack, still there on the floor beside his desk. He reached down and picked it up, opening it on his lap, and again removed the thin, rubber-banded packet of letters inside.

He set the bag aside and once again began going through the letters, rereading them, thinking how, perhaps, he might write to someone—to that wayward uncle of hers, Boyd, or the cousin he mentioned, Cousin Elizabeth—when something happened. At that moment, something fell, hitting his leg, then to the floor. He looked down.

Another letter had, apparently, somehow become stuck behind one of the envelopes he was shuffling about in his hands. He leaned down and picked it up, when his heart skipped a beat.

The letter was unopened and had been sent to Connelly at some address in New York. Then his eyes rose to the sender and his heart skipped again: It was from her—from that same Elizabeth McCullough, and mailed, according to the postmark, the previous year, from an address in Tucson.

He hesitated, wondering why in the world she hadn't—then put all that aside, opening a drawer and taking out a letter opener. He slipped the edge beneath the pale bond and slit the envelope open. He next set down the opener on his desk and, trying to still his shaking hands, withdrew the letter and opened it, and he began to read:

Dearest Cousin Connelly,

How wonderful it is hearing from you at this moment! Besides, what does it matter if anything makes any sense, now that you've written to me. I only regret that it's taken so long, and I can only imagine what you've endured, the meantime.

Sweetheart, I knew both your mother and father. Do you know when they were married they went on a two-week backpacking trip across Mexico (your mother told me that was the only thing they could afford), and they stopped by the ranch on their way home. Jack put your father on horseback and took him fishing into the hills above the ranch, while I taught your mother how to can peaches and shoot a Colt. They both even took a turn on resetting some fire-blistered wall stone around the original Walker homestead (which still lies in ruins at this moment), but your mother was already pregnant with Eric then, and they had to leave soon after.

Regardless, I recall we had a wonderful visit, and Jack and I talked with them several times on the phone after that. But they seemed so caught up in their new married lives, with you kids coming on and all, that when we tried to call them the last time, and found out someone else had their number, we didn't think much of it. We figured they had moved the family on somewhere, and they would contact us again when they were good and ready.

And now this.

My poor sweet dear, had we known when it happened, Jack and I would have moved mountains into valleys to get you two with us. As it was, I guess the Lord thought we already had enough to take care of, helping birth a brood of squalling midnight calves, but we always wanted a family; even went down to San Antonio a time or two to see about adopting. But one thing or the other kept getting in the way. But we had no idea about you and Eric. And now time has gone and done what it does best, which is to leave us behind, taking opportunity with it, as my own dear Jack has done to me, already several years gone. That's when he had his first and last heart attack, age of forty-seven years, riding fence up along Settlers Ridge; and wouldn't he be proud to know he had gone that way, rather than lying off sick and withered somewhere, till the end trickled from him like blood from a tick bite.

I closed everything up after that—that is, sold all the stock and let the cedar and mesquite eat up the sweet grass pastures that Jack had nurtured so hard along. Then I up and moved in with some of Jack's kin here in Tucson, doing a little teaching at the local university, and not really having any direction or purpose lately that would befit a correspondence of this sort.

Cousin, you say you're curious about me. Who I am. What I'm like. Am I even real or not. And that your own life has not been going so well lately. Well, that is such a mouthful of wonderment and revelation that I won't even try and fit all the necessary answers and opinions here. Because I can also ask the same things about you; though my own life has become more humdrum than (as I hesitate to imagine) the way yours may have turned out.

Yet we are both Walker stock, and that's a fact we must live with and, I believe, embrace; at least, in lieu of any other good and suspect fortune. In any event, I would very much like to meet with you and spend some time with you, even then, having no idea what your current circumstances are. I see you are now living in the North, and that is not the worst thing that can happen to you, though it lacks the potent for bragging. Still, I can come there if that suits you, or you can come down here. It's no matter to me. I know you probably have some good stories to tell me, and I can tell you some, if you've a mind. And I would so like to finally hold Emily and Michael's child in my arms (and Eric, if we can find him).

Connelly, how amazing it is to me that you have decided at this time in your life that you should come to know me, and vice versa; as I have lately been hungering for something back into my own life that I have been unable to put a finger on, until I read your letter. Then, hearing your words and imagining *what you are like, I knew there was something at work beyond my simple speculations and unfocused middle-age desires. And I am now only satisfied that it has happened, and want for nothing else now but to see you. So listen well, Cousin. Don't spend your time trying to put together an answer to this (as I am sure, as well, you are near out of pencil by now!), but call me. Right now when you read this. I enclose our house number at the bottom, and there is always someone wandering past the old black thing, should it go to ringing. Call me, girl, as I am riding literally burrs under the saddle till you do.*

With fondest thoughts of our (many) conversations to come,
Yours,
Liz

He sat there motionless. Not long. But long enough to try and briefly grasp at the quirkiness of fate. Of things critical and needed, and so close that we might reach out and touch them; that then pass by, unnoticed. Only, with neither logic nor reason, to return to us at some future time, now (as Cousin Liz might say) full of wonderment and revelation.

Then he dropped the letter on the desk and reached for the phone, his trembling finger punching in the number; when, after a moment of final indetermination, he heard the old black thing, somewhere far and away, go to ringing and ringing.

38 ♀ COUSINS

When Connelly opened her eyes, the first thing she saw was her mother leaning near the door, holding a stuffed pink bunny rabbit in both arms against her chest, and looking over at her. Then she closed her eyes, and opened them again, and saw another woman instead; but somehow there was the sense of her—the way she stood, the overall sense of the way she appeared, or her sense of self—that was her mother, even though she wasn't. Instead, she was a pretty, middle-aged woman: tall and slender, with her long brown hair pulled and clasped conveniently to the side. She was wearing a man's rumpled, long-sleeved linen shirt, jeans and cowboy boots. The jeans were weathered to a milky ink and worn long and tight over the boots. The boots (what she could see of them) were scuffed and still had traces of dried mud about the stitching. The woman was smiling so faintly, it appeared an afterthought, like her mother would smile sometimes.

"You're awake," she said. Then she stopped as if unsure what to say, before saying, "I'm your long-lost cousin, Liz." She hesitated again. "From Texas, remember? You wrote me that dear, sweet letter a while back, and I wrote you back, but I never heard from you after that. Then, just last week, someone called me and told me you were here. So now I'm here."

The entire time she was talking, Connelly only stared at her, without expression.

Then this woman who called herself Liz came over and laid the pink rabbit upon her chest, saying, "I wasn't sure what you'd like—"

Without thinking, Connelly grabbed the rabbit up and threw it at her, hitting her in the face and shoulder before it fell to the floor, and said, "I don't need your fucking *rabbit*."

The woman stood there a moment, seemingly amazed, the color draining from her face—the scarlet flush to chalk—in spite of herself. Then very slowly, carefully, she bent down and picked up the rabbit and set it on the metal nightstand next to the gray-plastic container of water.

"Well, at least you can still talk," she said quietly. "That's good. I like talk. It's how people get things done."

Then she turned and walked to the door, where she stopped and turned back again, looking at her. "Connelly, I don't know where you've been or what's happened to you. But I would like to know. That is, if you want me to. I'd like to try and understand. If you'd let me."

Then she turned and went out, closing the door behind her.

Now Connelly lay there a long while, listening to the faint hospital sounds, coming from under the door, that she knew by heart. By now she could even tell who was walking past, by the sound of their footsteps...And now *she* was here. Why had she come? *Why?* When that was the worst thing she could think of that could happen now. Now that Eric was dead (and he really was dead, as she'd told herself over and over, until she was sick of it), that was the *worst* thing that could happen now. Now she didn't need anyone. Not any longer. She'd decided that one night when she had finally accepted, inside herself, how it had all ended. She didn't need anyone now. Now it was too late. And Eric was dead. And she didn't need anyone now. Not now...until she slowly reached out and picked up the pink rabbit and looked at it. Then she pulled it to her—against her face, shutting her eyes and smelling its sweet-scented fur—and began to cry into it, holding it against her and crying.

*

She came back in the evening, after the sun had filled the curtained window with golden brightness, before dissolving slowly and then quickly (as she could imagine the sun sliding over the far watery earth) into darkness.

Before she came, Connelly wondered if she even *would* come back. Maybe she was too mad now and she was gone. Maybe she was on the plane right now, flying back to wherever she came from—when the door opened, and there she was again.

Connelly leaned back, relieved, but looking away from her, toward the darkened window.

After a moment, she heard her say, "Well, I see you and the rabbit finally made up."

Connelly turned toward her. "I didn't ask you to come here."

"No, you didn't. Someone else did. He told me he found the letter I'd sent you awhile back, unopened, and he read it and called me." She watched her cousin, watching her back, and saying, "The question is, now that I'm here, would you like me to leave? I will if you want that. I'll go right now. Go on with my life, as it is, and you can go on with yours. Happens all the time."

She stood there, waiting.

Connelly looked back at the dark window. "You can do what you want."

Cousin Liz said, "If it's all right with you, what I want right at this moment is to sit down a spell." Then she just came and sat down beside the bed, leaning back in the armchair, looking at her. "I been down at the car dealer, having the truck serviced, and there was a salesman there that near walked and talked me to death, looking at new ones. But I told him no. Jack was partial to that old Ford, and it doesn't use much oil."

Connelly looked over at her. "Your husband's dead?"

"That's in the letter," Liz said. "Had a heart attack a few years back, and I've been living with some of his kin in Tucson."

"Oh," she said. "Well, I'm sorry."

"And I'm sorry about Eric. I wish I could have met him, having seen the pretty look on your mama's face when she had him inside her."

Connelly shut her eyes and then opened them. She didn't want to talk about Eric now. She said, "What about the ranch?"

"I closed that down when Jack died. I just didn't have the desire for any of it then. But now I'm thinking about going back and, at least, living in the house again." She looked over. "That's why I came out here. See maybe if you wanted to go back there with me. I could use the company."

Connelly eyed her warily. "You mean just drive there? All the way to Texas?"

"That's the only way I know to get there," Liz said. "Less they let me put Jack's pickup on the airplane."

She leaned back against the pillow, astonished with the whole notion of it, spreading out before her, darkly unknowable and biding its time. She said, "But you don't even know me."

Liz said, "It's a nice piece there. I'm sure we'll know each other better by the other end."

She turned back to her. "No, I mean you don't *know* me. You don't know anything about me. You don't have any idea what you're getting into with me."

"Nor you with me, now that I consider it."

They were still sitting there in diffident silence when the girl came in with her food tray, setting it on the stand and positioning it over her. When she left, Connelly stared down at what was there. "What if I don't like it? What if I want to leave?"

Liz shrugged. "Bus tickets are cheap," she said. "And they'll take you most places you want to go."

Connelly looked up at her. "So there're no commitments then. No promises."

"Not unless you want to make them."

"Well I don't."

"Then I guess we're both just along for the ride."

Connelly hesitated, as if she were considering from among several equally reasonable options displayed right there on the food tray before her, before finally pushing it away. "All right then, I'll go. I'll go to Texas with you. But I probably won't like it."

"Whatever keeps your girth tight, sweetheart," Liz said back, picking a piece of lint off her pants leg.

*

But it wasn't working, Connelly realized as soon as they drove out of Los Angeles, heading east into the desert country; when the barren emptiness of that countryside seemed to fill her with her own too-familiar kind of emptiness. As mile after mile went by, moving ever-closer toward what Liz referred to (in that softly ironic manner she assumed that almost always hauntingly, lovingly, returned her mother's presence to her every time she heard it in her voice) as the Great Southwest, she envisioned them driving and driving and then suddenly dropping off the very edge of the sunblasted earth into an abysmal, everlasting emptiness they, or more likely she, could never escape.

Or worse, they would actually arrive somewhere—to a promised destination like Texas or somewhere—when, with an equal suddenness, it would somehow be taken away from her, as it was always taken away before. As she had learned so well how it was better not to hope, not to count on a thing, and then you wouldn't be disappointed again. And how it was better to stop it now, dead in its tracks, before it was too late. Before you got used to it, and started liking it, or loving it even, and then it was gone, and she had to start over again. She had learned that, over and over, until—when they finally reached the state line, where she knew, just over it, at any moment, or the next day or week, it *would* all be gone again, she would just wake up and it would be gone— she told Liz she'd changed her mind. She wanted to go back now. Back the way she'd come, which wasn't that far behind her yet, she added.

She told her this, sitting in front of Millie's Stateline Café, with what (she assumed) was the Great Southwest, spilling out before them just over the invisible state line and down the wavering highway. Liz looked then like she had been gut punched, having all the way there been chattering like a blue jay about the things they would do once they were "home," as she kept referring to it, until Connelly wanted to scream, with the suffocating nicety of the vision filling her mind then.

Now Liz sat there, leaning against the steering wheel, looking over at her. "You sure about that?"

"Yes."

"Well that was quick."

"Yeah, well, I thought about it and I realized it just wouldn't work out for me, Liz. For either of us. So it's better to stop it now, before it's too late."

She saw Liz sitting there, watching her, she felt, with some manner of reverse introspection she was not used to. As if she could peer into her mind and examine what was really going on there. Then Connelly realized that maybe this was what family was about. This was the difference between someone who just knew you, and had to believe what you told them, and someone who shared your very blood, and knew as well as they knew their own breathing what you were about. At least that's what she felt, sitting there with Liz watching her like that.

Then Liz said, "And you realized all this since the four hours ago we left the city, is that right?"

"Yes. It doesn't take me long. I mean, I've been on my own my whole life, so you just learn how to make decisions on the run, so to speak."

"I see."

Connelly shrugged and turned away, looking out her window. "You know, Liz, that doesn't mean we can't be friends and all. I mean, we can stay in touch, if you want." She looked back at her. "It's just that, I know from experience, I'd be better off on my own right now."

"That's fine." Liz nodded toward the café. "Millie's got good hamburgers. I stopped here on the way over to see you. You feel like a bite before you get on that bus? It'll most likely be dark before you get back to the city again."

"Whatever," she said, feeling her voice draw away from her, as if something else had taken over her power of speaking.

Then, inside the café, she excused herself and went to the bathroom, where she immediately broke down, sobbing in wretches and heaves over her unfixed fate and what she was doing now, doing to herself again, which she had no idea. She stood in front of the sink, looking at herself in the mirror, her horrible, wretched, red-eyed face, hating herself, and hating Liz now for making her hate herself, for making her have to decide about things that—seeing them now, so close, so face to face—were simply too much to bear, to deal with at that moment. After all, she'd just lost Eric, and now Liz wanted her to turn around and go live in Texas with her, just like that; and it was just too much to deal with. Too uncertain. So she hated her for making her deal with it—with everything—then. She hated her relaxed Texas manner, and how everything would be just fine, once they were both home. She hated her for that, especially.

After she splashed water on her face, she went back out and sat down in the booth, across from Liz, who was sitting here, laughing and talking with Millie herself, according to her name badge, just like they were long lost friends or something.

She saw Liz look over at her. "What do you want on your hamburger, honey?"

"I'm not hungry."

"We got real good hamburgers," said Millie, who was standing there, gaunt and frazzled as someone, she imagined, that would go live on the edge of the desert; and she was leaning to one side, snapping gum and grinning down at her.

Connelly looked up at her. "I said I'm not fucking hungry."

Millie got wide-eyed.

Liz said, "Sweetheart, what's the matter?"

"Nothing. I'm just not hungry, that's all."

"You were just a minute ago."

"Well, I changed my mind." She glanced over at her. "That's another thing you don't know about me, Liz. I change my mind a lot. I'm very capricious like that, you understand?" She tried to smile now. "Anyway, where I come from, a lot can happen in a minute. I mean, I've had some minutes where my whole life's changed around—you know? Can you understand what I'm saying, Liz, or is it too much for that Texas-thick homespun fucking head of yours?"

"Oh, *Lordy*," Millie said, shifting to her other leg and watching.

Liz sat there a moment, just looking at her. Then she said quietly, "No, I understand. I know you've gone through a lot. I know your world has probably been turned upside down more than I could ever imagine. But, sweetheart, that still doesn't give you the right to be rude to people. To be mean to them or lack manners. As if you were the only one who's ever had their life turned upside down."

"I didn't *say* that, Liz."

"Honey," Liz said, her voice rising, "to tell you the truth, you haven't said much of anything that's made sense since I've met you. In fact, about all I've seen you do is feel sorry for yourself—which you do real good, by the way—and treat everybody and everything else as if it just can't quite measure up to what's happened to poor little old you."

"I'm leaving," Connelly said, starting to get up.

"No—you're *not*, young lady!" Liz said in a voice that basically brought everything in Millie's to a dead halt.

"I don't have to listen to you."

"You *will* listen for one damn minute," Liz said, "and then I'll go next door, to that bus station, and buy you a ticket to any damn place you want to go."

"And I have my own money."

"You may have, but you don't have enough to keep from listening to what I have to say to you. As if you're the only one life's been mean to. Why, I'll bet you a walk to Georgia every single person sitting here, listening to us right now, can tell you something bad enough that's happened to them that would make you sit back and reconsider that notion. What—you think you're the only one who's lost someone? You're the only one who wakes up in the middle of the night, night after night, knowing they aren't there anymore, and what are you going to do now? When there's nothing you can do but lie there and take it till morning, then all day till night again. And on and on, until you just get sick with grieving, and you'd cut out your heart, if you knew that would lessen it. So what? So I lost the only man I ever loved like that. And so now I have to figure out how to go on and live my life, without going stark raving mad over it. Then I got your letter and for the first time since Jack died I had one little something that caught my interest again. You sounded like me in that letter. Like you were hurting and you just wanted to find a way to stop hurting. And that's how I was. So what I hoped was you and I could go figure out a way together. Nothing definite. No commitments and no promises. Just take it one day at a time and see what happens. Because you can't really understand how hard it was to walk away from fifty-seven thousand acres of heartache and toil that Jack and I loved more than anything, except each other. And he died loving it. And now I was taking you back there, maybe to let you see a little bit of where you came from; or maybe because I needed you, Connelly, I needed you *bad*, and I had only hoped that you might need me back, just a little, and that we might do something with that. But then maybe I was wrong. Or was I? I mean, don't you think you might need me, just a little? Or no? You have to decide. That is, whether or not you're gonna go take *your* money and go buy *your* bus ticket out of here, or whether you're gonna tell me, right now, what you want on your goddamned *hamburger*."

She stopped then, as sudden and breathtaking as a face-slap, and sat there, waiting.

Everyone around them in the diner, in fact, was seemingly stopped in midair, waiting as well.

Connelly, meanwhile, feeling pinned back to her seat, stared wide-eyed across at her. This was *it*, she realized. This was what it was about: Family. Mother. Love. Concern. Anger, even. This was it. Somewhere along she'd forgotten, and now she remembered. And now she had it again, as well. Right there in front of her. She finally had it again. After a moment, she swallowed and said with an unsure pliancy, "Mustard and onions?"

"Got it, honey," Millie said, slipping her pad into her apron pocket and turning away, gum snapping.

Now she saw Liz sitting there, red-faced, looking around them. After a terrible long minute, she watched her lean toward her and whisper like an embarrassing secret, "They got good rhubarb pie here too, you're interested. You ever ate rhubarb pie, girl?"

In spite of all, at that moment she felt her torn, twisted heart give way to itself, when she replied as quietly, "No ma'am."

They sat there now, in their bruised and settling silence, waiting for their hamburgers.

39 ♀ GONE TO TEXAS

The deeper they went into it (a different kind of wilderness, she realized, from where she came), the more the land receded and the sky took dominance. Not to say the land itself was not remarkable. She was astonished by the color and shape and coarse texture of it, land and sky melding, creating a vaster panorama of evermore-powerful nature, seeming to soak up Liz's pickup's sun-blanched green into its own greenness, traversing it, as all was absorbed in its entirety. Until she felt as if she would be overwhelmed.

*

They finally stopped in El Paso, where Liz checked them in to the downtown Camino Real with its Tiffany-blue, cut-glass dome, and where they both took long hot showers and ordered room service. In the afternoon, while Liz went shopping, Connelly tentatively lay in her new gift-shop-purchased bikini in a secluded corner of the rooftop pool, flipping through magazines, while warily watching the cute Latino waiters come and go, shifting easily from English to Spanish and spangled forms between; all the while observing the shifting, changing colors and strange designs flowing about her, and that gave her the feeling of having set down in some exotic new world.

In the morning Liz took her to the city museum; and it was there—wandering along hallways and through rooms filled with *retablos*, or small folksy oil paintings of the Catholic saints; and *santos* or *bultos*, the little hand-carved devotional statues; and bizarre potpourri of woven and hammered and fired and glazed ethnographics; and a collection of colorful tribal masks; and a mosaic of a prehistoric village made from shellacked chert gravel; and another collection of Milagros or devotional charms; and, finally, the five-hundred-year-old child's serape, stained with blood, announcing the arrival of the conquistadors—that she realized, for the first time, how far away she was moving from everything left behind, and closer to everything, before her, she knew nothing about.

*

From El Paso they followed the border into the Chihuahua Desert (She had asked Liz, having examined the glove-box maps, what it was like—that great emptiness following the Big Bend of Texas, south into Mexico). And seeing it there made her think of the night Clair was out, and she and Richard had stayed up, smoking a joint and reading Dante's *Inferno*. They baked a pan of chocolate chip cookies and ate them, passing the plastic milk jug and leather-bound poem back and forth, taking turns reading aloud the Italian pilgrim's quest to seek out his beloved Beatrice and live in eternal paradise.

Now she looked into the desert and tried to remember how many circles of Hell there were—eight, she thought, or was it nine?—and the warning above Hell's Gates: *Abandon all hope, ye who enter here*. She looked out and wondered what circle they were crossing now. The Plain of Fire, perhaps? Circle Seven, as best she could remember, with its rings of wretched sins, its dreary lusts.

They wandered back and forth, occasionally bumping into the Rio Grande, before turning back. One time on a whim, where the river was wide and shallow, she waded across to the other side and walked around for a while, with Liz behind her, watching her in silence from America. In the distance were the strangest looking mountains she had ever seen—enormous and misshapen, barren and brown, instinctively uninviting, yet oddly alluring. She walked down along the edge of the muddy river. There were people there, camping out. It looked like they had been there for a while, with an old International pickup and camper on its back, and small dilapidated bus with its attached awning sagging on rusted poles. The people were gathered around their campfire and cooking pot, watching her: several men and women, a scraggly throng of children. They seemed interested in what she was doing, and their expressions did not change when she approached them.

She raised her hand, acknowledging them.

One of the men nodded. Everyone else simply stared at her: this odd gringo girl, with her red and green hair, standing wet-legged before them.

She waved a hand toward the mountains, her voice echoing away from her in the bleak hollowness, surrounding. "*Qué llama usted ellos?*"

Everyone turned and looked toward the mountains, staring at them as if they had never seen them before. They looked back at her. The man smiled and said, "*El Despoblado.*" She looked at him, shaking her head; then she nodded her thanks and turned and waded back across the river. Liz sat waiting for her on a large flat rock beneath the twisted remnants of what appeared a very life-tortured tree.

"Have fun?" she inquired.

Connelly glanced back across the river, then over to Liz, whose self-taught Spanish, she knew from hearing her, was much more forgiving and encompassing than her own public school variety. "What does *El Despoblado* mean?"

Liz shrugged. "Like something empty or uninhabited." She looked around, frowning at the sun. "Well, honey, if you're done breaking the law, you about ready to go home?"

Connelly looked around, taking in the primitive setting one more time. "Ready as I'll ever be."

*

Liz had described the San Miguel Valley and its surroundings to her in such detail, driving there, that she thought she must already know exactly what it looked like. Indeed, when they began the ascent over a western range of small, but wild-looking mountains, she turned to Liz and told her, "The San Miguels."

Liz nodded.

Now the road was narrow and steep, with one switchback after another coming at them. These mountains, she saw, were very different from the barren brown mounds they had been traveling through. These were covered with enormous oak and cedar-brake and thick scrub; and in the deep draws were big pecan and cypress, while short stiff grasses grew on the steep rock-faced meadows above. Going into a turn, two motorcyclists roared around them on a dead-blind curve, and she held her breath, watching them leaning back sharply the opposite direction into the next curve and disappear around it forever. There was another humped rise before them when there appeared a sign that read: San Miguel Pass.

"This is it," Liz said, reaching over and squeezing her arm. "All of a sudden, five years seems like a long time gone from here."

They began the descent into the valley. There were more switchbacks, separated by sudden ravines, slowly evening out into broader concaved stretches of tangled tree and shrub, struggling en masse on the mountain facing. Various dead animals littered the roadside and buzzards gathered in pockets of feasting and flying in slow, lingering circles above them. The first civilization she saw was a tiny apple orchard, the dwarf apple trees in crooked rows across the sparse meadow. She looked at the orchard, passing, and thought it appeared to be struggling simply to remain there. Everything she saw, passing by, appeared like that: gritty and weathered in the long sun, struggling to remain. Before long, the road began to even out into longer stretches and broader curves, winding through the close rough hills. At one point, rounding another curve, a bridge appeared, and going over it she saw the San Miguel flowing like a wide, silky-green ribbon below. Enormous cypress grew along the banks, interspersed with splashes of white sun against the bright limestone banks, and they were over it.

Now the larger southern mountains, Liz had called the Bandras, and separating them from the long desolate and descending plain down into Mexico, appeared. They were always there, always in the distance, as they followed the river, running beside it, then pulling away. After several miles there was another bridge and, crossing it, she saw the waterfall in the distance, swallowed as suddenly by the sheer red and yellow cliffs, and the closer hills resumed, stretching off again into those distant, sky-piercing mountains. After a mile they came to the crossroads, or the Corners (she knew) as Liz had called it, and stopped at the four-way stop.

"This is what we got at this end of the valley rather than a town," Liz said. "Of course, Comanche Falls is at the eastern end, toward San Anton. That's also the county seat. Pretty little place."

There was the Rimrock Feed Store on one corner with its rusted weathercock staring back down at them, and wide front dock with two old sagging pickups backed up against it.

"I swear," said Liz, "those same two trucks were parked there the last time I drove out of here."

On the corner next to it, as Liz had explained, was the old brick blacksmith's shop, now turned into a welding and machine shop, as well as ranch equipment outlet. Across the narrow farm-to-market highway was the little limestone Drop Biscuit Café.

Liz said, "That's where your Aunt Sally—God rest her soul—always sniffed up her nose and said the pie crust wasn't flaky enough, and said Miriam Thompson was using sugar in her cornbread to lure the tourists."

To the right, Connelly knew by heart, was the quaint, tricolor-flagstone Raintree's Eat Gas Gro: Ida's Famous Valley Apple Pie, a combination gas station and grocery store, with its two small red-and-white gas pumps before it, round globes atop, with their red-winged horses in the center that would glow at night. The crank handles, just as Liz told her, were still mounted on the side

Liz said, "When I was a little girl, daddy or Uncle Max would always let me crank them around, and they'd say, 'Commence the petrol,' every time we filled up the old truck."

Connelly listened to her, remembering (driving for hours through that desert) what she'd said about time and families; and how some remained vibrant and widespread and deep-rooted for generations, or even centuries, or millenniums, possibly; and how others, like theirs, weren't so lucky, burning the bright flame (or, perhaps, the flickering matchstick) for their handful of time, before wars and disease and the unfairness of life and poor decisions and poorer genes and just plain bad luck took their toll.

How, in the beginning, an English empresario named Lord Richardson had received the original million-acre grant, which included the San Miguel watershed, from the Republic of Texas in 1843. The idea was simple: Provide access for the brave and the foolhardy to move deeper into Indian Territory, settle it, and thereby provide a buffer for the more-established settlements to the east, also under constant threat by their Kiowa and Comanche neighbors, who, Liz said, didn't think much of the idea.

"That valley, in particular, was just plain sacred to them," she said. "It was filled with the mineral springs that healed them, and the colored clays they used for paint and pottery, and it was a favorite hunting ground. And they were dead set against giving it up. Meanwhile, the white settlers, like John Walker, had pieces of paper that said they owned it now. So it was gonna be hell-no-end good to come of it. One side started killing, and then the other, and no one stopped. Those early Texans were tough and mean and opinionated, and, more than anything, they believed they were in the right. So did the Indians, but they happened to run out of people before they could prove it."

And how, in spite of the mutual deprivations, as Liz referred to what happened there, the Walker family had eventually flourished, reaching their peak just prior to the Civil War.

"Then we lost half our menfolk during that whole mess," Liz told her. "Never did recover. After that, we sort of limped into the Twentieth Century, and through it, until I looked up one day and there was just me standing there. That is, until I got your letter."

Now they sat there, in front of the red and white gas pumps, and Connelly heard her say, "I guess it takes a certain, special type of fool that would want to wrestle a living from this grub." She looked over and smiled (Connelly was learning) her sad, brave smile, when she was facing any uncertainty, and said, "Anyway, it's just you and me now, honey."

Connelly looked out her window, into the hills above. "Well, I think it's beautiful, in a sort of terrible, twisted way."

Liz laughed. "That's as good as I've heard anyone describe it. C'mon, let's go get the keys from Ida and Wilburt, and I'll introduce you."

"Ida and Wilburt?"

Liz nodded toward the store. "Ida won't bat an eye—and I've been gone these five years, still calling me a Walker, after all the time Jack and I were married. And Wilburt will tell you about the old days, and invite us to dinner, which is what we call lunch around here."

Connelly heard the screen door's low growl and the tinkling bell, and followed Liz inside. Now she stood there in the semi-darkness, looking around the old L-shaped room. To the right she saw the long cypress plank counter, with an old mechanical cash register at one end. A few shelves stood in orderly rows before it, carrying a mixture of food and sundries and some hardware. A reach-in cooler was at the far back of the shelving, and the oak barrels between the shelving and counter were filled, she saw, with iced soda pop and beer.

At the break in the L and forming, more or less, the room's divide sat a large black Franklin stove, surrounded by the small cluster of empty chairs where Liz had told her she'd sat beside her father and Uncle Max, sipping her grape Nehi, and listening to the men talk for hours. To the left were similar tables, covered by the same checkered table cloths, and more chairs. Beyond these, the grandfather clock, Liz had described, stood tall and severe-faced in a far corner. And Connelly stared at the long brass pendulum swinging methodically, eternally, below. Above the clock and, in fact, peering down at them both from various vantage points on all the high surrounding walls were the heads of the past local animal population displayed; while two enormous ceiling fans, one on either side of the room, turned in slow silent unison.

Next, an old woman appeared through a doorway behind the counter, small and wiry, wiping her hands with her patterned apron and adjusting her eyeglasses to see them better.

"Well, Liz Walker, I'll swear," said the woman (Connelly figured was Ida, since she didn't bat an eye). "And ain't it been a while."

She watched them hug, and then turn to her.

"Ida," Liz said, "this is Em Walker's daughter, Connelly; only, you recall, she's a Pierce now."

Ida clasped her hands in surprise, her pleasant face seeming filled with memory. "Sam Walker's kin, come home at last! And aren't you pretty as, I hear tell, Sam thought he was; and, I know, got you mama's beauty all over again."

Ida hugged her and kissed both of her cheeks, and then she held her at arms' length, looking at her. "Liz told us about your folk, sweetheart, and we're truly sorry to hear what happened. Why, it seems like yesterday, they both sat right at that table and had pie and coffee, twittering together like two lovebirds."

For some reason, the notion that her parents had once been there like that, so close and twittering together to where she was now, unnerved her, and she said, flustered, "Thank you, ma'am."

Then Ida waved her hands and went and stood in the doorway behind the counter and hollered: "Wilburt. *Wilburt*—Liz Walker's here. Yes—*that* Liz Walker. Now put down that ice tea glass and bring the key ring to her place. Key, Wilburt. Yes—k-e-y. Lord have mercy."

Connelly heard the gravelly voice in the distance, drawing closer: "So she finally showed up, did she?"

"Yes she did, and aren't you glad for it anyhow," Ida replied. She cackled and looked back at them. "I reckon he's done wore himself out worrying about you, Liz. I think he nearly got in his old truck and started out looking for you at least a dozen times."

"Now, Ida, you know that's a damned lie," Wilburt said, coming around the corner—tall and big-boned, his white hair bristling to a full peak above his broad forehead. He came out and hugged Liz, saying, "You're staying for dinner, ain't you?"

"Maybe supper, Wilburt," said Liz. "We're anxious to see the place."

"Well, like I told you along, cedar and mesquite's taken over the grass," he said. "And we chased some pasture-squatters out a year or two back. Had some blue northers blow in, so you got a few mile of the old fence down. Otherwise, it's mostly the same since Jack died."

Ida said, "Wilburt, this drop-dead pretty thing is Em Walker's daughter; though, you recall, she's a Pierce now."

Connelly felt herself pulled into powerful arms that hugged her enormously. When Wilburt released her, he laughed and said, "I reckon your great-great granddaddy just wasn't the ranching kind. And couldn't they have used him up there then. Why, I remember when I ran fence with Max and Colton Walker and Charlie Youngblood back in '55, after the war. We was all just kids then. Spent weeks up yonder beyond Purgatory Ridge, and then on over the divide. Back then, place had sweet grass to your chin, and Charolais bulls the size of freight cars. Everyone stocked their remuda from Walker mares back then."

"Lord have mercy," Ida said, shaking her head. Now she suddenly took up both of Connelly's hands into her own, telling her, "Child, I do believe you have the prettiest shade of purple in your hair I've ever seen."

Wilburt nodded in agreement beside her. "Reminds me of that Mexican rain sage up on Werther's Mountain at sunset," he said.

*

From the main highway they took the narrower FM county road south, until it again met the river and ran beside it. They followed its twisting course for two or three miles, when Liz suddenly slowed and turned onto a gravel drive and stopped. Now they sat there, staring back through the shadowy trees at the huge iron gate, with its great wide band of iron encircling the sinuously winding overhead *W*.

"Well, this is it," Liz said. "Your family homestead."

The pickup crept up to the gate and Liz got out, fiddling with the padlock, and swung it open. Then they drove on between large pastures on either side, overgrown with scrub brush and the young cedar. Not far along they came to a narrow bridge over the river that fronted the property, and Liz stopped again.

Connelly looked over at her. "Do you think it's safe?"

Liz smiled. "Well, let's go see."

They got out and walked onto the bridge. About thirty feet below ran the San Miguel River, wide and green, with the towering cottonwood and old-testament oak and nub-footed cypress and great swathing-limbed willow lining both banks. They stared down into the gentle current, and then peeked between the timbered superstructure and saw steel beams resting on the massive stone piers.

Liz said, "Great-Grandfather Franklin tore down the old wooden bridge that used to be here, and washed out every flood, and had some German engineers put this one in at the turn of the century; and Uncle Max always said you could take an army over it."

They drove on, crossing over the bridge and around the hill's curving base. The road wound up through stands of broadleaf forest and through more pastures overgrown with scrub. Once, a whitetail buck bounded across the road before them, disappearing into the tangled thicket like a fleeting phantom. They continued on, reaching the top of the hill, when she saw it—saw everything at once—and said, "Oh, Liz, stop. Please."

Liz stopped the truck and they sat there, looking out.

In the distance, across the wide rolling pasture before them, sat the old limestone house and barn. The homestead was positioned on the flattened top of a long gradual rise, and behind this abruptly began the steep incline of the mountains they had always seen in the distance, but were now looming just before them. Sheer limestone cliffs towered high above the ranch where hawks flew in haphazard circles about the airy heights. Precarious-looking rocky slopes, with wide talus aprons, pulled away from the cliffs, turning into the rising and dropping summit that disappeared off into the distant haze. The road circled around the small lake, or tank, as Liz called it, with its clustered mix of red maple and birch at the far end, and a small pier, now collapsed, resting partway across the water's serene surface.

Liz had tried to tell her about the house—a three-story, burnt-crème limestone she referred to as a sort of Romanesque revival, altered as necessary for that particular environment and locale, and based on the designs of the nineteenth-century architect Henry Richardson, with his grand Medievalesque forms, his daring motifs, mixing power and grace, and revealing the flock of cross-gabled roofs, spreading out among conical-roofed towers, and a myriad of Roman arches supported by their legion of strong squat columns—but Connelly had not been able to imagine it, to truly understand, until she saw it now, tucked back within those rugged burning hills, with its accompanying gambrel-roofed limestone barn, and as a place, Liz had added, of worn hardwood plank and rough stone where men in boots had walked for generations.

Finally, they drove around and parked in front of it.

The stone steps led onto the wide veranda that ran the width of the house, turning partway alongside it at both ends. The porch was empty except for a myriad of spider webs, stacked bowls of tumbleweed, and two hickory rocking chairs, sitting side by side and forgotten along it. The front door was tall and made of wide thick planks of hand-carved, unfinished cypress. There were panes of leaded glass in the top half with the iron-cast Circle-W brand leaded into its center.

Connelly said, "I've always wanted to open a door with a skeleton key."

"Here's your chance."

She unlocked the door and shoved it open, hearing it creak away from them in a wide arc on rusty hinges. She said, "If this place isn't haunted, then I don't know anything."

"We always did keep a few of the old family spirits around for company," Liz said. "I'll tell you, it gets awful lonesome out here."

She saw an enormous hall, capped by three wrought-iron chandeliers, pulling away, dividing the house into its left and right halves. Halfway along the hall to the right, a curving mahogany staircase ascended in a gradual arc back over it and out of sight. Everything, she thought, seemed fixed and ready to face eternity. Linens were draped and taped over all the furnishings, a forgotten museum; faces stared down at them as they toured the hall: stern, unforgiving countenances of men, and the more patient and receptive of women—her kin, she knew, near and far.

They walked through a mahogany-paneled office where she glanced Jack McCullough's PhD in Ranch Management hanging on the wall, right beside Liz's in American History, and other awards and pictures of them both getting awards; then out the opposite door and into the smoking room beyond, where (she imagined) men once gathered and talked, lighting up their cigars and pipes, through a parlor, and then on into the massive front library tower, and stood looking out through a series of double-hung windows that ran in an intermediate arc in the front half of the round room, with oak-shelved books filling the spaces between the windows, and around the wall to a height requiring a rolling ladder and platform to reach those dusty, furthermost volumes, ascending. The view through the windows, she saw, stretched down across the pastures and lake toward the distant forest.

Next, they wandered down adjacent hallways, through rooms Liz recalled little stories about, and entered the dining room, with a centered, uncovered table made of four-inch hickory plank and cypress ties that seated twenty; the high-back black-hickory chairs padded with horsehair and dyed burlap neatly in place; the air of past festivity lingering still, as if the room had witnessed so much, and now could not quite understand the purpose of so long a silence.

Then came the scullery with its iron sinks and hand pump and cutting tables, opening into a deep and narrow dry storage room. Liz took out her pocket Buck knife and cut the tape over one of the cabinets lining the wall and opened the tall doors. Stacks of white-glazed porcelain and red earthenware presented themselves; rows of heavy porcelain cups, hanging. Meanwhile, the kitchen, through an archway above, seemed a world unto itself, with its great river-rock fireplace covering an entire wall, an ancient double-barrel shotgun mounted over the cypress mantel; its double, gas-and-wood Red Chief stoves; its ground limestone counters, and eight-by-eight beveled butcher-block centerpiece, around which were clustered hand-hewn dwarf oak chairs; finally, its row of windows, opposite the fireplace, which offered up the startling vista of sunbaked mountains, looming and eternal.

They wandered upstairs, not saying much as they went, through bedroom after sitting room, sewing room after privy, until Liz had brought her to the far upstairs room of the rear tower, with its conical ceiling, high overhead, made of eight pie-shaped wedges of copper cladding over cypress beam. A dozen tiny octagon windows of colored, beveled glass laced the perimeter, allowing a rainbow of light beams to cross and crisscross the room, depending upon the set of the rising sun, the passing cloud. It was like standing inside a slowly shifting kaleidoscope.

Connelly turned toward her. "Oh, Liz, can this be mine? I mean, can I sleep here?"

Liz stood there, seeming pretty and wan in the colored light, leaned against the wall. She shook her head. "And why shouldn't that surprise me."

"What?"

"When they came, this is where they wanted to stay, your mama and daddy, and that was the bed they slept in." She shook her head. "Now I see you standing there, and I see them all over again; and isn't time funny coming back on itself like that."

She stood there a moment, not really thinking about the sequences of time, but rather seeing her mother and father, lying there in their naked, wet embrace, and time held still for those long nights of lovemaking, yet unrevealed.

*

Against Ida and Will's protestations (who wanted to fix them up a proper food basket to take with them), they had purchased grape Nehi and jars of peanut butter and jelly; then went over to the Drop Biscuit for a loaf of fresh-baked bread; now they spread everything out on the butcher block and ate sandwiches, before anything else.

As she ate, Connelly looked out the windows at the stark, lovely hills, and the mountains, she thought both bleak and inspiring, and then around the spare kitchen; and there was the tiniest initial feeling of connection, she felt, listening to Liz chatter on about having the co-op turn the electricity back on, and making up a grocery and necessity list for Comanche Falls, which was entirely lost when Liz said, "Then we've got to get you enrolled back in school. I would guess you've got some catching up to do."

"Can't we wait, Liz? I mean, at least until January?"

"I suppose we could," Liz said. "Everything's shutting down for the holidays anyway. And that'll give you more time to get settled in."

They finally compromised. Liz would speak with the counselors and they would do the placement testing before the holidays. Then she could start classes in January.

That was better, Connelly thought. She needed more time—for everything. For everything she was feeling and not understanding; and more time with Liz, just the two of them there, together and alone, before that would change as well, as it always did.

*

In the afternoon Liz took her on a tour of the immediate ranch-grounds: the enormous barn and calving shed and outbuildings and corrals, all charmingly arranged, and all now in such levels of disrepair that Liz questioned aloud the sensibility of her plan for resurrecting the old place.

"But that's for future worrying," she said. "There's something else I'd like to show you now."

A narrow road wound up the hillside, opening into a small courtyard, containing the remnants of a desert garden and a pretty little stone house where, Liz said, the ranch manager and his family lived when needed.

The door to the house was not locked and, opening it, they saw patches of dark red fur darting everywhere.

"Litter of fox," Liz said.

"Little darlings," said Connelly. "Don't they call them kits or something?"

"Among other things, if you're trying to raise chickens and have a few fresh eggs."

They softly shut back the door and continued on up the hillside, the road soon becoming a wide stone path, which eventually entered into the flattened mouth of a narrow, fierce-walled canyon; this ascending toward the first long grade of mountain above. Not far inside, they made out the outline of another long, low, stone structure ensconced back within the brush and briar and seemingly omnipresent cedar scrub. They worked their way slowly around the nearly impenetrable brake, until Liz had pieced together for her the outline of "John Walker's original homestead," now roofless and unbeholden to time, along with the attached long-shed and stable. She then showed her the piece of wall her parents had worked on for a week, before their time ran out and they went back to California.

Connelly stared at the short wall for a moment, and then looked away. "What happened to it all, Liz? It looks like there was a fire."

Liz took her arm in her own and they walked a short distance up a gentle rise behind the site. Beneath a spreading elm was a small, moss-covered historical marker built of stone and granite and, according to the attached metal plate, placed there by the San Miguel Historical Society.

Connelly, holding on to Liz, read aloud: "*The Parker-Walker Thanksgiving Day Massacre: On Thursday, November 27th, 1862, at this site, as well as the Twain Oak Lookout on Lost Woman Creek watershed, members of the Benjamin Walker and Nathaniel Parker families were attacked and murdered by a Comanche raiding party. Herein lie the remains of Connelly Walker and three of her children: Colton, age ten; Sarah, age seven; and Samantha, age of six months. Benjamin Walker Jr., age four, hid in a nearby corncrib, and was the only survivor.*" She stopped and looked at Liz. "She has my name."

"No, you have hers. Your mother stood right here once, where you're standing, and she obviously remembered it when you were born."

She looked back at the marker. "Well, it must have been terrible."

Liz said, "As I've been told, Ben Sr. was a captain in the Confederate cavalry at Fredericksburg at the time. But he'd taught his young wife how to line up the rifles by the door, and how to shoot them. The morning after, when the men rode up from Comanche Falls, they found two head-shot Indian ponies in the front yard. Uncle Max always said it must have been hell's own ride for the time. After the war, when Ben came home, he became a Ranger for twenty years before he could ever settle back into ranching. Died blind as a bat, ninety-six years old, at a nursing home in San Anton. Aunt Sally said Alice Tucker tended him as a girl. Said he never did talk about anything. Liked to listen to the baseball games on the radio."

In the twilight, they descended the hill to the main house, where they washed and then drove back over to Will and Ida Raintree's for supper.

40 ♀ A NEW BLOOD-SOAKED COUNTRY

At night she would lie in bed and listen to the long, drawing silence. There was an emptiness to the silence that seemed to invade her body, her anxious mind, until she was made to get up and go sit by one of the little windows, which she would swing open and stare out into whatever was there, abiding in the darkness. Bats and owls, usually, flicking by in the moonlight. Once, she heard what she thought was a woman screaming; and that Liz told her in the morning was probably just a mountain lion; and she thought—*that*, or perhaps a mountain lion *eating* a woman who was screaming.

Otherwise…the great encompassing silence of that place.

*

During the day, tiny airplanes flew over that Liz said the ranchers used to get around, because everything was so far apart. Once, they heard actual gunshots like thunder, echoing down to them from canyon to canyon.

"Hunters," Liz said. "If Jack was still alive, he'd be right up there with them." She shook her head. "I can still just *see* him, coming over Humphrey's Saddle on that old piss-ant sorrel of his, leading the pack mule, with his gutted buck slung over its back, and grinning like a badger."

She shook her head again.

*

Connelly realized, coming back there like that, after five years, had not been easy for her. Maybe that was one of the reasons she wanted company. She also realized, in the beginning, when Liz shut herself up in the office like that, to just let her be.

The first time, when she'd knocked at the door to ask her something and Liz told her to come in, she'd done so. And when she entered she saw her there, with papers and things scattered out before her on the desk, and she knew immediately they were Jack's papers and things; and then the look on Liz's face, trying to tell her, "Well, it's all right, honey."

But she'd excused herself and gone out anyway. After that, when the office door was shut, she left her alone.

Regardless, Liz only mentioned it one time after that—Jack, and what she was thinking about it all. They were sitting at the big hickory dining table, eating canned tomato soup and crackers one night, when Liz suddenly looked across the room, toward one of the doorways, and said, "It's just like he stepped right out of this room, and he's fixing to step back in, any minute."

She sighed and went back to her eating.

And that was that. She never mentioned him like that again. Like how much she was missing him. How much she was hurting. And how her entire life was changed around, and what would she do now? Never again.

Connelly had an image in her mind of Liz brushing off her two hands, cinching up her jeans, and going on. That is, she still loved him more than anything; and she probably still thought about him often, or all the time; but she was moved on now. There were things to do, living to do, and so she moved on.

Then she realized if she hadn't been paying attention she never would have noticed it at all.

*

Still, for her own self, there was something else besides the great emptiness, the aloneness, of that place that was bothering her. She could feel it inside her, as she'd felt it from the moment she first opened her eyes in the hospital, and realized she was still alive. Lying there in the hospital bed, she thought about it, and realized it was her secret. It was her small piece of knowledge that she had now, and she kept with her now, just like the gold-hearted locket she kept around her neck. There was also the question that came with it, that kept asking itself inside her head, and that she still couldn't answer, no matter how much she thought about it. It was vexing. And being alone at night in that high stone tower, staring out at that unfamiliar moon-washed landscape (feeling as if she'd been set down on the blue-lighted moon), didn't help matters any.

Regardless, she hoped Liz wouldn't see it; that is, how she really felt inside, but figured she probably did. She was always asking her if everything was all right, and was there anything she needed. She hated that. That Liz already had so much on her mind, and so much to do, and now this.

But rather than thinking about it too much, and worrying about it, she tried to help Liz out as much as she could. She tried to stay busy, which wasn't hard to do around there.

In the first couple of weeks they opened up the house again, taking down all the muslin sheets, covering everything, and dusting and sweeping and scrubbing everything down. They made several trips into Comanche Falls, buying supplies, going by the high school to enroll her. It was all nice, she thought. The picturesque little Texas town by the river. The old stone high school, with the hitching posts and corral behind it. It was all nice, she told Liz.

Then the way Liz looked at her, knowing all right, but not saying a word. As if she knew it was something, the one thing, she had to leave alone. The girl had to work this one out on her own, she seemed to know.

So, instead, one day Liz bought them both horses. They drove over to a rancher she knew and purchased two small bay mares, both five years old and fifteen hands high, that Liz said they needed in that kind of country. The rancher called them Sugar and Teets, and they just kept the names. After that, they went riding every day, each day a different direction; and she got to know the countryside better and better. Soon, she had to admit, helping out Liz and riding Teets into that terribly beautiful backcountry, she did start to feel a little better.

*

But at night the feeling returned, overwhelming her with the knowledge of what she knew, and didn't know, and what she would do about it. What *could* she do?

Also, it didn't help matters that lying there night after night and thinking about everything to do with the two of them, and what they were trying to do, seemed overwhelming as well. It was like a horrible mirror image of what she felt about herself. The fact that they were both there, surrounded by, as Liz said, "fifty-seven thousand acres of *mess*," didn't help at all, she thought, each and every night, lying there. It was just too much. And she had no idea what they would do about it. Just as she had no idea what she would do about her little piece of knowledge, which was simply this: When you almost die; that is, when you decide to give up on living, and you cross over the line (even a little) into death, and then come back, a part of you stays behind. A part of you stays dead. A part of you does not come back to life, even if you, your body and you, are made to do that.

That was her secret.

But the question that came after that—first, in the hospital, when she realized she wasn't dead, she wasn't with Eric like she wanted to be—was harder. And that was: What now? She wasn't supposed to be alive. At that moment (feeling the still muteness of his body beneath hers), she didn't *want* to be. So what now? What was she supposed to do now, since she had not made it there where she wanted so badly to go. And then, thinking about it, another question came to her, which was: Why? Why should she be the one still living, when the three of them were not? Why her? And why should she live at all, for what purpose, when every part of her (including the dead part), lying there night after night, knew it was all nothing but a *mess?*

*

But Liz, she felt, was closing in on her. Even though she was trying as hard as she could to pretend otherwise, she felt exactly like Liz was pretending back with her, even if she did seem to be losing patience. And there were moments she expected that woman to grab her and shake her and say: "Girl, get *on* with it! With the *living* part. You've done that other, dying part, and that didn't work so damn well, did it? So—get *on* with it now. What's holding you back?"

"I don't know, Liz," she imagined herself saying back. "I just don't see the purpose in it. I mean, I should have died back there, in Los Angeles, with Eric. Why didn't I? Why? And what am I supposed to do now? Because I didn't expect to be here. Anywhere, in fact."

When she imagined Liz looking at her and shaking her head. "All I can say, girl, is you're bringing forty mules to plow an acre of land, and don't you feel silly? Well, don't you?"

Of course, she knew Liz would never say that, at least to her, where she knew it might hurt her even more. And she felt comforted and a little relieved by that understanding.

Instead, on Thanksgiving Day they ate dinner at the Raintree's, with Will telling his wonderful stories (all to be taken, according to Ida, with a healthy pinch of doubt); and Ida clucking about them, with her roast gooseberry duck falling tender off the fork, and complaining she just couldn't make good biscuits or cobbler crust anymore, now that they'd gone and changed the flour processing somehow; then insisting they take a basket home with them for later.

That afternoon, when they got home, Liz suggested they take the horses up the Lost Woman Creek watershed and visit the Parker site.

"When I was a girl," she said, "folks would come round on Thanksgiving Day, morning or afternoon, and visit one site or the other and lay flowers and such. No one much goes either place anymore; especially the Parker site. Nothing up there, really, but a near-gone memory and a view."

So that afternoon they rode up the watershed to the outlook, beside the old twain oak, both sides, Liz had observed, thick as hogsheads and spreading in two opposing westerly directions out over the canyon precipice, following the line of hazy and diminishing, sun-reddened hills. Before that, Liz had showed her where the Parker cabin once stood, now a scattered pile of stone barely visible back through the underbrush, as well as the nearby memorial marker and common grave. And when she had apparently shown scant interest, Liz shrugged and walked back down beside the old tree.

Connelly followed her, when Liz turned on her and said, "So how long are you gonna keep at it?"

"At what?"

"Holding all the world's troubles inside you; while they're all fighting to get out; and you're fighting to keep them in."

"Is that what you think?" she answered, averting her eyes.

Liz smiled now and said, "Any event, I think Ida's cobbler's calling us."

They began the ambled ride back down the short steep mountain.

Once there, and the horses cared for, Liz suggested they eat their Thanksgiving supper leftovers on the library table, where they could watch the night come.

Sitting there, looking out over the cluttered pasture, Liz said, "I've always been amazed how, what seemed to be the worst sorts of problems, are sometimes made easier by talking them out, or even by the simple sound of another lone voice, talking it out, giving their side of the matter."

"Look, Liz," she said, "I know you only want me to feel at home here. And I *do* feel that. But there're things that sometimes talking doesn't help. They go deeper than that. And they're things that I just have to work through on my own. Do you understand?"

She saw the hint of hurt in Liz's face, and when she nodded how the hurt turned to a thin wavering line of resignation there, as she looked around the room. "Well, I for one plan on doing some serious reading tonight. There's a front moving in, and the norther rain falling, and nothing makes the cold, deep-night lusciousness of that sound so good like a good book in a warm bed—what do you think about it?"

Connelly shrugged. "I don't know. Maybe later."

"All right then."

She watched Liz moving around the curving tower wall, selecting two or three books for herself, when she found something else. "Why lookee here—and didn't Jack and I think this was lost some while back.

She came and sat down beside her. Connelly looked over and saw something odd—a small red-velvet volume that appeared to have been burned to a near fatal degree. The brown leather-enforced edges were scorched, and the binding was blackened and curled. Liz held it carefully in her hands and opened the cover, saying, "Miriam Walker made the note inside. That was another of your cousins, thrice-or-so-removed, and a pretty enough writing hand to make a robin cry. She wrote: *Being the Private Journal of Melissa Montgomery Parker, rescued from the ashes by Captain David McNeil, 2nd Cavalry, and telling her journey from Pittsburgh, Pennsylvania to Comanche Falls, Texas, 1858-1862.*"

Liz looked over at her, her eyes bright with interest. "And speak of coincidences, since we were just up there today."

"Who is she—Melissa?"

"The Parkers' teenage daughter. Of course, she died with the rest of her family on that Thanksgiving night. Her father, Nathaniel, was the most popular preacher in the valley then; I'm told, handsome as a carriage salesman, which always kept the pews filled. But, unfortunately, unlike Ben Walker's dark-eyed little firebrand with her line of Henry rifles, the Indians met no resistance with that poor peaceful brood."

She held out the diary. "Why don't you take it with you and read it when you can't help yourself. But treat it nice. Those Historical ladies have been after me for years to write an introduction and have it published. I guess now that I've re-found it again I'll have to start thinking of something to say."

Connelly took the little volume from her and thanked her; then she told her she was tired after their ride, kissed her good night, and left her sitting there in the darkening library, with lightening flashing with approaching intensity through the windows.

*

That night, with the thunder clapping hard down against the copper sheathing just above her, and the bright pressing explosions of light revealing the dark interior, she dreamed again of that dead part, rising up inside her, and taking her over inside; where she found herself standing alone in that storm, exposed on the rocky precipice and looking down into the dark abysmal sea below; and the deadness filling her mind, her heart, and telling her to jump ahead now, just jump; because that was the only meaning to it; that was the only purpose; otherwise, she would remain lost, as before. While she tried to hold herself together and wept into the lashing eternal torment surrounding her there. As the storm descended around her, unforgiving and demanding her to jump, as the deadness finally filled her up, overflowing; until there was no longer a point she could think of, no longer a reason to remain. And she jumped ahead, plunging down into the liquid blackness, feeling herself consumed…

She sat up in a breaking cry, reaching out one-handed into the darkness, and staring ahead, startled and afraid.

She realized the violent front had passed, and now she sat there listening only to cold norther rain falling; then slipped back beneath her sheets, pulling them up around her chin, staring out.

The dead part, she knew now, was the not wanting to let go part. Let go of them. Not wanting to proceed in her life without them. Even though she'd told herself, over and over, she *had* let go, she *had* gone on—she hadn't really. And when she cut her wrists and lay down across her dead brother, she was lying with the deadness of them, her parents, as well. They were all lying there, side by side, swathed in the deep stillness of the earth, and the forgotten silence of time, now lost. And she felt comforted by that. By the not caring. The not having to care. Comforted. And she shuddered.

A flicker of lightening filled the room and she sniffed, wondering. She thought: What was the point of burdened living, when all the meaning and purpose of it, for her, seemed to have gone away? Was taken away? What? That is, if life was really that cruel, that neglectful and uncaring, and everything that meant anything to her was taken away, why should she participate in it? As it seemed like the most awful trick imaginable, to be given life, and then have it filtered away (like Liz said they filtered dirty milk through cheesecloth), and all the essence squeezed from it, leaving you with only the dregs if it, and little else.

Knowing that, wondering what she might do about that, gave her an uneasy sense of herself, her impatience. Of *course* she had Liz now. And she finally had a home. So why couldn't she just accept that, be grateful for it, especially, and stop worrying and contemplating about things she could do nothing about? She twisted anxious about in her bed.

Then she stopped, holding in her breath a little, then releasing it. Well, she thought, maybe because she *could* do something about it. No matter what. No matter how bad. She could do something. And it wouldn't be the foolish mess she'd made with it before. Because she knew now. She knew, more or less, what to expect, and she knew exactly what she had to do about it. Now she suddenly felt filled up with a kind of wicked strength, feeling a little unclean and furtive, knowing that. That is, that she'd finally reached the end of it, and that was all there was of it, and what else could she do now?

But, of course, she always had that. The one option a burdensome, uncaring life could not take from you. She had that. But, at that moment, she didn't feel eased by that knowledge. For some reason, it just seemed to add to the awful weight of it already there.

Another aggravated, anxious minute passing, she reached out and turned on her nightstand lamp…and there it was, lying there where she'd laid it. She looked at it, the little fire-curled, mahogany-burnt diary, somehow surviving and arriving there, through the past century and a half of blind chance and endless circumstance, to her bedside.

She picked it up and stared at it. Now she leaned back against her pillow and opened up the cover, reading the note the pretty-penned Miriam Walker had left behind, and imagining the cavalry, led by that Captain McNeil, arriving on the awful scene. Then she turned the page when suddenly the delicately exuberant, variously slanted lavender script jumped out before her, as she read: *A Settler Girl's Thoughts and Whimsies; or, This Being the Most Private Journal of One Melissa Montgomery Parker (Me!)*

Connelly sniffed and again turned the page. The first entry, dated the 15th of March, 1858, from Pittsburgh, read: *So this is it, after all. I have finally reached the end of it, with nothing more to do. We are all going to this place called Texas…somewhere, I am inclined to imagine, at the very end of the earth. It is, according to my good father, God's will. He has been called upon to minister the needs of the people yet abiding there. So this is it. This is everything to do with it. God has spoken and we are leaving for Texas one week hence. I must confess I am beside myself with distress and the unknowable results of this journey…*

*

She read through the remainder of the night, finishing the journal not long before she heard Liz, faintly below, preparing her morning coffee and piece of toast.

The very last entry was Thanksgiving evening, 1862; the same night, she knew, Melissa was murdered with her family, and their cabin burned to the ground. It read: *The same Indians returned today. They knew there was feasting, I presume. Mother fed them some scraps, which they spit out, and then asked my father for whiskey. They used their sign, making their fist and jerking their thumb past their mouths. My father told them there was no whiskey, which did not appease them. But mother gave them blackberry cobbler and apple pie as recompense, and they ate it greedily amongst themselves, using their stained fingers as scoops, and then rode away. Their ponies looked tired and full of wet grass and ill-treated.*

Now I am tired. My belly is full, though father had jokingly chastised me throughout our meal, concerning the deadly sin of gluttony. I told him I cared not for his sins. It was Thanksgiving and I was hungry with the expectation of it; furthermore, I expected I would have leftover yams for breakfast. He laughed and reminded me how I need mind myself; that a blue norther was approaching, regardless. Tomorrow he and my grandfather and brothers must bring down our few cattle from the upper pasture. His laugh is so wonderful. And I am so tired. I will go to sleep now and dream of those yams...

After she'd finished, she laid the diary aside and lay there, for some reason, feeling somewhat guilty and ashamed. What was she thinking now? What did she feel? She thought about it, but couldn't decide. All she kept hearing was that yearning, hope-filled voice brimming over inside her head; and all she was aware was that voice's desire for life—however so it be—so overwhelming her own desire (now in some kind of shameful, trenchant retreat inside her) for oblivion. And she shook her head.

She rose before long (again, feeling Melissa's urgency to grab onto and fashion her own awkward, fated existence into something uniquely her own, pushing her along) and went downstairs to the bathroom, washing her face, and then on down to the kitchen where Liz sat, writing her morning letters; and she went over and kissed the side of her face; then she got her coffee.

"Well," Liz said, "I guess you rode out the storm okay."

"I guess," she said quietly. She sat down across from her, looking into her eyes.

"Everything all right?"

She nodded and sat there.

"Well," said Liz, "I'm going down valley this morning for some things. Want to come?"

She looked up. "I may take Teets back up Lost Woman today."

Liz glanced at her. "Is that right? Then you be careful up there. You never know when some groggy-eyed rattler's going to come out and try and catch some winter sun."

She promised her she would, and they sat there, having their coffee, not saying much else.

*

It took her almost an hour to reach the site again. Then she tied off Teets to a bush and worked her way back through the brush to the exact site of the cabin. Now she could see everything in her mind: the old porch and the cabin's outline. Working her way along, she discovered several mossy stone that Nathaniel and Eustace Parker had laid as foundation almost one hundred and fifty years prior. She closed her eyes and remembered the excitement Melissa and her family felt, moving into their new cabin, sleeping in it the first night, the sense of safety and well-being they felt. *A home at last!* the day's entry was closed out.

She went back down to the old split oak tree, looking out across the far, blue-tinged country before her. Bending down, she ran her hand along the rough bark, down into the deep cleft between the two trunks, feeling with her fingers. Now at the very brink of being forever swallowed up by the expanding rings, she found the remnants of the three initials—*M...M...P*—carved there. There were the ridges surrounding the furrowed paths Melissa had dug with her father's whittling knife, being handily chastised for returning it dull, and the whispered confession in her journal that night: *Although there would be no lack of mouths, surrounding me, speaking of its impropriety, at that moment today, leaned back so against the old fat tree, I dared to imagine another set of initials paired with my own. A boy—do I say? A boy to know? A boy to hold hands with and walk along the hackberry ridge? As I have never known such earnest desire (causing such a deep-clefted tingling of its own within me), and cannot imagine the source of this indecency, though it still pines within me, nevertheless.*

I am a "green child," according to father. Green as new corn. As such, I am obliged to think wholesome thoughts in preparation for my wholesome life. Alas, I must observe—what wholesomeness is there in this place? Though I felt not to mention it at the time (my entire nature incredulous at the circumstance), not two days on the trail out of Port Galveston, the oxen were halted as father intervened in a terrible quarrel. One man in our group had stabbed another for no worthy reason. A piquant wife was involved, I believe. Regardless, the man lay dead, pouring out his life's waters onto the ground, and we were made to commence our evening settlements early for his burial. Following the most decent rites, our trail master proclaimed the necessary justice, and the other poor fellow, a wretched drover named Sam Wells, was subsequently hung from a nearby cottonwood tree until dead. We buried him anon, though with a scarcity of ritual hardly likely to guarantee our place amongst civilized nature, and everyone went hastily to bed.

Thereupon, that being my first real view of this place where father had promised us pastures of peace and plenty. Instead, we have traveled to the road's long end and find ourselves in a new blood-soaked country, I could not previously imagine. And now I sit here, singed with guilt of my earlier desire to fashion, as yet, some unknown boy's initials above my own. To walk with him, hand in hand, in the cool gardens of twilight, and lay down my head awhile upon his comforting lap. Goodness!—is there no end to my impiety? Be it done.

Tonight I will say an extra prayer that God may protect me and us and have mercy on my wicked soul. And tomorrow I will help mother to salt the feral pork, hanging thusly purple-veined and swollen in the cellar. What more is there to do?

When she at last rode back down the mountain, she thought she understood the difference she now felt. That is, she now felt ready to walk in her own cool gardens of twilight. That, for whatever reason, she had been given another opportunity to do that. And thinking—what would *she,* her settler girl, have given for that? For new life stirring. For new hope. So fragile and precious. Now shifting in the saddle, guiding Teets around a last precarious switchback, overlooking her and Liz's ranch (and, she knew now, her home at last), was when she felt the deadness finally leave her. It lifted out of her like a dank spirit, and she suddenly realized she was ready to live again. More than anything, and for the first time in so, so long, she *wanted* to live. And that was the difference.

41 ♀ THE HELP

Days passing that early spring, as if she was coming awake after a very long sleep, she opened her eyes and there everything was—surprisingly, entirely different. This place. These people. As if she were seeing it—all of it—for the very first time. And she thought how she probably had Melissa Parker to thank for that, coming into such a place and somehow making it your own. Melissa had taught her about that.

Then she remembered how Mr. Gladdens, her academy painting instructor, told her how any artist worth his salt needed a sense of place, of belongingness, to succeed. Maybe that was part of it as well. She thought how one day she might try to paint again. She might. So maybe it was important that she had that then, or at least understood it better. Especially the belongingness part, which she considered, standing with Liz in the hair-coloring aisle of the downtown Comanche Falls Rexall Drug Store, picking out her particular brunette tint and saying, "I mean, what's the point *now*? *Here?*"

Because the sense of place part, she thought she had down; or at least some of the rules, or laws of nature, governing it. Such as: When two women, regardless of shared temperament or well-versed intelligence, find themselves a-straddle *such* a place of *such* proportions (regardless as well that it's fauna-less and flora-less), everything eventually breaks down. And that actually was the point—with the fences down, and the pastures overgrown with renegade scrub, and the well-house pump dying in the middle of morning showers, and the roof leaking, and the varmints inside the attic eating the house wiring, and (the straw that finally broke her) the toaster catching fire and burning up the last piece of Ida Raintree's homemade bread—Liz had driven down to Comanche Falls and hired three old out-of-work cowboys at ten dollars an hour.

She fired the first one the third day in a row he showed up drunk. Then she found the second one going through her lingerie drawer in her bedroom and sent him packing as well.

Connelly observed all this in bits and pieces, between going back to school, and listening to Liz fuss about it at supper, and couldn't help but smile about it. She also saw how the third cowboy, a broken-down, ex-rodeo bull-rider named Clyde McKinney, saw what was happening and stayed out of Liz's way, hanging out by the barn, pretending to fix things.

One Saturday morning after breakfast, she had wandered down by the barn, sipping coffee, and observing the way the stonemasons had fitted the wall-pieces together, just so, when Clyde wandered up to her. His gnarled hands were shaking, and his blood-shot eyes were filled with the wonder of his predicament.

"That mother a-yours is shorn hell on wheels," he said.

"She's not my mother, she's my cousin." She noticed the texture and color of the stone and of Clyde's leathery skin against it.

"Well, all I know is she run old Dill and Seyton off with nary a nod. Them boys is still turnin' circles."

For some reason she couldn't understand, she thought she liked Clyde. She thought as well Liz was probably going to run him off the coming week. Now she looked at him there, hunched down against the stone and staring warily back toward the house, and said, "Clyde, can you do anything? I mean, besides ride things?"

"Hell fire, can't well do that anymore."

"So what *can* you do?"

Clyde considered it. "I fixed a little fence there-bouts."

"Well," she said, "we have lots of fence down. My advice to you is start fixing it, and keep fixing it, and don't look up."

Clyde nodded. "Need a snuff-full a materials, I reckon."

"Liz has an account at the feed store. Why don't you get what you need and bring her the receipts."

The old man nodded again and shuffled off toward his pickup to make the drive cross valley.

*

The following weekend, while Liz was frying their eggs, she stepped out on the front porch, coffee cup in hand, when she saw a different old pickup, sitting sagging and askew, halfway down the driveway. Through the windshield's reflection, she could barely see the two heads inside, staring back at her. She sipped her coffee and waited and, after a respectful interval, the driver's side door opened gingerly, and a small bent-back man stepped out. Hispanic, she saw, probably in his late fifties, and, she guessed, even more probably an illegal. The look on his face was the epitome of discomfort and illicitness. As he approached, he removed the white straw cowboy hat from his head and wrung its rim round in his small hands. He was mostly bald with a half-ring of gray hair around the base of his perspiring skull, and had a neatly trimmed gray mustache. His eyes were two soft-edged almonds, floating in a bowl of honey. His smile was anxious and kind.

"*Señorita.*" He nodded, looking away.

She hesitated. "Can I help you?"

The man looked back at her, perplexed, and then turned, scanning the forest beyond the big pasture. He was looking at the land.

She wracked her brain for a translation. "*Le puedo ayudar yo?*"

He looked back, smiling. "I speak English, *señorita.*" He hesitated again and then said, "My name is Jesus Navarrete. That is my wife Angelina." He nodded toward the pickup, and then waved his hat toward her in a beckoning motion. The passenger door opened and his younger wife emerged and came hurryingly toward them, plum-plump and smiling. When she arrived, they both stood there, arm-in-arm at the base of the stairs, smiling up at her; and she half expected them to break into song.

"*Señorita,*" he said, "we have heard it said you are looking for help."

She hesitated. "Maybe we are. What can you do?"

"Oh, my wife—she cooks very good. And I do whatever is necessary."

She nodded. "I don't suppose you're legal. I mean, do you have your cards?"

He nodded fervently. "*Sí, señorita,* we are on the list."

"The list?"

He bowed his head. "There would be no trouble, *señorita*. I have heard it is a tradition in some places."

"I'm sure," she said.

Behind her, the front door opened and Liz came out. "Sweetheart, our eggs are getting cold. Is something wrong?"

"These are the Navarretes," Connelly told her. "They heard we needed help."

She saw the smile on Liz's face. "Do you have your cards?"

Connelly saw both their heads drop like stones. She said, "They're on the list, Liz."

Liz shook her head. "I'm sorry. I mean, we could certainly use the help, but—I'm sorry."

Angelina looked up at her husband, whispering, "*Qué dice ella?*"

"*No tienen nada,*" he whispered back.

And she began to quietly weep against his shoulder.

"Liz, couldn't we do something?"

"No, *señorita*," said Jesus, "we understand. We are sorry to bother you."

Next, with a gesture of great reluctance, he turned his wife around and headed her back toward their truck. Once they were seated again inside, they both sat there, staring out.

Liz said, "Are they just going to sit there?"

"Where can they go?"

"Home for starters," she said. "Sweetheart, I can't believe you're ready to break the law at the drop of a hat, or, in this case, that woman's tears. They're obviously plying our emotions and you've fallen for it."

"*No tienen nada,*" she said.

"Oh, stop it. Now let's go eat our cold breakfast and then go haul our water over from the Raintree's."

When they were finished eating and came back out on the porch, the old truck had not moved.

Liz said, "Well I'm going to go tell them something."

Connelly watched her tromp out to the pickup to speak with them. When Liz came back she avoided her eyes, looking hard off somewhere, saying, "He asked me if they could take a nap before they started back. I told him it was all right but they had to leave right after that." Then their eyes met and Liz said, "You ready to go haul that water?"

Liz went past her into the house. In the distance she saw Clyde, head down, stringing new fence wire on the new cedar posts he had set the day before. Then she looked back at the pickup sitting there with Mr. and Mrs. Navarrete sitting inside, looking back at her, and she turned and went into the house to help Liz gather the water jugs.

*

When they returned with the water—forty plastic gallon jugs, they had to fill and haul twice each week for their drinking and their cooking and their meager sponge baths—the pickup was still sitting there.

After they'd lugged the water inside, they began making egg salad sandwiches for dinner.

Liz sighed and said, "We may as well make them a few for the road. And there's a thermos for ice tea. You can take them out a basket and tell them *adios*."

When she brought out the basket the both of them got out and thanked her. They stood there, looking around.

Jesus said, "This is such a beautiful ranch. How many vaqueros does your cousin have to help her?"

"Just me," Connelly said. "And him."

They all looked over at Clyde's narrow bent back, stringing wire.

"That is not so many," Jesus said, smiling.

"No," she said, "not many."

*

That evening, with the pickup sitting there, dissolving into the surrounding darkness, Liz said, "Well, they can just sit there uncomfortable all night for all I care."

Connelly looked over at her. "I'll go speak to them. I'll tell them they just have to leave. They have no choice."

"I fixed them a supper basket," Liz said. "Just tell them to take it and go."

After supper she went out to the truck.

"*Señorita*," said Jesus, stepping out to greet him. "Isn't it a fine evening?"

"Jesus, you know we can't hire you. You understand that, right?"

"*Sí*—yes, we understand. We are almost ready to leave. We won't bother you again."

"Liz made you another basket—to take with you."
"You are too kind to us. We expect nothing."
He took the basket.
"Well, have a safe trip."
"Yes, of course," said Jesus.
She walked back to the house.
Liz was sitting in the kitchen. "Did they leave?"
"Almost."
"That's the same as staying," Liz said. "Any count, I imagine they're probably just as useless as that broken-down cowboy you have out there tangling up our fence wire."
"Clyde's all right."
Liz shook her head, seeming at a loss within their shared predicament.

*

Regardless, in the morning it was all different again. Connelly knew that the moment she opened her eyes and smelled something—delicious odors of cooking food, wafting the air—and then heard something else—someone on the roof, walking about. Then, in the distance—the sound of running water, and laughter.

She dressed herself quickly and went downstairs, into the kitchen, where she saw Liz, sitting at the table, drinking coffee, and looking up at her, exhausted and guilty.

Angelina, meanwhile, stood at the counter, pounding out corn tortillas for her huevos rancheros. Black skillets filled with spicy meat and sauces were bubbling on the gas stove. Connelly walked over to the sink and turned on the faucet, and cold water gushed out. She hadn't imagined it. She turned it off and turned around to Liz.

"He fixed the pump," she confirmed the obvious. "I held the flashlight for him while he did something to the wiring. Then he made gaskets out of some old leather in the barn to stop the leaking pipes. Then he came in here and fixed the toaster and the light switches. And now he's up on the roof, fixing that. He told me—how can anyone sleep when there's so much to do."

Connelly went and sat down beside her at the table and, immediately, Angelina was at her side, setting down her steaming coffee mug, smiling and bowing, before going back to the counter to finish their breakfast. She looked at her and then at Liz, who shrugged apologetically and said, "I told them, since no one's using the manager's place, they may as well stay there for the time being." She looked down. "Maybe after breakfast we'll go get it ready for them." Then she looked up at her, expectantly. "Well, go ahead and say it, you've a mind."

"I don't have anything to say."

"All right then."

Now she sat there in conspiratorial silence beside her, sure there was another rule or law, of a local nature, about necessity versus abidance, which she was also sure Liz understood, but didn't feel particularly set to mention right then, listening to Angelina sing quietly to herself in the corner.

42 ♀ GROWING GRASS

By summertime she was better understanding the rhythm of these things, the give and take of them, even if she didn't understand entirely their meaning or purpose, or how they fit together, or didn't fit.

Now she took Liz's digital camera and rode Teets up into that surrounding high country, taking pictures. She wasn't that particular—anything that caught her eye or mood at the moment. These she downloaded into her laptop computer Liz had bought her, finishing her junior year, fiddling with the tones and colors, and printed them out. She taped them on the walls of her round room and then watched them change as the sun moved across the sky, filling her room with colored light from morning until night. Sitting there, she made sketches of pieces of them, filling her pads with what she saw there: stunted trees, writhing stoically in their efforts to survive; parasitic cacti, clinging for life from a rotting stump; insects devouring an unrecognizable carcass; the blood-red sun burning down against forsaken, barren hills; the full morning light and the immense, starry darkness of the night, being the only things she could imagine able to fill up that land. She looked at these jumbled sketches and little scenes and tried to understand what she was trying to do and why. And once she thought she understood that, she began to paint.

Or tried to.

Now different kinds of problems arose. In frustration, she went back to Melissa's journal and studied the passages where the voice seemed to struggle to understand itself, what it was trying to say, and how to say it. It didn't look easy and she knew it wasn't. But over and over she saw how the other did not take the easy way out; how she struggled to understand exactly what was going on, the *essence* of that moment, and then struggled to capture it exactly in her words.

She figured her own art was the same. She just didn't know exactly how to capture it; everything she saw around her that had been so unfamiliar and different from what she knew before, but was now what she had to work with. She looked at the hanging photographs and the sketches scattered everywhere; then she looked out her little window, across the pasture to where Clyde was stringing new wire, and the big live oak beyond him, and the green tree-laden hills rising beyond that. She thought about the arguments she'd had with Mr. Gladdens, remembering his sly, cutting remarks about laziness in general, and taking the easy way out.

"Short cuts, for instance," he told her. "You can fool some of the people, using them, if that's what you want."

"So what are you saying?"

He had shrugged, sitting at his little open office window, blowing out the smelly black smoke. "It's no different than any other kind of sacrifice for what you love. You reach a point where you have to be willing to throw yourself on the sword."

"The sword," she repeated, smiling.

"That's right," he said, stubbing out his cigarette. "Sacrifice beyond the reasonably expected; beyond that sensibly defined." He looked at her. "You have to be willing to go all the way, sweetheart, or don't go at all. Take up flower arrangement, or something."

Liz laughed when they were out driving one day, and were having a conversation about art, and she told her about Mr. Gladdens' sword; but she said she thought she understood. Then they went on to talk about how maybe art could be extended into living. How maybe the way a person dealt with their life, fashioned it, could be art at well. She wasn't sure and neither was Liz. All she knew now was there was an impressionistic effect she was trying to capture, and it was driving her crazy. It had to do with the same sort of effect in her mind when she looked around that awful, beautiful place she now lived. What was it about there that repelled or, perhaps, frightened her, and, at the same time, drew her into it?

Sitting at her window she looked at the sky's odd, washed-out shade of blue, the light reflected off it, and what it did to the tortured, rolling landscape beneath. She pulled her easel over by the window and began to lay down the whites and grays and blues of that sky; these bleeding down through the very air that filled the spaces below. There was a way the hills looked at dusk: a dark, forbidding green she had never seen in California; and as the light fell she worked to capture that green, with the milky air somehow infused into it, and the big sky above. The last thing she ran was Clyde's brokenhearted barbed-wire fence along one corner of it, with Clyde—all flat brushes of thorn-bush browns and hill-grit grays and lonesome midnight-blue accents—bending over it.

It was dark outside when she finished.

Someone was knocking at her door. It was Liz poking in her head. "Angelina's made some of that God-forsaken, fire-breathing chili you like."

"All right," she said.

Liz came in and stood beside her, both of them staring at the painting.

"So you finally did it," she said.

"What?"

"Threw yourself on the sword."

*

When suddenly some rhythms, which didn't look that complicated to her from afar (observing them as she set up her easel, and trying to capture them from the center of the three mile pasture), fell out of synch. These were rhythms, she thought, that should have lent themselves to the easier side of nature, but now seemed complicated as calculus to her.

Like growing grass, for instance.

As the passing years had left much of the pastures and fields overgrown with wide brakes of cedar and scrub, useless for much of anything but hiding varmints and mosquito swarms, and leeching away precious groundwater. Jesus and Clyde, she saw, were both determined to wrest back from nature what, they regularly assured Liz, was any man's God-given right. To Connelly, watching them from her mid-pasture perspective, they seemed nearly feverish in their zeal to return the land to sweeping swaths of sweet-swaying Texas grasses, interspersed by park-like forests of girthy oak.

Each, she observed, had their own methods.

Clyde brought in a small bulldozer with a short slab wall of six-inch steel at one end, and a gaping backhoe mouth at the other, revealing an abrupt row of decaying-looking teeth. Limping stoveabout (as he had told her) from his years of falling off bucking horses and being stepped on by red-eyed bulls, Clyde surveyed the creeping illicit growth as if he was witnessing a greenhorn cantering a sorrel filly sideways through a cactus field; then slapped his cowboy hat against his dusty jeans, crawled upon the ragged dozer seat, and got to it. She observed how he spent days climbing up one hillside and down the other, ripping and plowing trash trees and shrubs from the ground into huge piles, upon which he poured gasoline and exploded them into infernos that rained soot and ash down upon him like soft spring rain. Already covered with mud and blood from whipping branches and maverick, runaway root systems, the soot layered and mixed, giving Clyde a crazed, apostle-like appearance of having survived some personal Armageddon.

Jesus, she saw meanwhile, only shook his head, laughing quietly to himself, and brought in a small herd of Angora and Mexican goats, an attentive black and white herding dog, he named Kip, to watch over them, and released them out into the undergrowth. In an almost gentle fashion, the goats began to nibble at the brush and cedar as if a wide, soft eraser was removing them from the sheeted landscape.

When Clyde saw the goats' monotonous, unrelenting progress, he began a renewed assault on his own parcel of hillsides, now seeming possessed in the undertaking. This, while Jesus quietly urged his goats to: "Eat—eat my little *cabritas*. That vaquero *jorobado* is gaining on you."

Connelly recognized their competition, the vying for supremacy in a hierarchy of two. Liz told her that Jesus apparently based his claim on cultural tenure; Clyde, on timing, having arrived there, at least, at that particular spot, first. When one day the four of them were sitting on the porch, eating sandwiches and drinking ice tea Angelina had made for their lunch, Clyde and Jesus discussed the varieties of grasses they would plant. Connelly listened to them, arguing amiably, until Jesus suddenly said, "Of course, as *peón de confianza*, I should have the final say."

THE BEAUTIFUL-UGLY

Now Clyde sulled and jumped up, wide-eyed. "You ain't no damn peon confa-*nanza*," he said, and tromped off. Soon they heard the bulldozer's engine crank over and begin to churn.

Meanwhile, Jesus only rose up and walked down to the end of the porch to stare off at the vista of his goats, grazing on the opposite hills.

"They'll work it out," Liz told her.

*

So occupied with her own attempts to wrest some meaning, on canvas, from that stubborn, hard-scrabble landscape, Connelly hardly noticed when Clyde's bulldozer broke down. It sat lopsided on the distant hillside where the old man spent hours scratching his head and slinging wrenches; until, one morning, she saw him back stringing barbed wire again, head down, seeming given in to it all.

Then the next morning, lingering over coffee with Liz, she came outside and set up her easel at the porch turn, when she spotted Jesus, up by Clyde's dozer, tinkering. She looked over and saw Clyde, head down, nailing wire.

Around noon the sound of the dozer engine came alive and Jesus drove the yellow, growling thing down before the barn and parked it; then he went back to his own work.

After that, she saw, Clyde eventually began using it again. He would spend an hour or so up on the half-ravaged hillside, then go back to his fencing, as if his heart just wasn't in it like before. Like maybe he felt bad or guilty about it, and it just wasn't the same now.

*

Then, some days later she and Liz were re-setting the cap-stone at one corner of the limestone fence, lining the driveway entrance, when they heard the shout. They looked up and saw Jesus running up the hillside, through the orchards beyond the barn. Coming down toward him was his goatherd, or what was left of it, fleeing in a panic. They followed Clyde, running as fast as his bowed, broken-down legs would carry him, up the hillside, into the line of cedar, and discovered a horrible scene: Goats lay dead-about everywhere, the swollen horror in their eyes still receding, their stomachs opened with scalpel precision, and intestines strewn about. The little herding dog Kip, as well, had been torn, literally, into pieces, apparently trying to protect his herd.

"Runoff dogs," Clyde said. "Pack of'em."

Jesus looked bewildered, like something misplaced, standing there.

Connelly felt Liz touch her arm and say, "Let's get the shovels, honey."

When they returned, Jesus had gathered the carcasses into a pile. Tear-lines had ploughed down through the mask of dirt on his face. Together, the three of them buried the remains. Clyde had apparently left, and Connelly thought it especially mean-hearted he had not stayed behind to help. But they continued on, finishing it, and walked back down to the barn.

"Why don't you take the afternoon off," Liz told him, putting away the shovels.

"No, *patrona*, not when there is so much to do," he said, quiet-voiced, and wandered away, distractedly.

*

Finally, in the late afternoon Connelly saw Clyde's pickup come rumbling up the driveway, his horse trailer behind. She watched him park alongside the barn. He backed down his old bay gelding and saddled it, tying on a bedroll and saddlebags. Then he tied on his scabbard, fit his slack-jawed Winchester rifle inside, and rode off.

As the days passed, and Clyde's old truck and trailer remained mute behind, Connelly began to wonder what they should do—perhaps go looking for him, or call the sheriff—she wasn't sure, and finally asked Liz, who only smiled at her and said, "He'll be along."

And that was that.

Clyde was out eight days. And when he did return, riding up at dusk to the front porch where they all sat talking, he threw down the gunny sack upon the cinnamon-and-ivory-colored flagstone; then he trailered his horse and drove home.

Jesus, meanwhile, had gone down and dumped the bag's contents—eight pair of blood-crusted dog ears wired together as a disturbing necklace—over the paving-stone ground.

The next morning, when Connelly stepped outside, she could see the two men in the distance, walking side by side down along the edge of the new pasture where tiny grass blades were sprouting, unfettered, all the way down to the old forest of girthy oak.

43 ♀ THOSE OTHER WALKERS

Liz had told her she wanted cattle—back there on the ranch—before July. And she had listened to the conversations the three of them, Liz and Clyde and Jesus, had about what breed to start with, and how many, and what kind of yearling mix they wanted, and who had the best bulls for sale.

And she knew she would never forget the day, that last day of June, she was sitting with her sketchpad on the porch, when the cattle trucks brought in the first hundred head of Black Angus, and unloaded them in the middle of the holding pasture.

She went out and watched the horsemen cutting the older cows from the yearlings, and driving them into separate, larger, feeding pastures. Everyone seemed excited and happy, she saw, working the cows.

Afterward, she went back and sat in her rocker, sketching again, while Liz stood farther down the porch, talking with the rancher she'd bought the cattle from. Then she gave him a check, and they shook hands, and the rancher left.

That's when she saw the other, younger cowboy, who had been standing down behind him, at the base of the stairs.

She remembered him from before, out there—black-hatted and long legs pushing determined down on the stirrups—neatly cutting the cattle left, then right; and she remembered what she'd thought about him, and the way she'd watched him; and now (after he'd returned her back his own quick, accusatory glance) she lowered her head back down, intent upon her drawing again, feeling her ears burn.

"Can I help you?" she heard Liz ask him.

His quiet voice said, "Heard you were hiring, ma'am."

"I might have room for one more," said Liz. "What's your name?"

"Will Walker."

Now Connelly looked up again—first at him; then at Liz from the side, the way she was looking down at him.

Liz said, "You any kin to Elmer or Bobby Walker?"

Head down, he nodded. "Elmer's my daddy. But he died—"

"I know what happened," Liz cut him off.

Then Connelly saw her expression, like she'd bit into something rancid and needed to spit.

He looked up and said, "I'm not looking for any favors."

"You came to the right place then," Liz told him.

*

After much pestering and probing on her part, Connelly finally got Liz to tell her about those "other" Walkers; or what she called "those Nueces Walkers, down South-Texas way."

"That was Ben's bad-gene older brother, Cyrus, hear tell, shot his company commander at Vicksburg and deserted, robbing banks all the way home. Then he packed up his family and moved south, across the Nueces River; and that's where the bunch of'em have been hiding out since: generations of rustlers and scalp-hunters and common un-lawed riffraff and wildcatters and offshore roughnecks and whatnot. But Uncle Max was always quick to point out the Lord didn't see fit to choose sides; and, as it was, the Cyrus Walkers didn't do much better than the Benjamin Walkers in the family preservation category. I knew there were Elmer and his brother Robert left. Then I heard Bobby got killed in a welding explosion; and Elmer went fast down after, dying ditch-drunk, lying on a red-ant pile, right there on the Carrizo Springs city limits, summer last."

Liz looked over at her now. "So why are you all of a sudden so interested in that bad-seed family bunch?"

Connelly shrugged. "It's just odd, don't you think? I mean, I started out with practically no family; then I got this big, tangled-up Texas family that, I'm learning now, are about all dead as well. So

THE BEAUTIFUL-UGLY

I'm almost back to where I started from. It's just a little weird, thinking about it, you know?"

Liz said she could see her point.

*

The truth was, she found herself wondering if he was, perhaps, a far-removed cousin like Liz, or maybe some sort of offshoot uncle; and she doodled family-tree pyramids on her drawing pad, numbering generations and arrowing across from third-removed this to fourth that, and never deciding; and she knew she couldn't ask Liz, who (she could tell) was suspicious about it from the start.

Because at the end of the previous school year, Liz had commented, "Now I just can't believe that none of these tall drinks here-bouts has asked you to the prom yet."

"Who would think?" she replied, grateful Liz chose not to directly inquire, concerning it. As several of those tall drinks *had* cornered her in their local manner (she thought, an odd mixture of shucking shyness and an almost brazen air of possessiveness), shuffling up to her in the school corridor and leaning hard into her, their lower lips pinch-packed with Skoal or plug of Red Man, squinty eyes averted off toward some unseen horizon, as they inquired in that increasingly decipherable mumbled twang, "Won' go the dance?"

"No thank you."

And they'd all given her that curt, showdy sort of nod they had, and ambled off, stiff-legged and erect, into the sunset.

So she'd happily spent prom night popping popcorn and watching a rented movie with Liz, who had given her that poor-thing look aside all evening, until she finally told her, "Look, Liz, I'm just not ready for that yet. That dating stuff. I mean, I guess I'll have to work through this whole boy-girl thing again, from the beginning, because where I've been, and the comparisons I've had, just don't work now."

Liz nodded understandingly. "Sweetheart, I'm not saying a thing about it. Why I'm nearly in the same fix, knowing someday I'd like to maybe meet someone again, and share things again, and just slap scared to death, thinking about what comes after."

So they both agreed to let it be for then; and they promised each other—if either of them ever did decide to look at *it* differently—the other would be the first to know.

And that seemed to momentarily cool the rising heat, she felt, surrounding the two of them, even *mentioning* men; and within herself, especially.

*

But now she was not so sure about it. As the summer deepened into the dangerous heat of July, she tried to sort through the tangle of feelings inside her, she realized she had reached a sort of junction, within herself and with herself, concerning the outcome of those feelings.

Of course, there was the confusion about the before and the now. Even though she had accepted, and even embraced, her new life there did not mean she was not suspicious of it. Questioning the verisimilitude of it. As well, there was the question of where it was taking her—this new, suspect life—and would there be enough there to grasp and cling to, arriving; as she expected no favors, nor their accompanying disappointments; and she knew stepping off edges, into ungrounded space, was not so unfathomable as the understanding, the discovery, she could be in one place, could remain there absolved the while, though surprised and daunted she might be.

*

Then there was him, that other Walker, who, after she'd failed to establish the exact genealogical connection between them, and especially after she'd given Liz her piquant little don't-need-boys speech, she decided was best to avoid, or even consider in any manner or form; which was not so hard, as he seemed intent on avoiding her as well; barely giving her a nod or glance after that first defining cut aside, which still lingered inside her like a tiny burning brand.

Instead, she stayed mostly in her tower hideaway, standing before her canvas and easel; working her way through the varying perspectives, the lights and shadows, of that place; but more often than not, she found herself wandering about her circle of round windows, pushing them slightly open, one after the other, to peek through them, out over the changing aspect of the countryside: seeing the paler green pastures down to the darker green woods; the blue lake shimmering and reflecting the bluer sky that seemed to hold dominion and change itself by the hour or minute; the black cattle and red horses grazing on the sweet, seed-tipped grasses; Jesus' goats and fowl, moving hither and thither in

THE BEAUTIFUL-UGLY

wavering pockets of bright cinnamon and gray-washed soot and tinted ivories and burning gold; and the men, on horseback or afoot, working the land and all on it like some great evolving painting before her eyes, turning its former forsaken self into something newly pleasurable and keen.

But as the days passed and she encountered him more and more—in the distance from her room, when the slouching fluidity of his form contrasted sharply beside Clyde and Jesus' stump-and-stubble presence; or suddenly up close, coming round some corner when they would both spy the other, off—she began to notice the tiniest tingle of excitement she felt, experiencing that, over and over.

Then when she didn't know where he was or what he was doing, she noticed as well, that little itch of irritation welling inside her, until she eventually sought him out, pretending to be otherwise occupied with things.

Meanwhile, remembering Liz's words concerning the manner and makeup of those Nueces Walkers, she half-expected trouble to come tumbling down, or more likely exploding up, around him at any moment. And when nothing happened, nothing but the common and ordinary tasks and rhythms of ranching (as she was now perceiving with the deepness of the passing summer) she wondered even more about what he was after with himself, and where he would take it.

As she saw the others there had accepted him without much comment. He mingled shoulder to shoulder with Clyde and Jesus in that mute, purposeful way men had of doing unpleasurable things pleasurably together. And Angelina was beside herself with making sure "*Señor* Will" had enough to eat at dinner, and never letting his tea glass go three sups down (to Clyde's empty-glass consternation, sitting beside him). While Liz, especially, seemed to have warmed to him, finding out that Elmer had had him working ranches since he was eight (The only time he had mumbled something, in their presence, about his past, saying it was to "keep him out of the oil business entirely, and his father's hard-living ways in particular, and trouble in general."); and Connelly observed the way Liz would now ask his opinion of things, and his deferential replies back, almost as if it hurt him to be noticed and regarded in that manner, preferring to be left entirely alone.

"He's a quiet one, all right," Liz said to her out driving, running errands, one morning. "Like he's trying to do everything he can to put distance between where he came from and where he's going."

But where that might be, lying there night after night in her tower bed, she could only wonder. That's when she would rise from her bed and go to the little round window overlooking the enormous, moon-washed barn and surrounding outbuildings, picking out the little stone tool shed Liz had let him take over and fix up for himself.

He'd seemed so grateful when she'd done that, but she only told him, "It's bunk and bite, Will. You'll work it off."

"Yes ma'am," he replied.

Connelly had watched how, after the long day was over, he would set to work, fixing up the little place: re-grouting all the stone walls, and putting on a new red-tile roof, and repairing the chimney, and finally getting it ready inside (which, frustratingly, was the only part she could not observe in detail).

He, at last, hung curtains, she saw—white ones with green trim—over the two windows; and it was everything she could do to keep from going by, while the men were away, and peeking through one of them to see.

*

What she did see, however, was how twice each week—on Tuesday and Thursday nights—he would get in his old fender-wired truck and drive away somewhere. And this was especially irksome to her, not knowing.

Until one night, as she stood on the porch, watching Will's truck fling gravel over the last patch of visible driveway, Clyde ambled by on the way to his own truck, heading out. And he stopped below her and chuckled. "That hud's hot on it, all right."

She looked down at him. "On what, Clyde? What do you mean?"

"Gone a sparkin', what it's called, sweet darling," he said, grinning back up at her. "Down Falls way and well a woman, what I hear. And him hardly nineteen and a lick."

"A girlfriend, you mean?"

"Yep."

"He told you that?"

And the way Clyde's eyes brushed over her. "Yep." Hesitating then, looking off into the dwindling twilight, before he said,

"Surprisin' too, as he don't seem much to do with that sort of thing. Why he even said you's spoiled a house brat as he'd seen awhile."

She felt her face suddenly soak up the lingering, surrounding heat of the day, and said, "Did he say anything else?"

Clyde only offered up one long splurgeful spit of tobacco juice into the nearby powdery dust, eyeing her winsomely back, as he swiped a trembling backhand across the already stained grizzle of his chin. "Nope."

Then he wandered off toward his truck and home.

Meanwhile, she climbed the circle of stairs to her room in a quick, angry flush, throwing herself down on her bed and heatedly recalling the details of how he'd so carefully avoided her since arriving there (seeming oh so needful and earnest, standing there), and now knowing why; knowing he had apparently decided everything about her, with hardly a nod of recognition toward her, or anything resembling concern or even curiosity about her, the entire time.

But now she knew.

And now, through supper and after, sitting awhile with Liz on the porch, but hardly able to maintain a thought or line of conversation, she soon excused herself, and went back to her room to spend a fretful, slow-burning night filled with thrilling fits and blood-eyed promises to herself, and against him.

*

In the morning, feeling the deserving calm and purposeful resolve from having worked through and through such feelings like a pan of well-kneaded dough, she rose and dressed and went down for a cup of coffee with Angelina in the kitchen; then she wandered into the library for a book, going out toward the main hallway where, as luck would have it, she encountered him—that Will so-called Walker—standing there across the hall from her, black hat in hands, before one of her paintings.

She leaned against the doorframe, observing him, knowing he was probably there to see Liz about something, and finally shook her head and said, "Do you have any idea what you're looking at?"

He turned and looked back at her, and she cradled more tightly against herself the book she was holding. Blue, she thought. His eyes were stone hard and cold blue, and unforgiving, and not (she decided then) in any additional sense attractive; while she felt her own dark eyes burning, as if with a new, different kind of fever.

"I know what I like and don't like."

"Is that right?"

She inwardly cringed at the pettiness of the moment, even as she was trying to chase down certain elusive words inside herself, fluttering about. Then she remembered what Clyde said, and finally stared (she hoped) with indifference back at him, feeling that advantage of knowing things he did not.

But he didn't seem to notice, or care much, regardless, and said only, "What are you reading?"

Jerk, she thought. Asshole. "St. Vincent Millay."

He stood there.

She frowned and said, "She's a poet."

He stared back at her.

"That's someone who writes poetry."

He vaguely nodded.

She shrugged now, through with him, and walked past him down the hallway.

Not far—when from behind her came his timbered voice: "'*All I could see from where I stood, was three long mountains and a wood.*'"

She stopped and turned around, staring at him.

He went on, "'*I turned and looked another way—*'"

When she heard herself whisper, "'*And saw three islands in a bay.*'"

Now they both stood there.

He sniffed and wrung his rumpled hat rim in his hands. "My mother—at least, before weak blood and Elmer's drinking brought her down—wrote some stuff. Got three of her skinny books. She read to me when I didn't know blank verse from baby blankets. Actually, I lean more toward those saccharine-starved metaphysicians. Their uncharted imagery, as mama would say."

Connelly felt the swath of heat rise inside her, for some reason, *hating* him then, just hating him, everything about him, or at least what she knew.

She said meanly, "Don't you have cows or something to take care of?"

He stood there, motionless, watching her back, seeming, at worst, amused, or, at best, uncertain, or unwilling, about committing himself one way or the other, concerning her.

She changed her mind then, going back down the hall and brushing past him again (that being, she realized, the closest she'd ever been to him), before going outside into the early morning August heat to seek a cooler place to read.

*

But whatever she expected as an outcome to their initial confrontation, or muddled confluence, or whatever it was that happened in that hallway, what she saw happen next was, she felt, entirely opposite of that, and was the worst thing she could imagine right then.

Which was, nothing. Nothing at all. She suddenly started school again, at the end of August; and Liz suddenly had delivered two hundred additional black, squalling and bawling heads into the holding pasture, and everything was at loose and ordinary ends for days, and then weeks, into September.

When, finally and at last, she turned seventeen.

That's when Liz decided to throw a barbeque, inviting everyone in the valley to celebrate the birthday. She realized, as well, they had not done a proper housewarming since returning.

"Don't worry none, sweetheart," Liz told her, knowing how she was about such things. "It'll be just some little old put-together thing." And she began to make calls.

The barbeque took place on the last Saturday in September, when the olden summer heat was becoming forgetful, and the sharp new mind of fall lingered ready at the distant edges of the paling sky, and around the furring outlines of the big cottonwood and willow, swaying down into the shallow, green-running river.

Connelly observed the beginnings of the day from her room, seeing the honking line of trucks and cars arrive in the dark, making a big circle in the three-mile pasture, and commence preparations.

She dressed in her birthday outfit of old jeans and boots and a fraying T-shirt, and went down to eat breakfast with Liz, and get going with it.

Outside, as dawn broke, everything seemed to be happening at once: men were digging and lining and firing up the pits to roast the freshly slaughtered goat and pig carcasses, lying canvas-covered, side-a-side, on the back of a flatbed deuce and half; others were setting up the band stage and long row of picnic tables and benches; others were marking off the lines of the parking lot and horseshoe pits and the quarter horse racing lanes with chalk runners; while still others were setting up the ice tubs for drinks and melons, and lighting the cooking grills; and women were back and forth, between the big house and pasture, with Liz at one end and Angelina at the other, directing the casual, purposeful, army.

Connelly helped where she could—toting basins of scrambled eggs and platters of pancakes to the wood tables for the workers' breakfast; then toting the dirty everything away—but mostly wandering anxious about, taking pictures and observing how it all came together, seeing one framed scene after another in her mind (the movement and meshing textures and colors and shapes and sounds of it); until the line of cars and trucks, entering, began about midmorning, and didn't slow down until the noon dinner.

By then everything seemed to have caught its second breath and rhythm, and the festivities rose up, churning with a full-swinging motion into the long hot afternoon. The swing-and-stomp band began to play, filling the air with sweet-moaning fiddle and twanging guitar and the deep, steady throb of percussion, pulling people to their feet to dance before the swaying stage. In the calving pen, rodeo clowns entertained the children with their lariats and shenanigans; then conducted the sheep-riding and greased-pig events; meanwhile, the adults threw horseshoes and raced their full-chested ponies, side by side, down the sunbaked lanes; others, meanwhile, gathered at the holding corral to watch all the horse bucking and barrel racing and calf tying; or wandered through the open barn to witness the dessert and canning competitions, followed by the "sweet silent auction" for the orphans' home in Kerrville.

*

By the evening, when she knew he had stayed away, and he would be away until late at night when the darkened silence was full set, Connelly slipped away and climbed the long, dragging stairs to her bedroom; and she lay there, not exactly sure what she felt, or should have, but knowing it was not what she wanted to feel then. She was still lying there in her remorseful curl upon the bed, when she heard the knock at the door, and knew it was Liz, who came in (she could hear) in the briefest swirl of scraping denim and shuffling boots over the wide plank.

She heard her concerned voice: "Sweetheart, what's the matter? You just disappeared and no one knew where you'd gone."

"I'm all right, Liz. I'll be down soon."

With an aching, inward anguish, she felt her sit down beside her on the bed and say, "Did something happen? Or maybe there were just too many folk out there, after all. They don't mean any harm."

She sat up then, wiping her eyes. "Oh, no, Liz—it's wonderful. It's all so wonderful, you'll never know. Thank you."

She hugged her.

Then she saw Liz still studying her. "Well, what about Teet's new saddle—hand-tooled Rondo leather, I thought it would make a real pretty present—"

"No, Liz, that's wonderful too. Please—I'm just feeling a little tired after everything, and I—I—oh, *Liz*," she suddenly gushed, "I love him so much. What am I gonna *do?*"

She broke down entirely then, falling and sobbing hard against her.

"Oh my Lord above," Liz said, taken back, holding her. "Tell me, girl. Tell me who's taken your heart."

Between catching breaths and choking back tears, she said, "W—Will."

Then she heard Liz moan and say, "Katie bar the door—*please* don't tell me that. Just now seventeen and she falls for the only Nueces Walker left to bury."

"Don't say that, Liz."

"I should have known, the way you two were hissing and spitting about each other like two long hot cats in a short alley." Liz stopped now and looked at her. "He hasn't touched you, has he? Tell me that sull-eyed varmint's laid a finger on you and I'll—"

"Are you joking? He can't *stand* me. He thinks I'm a spoiled house brat. Anyway, don't think about it like that—about me. I told you, the things I've done, had to do—well, just don't see it like that. Like anything normal."

"Maybe not, but, like I told you before, people move on in life. And just because certain things have presented themselves in a certain way once, doesn't mean it stays that way."

"What I'm saying is, I already know about men. Bad men and good men. And I know which kind I prefer."

"Sweetheart," Liz said, taking up her hands in her own, "no matter what's happened to you, just remember, you have your whole life to live yet. And you and I are planning that life together, aren't we? A good, normal life now?"

After she saw Liz wasn't letting it go, she nodded. Then she sighed and said, "It doesn't matter anyway. Like I told you, he doesn't care about me at all. And, besides, he already has someone else."

"Who else—Will Walker? Why, he told me he doesn't have time to make cents from dollars after working around here all day."

"What about when he goes into town on Tuesdays and Thursdays? Clyde says he's going to see her."

Liz laughed and shook her head. "Listening to Clyde should have been your first indication things had gone terrible wrong." Then she hesitated and said, "Now Will didn't want anyone to know this, but he came to me for advice, so I do know. You see, he's working with a tutor those nights to get his high school diploma. And after that he wants to go on and be the first South-Texas Walker to get his management degree in scientific ranching. And that's all that's about, baby."

At that moment, Connelly felt every thought, feeling, inside her go pouring out some sudden, unstopped breach, wondering: *What had she done? What had she been thinking?* Then not wanting to consider the obvious answers to herself. She looked up at Liz. "Well, at least his opinion about me won't have to change now."

Liz held her hands. "All I know is this, Ms. Connelly Pierce. When the right person discovers you, you knowing it's right will be the easiest thing to understand. And you won't have to worry about it. And you won't have to move any mountains or change a hair on your head. It'll just be right. And you'll know it is. And that moment will overcome any and all obstacles, arriving, I promise you."

But she didn't feel any better after hearing that. In fact, she felt perfectly awful about everything to do with it. But she pretended she was better for Liz's sake, and because she didn't want to talk about it anymore.

After Liz had spit-cleaned her tear-run face with her hanky, the two of them rose up together and went back down to the barbeque and their waiting guests.

44 ♀ PULLING CALVES

There was a day-by-day contentment she felt now, causing her to look around herself and wonder at the very simpleness of it, never forgetting where she'd been, and always amazed that she'd finally arrived there—at that moment and place—at all. It was October roundup now, and each morning she watched Liz and the men ride off toward the near mountain pastures to gather cattle, while she gathered her books for school. Then she would get in the old Ford and drive herself there, sitting all day in classes and laboratories, trying to pay attention, while she thought about how she felt now, and then thought about him, that Will so-called Walker, wondering what he was doing, right at that very moment, and how he'd ridden off that very morning, not looking back.

One morning after they'd gone, she suddenly went over to his little house and let herself in. She stood there, in the center of the single little room, looking around, seeing his desk where his homework assignment lay scattered, and the old stuff chair, Liz had given him, where he sat and read. She went over and picked up the book, lying open there, and saw it was the scene in Homer where Odysseus was home at last, preparing to confront the ravaging, unwanted suitors; and she laid the book back down.

Then she went over to his narrow, made-up bed and lay down, pressing her face into the feather pillow, smelling him there with her eyes closed, imagining him there (while, as well, feeling her own deep-clefted tingling inside her). Finally, rising up and straightening back the bed, she went out, climbing into the old truck, and driving herself down-valley to sit in classes, and try and pay attention.

*

The following weekend she rode Teets around the working corral's far perimeter, half-watching them inside, roping and dragging calves to the branding pit, where (with her eyes averted) she knew the hot iron sizzled, and the tender ears were notched, and the long needles were shoved into so many squirming rumps, even as she could hear them bawl like babies from afar.

Then, in the afternoon, after she saw Will giving her one of his spoiled-house-brat looks, she told Liz she wanted to help.

"Honey," Liz said, "with your school and helping around the house, you're doing plenty."

So later, when she saw Clyde riding out into the big west pasture, she hopped on Teets and caught up with him after a mile; and she asked him about teaching her to cut.

He laughed and said, "Not on that thing."

"What's wrong with Teets?"

"Why'n, got 'Rabian blood," he said, getting all puffed up in his saddle. "Good for a pasture ride, but no cow sense."

She sighed and rode beside him. "Where you going?"

He nodded ahead, and then she saw the circle of buzzards in the sky before them.

It took them another half hour to get to the cactus-and-greasewood-rimmed hollow where they found the swollen heifer, lying on her side in her own pool of blood, kicking.

Connelly sat in the saddle and watched Clyde get down and examine her. "Say, baby's crossways a-her," he said, his right hand lifting his hat and shifting it slightly backwards on his head. He looked up at her. "Why don't you head on back now, honey, and I'll be along after."

She looked down at him, and then at the young cow, who looked out terror-eyed and alone, lying there in the blood-soaked dirt; and she turned Teets around and headed up from the hollow, back onto the rolling plain, not five minutes toward the ranch when she heard the single rifle shot, echoing off behind her. And she kept riding at a slow gallop, not looking back.

*

After that occurrence, she told Liz she could do that. She could help watch the expectant cows and heifers through the night (like, she knew, everyone else was taking turns doing), and she could go for help, if necessary. "I'll bring my homework out to the barn," she said. "I'll be fine."

Liz finally agreed and took her out there to show her what to do and what to watch for. "Just come get me if you're not sure," said Liz, still unsure about it.

The next morning, when her alarm went off at three a.m., Connelly rose, yawning and stretching and pulling sweats on over her underwear, and slipping her feet into her flip-flops; then she gathered up her schoolwork and trudged down the stairs and outside and over to the barn where Jesus was occupied with some task.

"Now a nice little catnap before breakfast," he said, walking out, whistling in the dark.

After he had gone, the barn seemed to grow even more empty and cavernous around her. Then she remembered what Liz had told her to do first, and she found the flashlight and went out into the calving pen to check on the animals there.

Everyone seemed fine, the beam of light revealing them lying there in a group, chewing their cuds and watching her back; and she went back inside and looked in the stalls. There was a cow and two heifers in separate stalls, and only the heifer in the center was standing. She was the smallest, and she stood there, staring back at her, as if she were a little startled by her presence.

"Are you all right?" she asked her.

Then the young black-faced mother-to-be swung away, heavy-sided, turning her back on her, and staring out, still startled, through the opposite gate.

Connelly went over and sat down in the nylon folding chair and looked around. Through the open barn door she could see the lightening flash somewhere off in the distance. Then she heard the low rumble and knew the morning rain would come before the light. She thought about how everything would look then—fresh-washed; new day beginning—and she realized, for the first time, she had never seen anything, anywhere, so beautiful. And the flash and rumble came again, closer now, as she picked up her composition book and began to read about Gogol and his dead souls, thinking that this was the perfect time and place for a different sort of dead soul to wander such a landscape, seeking reunion with their disconnected self, or perhaps a passage onward to that further realm. She shuddered then and quickly became absorbed in her reading.

*

The clap of thunder woke her up, and she jerked in the chair with a start, looking around. She wondered how long she'd slept and saw the gray-black morning outside, where she also saw the rain beginning to fall in slow rhythmic sheets all the way down to the stock tank; and the wind gusting then, causing the red maple and birch, surrounding the water, to throw out their arms and back their heads in a quick-frenzied jig.

In front of her the small heifer turned abruptly and kicked. Connelly stood up, setting down her book, and went over to the steel-pipe gate, looking inside, when she gasped. The heifer turned, again trying to kick her own belly, while the enormous water sac hung and swayed low from her vulva.

"Oh," she said. "Oh."

She turned and started to run out the front barn door, to the house, to wake Liz. Then a crack of near lightening turned her around, and she ran out through the smaller back sliding door, into the rain, and toward Will's little stone shed, instead.

She ran up on the porch and stood there, undecided, and then knocked. She waited moments and then knocked harder again.

The door opened and she saw him there, standing there in his underwear, leaning against the frame.

"What?" he said, brusque-voiced.

"She's having it now." She stood there and then said, "There's—I think Liz called it the water sac."

She could see the outline of his face looking at her. "All right. I'll be over in a minute."

She turned and ran back out into the rain, back through the barn door, over to the stall. She saw the water sac had broken and the heifer was turning about one way, then the other.

"He's coming," she told her. But it didn't seem to make any difference. The animal grunted heavily and swung about.

When Will came through the door, Connelly watched him closely. He was wearing his old boots and jeans and a pullover shirt speckled with blue paint. He stood there beside her, looking over casually into the stall; and she could still see the sleep on his face and in his dark blue eyes, and his hair mussed.

She said, "Is she all right?"

He seemed amused by that, looking over at her. "Would you be, fixing to squeeze eighty pounds of trouble through a ten-pound hole?"

She watched him enter the stall, talking gently to the heifer. "Why you're just a little bitty thing—what you doin' gettin' yourself knocked up like this? You should be out runnin' round with young bulls and such, not in here fixin' to be a mama. Why I never."

And the entire time he was going gently around her, feeling down along her sides, snapping a rope to her halter ring and tying her off to one of the steel bars, dividing the stalls. He took a plastic bucket hanging over one of the posts and handed it to her. "Get me some hot soapy water, would you."

She took the bucket over to the stainless sink and rinsed it and began filling it with hot water, squirting in some dish soap and making suds. When she carried it back to the stall, going inside now, she saw that he'd tied off the heifer's tail to the halter, getting it out of the way.

He said, "Don't set it too near or she'll kick it over."

She set the bucket back a little and stood there, watching him take a long-handled nylon brush and scrub down the heifer's entire posterior. Then he went over to the sink and scrubbed down his hands and arms. He came back, pulling plastic gloves over his hands, and said, "Lube me up, would you, honey."

"Do what?"

He nodded toward a wire rack, hanging on the steel crossbar, and she went over and pulled out the big bottle of lubricant. Then he stood there, hands out, as she squirted it over the rubber gloves, and he rubbed them slickly together.

"That's good," he said.

Now she stood back, eyes wide open, while he carefully inserted his fingers, then hand and forearm, into the heifer's vagina. She listened to him whistling quietly to himself, as he examined the insides of the young cow. He looked back at her and winked. "I feel little feet."

"Oh my God," she whispered, suddenly feeling dizzy-headed.

He pulled out his arm and hand. "We're gonna have to help her out, though."

"What do you mean?"

"Well she's dilated, but she's small—her birth canal and all—so we're gonna have to help her."

"What do we do?"

He grinned. "I'll show you."

He took his time. She noticed he didn't seem to be in any hurry, but every movement was purposeful and exact. He went out of the stall, over to the working table, and drew two sections of stainless chain and triangular handles from a soaking bucket. He came back into the stall and, once again, nodded for her to squirt lubricant over his gloved hands and now the chain. Then he ran his hands up and down the chain, until everything was covered. Meanwhile, the heifer was becoming more agitated, grunting and swaying and trying to kick out.

"Easy, sweetheart," he said. "We're all in this together."

One after the other, he inserted the chains into the vagina, and worked them back, one-handed, and worked to tie them off.

She said, "You're putting those on the calf?"

He nodded, working. "Right above the fetlock joint. Then I do me a little half-hitch below, just to be sure."

She had no idea what he was talking about; but he seemed to understand, and smiled back at her. "I can show you sometime. It's not hard."

Not hardly, she thought.

Once the two chains were dangling through the vulva, Will took a section of coiled nylon rope, hanging on the stall pipe, and began tying it around the heifer. He placed it over her neck and ran the two ends down between the front legs, then crossed them up over her back, and down between her hind legs. Now he pulled on the two ends of rope, tightening, and the heifer began to draw together, her legs crumpling beneath her.

"C'mon, sweetheart," he said. "Time to be a mama."

After a minute or so of gasping and heaving and going back and forth, the animal lay down on her right side; now lying there, heaving and pawing the air and straw with her hooves.

There was a small aluminum sectional ladder leaning against the wall, just outside the stall, and Will placed it against the heifer's rump, forming a T, and draped the chains and attached handles over it.

Finally, he drew off and discarded the plastic gloves he'd worn, and put on clean ones.

Knowing now, Connelly squirted lubricant over the gloves and stood there watching him as he rubbed his hands together. She saw the way he was looking at her.

"You ready?" he said.

"For what?"

He nodded toward the grunting heifer. "Pull a calf."

She looked down at the waiting, heaving animal, in obvious labor, and said, "You're joking, right?"

He stood there, shifting his weight to one leg, watching her.

She sighed. "OK—what do I do?"

"Get down on your fanny and put your feet against the ladder."

She sat down on the straw and positioned her feet.

He said, "Next time you might wanna wear something besides flip-flops."

"Uh-huh, next time."

He squatted down beside her and handed her both steel handles. "Best to pull the down leg first—that'd be your right hand."

Her hands were shaking and she thought she was going to be sick.

She heard him say, "You're doing fine. Better than me on my first pull."

Then she looked up into his eyes, his face right before hers, and for the moment she forgot everything else. She forgot she was sitting on a pile of straw, in her sweats and flip-flops, preparing to pull a baby calf out of its mother with chains. She looked up into his eyes and felt herself sway forward, toward him, her lips parting—when the thunder rumbled right above them, causing the entire barn, the concrete floor she was sitting, to tremble. And she realized, and sat back, gripping the chain.

She watched him move behind the heifer and insert his hand and forearm back inside the vagina. "C'mon, sweet baby, time to dial it up."

After a minute he said, "Okay, start pulling that right hand, slow and steady."

She pulled, and nothing happened.

"You need to pull harder."

"What if I hurt it?"

"You won't."

She pulled harder, gasping with the effort.

"You pulling?"

"*Yes.*"

He glanced back. "Use both hands, girl."

She grabbed the handle with both hands and pulled, feeling the muscles in her back straining. She gritted her teeth, pulling, when she felt something slip forward.

"Don't back off!" he said. "Keep the pressure on, or it'll climb back up inside her."

She kept pulling.

He said, "You got the down leg out, now pull the up'n."

She shifted, pulling the left handle and chain. She knew better now what she was doing, and she soon felt the right, up, leg also slip toward her.

"I can feel it!" she said, excited.

"Uh-huh. Now pull that down shoulder through."

She pulled and pulled until her arms were aching, but she didn't say anything, and she wondered if she could go on.

"There it went," he said, feeling with his hand. "Now the up shoulder."

On and on, pulling and pulling, until...like the tiniest unfolding miracle, before her, she saw the pointed black tip of one hoof emerge; then the other.

"I see it, Will. I see them both."

"What it's about, girl."

On it came, until she saw where he'd attached the chains, and then on, when she saw the snubbed black nose, and then the full face of the calf emerge, and she knew she would pass out within the moment. "Oh," she said, her head swirling inside.

"Don't let up," he told her.

"I can't, Will. I *can't.*"

Then he was suddenly back beside her, taking one of the handles from her. "You pull that one and I'll do this."

"All right," she gasped.

Everything was turning about her now: the entire barn was turning, as she pulled, exhausted. Somewhere in the distance she could hear the falling rain; and she heard him laughing beside her; and then she saw the calf slide forward—all slippery and wet—and she cried out now, both crying and laughing, as the calf came entirely out over her legs, squirming with life. Together they were leaning forward, wiping the mucous from its face and nostrils, helping it to breath. Now it looked up at her, all black-eyed and wet-faced and steaming.

"Did good, girl," he said, smiling. "Got yourself a little bull."

Still dizzy-headed, she looked at him and heard her own voice pour out of her, just like the little bull had only the moment past pour out of his mama: "*I love you, Will Walker.*"

Suddenly there was the slick tangle of her and him and the startled calf; and he was kissing her, and she was trying to pull him to her and her to him, and they were rolling about in the hay then, slipping and sliding this way and that, covered in the lubricant and the blood and the oils of birth.

"I should stop," he said, panting, holding her back.

"*No,*" she said urgently, shaking her head.

The moments merged, one into the next, opaque and dreamlike, like the slow-falling raindrops merging outside the barn; until she knew something had happened—*was* happening—but she had no idea. She just saw them, felt them, flowing one into the next, unknowing...seeing his face framed by the massive timbered barn-joists beyond...and hearing the blood pounding in her ears...and now vaguely conscious of him there—close above her and entering her below—as her fingertips brushed the lock of hair from his face, and they finally rolled together as one in the deep, sweet-smelling straw.

Afterward, he kissed her and held her against himself, and they looked over at the calf, lying there, watching and waiting for them to be finished. They laughed, seeing it.

After they'd both washed up at the sink, he showed her how to clean up the little bull with towels and use a hair dryer to fluff up its silky black coat. "I'm going to call him Leo," she said happily, waving the dryer over the ruffling hair, "Count Leo, after Tolstoy."

"No profit in naming bulls," Will said. "Could end up a steer or go to market."

"Not this one."

"Then you ought to call it Lucky."

"No, I'm the lucky one," she said, turning the dryer off and laying it aside. Then she turned and pulled him to her, kissing him again.

He winced, standing there, and said, "Now all we got to do is deal with Liz."

"No," Connelly said. "Not if I'm happy. Not if it's what I really want."

"Is it?" he said.

She stood there, holding herself against him, smiling wanly. "I'm not going to say it out loud, Will Walker," she said. "I'm not going to say how much I really want you, how much I love you and want you—just for myself—more than anything; because all my life, the things I've wanted that badly have always, somehow, someway, left me. And then I had nothing again. So I'm not going to say it now."

His eyes observed her closely and deeply a moment, and then he said softly, "Girl, don't you know you got to feed your little count his colostrum?"

"What's that?"

"His first milk. Kind of like an energy drink, but with a laxative."

"Oh," she said, leaning against him.

So she feed little Leo his first milk, with him butting his head impatiently and gluttonously against her and the bottle; and she kissed him afterward between his dark, bright eyes; then she kissed Will again and walked back to the house, alone, through the quiet-falling, new-morning rain.

*

There was a slender peace to her life now, she had never imagined possible. And she didn't know where or how you held on to such a life, or perhaps it held on to you, she wasn't sure. Regardless, Liz didn't help her much, understanding it; and also understanding how she slipped out, night after night, to share Will's narrow bed; though seeming more aggravated that she had not first confided in her, as they'd agreed. Liz just brought her down to her doctor, and got her prescription for birth control pills, and then told her plainly, driving back, "I told that Will Walker I've been turning bulls into steers my whole life, when they didn't use good sense climbing on top of things."

"Oh—*Liz*."

"All I'm saying, sweetheart, is I know I can't change the course of nature, even if I wanted to. And maybe since both of you came out of trouble, you'll know enough to leave it where you find it. But I can advise on taking certain precautions. You both want to finish your school, and maybe then start a family, I guess."

"We haven't really talked about it," Connelly said. "But he is using protection, if that's what you're trying to ask me."

"It is," said Liz. "And now I know, I'm finished talking about it."

"Good, because I don't have anything else to say about it."

She saw it as a sort of fragile thread she was following along, somewhere, one day at a time; always amazed when she woke in the mornings and found it still there, waiting for her to pick up and follow again. As now her days were filled with all she had ever wanted them to be, which was the love of some kind of family, and her art.

She saw the love as an encompassing thing, within that place she lived, and those that lived there with her: Liz and Clyde, Jesus and Angelina, Wilburt and Ida, and all the others she'd met so far and would meet; and then there was Will's love, which, she realized, was something at the center of all that love (even while holding itself a little apart) that she counted on and needed and filled herself with, from the moment she opened her eyes, until she shut them at night. And even then she dreamed of him through the night. And all the day when he was not with her; as the time he and Clyde drove three days over to Bandera to help with another rancher's roundup; and how she waited, enduring every aching moment apart, until Clyde's pickup appeared, rumbling up the long drive, returning him to her; when she still waited, as long as she could bear, then ran out behind the barn where he was showering behind the makeshift stone wall and beneath the cold-water nozzle Jesus had plumbed there; and she ran headlong—in her jeans and boots and radial-symmetric T-shirt, showing the Circle of Life, according to Buddha or somebody—into his arms, burying her mouth against his, feeling the cold water *sizzling* down her full-burning body, pressing against his cool hard nakedness.

45 ♀ WORKING HER ART

Then there was her art, and the cold-sunned November day she finally cornered Clyde into showing her where the colored clay deposits were. The Indian clay. As he had been puffed up and bragging to her about knowing their whereabouts for a while, and now told her he had things to do. Then she reminded him how he had been promising her for some time, and how some time more from now he would still have things to do, until finally he was made to relent; as a last attempt to avoid her and the obligation, he shifted his stance, his back hand smearing tobacco juice across his chin, and looked at her wince-eyed and sour-lipped. "Yew kin still ride, can't yew?"

"I'll manage," she told him.

While he saddled up Teets and his old gelding, Whiskers, she ran to her bedroom and grabbed the gunny sack of small aluminum painter's pails she'd purchased weeks before at the feed store, and ran back.

First, they cut down and across the falling land, catching the river where the limestone banks rose like ivory cathedrals and stubble oak grew horizontal from clefts below the rim. They followed the jagged precipice for a while, and she wondered was it really necessary to take that route, or was he just trying to scare her? She looked back up the hillside above them and figured the brush was so thick they could never penetrate that; and then she decided there was no other way, and hoped Teets could make it all right. She peered down the sheer wall, edging slowly past to her right. The river below was an emerald ribbon, running between banks of sun-burnished gold and silver. And beyond that, through the trees, she caught glimpses of the farm road and the pastures beyond where cattle grazed in blue-green grass up to their bellies.

She was grateful when Clyde began to work Whiskers down and through one of the cuts. But when she pulled her reins, Teets bobbed her head in disagreement, and stood there, confused at what she was doing; meanwhile, Connelly sat there, looking around, fixing the spot in her mind. Only then did she loosen the reins and allow the little mare to amble forward, following the other horse.

At the bottom, Clyde turned back downstream, following that part of the river they had already passed. Not far along, the river turned away, the curving bank appearing to dissolve ahead of them into the wall of rock. Clyde dismounted and she did as well, tying her horse to the brush as he had done. She untied the gunny sack and followed him through the brush. Watching him struggle, gimp-legged, she smiled, knowing how much he hated walking anywhere.

When they came out the other side, he stopped and pointed. "See how them holler ledges cuts back into the bank?"

She nodded.

"Well, folks here-bouts calls'em pots. Now down here by the river you got the old blue clay pots, and then the whites and grays. Different colors and shades, all of it, depending on what pot you're in to."

"What about the reds and yellows?" she asked.

"Them's up higher in the arroyos," he said. "We'll go there afterids, you wont."

"I wont," she said, smiling and winking at him.

He grinned, showing his missing teeth. "Just be careful, sweet darlin'. Snakes lie down along the edges a-them pots a frog watchin'. Grab a snake, say, let it go."

"I'll remember that."

She began to work her way along the rock bank which rose in a steep curve out of the water and turned back into the sheer wall above. When she came to the first cut, she set down the sack, got down on her knees, and reached back until she felt the clay, curling her fingers into it. She withdrew her hand and saw the shimmering blue-gray paste on her fingers.

"This is so cool," she said. She raised her hand and shouted: "Clyde—it's beautiful!"

He laughed and nodded, waving her on.

When she had filled the first pail, he called out to her, "Pretty girl, put a little river water on top to keep it wet."

She nodded, shimmying herself down to the river's edge, and dipping the pail down into the water. Afterward, back up the bank, she made sure the lid was secure, and set it down.

For an hour she searched the pots along the river, collecting three shades of blue, two gray, and a pail of creamy white, which had curious streaks of stone-ground caramel in it like ice cream. By the time she made it back to Clyde, he was stretched-out, sleeping beside the river. She touched his boot with her boot. He woke up and immediately began to chew on the worried plug, left sedentary in his mouth while he slept.

"You still hankerin' to make them arroyos today?"

"If we can."

He stood with an arthritic-laden struggle and spit. "Let's ride then."

Back on the ridge, Clyde turned back upriver and they edged along it for another half hour before the land opened up into a cautered bowl with a narrow gulch at its far end. Clyde heeled his horse and took off and she followed, going fast up the gulch. She gripped the reins and bent to the left and right as brush and small tree limbs tried to yank her away. Going around one bend after the other, she kept losing sight of Clyde and his horse; but Teets seemed determined not to fall behind, and she gave the horse its head, holding on. Eventually Clyde began to slacken his pace before her and she did the same.

When the gulch began to broaden into a wider, soft-humped valley, she rode up beside him, and they rode together, the horses' hooves making a clickity-clack sound over the caliche bottom. When the valley began to turn up sharper against the rising hills that held it, Clyde pulled away and rode at an angle up the eastern slope, and she followed.

Now they went up and down a series of small greasewood hills that eventually began to break apart, divided by jagged widening cracks where the earth had once split apart in some prehistoric upheaval, leaving the land in strips and tatters. She saw that Clyde appeared to ride through this ominous place without concern, and she felt comforted as well, tagging a little ways behind him.

When they reached the mouth of the first arroyo, she saw that he rode past it with nary a glance. At the second, he paused, reining in his horse, looking up the opening in the earth, then changed his mind and rode on. At the third, he jerked his reins and kicked and she followed him, seeing his horse ahead, kicking clumps of dirt into the air behind it. Encountering the first stagnant pool of water, Clyde slowed his horse and she came up behind him, her horse nickering and cantering sideways to avoid the muddy bog. They trotted around the pool and rode on, encountering another, larger, pool, where she saw tiny fish, swimming along the edge. Passing this, the walls of the arroyo began to rise above them, until they rode in deep cool shade, and the air smelled wet with some sweet fragrance. She was lost in her thoughts when Clyde was suddenly dismounting before her. She did the same, observing the water leeching from the red and yellow stone walls on either side, and trickling down into the hollowed center where it formed the tiniest of streams. They walked along for a while over the slick surface beside the stream.

She pointed and said, "Are those more pots? Those openings at the base?"

"Some is. There's better'uns ahead."

They finally stopped in an opening where the arroyo forked. A miniature waterfall trickled over the facing of the one to the left. Clyde dropped his horse reins, allowing Whiskers to drink in the clear pool, filling the opening's center.

"They ain't goin' nowheres in here," he told her.

She dropped her reins and untied the burlap sack from the saddle horn. She carried it over to a flat rock and opened it, setting out the empty pails.

"This here clay's yeller as mustard and red as turnip blood," he said. "Gits set in a horse's hoof, it'll swell and bust wide open, you don't dig it out."

She began to search the crevices along the canyon's base and found the clay filling the cracks between the rock. She dug it out with her fingers and tried to see its exact tone, but there wasn't enough light. She saw it was some sort of red and filled the pail. Then she went down to the stream and topped it off with the cool filtered water and tamped on the lid. She went on now, filling the rest of her pails with different colors she discovered under the rock ledges. One of the reds, she saw, had gold-colored flecks; and the lustrous yellow she found had silver and black glitter that made her catch her breath when she held it up to her eyes.

When she was finished, she walked back down to where Clyde and the horses were waiting. Clyde was seated on a small rock, rolling up a cigarette. He put it in his mouth and pulled a match from his shirt pocket, grazing it with his thumbnail, lighting his smoke.

"Do any good?" he asked.

"Clyde, these are so wonderful. I can't wait to use them."

He nodded, pushing his hat back off his forehead. "Injuns painted and pottered everything they could with that stuff. You may as well have a go."

They sat there in the shadows, listening.

She looked away and then back. "Clyde, were you ever married?"

He took a slow drag off his rumpled cigarette and nodded again. "Oncet."

She waited and then said, "What was her name?"

"Rosa," he said. "Little Meskin girl. Foreman's daughter for this outfit I's workin' for up outside Dalhart. I's twenty and she's eighteen. Lived in an old trailer house. But she loved fixin' it up, plantin' flowers in the summer."

He sat there.

"So what happened?"

"Oh, she died a pneumonia one winter when I's out savin' cows too damn dumb to help themselves. After I buried her, I went back to that trailer, but I couldn't stay there, starin' at all her purties, smellin' her there like lilacs in the spring. I burned that summitch to the ground and drove down to Dallas and started rodeoin'." He looked over at her. "Sweet darlin', we aim to make it back before early dark, we best git goin'."

They got up and caught the horses and began the long ride back through the early November dusk.

*

On Thanksgiving day all the settings around John Walker's long, polished, hickory-plank table were filled; and sitting there, looking around at those faces, Connelly wondered if this was how traditions in families began, or began again for those that had to regain their sense of place and order. And she thought how all families were of a type; that is, they had their own tones and textures and their own voices that made them up; and no matter how large or small, or happy or sad, they were all, ultimately, unique unto themselves, existing for their selves and their purposes, apart, but part of some greater order and connection and fabric of the whole that was any society. And even those societies rose and connected to the larger design, still, that were cultures and civilizations that ultimately rose and fell; and sometimes were lost in the dusts of millennia; and sometimes, someway, discovered their sense of place and order anew, and began again; as she cut into her slice of stuffed jalapeño goose, looking around the table.

In the late afternoon they assembled their short caravan and drove with their assorted desserts and chilled wines and twenty-gallon canister of jerk-leg coffee down to Franklin Walker's German bridge, to the high meadow overlooking the wide green ribbon of the San Miguel, and spread out their blankets until dark.

It was there, with the swelling dusk and the first fingers of rising damp from the river closing over their sudden camp, that Will Walker whispered to her their future. They were lying a little apart from the others when he slipped the best ring he could manage on her finger.

"Consider that a till ring," he said.

"What's that supposed to mean?"

"That means it'll have to do till I can afford a decent one."

She pressed herself against him. "I don't need rings, Will Walker."

"Anyway, according to Cousin Liz we've got all the time in the world to work it through."

She looked up at him. "Well, Liz Walker doesn't have my sense of time and circumstance," she said. "And I've told you, Will, I've already lived a different kind of life until now; and now I want something else; something ordinary and sane, for once; and something just mine and yours. I want that, Will."

He touched his finger to her lips. "I'm not going anywhere."

She leaned her head back against him. "But that's the problem. That's what I learned all those years. We're already there. We just don't know it yet."

*

On late Saturday afternoon Connelly had to drive herself into town because everyone was busy with something. She needed plaster of Paris and glue to mix her gesso base, and primer lacquer spray to preserve the clay's colors, and some other things; and the cattle trucks were there loading; and even Liz's truck was busy being serviced by Clyde, who told her to take his rig. "Key's in the ignition, sweetheart," he said, buried beneath the hood.

It was a dually Ford with a fifth wheel that had an AM radio she listened to Clyde's country music station. Driving to town she thought about what she was doing. What she and Will had decided to do, which was for her to enroll in the UT arts program in Austin, while Will would head a little farther east to A&M and their Ranch Management program. That was their plan, and they had stayed up late the previous night talking about it. Liz was with them and assured them it would all be coot crazy for a while, but they would be all right.

Then they told her about their decision to marry the following year, and what did she think of that?

Liz shook her head. "I don't think anything except what puts your minds at ease by day's end. That is, seeking the balance of it; and I think, there, Will's got the grounding sense to occasionally pull you back down to his earth, Connelly Pierce; meanwhile, you've got the awkward airy and impetus to drag him up into your fanciful heights, on occasion; while both of you keep it fresh and common, as what makes it good. You'll both do fine, and I also think I may as well start putting things together now before you're both near eat up with anticipation."

That was the moment of completion, of closure, Connelly realized then she had aspired. Kissing Will and Liz good night, she climbed the rounding stairs to her room and lay there, with the cold-sounding, late-November wind dragging, creaking, past her windows; as she imagined the now dark forbidding hills, beyond, that she loved so much, seeing at first light. She snuggled deeper beneath the feather duvet and closed her eyes. So long, she thought, drifting. It had all been so long and so precarious till then, lying there, feeling the deepening waves of sleep moving rapidly upon her, even as she could feel her long past (once so critical to everything about her) now shrinking before the rising, dominant future. And visions of things, previously unimagined, rose up before her, delighting her encumbered mind, relaxing, freeing itself...children in the river meadow, playful about and mixing among Jesus' goats...and the people, with their faces indistinct in the distance, she thought she knew, coming toward her from the green river below...until everyone and everything surrounded her and she wondered: was this some sort of heaven, or earthly paradise, or what? Standing there in that bright-colored, sun-warmed place, surrounded by those still faceless people she thought she knew. Or was this just another one of her mind-paintings, she had created for years, to help her sleep? She wondered that in her ease, drifting along as a small boat drifted in the abiding, unstopped current; and she slept.

*

She found everything she needed at the crafts and variety store on Main Street. Next, she drove over to the grocery store to get some things for Angelina. When she came out of the store, she saw the two of them leaning against the front of Clyde's pickup. One was short, the other tall. Both were covered with dust and sweat and wore rumpled cowboy hats with curled-up sides. She hesitated, and then started to walk past them. The tall one blocked her path.

He said, "Me and Harley's wonderin' what some little old gal's doin' drivin' Clyde McKinney's rig. You ain't stole it now, have you?"

"Not hardly," she said, standing there, smelling whiskey.

"*Whoo-wee!*" shouted Harley, skipping a step.

"Cause you too damn *fine* lookin' to hook up with some old broken-down hud like Clyde."

"Fuck off," she told him, brushing past.

With the howling and chortling behind her, she placed the bag of groceries in the rear bed beside the other bag and got inside the truck. Outside, the cowboy named Harley was gleefully dancing a jig beside his partner, who was staring at her through the windshield. She started the engine, put the transmission in reverse, and turned around to back away from the storefront. When she turned back around, she saw the tall cowboy standing in front of her, blocking her exit. Harley, meanwhile, was standing on the sidewalk, swinging his hat in circles, egging her on. She swallowed and put the transmission in drive. The next thing she knew she had floored the accelerator—the truck lurching; the big engine roaring in response—and shot ahead. She saw the tall cowboy jump and come over the top of the hood. His hat flew off and for several seconds he was prostrate across the hood, trying to hang on, while one side of his face was pressed against the windshield before her. Her mind racing, she jerked the steering wheel to the left and the cowboy went to the right, tumbling off the hood. She continued on across the parking lot to the street. In her rearview mirror she saw Harley behind her, still dancing his jig, waving his hat about his head, while his partner was getting up slowly off the ground.

What gives some of us bad ends, she could hear Liz say about it, and continued up the street.

She drove out of town and caught the farm road, heading back up valley. Her hands were shaking and she kept looking in her rearview mirror, until she saw the distant black dot, growing larger, on the horizon. She pushed the accelerator to the floor and the engine began to cough and sputter, and her mind raced about what to do. There was no one else on the road. She looked around and saw a ranch house in the distance, beyond a field of clover, but she didn't know how to get over to it. She looked in the mirror and could now see the shape of the new pickup, growing. Her eyes scanned the countryside around her, as if something or someone would come to her aid. The road began to curve and, in the distance, a signpost appeared and grew larger. She slowed down and it read: Henry Spring Road. She could see nothing behind her and she turned onto it.

The feeder road was narrow and winding and she soon felt she was being swallowed up by the overhead branches that formed an arc. There was no sun here and the light that filtered through seemed washed in turbid gloom. She looked behind her...nothing was there, and she began to breathe easier. The road dipped, crossing a dry bed that would fill with water when it rained. There was a yellow sign there with black marks showing how deep was the water, and she went up the other side and over a hill. She went down the hill and around the curve and, ahead of her, crossing Henry Spring, the bridge was washed out and the road was closed.

"*Damnit*," she said, stopping the truck at the barricade. She turned off the engine and rolled down the window and listened. After a moment she could hear the breeze shifting the leaves about and not much else. She sat there and waited. She wondered how long should she wait? And then what? Should she try to make it home? Or maybe back to Comanche Falls, to the sheriff's office, Liz had shown her, by the courthouse? She sat there, wondering, when she thought she heard something; then she could make out the sound of it, approaching. Seconds passed and the truck came into view behind her, moving slowly, knowing the bridge was out, knowing there was no need to hurry.

She rolled up the window and only then realized there were no door locks. Clyde had removed them, probably from locking himself out. And she said: "Damn you, Clyde."

Then she realized it didn't really matter. The locks didn't matter.

The big new pickup pulled in behind her at an angle, blocking her, and the engine was turned off. Both of them sat there a moment. She glanced back and could see them there, sitting there and talking. Next, both of the pickup doors opened simultaneously and they got out. She was hardly aware of how hard she was breathing. For some reason, when they came and stood on either side of Clyde's truck, she scooted to the center of the seat—inches of separation from them—and stiffened herself and waited.

The tall one said through the glass, "Girl, you tore my ass up with old Clyde's truck."

The short one snorted a laugh.

She waited—her hands rolled into fists, her chest rising and falling—staring straight ahead.

When they both came through the doors at the same moment, she lashed out—both directions at once—then tried to raise her legs to kick one of them. A hand jerked her hair and another hand slapped her hard across the face and her head fell back. They were both pushed against her, each one holding an arm. She felt their mouths against her face, rough hands squeezing her breasts, and smelled their breath. Someone's sour tongue was in her mouth, her ears. A husky voice said: "Undo her dungarees, Harley."

"No—*please*," she whispered.

She felt the hands fumbling with the buttons on her jeans. Then she felt the hand below, the fingers probing inside her; and through her mind suddenly flashed the moment, years before, when other, smaller hands and fingers admonished her so.

She was crying now. Everything, turning around inside her, seemed filthy and wet and frightening to her. She sat there shaking. "Please," she said. "Don't hurt me."

After a while she felt the fingers withdraw.

"Shoot," he said quietly, "she done peed herself."

Everyone sat there.

He said, "You ain't nothin' but some little city *bitch*. C'mon, Harley."

She was barely aware of them getting out of the truck. Without looking, she quickly buttoned back her pants, but knew she dared not breathe, otherwise, sitting there. They were somewhere outside, and she stared straight ahead, her entire body shaking, waiting for them to go, trying still to contain the incredible feeling of relief ready to burst from just beneath her skin, waiting. *Please go,* she thought. *Just go.* And sitting there, forcing herself to look ahead—moments passing; the line of dark forest just before her; the patch of blue sky through the trees, in the furthest corner of her vision—when her eyes shifted to meet the imperceptible shift of his eyes, and she knew at once her mistake.

"No," she said.

He turned and leapt back through the door opening, catching her by the arm and dragging her off the seat and outside. She swung her free arm, feeling her fingernails raking into the claylike flesh of his face, hearing him cry out. He swung his hand and her head jarred and twisted aside. He slapped her again—harder—and she was on the ground, as he reached down, ripping at her shirtfront.

She heard close voices: "Want me some!" "No, Dix, no!" And then saw the taller one knocking the smaller one back and down and kicking him. Then the taller one turned and came back to her, kicking out at her as she tried to turn away, when she felt something collapse inside her, like the too-brittle protective covering of something, collapsing in on itself.

She only tried now to protect herself, raise her arms that felt leaden and weak and refused to do what she wanted, as he kicked and punched at her. She could see his angry face in a blur, with her fingernail bloodline drawn in a barbed-wire jag down the side; and it flashed through her mind how she had spent her whole life fighting things off she didn't want; when he put his hand over her mouth and she bit him, tasting dirt and blood.

He hollered and swung close-fisted now, and she realized then he was going to kill her. He was going to do that. And suddenly she felt an incredible sense of loss—of self, of possibility—sweep through her, knowing that, and thinking oddly in that last moment of Melissa Montgomery Parker, dreaming of her breakfast yams. Thinking: *Was this how she felt when she died? Was it?* When she was jerked to her feet and backhanded one last time, turning her away from him—when her world gave way beneath her. She had slipped off the edge of the bank, free at last from the entangling wrath behind, and was now careening down the sheer drop, to the tousle of waiting, spring-dappled boulders below.

46 ♀ THE QUALITY OF THINGS UNDEFINED

Just before dark, the old rancher was slow-driving his truck, checking fence line down farm-market, when Dix Newsome's fancy new rig came bursting out of Henry Spring, nearly hitting him in the process.

"Damnit, Chuck, you need to get a handle on that boy," he commented, watching the rear of Dix's black Chevy fishtail into the dusky twilight.

Then he sat there, recalling a conversation he'd had with Chuck Newsome, and his brother Mel, over at the Cattlemen's Coffeehouse, just about such things. Not necessarily about these new breeds of spoiled, self-minded kids, coming along—kids, he told Chuck and Mel, with plenty pocket change and no head sense—but, rather, the changing ways that got them there. And he stopped then, not saying another word about it, but the three of them understanding he was talking about the Newsome brothers' decision to give up real ranching and turn their place into a big-game-hunter's paradise, complete with TV commercials, bragging about them up in Dallas and Houston, and fifteen-foot game fence to keep their African deer and tiger inside.

Chuck had argued back that they now did half the work and got twice the pay. "Why," he said, "we got businessmen that pay twenty-five thousand for a head."

Mel said, "Old days, only thing occasional boy passin' through wanted was chuck-wagon beans and biscuits, and shot at a whitetail. Now these new slickers want aged steak and French wine and silk sheets to fart into at night, and then a kudzu or big cat waiting for them in the morning. It's all different now, Tom. And it's easier too."

"Well, I reckon so," he said, shutting up about it. Still, he thought, easier didn't make it better, did it? And he was wondering about that again, driving slowly up Henry Spring, with one discerning eye scanning fence line, and the other watching the road, when he saw it ahead and stopped. He said aloud to himself, "Why, that's Clyde McKinney's old rig."

He sat there, wondering why Clyde would leave his truck parked at the washout with both his doors open like two big ears showing. It didn't make no sense, seeing that. And he sat there, wondering.

Slowly, he pulled his truck up behind Clyde's and stopped, shutting the engine. He sat there some more, looking around, and then he got out and went over and looked inside. Keys still in the switch, he saw. He looked in the bed, snooping in the bags. Green tea and baby oranges and craft whatnot—didn't look like Clyde none. He stood there.

It was darker than it was light when he went and stood over the near-dry spring bed, looking down. His old eyes scanned the bottom, a dozen or so feet below, trying to make anything out among the rock and barely trickling pools of water, when the shape of something there stood apart. He went back to his truck and got his flashlight out of the glove box, and then went back to the bank, shining it down, able to see it clear now.

"Eh—God," he said and turned and scrambled along the side of the bank, finding the boys' fishing path down, and followed it, making his way over and among the tangle of rock and boulder. Finally, he stood above her there, noticing how one of her thin arms extended out from her, over a flat stone, with a single index finger hardly touching onto the surface of a tiny water pool, as if testing it.

He knelt down, pulling the hand and arm up from the water, feeling her pulse...after a moment thinking he detected the faintest of ill-timed beats, lingering. He pondered what to do. Afraid to move her at all after such a fall; cursing himself for not keeping his cell phone with him as his wife had pestered him to; and knowing, if he didn't do something, she'd never last him driving into town for help. He shined the light in her face, and said, "We got us a short rough piece ahead, young lady. But it's all we got, and I'm sorry."

Then, as carefully as he was able, he picked her up, thinking how fragile and all to pieces she felt in his arms, and began to make his way back through the rock and up the steep bank.

He was wheezing hard at the top, but kept on going to his truck, letting down the tailgate, and stretching her out upon it. Then he climbed in the bed and spread out an oil canvas he kept there to cover things, and laid her atop it. He took one last look at her there, seeming so small and broken up, and shook his head. Then he jumped, groaning with his arthritic pain, down out of the bed, shut the tailgate back, and climbed into the cab.

He was five minutes back along ten minutes of Henry Spring Road to the market road, where he barely jammed his brakes, entering onto the highway sideways, with tires squealing and rubber grinding off onto the weathered asphalt, as he corrected himself and headed for town in a roar and rattle, sway and shimmy.

*

Liz had earlier bartered a dozen market heifers for two breeding mares, and sent Will over to Uvalde with the trailer to pick them up. Now, with the sun gone down, and with his two girls safely loaded and heading north again, he looked out over the rolling, brushy hill-country and thought about the past few years of a life that should have stopped working some time back, but somehow didn't.

He knew it had all gone south fast, after his mother had died and Elmer set himself down to some serious bottle-hugging. She was always the great tempering in his life, thought Will; what you could do with someone like that, anyway. But she had always seen a thin piece of Elmer that no one else was allowed, even his own son, and she worked that piece for all it was worth, until it was wore out, and then she was, and there wasn't much left to do with anything, but put your few miserly affairs in order, hug your boy one last time, and then shut your eyes and let it go.

Will remembered that last day Elmer showed up at Nueces Riddling High School drunk as a southpaw preacher and took a swing at him in front of his algebra class. There wasn't much left to decide over then; and after he knocked old Elmer out hard and cold across Mr. Wilson's cluttered desk, he stopped by the house only long enough to grab his gear, then head down into Zapata County and hire on with some San Ygnacio outfit as a river runner; which basically sent him packing across the Rio Grande to get back their cattle and horses on those nights the Mexicans weren't stealing them in the first place.

He recalled a hard couple of years, following, when things could have gone either way of bad and worse. He spent a little time in jail, and a little more time unloading marijuana from the backs of tiny planes, sitting on red-dirt landing strips in the middle of a million acres of nowhere particular. Then his best buddy got caught up between a couple of rival north-south smugglers, got himself kidnapped; and Will spent an anxious couple of weeks, waiting and watching, as his friend came back to him in America, a piece at a time.

After that, whatever romantic, adventurous notions he had harbored seemed to sour with the settling, and he found himself wandering north again. He ended up working at a sheep tannery on the outskirts of San Antonio where he spent fourteen-hour days, hanging eighty-pound, maggot-husked, chemical-dripping skins in what his Mexican co-workers referred to as *caja caliente*, or the hot box—a long, narrow, dark, hundred-forty-degree curing attic, with high rows of rusty hooks that he mostly caught his hands on, until they swelled up like big red Del Rio onions, and he said fuck it and quit.

*

Usually on a drunk, Elmer had often gone on about them "fancy Walkers, up San Miguel way." And, growing up as he had, Will often wondered about them; gathering from the pain-revealing intensity of Elmer's jealous babble that they were probably normal and decent, hard-working folk. He knew through the cowboy grapevine about the Circle-W spread, and about Liz and Jack, who treated you fair. Then he heard Jack died and Liz shut things down, and he figured that was probably it; that is, until the day he quit the tannery and drove over the small, rugged mountains into San Miguel valley. There, having a beer at Buster's Honky-tonk was when he heard Liz Walker, or rightly McCullough, was back in the valley and trying to start things up again. After finishing his beer,

Will got into his pickup and drove up-valley, looking for the Circle-W.

Now, dropping back into that darkened valley, glancing in his rearview at the trailer, he recalled how nervous he was, talking with Liz that first time. He wasn't worried she might not hire him, or even her finding out who he was. What bothered him was that, somehow, someway, she might reject him in one of the endless ways he had been rejected since his mother died. And since Liz was the only other Walker still around and capable of doing that, he felt there was a lot at stake, meeting her.

But she had proven fair, as he'd heard; and if it wasn't for that one other particular detail in the matter he would have settled in with little or no trouble at all.

Will swallowed and gripped the steering wheel, remembering the first moment he saw her, sitting there in that rocking chair, staring down her pretty nose at him. He wasn't sure if that was the exact moment he fell in love with her, or if it had been a slightly more drawn out affair. All he knew was that—from the time they commenced fussing and fighting with each other, up until the moment she was sitting beside him in the barn, with that hard-born little bull across her legs, telling him she loved him—he had felt himself vanquished by Miss Connelly Pierce's presence, and was powerless to defy it.

Naturally, in the face of such beauty, and, in fact, before such an undefinable quality of womanhood, he did the only thing he knew to do and still be able to maintain some semblance of male dignity. He pretended not to care a whit for her; in fact, he pretended to offer up the barest headshake of disproval, commenting on the spoiled house-bratedness of her daily existence to Clyde McKinney, who, he knew exactly, would run back and tattle to her, which he did. And Will could feel the lump in his throat, recalling the way she'd swelled up with all the feminine indignation she could muster, before him, causing the love he'd been harboring for her to also swell, till it was nearly too much to bear, seeing her so.

Beneath the dark umbrella of the century-oak stand, he drove up the ranch driveway, crossing the bridge over unseen water, and continued on up among the rising foothills. He thought at last of the conversations they'd lately had, concerning their future, and how the nature of such speculation was alien to him in general, and downright unsettling in the closer examination of its parts and details.

Never, he thought, never in his wildest moments did he think he would ever have the opportunity to actually plan out a life with someone, and certainly not someone like her; like his own sweet-scented, wet-lipped, girl-woman (as he loved to work over that string of words in his mind, listening to the tiniest parts of them, and all they implied for him); but he was doing that with her; and her telling him, the while, not to tell Liz a thing, until absolutely necessary; when she would run right to Liz and tell her all of it anyway: how much she loved him; and how they would work out going to separate schools; and how they wanted to marry in the great hall of the ranch house, and do a hard-cider toast to past generations, as well as their own and those to come, out on the gallery afterwards; and finally how many kids she wanted (four, at least—two boys first, as guardians and protectors of the two girls that would follow—and then arguing with Liz when she was told how it might not work out with such mathematical and biological exactness); and on with all the rest of it, until Will wondered what exactly he was caught up in. What kind of wonderful devil's wind was this? What enchantment? Because he knew it could not be of the ordinary physical earth, and the ordinary living upon it, and what it had previously presented him. He knew that. It was, rather, something—a word—he heard somewhere; that is, something called *Meta*, something after, something beyond; but nothing to do with the ordinary of anything, as best he could tell.

So preoccupied as he approached the ranch house up the long curving drive, it was unclear exactly when he felt something not right. Something out of place. He first noticed the big barn-light was off. Then he realized that although the entrance light to the house was on, there were no lights shining from inside, and especially no light shining through the round windows of her tower bedroom. Now what? He began to look around, seeing no vehicles parked there, wondering.

It wasn't until he was pulling up before the barn that he saw Angelina come out of the house and down the steps toward him. It his headlights he saw her crying, and felt the shift within him, and then the tightening. Leaving the headlights on and the engine running, he got out of the truck, as she ran fast against him, holding hard to him.

"Oh, Will—*así que horrible!*" she cried out, sobbing and holding herself against him. "*Mi pequeña pájarita—le hicieron daño!*"

Their little bird was hurt—he grasped at the translation in his mind. Little bird was her pet-name for Connelly, the way she was always fluttering about them, as from limb to limb, singing along to her strange talking music, Angelina referred to as heep-hop.

Will said, "*¿Dónde está ella?*"

"*En el hospital,*" she managed, before throwing herself back against him, overcome.

He was finally able to make her return to the house; then he turned and quickly disconnected the horse trailer, jamming a chock under one wheel, before he hopped back into his pickup and tore down the driveway, throwing gravel into the air behind him.

47 ♀ AT BUSTER'S

The drive down-valley to the medical center felt like a single unrealized moment to him, stretched and then stretched some more. Hunched over the steering wheel, eyes fastened to some unseen spot on the road before him, he crossed over Comanche Falls city limits doing a hundred-three, before he caught himself, taking deeper breaths, wondering.

All his senses seemed as fragmented and disjointed as the seconds, ticking past, he tried to connect and detect any measure of meaning or hope. At one point, he found himself outside his curb-parked truck, running toward the hospital entrance. He ran inside, ran up to the counter, to the lady sitting there, and said, "A girl was just brought here—Connelly Pierce—where is she?"

She looked implacably out at him, as if accustomed to such off-shot, unrestrained inquiry, and then typed something calmly into her computer. She looked back at him. "She's in surgery now."

"Where?"

She pointed. "Down that hallway, to the left."

He ran, trying not to think. Then thinking: *Please. Please.*

He didn't stop running until he rounded the corner and saw Liz standing there, across the waiting room. She saw him as well, and he walked slowly toward her. He searched her face for a sign, any thread of familiar agreement between them, but all he could see was a sort of bruised resignation. He finally stood in front of her.

She shook her head. "She only went in an hour ago."

He stood there. "What happened?"

Liz shrugged. "All Clyde would tell me was that Tom Hall told the sheriff he found her at the bottom of Henry Spring. He told him she didn't look like she got there on her own."

Now they both stood there, as if either of them were afraid to move first. He said, "So how bad?"

She shook her head again, now closing her eyes, and he took her into his arms.

He felt her pull him to her, as she whispered in his ear, "I have an old friend here, Will. One of the nurses. We grew up together. And she came out here and she told me I needed to pray real hard. She told me that."

He felt her shaking against him and he held her until she quieted. Then he said, "Where's Clyde, Liz?"

She pulled away from him, pulling a handkerchief from her rear pocket and daubing her eyes. "Oh, you know Clyde. He'd rather take a licking than sit in a waiting room. He and Jesus are outside somewhere."

Will went out and found them sitting inside Jesus' truck. Clyde was rolling a cigarette and nodded at him through the open widow, saying, "Is sweet darlin' still in the cuttin' room?"

Will nodded and stood there, looking around. "What about it, old man?"

Clyde took his time, licking the paper and rolling up the tobacco tightly inside. He struck a small-box match with his fingernail and lit the cigarette, sucking in and releasing the smoke. He looked out at Will. "Say she got herself crossed up somewheres."

"I'd say," said Will. "What about Tom Hall?"

He saw the way Clyde was eyeing him, smoking. "Tom said, just before he saw my rig at the washout, both doors agape, Dix Newsome's fancy comer almost hit him, pulling out Spring Road."

"Is that right?" Will said. "I don't know him."

"Chuck Newsome's boy. Right handsome feller, bout your size, don't give a shit or who knows it. Reckon the sheriff'll call his daddy and bring him in for a little talk."

"That right?"

"You're startin' to repeat yourself," Clyde said. "Wont to go back inside?"

"I don't think so." He looked back at Clyde. "Thanks, old man." He hesitated and said, "If you see her—I mean, before I do—tell her I asked about her, would you?"

He turned and walked off. Behind him, he heard Clyde say, "Now, son—"

And he just kept walking.

*

Will knew, except for a couple of Mexican Tejano joints, Buster's was the only place between the valley and San Anton to really stretch out and wet your whistle. However, he had not been back there since stopping off for an afternoon beer, first arriving in the valley. Then, there had been one other customer sitting at the far end of the bar, and the bartender. Now the honky-tonk was filled. The band was playing a ZZ Top cover about bad and good and Hollywood, and people were dancing, and there was barely room to squeeze his way through to the bar.

When one of the bartenders finally got to him, Will pointed at someone's bottle, and the bartender nodded and brought one over. Paying for it, Will smiled and leaned forward. "You see old Dix tonight?"

The bartender tilted upward his head, indicating behind him. "Back there by the pool tables like always."

Will nodded and began to thread his way back through the crowd again, toward the three pool tables. They sat in an elevated alcove, to the left of the main bar floor, surrounded by the tall, beveled-green windows, overlooking Main Street.

When he got there he stood back and watched. It didn't take long before he laid his quarters down on the edge of one table and waited.

When it was his turn, Will put his quarters in and racked the balls. His opponent was leaned into a corner nook, pressing himself up against a girl in new jeans and a newer hat. He looked around at Will, his eyes slit with drink, and squawked, "You about ready there, hud? That is, to have your ass handed to you?" He turned back to the girl and nuzzled her neck as she blossomed and giggled in his embrace.

"Now, Dix," she cried, "don't mess my face."

"I'm gon mess more'n that, Carla-Jean Hougherty, right after I hand old hud here back his ass. Idn't that right, friend?" When Will didn't say anything, Dix said, sullen-voiced, "That's twenty dollars front, cowboy. Harley there holds the money."

"That's right," Harley said. "I hold the money."

After Will handed over the bill, he broke the rack and proceeded to run the table.

Harley leaned near, saying, "Whoo-wee! Dix, look at him go!"

"I see it," said Dix.

When the eight ball dropped in, and the white cue spun and stopped, Will said, "Say double or nothin'?"

Dix stood there. "What are you, a fuckin' hustler? Some city rack-rat or what?"

Will shook his head. "Just someone lookin' for a little friendly action, Dix. You know how it is." He smiled. "Now are you in or out?"

"In, but you need to know, if you run the table again like that, some of these boys here might go to wonderin'."

"I'll remember that," Will said.

It wasn't until he again broke and began the second run that Will first seemed to notice the ugly wavering scratch down Dix's left cheek, disappearing down his neck. Then he said, "That's quite the little tattoo you got there, Dix. You pick up something you couldn't put down?"

"Like that," Dix said, absorbed in the play. He glanced up. "Anyhow, she got her lesson taught."

"That right?" Will said, eyes ahead, moving methodically around the table. "You taught her, did you?"

"Oh, we taught her all right," Harley said, his own eyes sparkling. "We taught her all she could take."

"You shut up, Harley," Dix said. "You talk too fuckin' much."

"Whoo-wee!" said Harley. "We showed her, didn't we, Dix?"

"I told you to shut the fuck up, Harley."

"We got us some finger honey least, didn't we?"

When Dix started to move toward Harley to shut him up, Will happened to be standing on that side of the pool table, and extended out his cue, blocking him.

Dix stood there, newly surprised. "What's your problem, friend?"

Will smiled and withdrew the cue, now looking back down at the table. For a moment his lips squeezed tight together, then released. "No problem. None at all. 'Cept—that girl, Dix. That girl

THE BEAUTIFUL-UGLY

you knocked over Henry Spring was the same girl I just asked to be my wife, you sonofabitch."

As Will leaned down and once again hard sank the eight ball, Dix stood there, as if trying to understand exactly what he'd heard. Then Will straightened up and said, "Anyway, I just wanted you to know why all this happened."

Before Dix could stop looking startled, Will reversed the cue stick in his hands and swung about in a half circle, bringing the thick butt down against his nose, cracking it open through the bone, and sending him backwards through the big green window onto the street, as if everything had been suddenly caught up and sucked out in some giant vacuum. Then Will turned the other way, bringing the cue against the side of Harley's astonished face, sending him reeling backwards as well.

In a flurry, Will found himself covered in cowboys, pulling him to the floor and held there, hearing the voices as if from some great distance: saying that Dix was sure nuff dead as Griever's grandma; and Harley wasn't much better, though thicker skulled, so to pitch some beer in his face; which someone must have done, because Will heard him start to scuffle about and moan pitiably and then commence crying. Then another voice asked if the sheriff was called, and that was affirmed. As Will lay there, listening to the voices and considering only what was now lost, which was everything. Everything lost. Everything gone in a heartbeat. Lying there with the heavy knees pressed against his back. Listening to his own heart pounding through his ears into the surrounding din.

48 ♀ WHAT HAPPENED WHEN SHE DIED

Her last, odd thought, passing, was: *Where, Will?*

Connelly felt him hit her, and felt herself turning—when, in one dizzying moment, there was nothing below her. She was falling through space and, in a flashing by, she saw the swirl of the spring's gulley below and trees like giant, rushing, green clouds…when suddenly everything seemed to slow down. She was in the air, turning in the air, and she saw the large flat boulder beside the tiny pool of water…coming closer…closer…when it all stopped…

Everything was stopped now, and, lying there, she thought she could understand that. That she'd fallen, and landed, and everything was stopped. She thought she could. But it seemed different now, understanding things. It was different.

Somehow she was able to shift her line of sight slightly downward, and she saw her finger there, barely touching the surface of the water. She thought how lovely it looked, resting there on the smooth surface, just the index tip, resting. Tiny minnows, she could see, flocking now to the commotion, swimming in zigs and zags about her fingertip, as if trying to understand exactly what had just now invaded their world. She thought: this was their giant meteor, striking.

Then her finger twitched. She saw that—sending out tiny waves, scattering the minnows. But she didn't want them to go; she wanted them to stay there with her, the way she felt about it all.

And she tried to call to them but found she couldn't do that now. She couldn't speak at all, or even move her lips the tiniest bit. She could only lie there and watch them move away from her, leaving her, and felt sad with knowing that. That she was alone, entirely alone, with nothing she could do about it.

Her finger twitched again. Or she thought it did. Not much. Only the teeniest, tiniest bit, she decided, or had she imagined it? She wasn't sure. And she lay there, wondering if she'd really seen anything at all...when something happened.

First came the strangest feeling inside her, the changing inside her, like a wound, bleeding. That was the only way she could think of it, because she could feel her own bleeding occurring. More like a seeping than anything. Her own blood was now seeping out inside her, into places it should not be. Somehow she knew that. She could *feel* the seeping. And this other feeling was like that, only warmer and not so darkly menacing to her. More a filling up than anything. Filling her with a wonderful warmth, entirely; until she thought she was completely filled with it; and then she was overflowing with it. She felt herself a fountain, overflowing. She felt it pouring out of her, going...she wasn't sure. But she was staring down at her strange little finger, now quivering continuously in the water like an electrical current was going right through the tip of it; that is, from inside her, through her fingertip, into the tiny pool of water. A sort of conduit between her and the water. And then she realized—she was going into the water, or the overflowing feeling inside her was going there, she wasn't sure. All she knew was that something inside her was seeping and then flowing down through her arm, through her hand, through her fingertip, and into the water. Something. So she shut her eyes and felt the flowing out, waiting, and listening, and trying to understand.

It wasn't long before she heard the noise: the lapping and gurgling about her. And slowly, cautiously, she opened her eyes again...Amazing! So amazing! She was inside the water now. All of her was there—inside the water; that is, beneath the surface of it— and she felt herself pulled along in the current; part of it now; part of everything to do with it. Not so much like a fish, like one of her darting minnows, but more like being *of* the water itself. How could she understand that? She couldn't. Even as she was pulled along by its force, she could only think of it as being dissolved into it (when through her mind passed the vision of Angelina, beside her in the kitchen, mixing her brown sugar into the hot tea, dissolving). But more. As if the entire myriad of atoms that made her up, her flesh and bones and blood, were now attaching themselves to the water atoms, and everything was flowing downstream together. She wasn't *of* body anymore. She could not see herself or feel herself or make herself do a single thing. But, somehow, she knew *of* herself. And she was of the water. And the water was of her. And everything was now of the current, the force and flowing of it, going downstream, and gaining speed. That was all she could think of it. That was all. And it was a joy unto her mind, her consciousness, beyond all the joys, combined, she had ever known. A completeness. An ending, of sorts. Something—she stopped, realizing she couldn't think clearly. She could hardly think at all, in fact. Because she was of the water now. And it was so hard to think at all, even as she fought to do so. So hard...letting herself go now...drifting along.

Later, a noise. Or was it later? Or, maybe, before? As she had been trying to think about that now, about time, about how long she was in the water, and how long this took or that took; and then she realized it didn't matter now. How long. It didn't matter. Regardless, at first the noise was so imperceptible she had trouble separating it from the other sounds about her. But she listened and was finally able to tell the difference, hearing it distinct: a far, deep rumbling. A distant roaring, growing louder at every widening turn. And she wondered.

When she entered the larger water, feeling the bigness of it, the heavy awkward *greenness* of it, enveloping her, she thought: *Oh, my.* Then she realized what. It was the San Miguel that ran across the front of their property. Henry Spring, which seeped from a high granite crack and had dripped for centuries from the ceilings of hidden mountain caves into the sunlight, eventually made its way down through the hills to the river, which, she knew, continued its downward flow to the San Antonio River, then on into the Guadalupe, and eventually into the Gulf of Mexico.

Liz had told her that (*Oh, Liz!* She missed her so, thinking of her at that moment.). Then she remembered the big map of Texas in the ranch house's main hall. It was an old yellow-parchment map, mounted in a carved, dark-wood frame, and beneath a muted glass; and she remembered reading in one corner of it: *John C. Reilly & Associates, Cartography and Fine Books, San Antonio, Texas, 1884.*

Now that was a map! Liz had told her, laughing. A really old map.

On it she had seen all the rivers in Texas: the Colorado and Brazos and Trinity and Sabine and Red and all the others, flowing into the giant basin that was the Gulf. And now she wondered if that was what she was doing; because the noise, the distant roaring, she'd heard, was growing louder and louder, as she was pulled along, faster and faster. And she imagined all the rivers on the map combining into one giant river (knowing perfectly well that was not likely to occur), and racing toward the Gulf, pulling her along with them.

Because as she looked around her, she realized where she now traveled was much too large for one river, or even a combining of the rivers; far wider that the surging Amazon's mouth (as she'd witnessed on television), pulling everything along. Somehow she realized that, could hear and see that—the great roaring; the immense sweeping ahead—until, at last, she could see it all before her, and she felt her bodiless self cringe before the coming of it: the shuddering, pounding, Niagaric dumping of enormous water into an even more fathomless water below, opening up before her, taking her now into that all-encompassing, all-comforting great green sea; able to feel the undesired comfort of it, even as she quaked in its abysmal embrace, closing round her, descending.

Down...down she fell within that liquid galaxy, or so she thought. Actually, she wasn't sure now whether she was going down, sideways, or up, as in all the depthless, height-less, blue-greenness of it there was no way to tell her position or direction. But she felt herself moving along, soon feeling the closing in about her; the quickening, womb-like tunneling of water, as an embracing vortex, she was entering, turning her round and round; until she could also hear the strange humming, the frightening vibration, like some magnificent colony of water-bees was busy making enormous and ascending seashell combs of water-honey, grow louder and louder, feeling it vibrate stronger. Only then did she once again hold her breath and close her eyes, turning round-a-swirl...when— as before when she'd fallen off the high bank of Henry Spring and everything stopped—it stopped again. No noise. No movement. Nothing now. But she was there, somewhere there, but afraid to look, afraid to open her eyes, after all that had happened since then, but knowing at some point she had to do that; she just couldn't stand there; and she was now standing, she realized—but where?

Slowly she opened her eyes...finding herself in a place of multifarious shadows and mists; where even the air she breathed seemed transmuted and bent, entering inside her more as an artifice than a physical necessity. All an unreality. But then, somehow, more real, more driven within her (she deeply felt), than all the life and living she had known, gathered on a pinhead. That place. That magical conundrum.

She stood there, looking about her, for some reason, remembering that wonderful scene in *The Abyss* when Ed Harris was standing at the bottom of the ocean, behind some sort of protective curtain of air, and staring at (she was never quite sure) some sort of effervescent butterfly, not talking, not really understanding the particulars, but *knowing,* as she was now was standing there, knowing.

When suddenly he was there—a mist among mists—standing not too far before her.

"No," she said, overcome, throwing her hands over her eyes.

"Now, Sister," he said.

"No, Eric," she said, breaking into tears with the understanding of it. "No, *please.*"

"Don't be afraid."

"I'm not," she said, still crying, still holding her hands over her face.

After a moment, when she could feel him standing there, waiting patiently for her to finish, she made herself stop crying and stood there, sniffling and feeling foolish.

She heard him say, "You can look at me if you want. You can do that."

She did. She lowered her hands and looked at him, seeing him not as she remembered—purple tatted and gold earrings glittering like tiny false hopes in the sun, as he shuffled down Hollywood Boulevard with his bleached, spiked hair and hollowed cheeks and gaunt-haunted eyes—but different.

She said, "You look like I always wished you would look. I mean, if nothing bad had happened to you. To us. You look...normal."

THE BEAUTIFUL-UGLY

Suddenly all she wanted was to rush to him and hold him in her arms. She felt that desire overwhelming her, even as she knew, for some reason, she could not do that. She felt herself held there, right in that spot, unable to move at all; certainly unable to hold him as she ached to do.

She whispered, "Can I touch you?"

He stood there, watching her with the most gentle, understanding expression, and shook his head. "Not from that side. I mean, that would be, like, the most ultimate fireworks, Sis." And he smiled.

"All right," she said, disappointed.

He shrugged. "It's really weird. I haven't quite figured it out yet, but there's something about life—I mean, being alive—that we can't quite handle here. It's something, I'm led to believe, if we try and return too close to, we just wouldn't be able to deal with it. I'm not sure, but something's letting us know that." He smiled again, his nostrils flaring. "Plus there's the odor thing."

"Odor?"

He nodded. "The richness of scent about you, within you, I find overwhelming; almost as the sweetness of death and decomposition would be for the living; or maybe falling into a vat of rose oil, I don't know. But we can't handle that either."

"You're telling me I stink."

He quietly laughed and shook his head. "It's just that life has an actual smell to it, Con. I'm afraid, something too intense and too complex for our tender senses. And if you came too near, I know I would just *drown* in the abundance of it. Can you understand me?"

"I think so."

"Good," he said. She saw the way his eyes were looking over her, as he said, "I miss you, Con."

"Oh—*Eric,* I miss you so terribly. Why can't I stay here with you?"

"But you can, of course, if that's what you want."

"I do want that," she said. "I want to stay with you forever."

He was smiling, shaking his head. "I'm not sure if they could handle you here on a permanent basis, Sis."

"I'll behave. I promise."

He nodded, although, she thought he seemed to be considering something else, watching her. He said, "The way it works is, sometimes they give you a choice. Not always. But they do, under special circumstances. They let you decide whether you'll stay or go, especially when there's a complication; such as, the mixing of the lives involved. Then they prefer you decide. They prefer you have that responsibility."

"What are you talking about, Eric?"

He looked at her quizzically. "You mean, you don't know?"

She searched his face, offering the barest shake of her head.

He said, hush-voiced, "Sister, you're with child."

She felt her heart and stomach rivened through, hearing that, seeing his face saying that. And, with that, the knowledge they shared of an opportunity, a beginning, once lost, and now perhaps regained.

"No," she said. "That's not fair, Eric. Not after everything else."

"Well, that's the complication I mentioned, and why you must decide. No one else."

"Decide what?" she said. "I lost you once and now I have to decide whether to lose you again? How cruel can they be? How awful?"

He sighed. "And unfortunately it's one of those all or nothing choices, Con. As it has to be."

"But that's not *fair*, Eric."

"But don't you see what *is* fair is that you have the chance to do it right this time. You can do it the way we, together, were never allowed. You can do that, Con."

She was shaking her head, her eyes closed, wanting it to be different. Wanting it to be anything else. "All I know is I can't lose you again. I can't decide to do that." She could *feel* him there, watching her, waiting for her to decide. "Tell me what I should do, Eric. *Please.*"

"I can't do that, Sister, even if they should let me. That making of human choices, that faculty, among others, is taken from you when they take your life. But you—sweet-smelling, human-thinking girl—still have that choice. That power to decide. As well, I'm sure, as the inevitability of consequence that follows it."

She had opened her eyes again and was watching him, trying to see the difference between them, he was referring.

He smiled and shook his head, all-aware. "Don't try and understand it that way. Rather, understand that you should only feel what's closest to you, to your heart, and then decide."

"But that's you. It's only been you my whole life."

Only then could she hear him think: *But now, Sister? But now?*

And, hearing that, or thinking that, there followed the sudden rush of Will's face returning to her mind—all of him returning, standing there, smiling and talking to her, hip-cocked, as he did sometimes; this living father of the living child inside her.

She lowered her head with the gathering effect of it. The understanding.

After that moment passed, Eric said, "You've a good man, Sister."

She felt the tears welling in her eyes, knowing in a heartbeat what she'd decided. After all, the only thing could she decide. Now she sniffed and looked up, wiping her eyes. "So how're mom and dad?"

"Rooting for you, as always. They send their love."

"Oh, Eric, tell them I—"

"I know," he said. "They know."

Now they stood there, her feeling the separation, always apparent between them, widening. And she knew it was time. Once you decide, she realized, you have to leave. Quickly. That was the rule. Something was making her feel that. As well, she felt the distant throbbing agony of her injured self, her living self, returning, and shuddered. She said, "So, how?"

"Simple." He raised up his arm, extending out his hand, his finger. "Just touch your fingertip to mine."

"That's all?"

He smiled. "Believe me, that's enough."

She hesitated. "And you're sure there's nothing else? No other way we can—"

She stopped then, ending it.

"I love you, Sister."

"I love you," came her whisping voice. "Always."

Slowly, with a diminishing reluctance, she raised up her arm, extending her own hand and finger, saying at last, "*Eric?*", and touching her fingertip to her brother's…A flash and tumult came over her, lunging out and pulling her back, she felt, out of something, from somewhere; and briefly she envisioned chains about her wrists, chains as she'd pulled her own little Count Leo to life, that were now pulling her to life as well…pulling…pulling, when she burst back into—*there,* feeling herself there, steaming and wet-faced and startled—and Liz's sobbing voice saying, "*You're back. Oh God, you came back to me.*" And the hospital room turning in circles about her; and Liz holding her tightly against her on the bed; and feeling her cousin's hot tears burning down both her cheeks.

49 ♀ A FAN OF FRIDA KAHLO

When Connelly woke up in the Christus Santa Rosa Hospital in San Antonio and discovered she could barely move her legs, Liz (she knew, trying to be calm about it) told her she was lucky she could move anything at all.

"You were Coma Girl for near two weeks," she said. "They had to operate on you twice, back in the valley, just to stabilize you enough to move you down here."

Connelly lay there, listening to her talk, and trying to move her legs. She could feel her hands touching them; otherwise, that was it. But she was still groggy from coming awake and didn't want to think about her legs then. She was actually afraid to think about them and tried to think of something else.

She told Liz, "By the way, I'm pregnant."

"How do you know that?"

"I just do. Where's Will?"

"We'll talk about that later as well," Liz said.

"He did something, didn't he? You can tell me, Liz. I can handle it, I promise."

Liz took her time, arranging and tucking the sheets about her. "He went out and killed the man who did this to you."

"He killed him," she repeated the words as if they were from some twisted alien language handed her to use.

Liz nodded.

"Then he's in jail."

"I suspect the sheriff's putting up with him," she said. "But I've been so busy with you I ain't had time to worry about that."

She was going to ask her more about it, figuring Liz would say as little about it as she could get by with, when the nurse came and told her they had to prepare her for another MRI.

*

Inside the close imaging tube, she listened to the chanting monks through her headphones, while in the distance she could hear the weird array of synthetic-sounding buzzes and thumps, as they scanned her spine; and she thought about Will. Was he all right? What would happen to him? Listening to the chanting monks.

The following morning they operated on her for the third time, placing titanium screws within and bone grafts upon her cracked S-1 and S-2 sacral vertebrae.

The day after was when her doctor told her about her legs. He was a youngish-looking, gray-haired man that also looked a little busy and preoccupied. He said, "You have a mild contusion to your spinal cord at the lumbar vertebrae L-4 and L-5."

"What's a contusion?" she asked him.

"A bruise."

"Oh," she said. "Is that why I can't move my legs much?"

"Yes. It's called an autonomic response, or lack thereof, in your case."

She waited, but when he didn't say anything else—merely stood there beside her bed, busily writing something on a clipboard, ignoring her with his busy, preoccupied face—she asked him, "So will I ever walk again?"

He looked at her as if surprised she would ask him that. "Of course. With time and therapy you should be good as new. You're a very lucky young lady." He became busy writing again and said, "By the way, are you aware that you're pregnant?"

"Yes."

He nodded, glancing up at her from the clipboard. "Well, my advice would be to terminate the pregnancy. In your current condition, it would only make matters worse to attempt to carry the fetus to term."

"But I don't have to," she said quickly. "I mean, that's my choice, right?"

He frowned. "Yes, it's your choice, but I would advise against it as the least reasonable approach."

"Thank you," she told him.

After he'd gone, she looked at Liz and said, "All I know is, I don't want to kill my baby. Mine and Will's. I don't, Liz."

Liz said, "Honey, you've got plenty of time to think about that."

"No," she said, trying hard not to cry. "It's more than you know, Liz. I mean, having it and holding it as it grows up and loving it all the time and raising it *my* way, not everyone else's. It's more than you know."

"Now you see," Liz said, shaking her head. "That's just what the doctor was trying to tell you. You've hardly got started with the having part, when the talking part's already upset you."

She wiped her eyes and promised her she would do better. Then she asked her to find out the mailing address for the sheriff's office in San Miguel, because she wanted to write Will there.

That evening, after Liz gave her the address scribbled on a piece of paper, she wrote to him, telling him that she was pregnant; then telling him a little of what else she had been through, but that she was all right, and that she loved him, and to take care of himself, and concluding with a general observation on their shared predicament: *Wonderful. You're in jail, and our lives are turned upside down, and now we have to decide on matters of life and death, with our own flesh and blood, nevertheless. Just wonderful, huh?*

Days later, he wrote her back: *Well, I love you and trust you, so whatever you decide.*

Damn you—no, Will Walker! she scribbled him back in a fury. *You are half of this process and I won't let you lie up there in that jail cell and make me decide how to finish this. What do you want? Tell me what you want, Will?*, twice underlining the you's in both sentences.

This time it took him nearly the week to answer, finally sending her a postcard with a turn-of-the-century snapshot of the ivory-and-jade-tinted waterfalls below town that said only: *I would have to reject the notion of losing either of you.*

*

During her remaining time at the hospital, Connelly went to physical therapy twice each day, where she was dropped into the heated whirlpool, and rolled and twisted and pulled about the therapy table like one of Angelina's pork loins. After the first week, they helped her stand up behind the metal walker and shuffle up and down the hallway, mingling with the other patients shuffling along, until she envisioned them all as floating specters, with their white gowns flapping out behind them, emerging from out the hospital walls to spend their daily torturous hour upon the earth, moaning and groaning the while their common fate, before silently fading back into the walls to once again endure their forsaken, remorseful respite.

She never complained, and did, as best she was able, whatever they asked of her. And it was moving along the hall each day, breathing in that soured gray air of futile hope and commensurate recovery, that she also began to understand, closely and deeply, what she had only surmised, instinctively so, in writing and talking with Will and Liz, initially. That was—no matter how hard she tried to make it otherwise—how her life was never fully her own, never fully in her control; and probably not much at all; and when she was most sure about it was the hazard most quietly ominous and prevailing. She saw that now, looking back and trying to understand how it could have been different: What if she had not gone in to town that day? What if she had turned a different way and ended up in a different place? What if she had said or done something differently? What if—as the lamenting, moaning specters floated past her open door.

*

But then, of course, she would never have seen Eric again. And when she lay there at night, hearing the silence that can only come from those so gathered, shared so together in drug-numbed pain and the inveterate staring down mortality, she thought again and again of him and what happened. Or did it? Until she finally decided the experience had been too intense, too absolutely real unto itself, to describe or consider in any ordinary earthly manner she had heretofore been privy or used for such purposes.

So when she nightly considered it, she stopped thinking of the veracity of its realness, its proof either way, and thought only of that intimate actuality of having gone there, experienced what she did, and then returned to where she was now. To her own life. Her own existence. As (she knew like a whispered secret between them) was his purpose, his agreement with…whomever, before seeing her again, having to experience freshly raw and again that agony of parting, as hurting and intrusive as the scalpel's opening of her wet guts for that thoughtless circle of unseen eyes to stare within. That is, for her to understand the difference, and still decide to go on living because of that difference, rather the spite of it.

As she came to understand all too well the day they rolled her in the wheelchair out to Liz's truck, and she returned to the valley. To her living life there. When, at first, she could hardly contain herself, it being Christmas week and a dusting of snow lay over the hills and pastures like a welcoming surprise; and she looked out at the new, familiar countryside, feeling as if she'd been away for some untold age.

Meanwhile, at the ranch a welcome-home banner hung over the porch entrance and everyone was waiting for her. In spite of her protests, Clyde and Jesus carried her up the steps and straight into the small sitting room where Liz had had her bed relocated, and where she could see the big decorated spruce tree through the doorway into the larger parlor.

"It's so beautiful," she said, smelling the minty fragrance, as everyone gathered around her bed.

"*¿Tienen usted hambre?*" Angelina asked her.

"*Sí, paso hambre,*" Connelly told her. "I didn't eat any breakfast. I was too excited. But now I'm starving."

Angelina dashed into the kitchen and immediately returned with the tray and hot platter of tortillas and eggs and little crock of guava jam she had already prepared; and it was while she was eating this, surrounded by everyone smiling and talking in quiet, happy voices, that Connelly suddenly had the feeling of being overcome by all of it. By everything that had happened and almost happened, and by everything that might happen now. It was just *everything*. And she put her hands over her face, weeping in silent shame, as she heard Liz shoo everyone away, and felt the tray taken off her lap, and Liz sit down beside her.

"You know you're home now," Liz said softly. "That's all that matters."

"I'm sorry," Connelly said. "I just can't—" Unable to explain what she felt. That, being the sudden overwhelming nature of it. Of ordinary life. As Eric had intimated, and she felt coming inside her now as strongly as the gushing river of her twained existence she was so recently swept along; the purpose of it being simply to live it, to take the shapeless clay of it and mold it to some use. Nothing more. And she didn't know why that was then so hard to consider. Why it bothered her so much. When it should have been the easiest, most wonderful thing she could imagine. She finally decided that perhaps some of Eric's other-worldly sensitivity still clung to her, as the odoriferous richness of it, the layered complexity of it, being too much for her still-fragile nature.

Though she saw it nothing much to Liz, who only held her, gently rocking, and said, "None of us can, sweetheart. So don't you worry about it none. Just take your time with it, that's all. You take your time."

*

The first time she felt the baby move inside her she was sitting in the kitchen, having tea and watching Angelina prepare her venison chili (that Jesus referred to as *tazón de fuego,* or bowl of fire) when she sat upright at the table, touching her stomach, and said, "Oh, my God."

"*¿Qué pasa, mi amor?*" said Angelina, stepping toward her.

"Feet," she replied. "Very tiny feet."

"*Ah, mi Dios,*" Angelina gushed in a whisper.

As, weeks passing, many voices surrounding her seemed to be speaking to the higher deities. At Sunday Mass each week she lit a candle for Will, calling upon the wax of Christ's body and the flame of his divine love to help Will as he saw fit, until an agreement was finally reached between the attorneys and she felt at least somewhat vindicated.

Liz told her that Dix Newsome's family was now supportive of Will's case not going to trial, as the bad publicity of what Dix had done might hurt their burgeoning exotic-hunting enterprise; so the deal had been reached and Will pleaded guilty to voluntary manslaughter and was sent to the Walls Unit in Huntsville for six years, or three long, as the Stetson-hatted Austin lawyer Liz had hired told them both, "if he minds his manners better inside than he did out."

Unfortunately, Connelly was not able to see Will before they whisked him away. Then both Liz and her doctor told her, in fact, it would be better if she didn't visit the prison until after the baby was born. So she set herself for the wait, writing him letters, and enduring Liz's brand of homeschooling for the greater part of the day; afterward, taking longer and longer solitary walks down the driveway; first, with the walker; then, the hickory cane that Clyde (after several weeks of hard-cider sipping and evening-porch sitting) had whittled and polished for her, finally engraving her initials: CPW, inside the curve of the handle, mimicking what he had seen her place at the bottom, right-hand corners of her own inspired, hard-wrought creations.

It was spring now and, walking alone in the twilight, she had mixed feelings of the abundance and dearth about her and inside her. The hill country air seemed as pregnant as herself with the advent of promised life. But there was also the notion of final loss, lingering at the pasture's edge, and at the edge of her fomenting mind. It was something she had encountered her first conscious night in the hospital, and every night since; coming to her in ever-darker dreams and itchy waves of anxiety that made her want to climb out of the bed and her own skin, when neither was possible. Then was she made to lie there and try and calm herself; try and think kind and beneficent thoughts; when all she wanted to do was scream and strike out at something or someone, lying there, uneasy and unsure.

She wondered what it meant. Or did it mean anything at all? In fact, the only thing she was sure of was something had happened to her (something indeed had happened, she thought, leaning hard on the cane as she shuffled along), but whether it meant anything or was meaningless as a handful of red Texas dirt, she didn't know. Everything had seemed real, occurring; as real as anything had ever been to her. But then, maybe not. And why did she feel like that now? Like she would veritably explode, in the next instant, if something else didn't happen. Something, she had no idea. But something.

As lately her letters to Will must have contained some sense of this frustration and anger and confusion, as he had written her back that, all things considered, was she all right? She seemed somehow bothered by things. He wasn't sure.

I'm the same, she wrote him back. *I'm the same goddamned person I've always been.*

Sorry, girl, he replied, and didn't mention it again.

She thought how her life had always seemed at odds with itself. How, at particular intervals through it, it seemed intent upon tearing itself down, even as it was discovering new reasons for going on. Like now—like nearly ending itself, even as it was building itself, its reason for being, back up with the new life inside her. Crazy, she thought. It was absolutely crazy that she was going to be a mother, as her mother had been a mother to her and Eric; and what did that mean as well? Again, the answers seemed as evasive and contrary as those concerning the remainder of her current existence seemed to be. She and Liz bought some books on motherhood, and they enrolled in a breathing and birthing class; but she finally decided the majority of her response to this corporeal inevitability ever-growing inside her would be to just remember those ways of her own mother, which she now considered from the dooming aspect of her third trimester, when everything seemed too-fragile and overly brittle and slowing down. As she waited, exhausted and uncomfortable, until that brilliant blue-sky June afternoon, when her pain-wracked face leaned against Liz's rattling pickup window, and she screamed: "Goddamn you, Will Walker!"

"He can't hear you none, sweetheart," said Liz, the truck squealing into the valley hospital's emergency entrance.

"I don't care!" she argued back. "I don't—ohhh!—goddamn you, Wi—ohhh!"

*

The first night there, after everyone had finally gone away, she placed her son's delicate rosy lips over one of her own small painful nipples and watched him suckle her like a little pig; somehow feeling oddly intruded upon, this sudden sharing of her body with this helpless, insistent little stranger; these feelings then melting into an inexpressible sense of union, of shared moment, a sharing of the private selfishness that was between them now— mother and son—and no one else.

She whispered, "You don't even have a name." Running her fingers through his scant of reddish hair. Then she thought and said, "Of course, you're Will Jr.—William Eric Michael Walker. And don't you have the load to carry from the outset."

She held him up now, looking into his scrunchy, milk-drunk face; then she brought him to her, kissing his forehead, and placed him over her shoulder and patted his back until she heard the tiny burp, giving him a squeeze against her for the effort.

*

At the end of the summer, just before she was to begin classes at University of Texas in Austin, she bundled Will Jr. and drove up to the Huntsville prison for the first time.

There, she sat watching father and son get to know each other.

"He's got your eyes," she said.

"You think so?"

She nodded. "Beady and suspicious."

"His eyes are big and lovely and blue," said Will, ignoring her mood. "So are you feeling any better these days?"

"No."

*

She thought her doctor's diagnosis of postpartum depression didn't begin to explain the moody hormonal roller coaster she was feeling as a routine. That seemed to be getting worse. Leaving her with a growing desperation to find something, anything, that would catch her attention, even a little, and divert her the while; but mostly calm the simmering anger and frustration inside her, as she had finally worked through to it as best she could, at being pulled back into that mindless manner of chaotic, violent living she came out of and thought for sure she was beyond. She was done with forever. At least, she thought that.

Oddly, when she drove Will's pickup away to college that first year, what she did feel was vague, guilty pangs of relief that she had only herself to worry about now. That Liz and Angelina would take over the responsibility of little Will, even for a while, and even though where she was headed did not interest her in the least. That being her own self held no interest for her, and what she was pursuing, more out of habit that any lingering desire for (as Clyde referred to it) picture-making

She told Liz she would stick with her previous plan and major in fine arts, in spite of the fact, at least, since her encounter with Dix and Harley, she had stopped painting and had no interest in anything to do with that sort of thing. But she couldn't think of anything else to replace it. It all seemed now equally inane to her. Art. Science. Business. It was all the same. And she couldn't understand everyone else's fervor and furor over what they were doing with it and the rest of their silly, meaningless lives, thinking: *What's the purpose? What's the fucking point of it?*

Regardless, painting seemed the path of least resistance. She knew she could turn things out, just get through it, expending the least amount of effort, which she proceeded to do. Unfortunately, she also spent an equal amount of time warding off the untoward proffering of her painting professor, scraggly bearded, cornering her and her oft-brandished hickory cane throughout the semester to hiss out his garlic-breathed tensions between the living image and the captured, stylized surface; his nicotine-stained fingers extended, wavering and fluttering helplessly in the air behind like a twisted flock of stick-birds caught in an abrupt wind; and she felt actually relieved, during semester break, driving Will Jr. up again to visit his "jailhouse daddy," as she described him to her cooing, babbling son, strapped on the seat beside her.

Will by now was resigned to the change come over her, telling her he accepted it, as his own imprisonment, as part of the cost they'd paid—were paying—for the opportunity to experience whatever would come after for them.

"Opportunity," she repeated, flat-voiced. "After."

He ignored her, bouncing his son on his knee, and observed, "Anyway, this is becoming something like a tradition for us, don't you think?"

"Well," she said, taking the things from the bag—the ranch magazines and jar of instant coffee and peanut-butter crackers—he'd asked her to bring him, "I guess we have to start somewhere."

*

Her second semester seemed a little better. Fortunately, this time around, her painting instructor was a calming, non-intrusive woman, a visiting artist who, partway along, mentioned that she was beginning to see elements of Latin surrealism appear in her work.

"Are you a fan of Frida Kahlo or, perhaps, Remedios Varo?" she asked.

She didn't know. For one thing, she never concerned herself about the origins of her art, her inspiration or whatever. She could have cared less about that. It had always been just shutting her eyes and allowing that initial image—as tiny as Lady Julian's acorn—to appear, and then to grow, and to follow it along. That was her art, the following along, the knowing how to follow and keep quiet, and see what would happen next. That was the gain for her. The thrilling recompense. That occasional pursuit of unknown prey through an unfamiliar wood.

And that was now what brought her back to it; at first, mildly disarming and distracting to her; then growing, loosening up her tangled mind, opening up her sense of awareness, in the process.

Though, initially, she didn't see it as an actual improvement. To the contrary, there was the slight restlessness she felt, the faintest urgency that began to take shape in the images that came into her mind from absolutely nowhere and at first startled her. Soon, everything was affected: the design and color and texture of surfaces surrounding her; the juxtaposed features of people's faces and the odd, mixing and mincing variety of their bodily forms; the immobile face of her roommate's enormous Maine Coon cat that, when she returned to the dorm one day, had looked up at her from the other girl's bed—and smiled.

Unnerved, she tried to stop it, focusing instead on breathing deeply through her nose, and walking about the university grounds without Clyde's cane to support her; and that mixture of discomforted concentration seemed to divert her mind just enough to, at least, somewhat restrain the weird, syncopated trickle of hallucinations, or surreal distortions, or whatever it was leaking from her subconscious and leaving behind her little shimmering pools of imaginings as she walked about.

Then, after a while, she discovered she could control it somewhat; that is, at will she could take what was around her and create random, shuffling, shape-shifting patterns or more intricate designs in her mind, and then whimsically modify them in ever-intensifying degrees, before letting go. And she began to form the nervous habit of transposing heads and limbs among those more tedious, frustrating souls surrounding her from one ill-fitting, ill-gendered torso to another; or replacing them variously with rat and goat and walrus heads, and crab claws and mice paws for hands, and a Daffy Duck's splayed orange webs for feet; or, as she walked among the university buildings, turning their entire facades of windows and doors on their sides, then tilting forward their mason walls to view the intersecting floors of animated activity behind; or floating billowy, cotton-candied tree-puffs in a winding caravan—high above the unsuspecting swarms of bug-eyed, antennaed student insects, hunchbacked and clutching their books and packs as they transversed the wide, sugar-grassed, candy-gardened campus between classes—across the raspberry-sherbet-colored sky...until, like a bothersome tic, she knew she had to make herself stop. Just *stop*. And she shut her eyes, breathing deeply, and wondering: *What now? What next?*

"Are you a fan of Frida Kahlo or, perhaps, Remedios Varo?" her professor asked her.

Startled and embarrassed, she immediately returned to her more easily interpreted and acceptable abstract and representational endeavors, trying to put the rest of it out of her mind; at last, finishing the school year and going back to the ranch, and to everyone waiting for her, including her year-old, yellow-haired son, toddling breakneck down the center of the great wide hall to greet her—pink-naked and happy-faced, and peeing as he came.

*

Still, moving into the summer, there remained inside her that oddest sense of inertia—of something held in place there and fighting to break free, to unleash its own momentum and move according to its own path. She felt that and the unresolved agitation accompanying it, as she rode Teets up to Melissa's oak to sit and ponder, ill-at-ease with herself and everything in general, and still feel it inside her like a kiltered pendulum—swinging offset and pushing to free itself.

And she wondered.

*

Another day she took Will Jr. for a walk up the canyon trail to the remains of the family homestead. She held him in front of the historical marker and told him, "Will Jr., this is where your ancestors decided to start their new lives. And, I guess, this is where some of them ended them as well."

Holding him in her arms, she walked over to the briar and cedar patch, trying to peer inside.

"Somewhere in that pile of stone is our first family home and connectibles. And see there." She pointed to the side. That little piece of yard wall is what your grandma and grandpa—that's *my* mommy and daddy, Will—well, anyway, that's the piece they worked on when they passed this way. But, you see, your grandma was pregnant with your Uncle Eric. That's *my* brother, Will. So they had to stop."

She stopped now, staring at the little piece of wall nearly swallowed up by the surrounding tangle of undergrowth, and said, soft-voiced, "I always wondered what they might have thought, being here, and doing that; and if things had been different for them, if they had worked out differently, then maybe they—"

She stood there when she again felt the dull pressure inside her, building, and the anxious sweep through her; then, unable to contain herself any longer, she sat her son down in a small patch of sand and limestone shale, and got down on her knees and began to pull at the little weeds about, and then pull at the baby scrub and sapling cedar.

THE BEAUTIFUL-UGLY

She was still there pulling, her hands chafed and bleeding, when Liz came looking for her at sunset, gathering up little Will in her arms, and saying, "What in the world?"

Connelly looked distractedly up at her, flushed and breathless. "I want to finish it," she said. "I want to finish what they started."

50 ♀ FINISHING WHAT THEY STARTED

It took her a week just to clear herself enough space alongside the half-tumbled wall to begin fitting back the fallen jigsaw-puzzle pieces; then she had to keep stopping, hoe in hand, to defend the smidge of ground she'd only now claimed from the sudden, high-rattling coil of snake before her. But she finally made it back to where her parents had once stood and worked, side by side in the rising heat, as she now stood; and she placed her leather-gloved hands atop the flat-fitted wall and closed her eyes, allowing her tears to fall noiselessly down; trying only to hear and feel them there, working and talking and laughing together (her mother, perhaps, stopping to touch her hand against the bare swell of her stomach); trying to understand, before she finally went on through the long afternoon silence, fitting the stone, fitting the stone.

Occasionally, one or the other of them would wander up there and try and help her awhile. She knew they wanted to help. Or maybe they just wanted her to stop, stop acting foolish, and come back inside out of the sun. But she also knew how busy they were. Liz had hired on two more horsemen to help Clyde and Jesus handle the growing black and red and fawn-colored herds that, she noticed, had multiplied in her absence. So she mostly worked alone; although, she didn't mind, giving her ample time to sort through that cornucopia of nonsense and trivia, coursing through her mind.

THE BEAUTIFUL-UGLY

There was a flat piece of shaded ground beneath an old leaning Buttonwood tree that she placed Will Jr.'s playpen, and put her son inside with his playthings, where she could watch him, and now and then go sit by him. She knew he was a happy boy, perhaps feigning indifference, as would his daddy, to those uncontestable bars that held him in. And sometimes she would find him asleep, thumb in mouth and using his teddy bear for a pillow, and she would just sit there awhile, watching his spare breathing of that stone-dry air.

*

Near the end of the second week, Clyde surprised her one morning, driving his snaggle-toothed dozer up the wide trail to where she worked and, changing out his worn chew of tobacco for a fresh "gullet-plug," said, "Sweet darlin', you take your whatnot-stick and we'll, say, work round the edge a ways and grade it useable down some."

She nodded and—with Will Jr. feeling the change in the air, and standing up to grip his wooden bars and shout encouragement from the side—she and Clyde spent the rest of the morning clearing and grading the homestead perimeter.

Now, with her poking her snake-stick about and guiding him, what had taken her wearisome hours and days thus far now melted into minutes beneath the relentless steel dozer blade. Seeing it, she thought it was like peeling back pages of history, until even that separation dissolved, and she found herself as close as she could imagine to whatever had occurred there, the pureness of the event, lost in time.

After their noon dinner, Liz and Jesus and Angelina joined them, and they now all stood looking at what was there. They saw the two large front rooms of the old house connected to the stables and milking shed by a narrow pavestone gallery. There were two tumbled-down fireplaces; one in the front, living and sleeping room; the other in the rear, cooking and eating room. Everything beyond the stone walls themselves had been long before burned or stripped from the premises, including the wood window casings and square-timbered ceiling joists, and they spent the hour picking over the fire-scorched remains—finding a single yellow-blistered porcelain cup, as well as a .44 caliber shell casing—laying out exactly how it had been, how it eventually might be returned to that state again, though agreeing it would be a monumental task, regardless.

Connelly told Liz, "I don't care. Even if it takes me a dozen years, I don't care."

Then they all spent the afternoon stacking stone into their accorded piles, before gathering up little Will and walking in silent contemplation back to the house, where they ate cold sandwiches for supper, and where no one seemed inclined to talk about it, except to mention her health seemed to be improving with the effort.

*

As, with the passing weeks, she did indeed feel her strength returning. She had previously moved back into her tower bedroom, placing her son's crib in one corner. Then, in the morning, after attending to his needs, she would lay out her mat on the floor and do her stretches and strengthening exercises. After breakfast she and her son would wander together back up the hillside, to the ruins, and begin again, spending most of their day there. That's when she could feel her strength coming back inside her body, building the rock wall, stopping occasionally to take walks up the high canyon where a stand of wandering elm had established themselves. There, also, was the stream and disappearing pool where, according to Liz, the John Walker party, arriving, had first quenched their thirst and rested their weary bones in the wetted shade. And sometimes she and little Will would nap there, before returning below and to their work.

Of course she knew exactly that the odds of her ever rebuilding the stone cabin and its attaching structures to their original condition were highly unlikely. Likely impossible, in fact. She had neither the skills nor the strength to achieve that eventual desire, but she didn't mind. She enjoyed merely being there, and little Will seemed to like it, and so she continued to work through the summer, into August, when she knew it was almost time for them to drive up to the prison and be with that other Will. In fact, so content was she there, being there with her son and doing whatever she was able, she hardly noticed that last Saturday morning, the arriving caravan.

It was, in fact, Will Jr. who said, "Uh-oh, Mommy." And pointed.

THE BEAUTIFUL-UGLY

Then she looked and saw the line of cars and trucks pulling into the ranch yard below. She watched as the gaggle of men piled out and began unloading their toolboxes and wheelbarrows of materials and making their way up the trail toward them. There were at least forty of them, coming in two's and three's, with little Will again saying, "Uh-oh, Mommy."

The first man to her said good-naturedly, "Morning, Ms. Connelly. Heard you had yourself a little project going up here. Mind if we lend a hand?"

All she had time to do was grab her son and move out of the way, as the men came on, streaming past her, nodding and smiling at her and talking together as they strung out along the structure perimeter and set to work. Within minutes the entire setting took on the appearance of a rising hill of ants, with the masons mixing their mortar for the walls, and the carpenters re-casing the windows and doors. More were arriving below, she saw. She had gone with her son and stood beneath the Buttonwood tree, watching as more cars and trucks came, along with a trailered backhoe, and then the deuce-and-a-half from the lumber yard, rumbling last up the driveway, loaded with thick timber joists and long, forest-green sheets of aluminum for the roof.

She was watching the backhoe, splayed legged and eating its way slowly up the hill from the barn to the cabin; then digging the septic tank behind for the little attached privy; and the plumbers following, laying the plastic waterline in its sandy base, when Liz came up with the other women. They set up the tables of food and drink, and then Liz came over to her.

Connelly hugged her and said, "Thank you, Liz."

Liz waved her hand and said, "Listen, I just got tired listening to Miriam Harrison—who, you recall, chairs the Ladies' Historical Society—over at Gunderson's Market, squeezing tomatoes and going on how they'd been looking and looking for a bona fide restoration project for them to take on this year, and couldn't find a thing. So I told her to stop complaining and for them to send their husbands up here to help you out. Of course, they'll want to put up one of their plaques, patting themselves on the back, and give those historical tours once a year during the springtime, open-house jamboree, but I didn't think you'd mind."

"No," said Connelly. "I don't mind."

"Good," Liz said. "Now let's go pass out bottled water to the men and make them feel important."

*

When she went back to school she at first felt herself oddly torn with the sense of some manner of hard-wrought fulfillment mixing with another, stranger kind of despondency; turning, as the days passed, only into a deeper and darker feeling of desolation, and continuing the downward slide into the sealed black box of unredeemable loss. For days pretending she was sick and staying hidden in her dorm bed. For days. Until she made herself get up and do things again she didn't understand the purpose of. She was just doing them without feeling, without awareness or consequence.

She understood that the fulfillment was about finishing the stone cabin, and all that came with that. And she had thought that would change things. She thought accomplishing that would make a difference for her, and it had, for a while. Like a noxious disease in momentary remission, it had heedlessly and indifferently given her a measure of hope, before taking it back. Quickly. Without mercy. She saw that, feeling the gnawing edge of her anger and frustration returning, and tried to understand it.

She recalled the former feelings of inertia that had plagued her in the early summer, and that she had temporarily alleviated by working at the cabin. But now she understood it wasn't quite like that. Not quite a feeling of inertia, but of something else, like a sense of approaching expurgation, building in the deepest part of her stomach and wanting to break free. But she still wasn't sure.

Then Liz called her.

It was evening and she was lying in bed, trying to work through some preliminary sketches for an assignment, when her cell phone rang; and she saw Liz's pretty, sassy face appear on the little window, and she set herself, not wanting her to suspect anything.

Then she listened to her going on about how things were going, and how Will Jr. was into one thing after the other—keeping both her and Angelina bumping into each other, trying to stay up with him—and then on about why she'd *really* called, which was to tell her she was having some period furniture built for the cabin. That way, said Liz, if you and Will Jr. ever felt like camping out up there on occasion, you could do that. Connelly could tell by the sound of her voice that wasn't really why she called at all; and she waited, listening to Liz hem and haw, until she said, offhandedly, "David said he'd have it done in a week or so. The furniture, I mean."

Then Connelly smiled and said, "David."

She waited again.

"Well, that's just that carpenter you met that day. The one you told me first said hello to you and they were all there to help. You remember?"

"Oh, *that* David," she said. "As in the one you told me whose wife died the same year as Jack. The good looking one."

"Well I didn't notice that none," said Liz.

"I don't suppose. Anyway, has he asked you out yet?"

"Well, I wouldn't call it exactly *out*. I had him over for a chicken-fried supper one night, and he invited me over to his place for TV dinners and a rent movie another. And then we went down to San Anton to watch a basketball game one time; and then we had to spend the night there, it being too late to come home and all. But I'd hardly call it, say, *out*."

"*Christ*, Liz, you're practically engaged already."

"Oh, would you stop," she said, sounding happy-voiced. "But, I'll admit, it is refreshing to talk to a man about something besides cattle, which he has no interest in. Nor land, for that matter; as that's to remain for you and Will and Will Jr. to steward in your own way and time. Anyway, there's the potential for things, you understand, and I just wanted you to know that up front."

"Well, thank you, Liz," she replied, knowing the other was digging at her again for not telling her first about Will.

"It's just the potential, you understand," Liz said again.

Soon after they hung up, Connelly tried to go back to her drawings, but finally set them aside and lay there, thinking; finally coming back to that word Liz had mentioned—*potential*.

Why did that make her think of something? And she lay there and lay there, and then she remembered: Eric and his science project, his parallel and series electrical project.

She closed her eyes and saw herself sitting half-bored on her brother's bed, and her brother, like a little bespectacled professor, sitting beside her and holding up the piece of painted plywood covered with wires and switches and little ornamental bulbs, telling her about the potentiality of electricity, which was also known as voltage, he said.

"What's that?" she asked him, mildly intrigued by something she thought she'd heard before, but wasn't sure.

"It's a measurement of energy," he said. "Like an amount of pressure, trying to release itself. See, Con." And he threw the switch and the little light bulbs began to glow. "On this side you have potential, and on the other side it's gone. It's zero now."

"Where'd it go?"

"It used itself up lighting the bulbs, or sometimes it can go to ground and just be wasted."

"Oh."

"Of course it's still really there—the electricity, the energy—you can't destroy that, Con. But now you have to send it back to the electric company so they can give it more potential."

"Uh-huh. Make the lights come on again, Eric."

"All right."

And once again he threw the tiny toggle switch and the row of ornamental lights began to glow.

*

As the fall deepened into winter she thought about that: the potentiality within things. Like that handful of electrons circling and circling about themselves, biding their time and waiting to free themselves, maybe to use their energy for something worthwhile. Or perhaps go to ground and be wasted.

Then she realized how, at the most critical point, she had gone to ground. Literally. Dix had hit her and knocked her over the bank, and she had fallen the ten or twelve feet to the rocks below, and she had gone to ground and was wasted, or her potential was. And that was it. That was the hollow, horrible feeling deep inside her stomach, pushing and pushing and wanting to come out. Not potential, but rather that promise which she once had and was lost. Wasted, she thought. Like all those other groundings she'd had her whole life, time and again, year after year, when the potential had renewed itself, full of hope and possibility (though each time, perhaps, a little less so), and then gone to ground. Or been knocked there, as it was.

The occasion with Dix was only the latest in that long line, and maybe the worst, causing her, once and for all, to lose her nerve. And even more—her desire. Because it was something not of her making; and now felt it was something beyond her reach anymore, leaving her with those feelings now, accumulative and insurmountable, of desolation and loss. And so Eric was wrong, she thought at last. Energy could be destroyed. The potential inside her. It could be. She was proof of that. Wasn't she?

*

Without telling Liz, she went a couple of times to a therapist in Austin, but she saw right away how that only brought up those bad old feelings again of those days and events before, and she stopped going; even when the therapist told her it would take time to work through them together. It would take time. But she knew she couldn't do that again. She knew she was through with it—that part of her life, in that way—she was through with it.

Besides, she also knew she didn't need a doctor to help her pinpoint or understand that black ravaged hole inside her that was once something else, but was now only that. And the week after she stopped seeing the therapist, she saw her counselor and talked with her about changing her art major into something else as well. The art wasn't working, she told her. Her art. The way it was coming out, wasn't working. And maybe it never had worked. But then she didn't know what else to do, except maybe (as Mr. Gladdens had warned her) end up painting advertising murals on the sides of chowder houses, or go teach art history to a bunch of self-satisfied poseurs that could care less about the vicissitudes of a damned thing. Maybe that.

The counselor told her to wait. It was winter solstice, she said. Why didn't she go home for those holidays, and they could talk when she returned. So she returned home, in anxious turmoil, nothing resolved.

*

However, the winter tranquility of that place did make her feel better. Her second day there she asked Jesus what she could do, and he handed her a shovel and told her to clean stalls. So she put Will Jr. in one stall, already scrubbed and fresh-strawed, and set to work, shoveling out and scrubbing down the other stalls, one after the other, spreading fresh straw after.

Her third morning there she rode with Clyde out to fence-mend and put new hinges on a gate; returning, they met Liz riding toward them, and the three of them rode up the canyon to the old homestead so Liz could show her the new furniture David had made for it. There, wandering through the rooms, Connelly ran her hands over the hand-hewn wooden bed and locker, and little wooden desk and chair, with the oil lamp in one corner.

In the kitchen were the small eating table and four chairs, and there was a small antique cook stove that Liz had found somewhere and had installed, and dishes and pots and pans from the main house.

She told Liz, "I want to sleep here tonight with little Will."

"You sure?" Liz asked her. "Channel Four says we got a mean blue'n headed toward us, and my broke elbow's aching like a hollow tooth."

"We'll be all right. I'll bring my old art bag and Will can finger paint. I'll bring something to read. It'll be fun."

"I reckon," said Liz.

And Clyde began to tote in cedar kindling and hardwood sticks from the covered gallery, filling the wood box by the stove.

*

That night, as the cold front moved upon them, she listened to little Will run and holler back and forth through the cabin, while she built a kindling fire in the stove. She watched the dry sticks crackle and flame, then added larger pieces and replaced the lid, adjusting the damper.

She made them toasted cheese sandwiches on the flat grill, and boiled water for hot chocolate.

After they ate and she cleaned up, she said to her son, "Do you want mommy to read to you in bed?"

He ran off then, looking for his storybooks.

*

The winter storm arrived around midnight, barreling down off the high northern prairies, up the narrow canyon, and smashed against them like a herd of giant rumbling tumbling sage-demons, passing by, flashing and blinking their enormous gaze through the cabin windows.

"Oh, Mommy," Will Jr. said, as both their noses poked out over Angelina's fresh-smelling, windblown sheets.

In the morning there was the view she loved after a storm, with everything washed bright and clean. She sat on the cabin porch, having her coffee, and watching her son playing down along the descending trail. A few of Jesus' goat herd had worked their way up that far. For some reason she couldn't fathom, they seemed to relish the tiny daggered briars that grew from between the rock and were there eating them now. Little Will had wandered among them, the nannies nibbling like sweet bitches at his untucked shirt and fleecy hair. She observed this, seeing it as it actually was, when something else happened inside her—something shifted there—and she was seeing something entirely different now.

Next, she was setting down her cup and struggling to her feet. She ran back inside and through the cabin, into the kitchen corner where she had placed her art bag the previous evening. She grabbed it up and ran back outside.

Seated on the porch, she hurriedly began to mix the colors, trying to capture that particular red of the Spanish goat hair, like Angelina's *mole* sauce with its toasted poblano chilies mixed with melted chocolate into the rich mahogany hues. Next, she daubed her brush into the paint and lifted it, hesitating and taking a deep breath, and then lowered it toward the waiting canvas. Soon she was working in a frenzy, her eyes following her son's stilted movements across her field of vision, surrounded by the biting, bumptious creatures, until there was revealed before her the frazzled, dazzling melee of flaring nostrils and gnashing teeth, consuming the child whole.

*

As the winter and then spring months turned into summer, she was only partly aware of what was taking place on canvas after canvas appearing before her, and then left abandoned against the cabin walls, inside the wooden locker, the bare stables behind. Bright, wild scenes of mad distortion and foul display, and others of some kind of prolonged, anguished pouring out appeared as if by magic, filling up what had only been the commonest space, previously.

First Liz came—glancing about herself with diffident interest at the suggested faces and bodies of children, and of the same girl or group of girls, and others, often older and faceless and lingering in the background, as if unsure of their purpose there—and merely shrugged and brought Will Jr. away with her, the while.

Then came Angelina, weeping in silence before the unfolding tragedy, as she wrung her hands and whispered, "*Ah, mi Dios*," wandering among the tangled bizarre scenes of naked carnal lunacy (as she herself, gasping and panting and clutching at her breast, witnessed them) upon display; until she happened to look up and noticed that, at that very moment, her little bird was capturing *her*—Angelina Consuelo Navarrete's—likeness, including her embroidered virgin-white Chiapas blouse and long purple-pleated Pica skirt, even as she stood there barefoot before her; though now pulling her down with her, she realized, into her own unimaginable and horrifying madness. And she cried out and ran away in a fright, vowing never to return.

*

It was during this coming and going that Connelly began to try and more carefully observe and understand this mad fit, this retching, indeed, expurgation, in progress; as if her life, like that great strange river she had descended to reunite one last time with Eric, had been tilted back on his source, with the waters returning there and flushing forth in an unstoppable torrent until emptied; until there remained nothing inside her but that final fading Technicolor scream that she painted out one morning, and then set down her brushes and went walking.

That was also the afternoon Liz took the photograph of her holding Will Jr. naked against her naked self; and she saw that and felt what was inside her now, which was something new and quiet and at some stasis of peace with itself; finally returning to the cabin and painting her mother-and-son portrait, with the descending blued and grayed layers, darkening into something unrevealed and unrequited from outside itself.

Until she found herself moving through the remaining summer, though the flow continuing inside her, but guiding more its direction, controlled and purposeful and moving ahead with more a sense of ease and calm elation and that tingled thrill of creation, from this to that.

At one point, she put aside her paints and began to build collages from whatever scraps of materials she found about herself. She went back to her bright-colored river clays, experimenting with those rare, raw forms her subconscious daily dredged. She bought a wood carving set and began to whittle and scrape until the images swelling forth from her mind began to equally swell forth from within the plump fragrant blocks the lumber yard gave her free.

Then one day she noticed Clyde welding something clamped on the tailgate of his pickup; and she saw the bright sparks shooting out and the twisted glowing metal being transmogrified into something else entirely, something useable and strong; and she went by him, leaning winsomely near him and said, "Clyde, teach me how to weld."

Clyde raised his eye-shield, spitting off brown juice, and said, "Sweet darlin', Lincoln rigs and at-cetlin' torchins ain't the right sort a thing a girl ought to be messin' with. 'Specially one, say, got themselves jeg-legged up, the while back."

She gritted her teeth. "Now Clyde McKinney, now I just don't have *time* for this."

As she felt herself in the full throat of her life, no more able to lessen its gathering speed, than she was to deny its heady though promising particulars

And Clyde sulled his hour, then got down to it.

51 ♀ PEDDLING HER ART

Through both her and Liz's letters, and Connelly's visits, Will had been able to halfway piece together and follow his young bride-to-be's comings and goings while he was away. And this referred not so much to her physical wanderings (although, anything, any bite or scrap of information, about her daily existence intrigued and often mystified him); rather, the mental and emotional journey she was obviously involved, and that he tried desperately to follow behind, as long as he was able and she allowed, until she finally told him: "It's nothing, Will. It's just something I have to work through. Just me. Like you having to be here and deal with this. You understand that, don't you?"

He told her he did, although he still didn't enjoy the feeling of being left behind somewhere, from wherever or whatever it was she was moving toward, or perhaps from, for herself. Though he bided his time, wondering; while also understanding how that was the hardest thing for him, being around her, having to also bide his mood, his sense of—how could he say?—pure joy at them both just being there, both of them having survived that far, and maybe they could now survive even farther, and someday be together again. Feeling that. Though having to mostly hide it from her, as it always annoyed her, seeing him so at ease with their circumstances.

"You're in this fucking place, Will," she commented during one of her earlier visits. "And you're acting like someone's done you the biggest fucking favor in the world."

When just seeing her there, able to say that to him, almost taking his breath away, as he was made to look away, shaking his head, and swallowing his smile.

Still, most mystifying to him was when, well into his third year there, she came to him, yet changed again. She seemed more at ease now with herself and with everything, really. She had gone there—wherever *there* was—and now she was back. But he knew better than to mention it, though grateful and breathing easier for it, saying only, "Pretty girl, I can't tell you how good peanut butter tastes, once you've eaten it with a prison spoon."

"Oh, really," she said (and he thought) with that particular supercilious smugness of someone who'd left the absolute world behind, and then returned as something or someone of their own kind and making.

"Oh, sure," he said back, taking his son from her. "By the way, smarty pants, they signed my papers. I'll be home come November."

*

Home. How often had he mulled that one word over in his mind, seeming in the beginning like the cruelest word imaginable; then, as time passed, becoming something else; until it became the one special word that most sustained him.

Home.

Arriving there late one morning, after Connelly, alone, had picked him up before daylight and driven him there; though, having her pull off the freeway at the first rest stop not far along so he could walk around, telling her, "I just want to do that. I just want to feel myself free-walking, because *I* want to do it, and no one telling me."

He walked the length of the rest area, and back again. Then he got back into the truck. "All right. I'm ready. Let's go home."

What he discovered was, no matter how hard you try to slow it down, once you've been gone from something, it comes back at you at its own speed, unconcerned where you've been or how you feel about it. It comes at you.

Everyone, outside, seemed to be living breakneck fast to him. Even on the ranch where there was usually a sustainable pace and rhythm, everything now seemed like the most frenzied city. Then, his long-abiding fiancé telling him his second morning home how she decided she wanted to marry him over her semester break didn't change that perspective.

They were sitting out on the porch when she told him. "And I want to be married in the big hall," she told him. "So all those other Walkers, and all those other kin hanging on the wall, can see it."

"You sure?" he asked her.

She looked at him. "Why, do you want a church wedding?"

"No, I mean the getting married part. I mean, maybe we should wait," he said. "Give things time to settle down."

"I've been waiting three years, Will Walker," she said. "I just turned twenty, and I've been having your son inside me and outside me all this time. And he wants a daddy. And I want—I want you, Will."

"You have me. And I ain't goin' nowhere this time."

"That's not what I mean. What I mean is—"

She stopped, looking at him, and then quietly rose and went inside the house.

He was still sitting there when Angelina came out with his coffee. Then she sat down beside him while he sipped it, and he could tell she was anxious about something, finally leaning toward him and whispering, "Oh, *Señor* Will, *¡Usted debe ver algo!*"

"*¿Qué?*"

Next, she had her arm through his, leading him up the trail into the east shed where he soon saw the pretty limestone cabin, with its metal-green roof, sitting on the flattened rise, before the steep ascent. Of course he knew the cabin had been rebuilt, because she had told him all about it on her visits, and showed him photographs. But now, seeing it there, it gave him a different feeling altogether; although, he was still sorting through exactly what that was, when Angelina opened the door and waved him inside.

When he stepped through the door the sunlight was beginning its first cool gray filtering within, and he stood there a moment, letting his eyes adjust. Then, at one point, he became aware of something else: the steadily intensifying colors and shapes, surrounding him, and that, after moments passing, burst forward from the shadows, as with a single leap, to confront him. And he fought the urge to step back.

"Oh, *Señor* Will," Angelina said, anguish voiced, waving her hand and the white handkerchief it held out before her as to reveal the final misfortune befallen them. "*Así que horrible.*"

She sniffed now, daubing the corner of her eye with a handkerchief.

He stepped farther into the room, looking around him, mesmerized by what he saw, but knowing, understanding, nothing more than that. After a minute, the first clear thoughts came into his head: *So this is it. This is where she's been all along. This is what she's been doing.*

He remembered how he figured out she had been working through something. There was something inside her she had been working through. And this was the result. And he stood there, pondering that, when he realized something else. That was—he couldn't understand this at all. Not really. Not the way she obviously had understood it and dealt with it. Not that way. And maybe not any way. Ever.

He turned and said, "Angie, please go back to the house."

She nodded and turned, going out.

He remained there awhile, going through the cabin and dog-run gallery and into the little stable, seeing everything that was there. When he went back into the cabin he saw her sitting on the edge of the bed, waiting for him.

She said, "I figured Angelina would drag you up here soon enough. She told me she says a special prayer to her private saint each day for me, and he's promised her I'll make a full recovery."

Will said, "These are wonderful, Con. Has anyone else seen them?"

She shook her head. "I just want to marry you, Will. I'm through fighting the world. I just want to marry you and live my life with you. That's all. Do you understand me?"

He told her he did.

*

It snowed on their wedding day. The old house was filled with everyone they knew, the big hall overflowing with people into the side rooms where the fireplaces crackled and the piano music played. Will stood at the head of the hall, with Clyde fidgeting beside him in his yellow-rose necktie and his least threadbare brown suit, and watched them both come down the hall toward him. Wilburt Raintree was giving her away, holding her arm as delicately as he would hold his number-two perch fly rod, and looking solemn as Moses and, Will thought, regal as a picture he'd once seen of Sitting Bull in a museum. Though his eyes did not tarry on the old man, beside whom, she moved toward him like an ethereal spirit, a floating, veiled drift of white, and he swallowed.

When she stood beside him and he lifted back her veil, Will wondered if his knees would endure the strain, or buckle beneath him. Then he looked down into her eyes and saw her looking back, curious and unafraid, with that ever-winsome edge of some mystery to her smile, and wished he could know every thought passing there through her mind at that moment and the moment after.

As he listened to the priest offer up the vows, and their voices following in turn, he recalled another moment the previous week they had gone walking down by the tank, the little lake in the west pasture. The sun was down over the trees and they stood on the new pier Clyde and Jesus had recently built, looking out over the still water. There were pairs of geese walking the far side, nibbling at bugs, and wild mallards settling for the night among cattail reeds along one curve of the lake, when he looked over at her and said, "What are you thinking right now, lady?"

She looked back at him with that same unabashed expression, that same full-lipped edge of whatever, and said, "Nothing, really, Will. I'm just seeing things."

"Seeing?"

She nodded. "Just seeing the way things are. The way I can use them."

"You mean paint them?"

She nodded again and sighed. "Sometimes I believe it's an actual sickness, Will. This alternative reasoning always going on inside me. How I can use something. How I can capture it. Always that. I've been that way all my life. This sick woman you're going to marry. Of course, you have to understand—if I didn't do that, if I didn't paint, I'd already be dead. I wouldn't have made it this far. It's like it made me crazy and kept me sane all at once. So maybe there is some redeeming value to it, after all."

She stopped talking about it then, as if she'd already said too much, allowed him to see too much. But she'd said enough, he knew. As it was perfectly clear to him now that, although he might not ever understand her entirely like that, he would love her for it.

He would marry her and love her and hold her tightly to him until only time or some misfortune ripped her from his arms. Because he knew then that's what she tried to tell him that day out on the porch, talking about time and their future. That is, that nothing was guaranteed. And certainly nothing was permanent. And you could only do what you desired most, if you were lucky, before something else happened. He knew then, standing there on that new-smelling, cypress-wood pier with her, he would do whatever he could to support her in that. In her sublime sickness. Her crazy, sane art. He would do what he could.

"I now pronounce you husband and wife," the priest told them. "Will Walker and Connelly Pierce-Walker, you may now, before the eyes of God, kiss each other as one."

*

With his parole and her school schedule, they agreed to wait until both had been settled before taking a proper honeymoon. Instead, they spent the weekend in San Antonio, lounging about the Riverwalk, eating tacos and refried beans, and talking of things to come. Then they returned home, when she hugged and kissed everyone and almost immediately drove off to finish her school year, and he went back to ranching.

Though he felt himself preoccupied by things she'd said and what he'd resolved to do about them. So he went and talked with Liz about it, and she agreed they should probably try and do something about it, "although, she won't like it none when she finds out," she said.

"She won't find out," Will told her. "Just make sure Angelina doesn't write her any weepy letters about it and we'll be fine."

After that, they relocated all her artwork from the cabin to the main house. There, going through it, and initially trying to categorize and arrange it according to medium and whatever other kind of type and method they could fathom from it; then finally dividing everything up under the three generic headings of Strange Though Obviously Beautiful, Disturbing Though Most Likely Therapeutic, and Unknown.

They talked about it and Liz said the only gallery in the valley was Henry Merewether's Western Art and Memorabilia, at the edge of town. "Though he mostly sells cow skulls to tourists," said Liz, "who, I reckon, get them home and then realize what they've done."

So they selected a sampling of the paintings and drove down valley.

There, Henry looked at the pieces and drew back. "What am I supposed to do with these?" he nattily snapped at them both, as if forced to ponder such dark souls of torture and dement, they threatened to leap up and pull him back down into their chambers of awful ambiguity, their recesses of salacious compromise.

"Well, Henry," Liz told him, "you could shove them up your behind, but then we'd probably have to work out some sort of consignment."

"Now, Liz, there's no need to go standing up in your stirrups. This is just not the sort of thing I handle. You know I do Western realism, Remington knockoffs, and cowboys and Indians and prairie sunsets; not this sort of thing. Why, the sheriff's liable to arrest me if I's to try and put these on display."

Afterward, they both had pie and coffee at the Drop Biscuit to commiserate their shared predicament. There, halfway through his second cup, Will had an idea.

*

On his same gallery at Huntsville, three cells down, there had been an older man doing twelve years for forgery named Winston Johns. Will used to go sit in Johns' cell and talk about football and ice-fishing, while watching him do his small, eclectic pen-and-ink drawings of birds and insects. Will thought the bizarre detail of the drawings was amazing. Johns had trained as a zoologist before he had apparently convinced himself doing small, eclectic drawings of people's signatures was more profitable. But he preferred not to talk about that. He grew up in Beaver Dam, Wisconsin, and was a fervent Cheesehead; so they talked about football and ice-fishing, as well as what they would do when they got out.

Johns was already selling his stuff. There was a dealer in Madison he sent them to, and before he was released, the year before Will, he had caught the interest of one of the wandering curators of the Whitney Biennial, who put him in that year's show.

He had written Will after his release. He was living in New York City now, where, although he was still a Cheesehead, and missed his ice-fishing, his tortuously cartoonish caterpillars and abstract robin's head drawings were fetching five large, each; twice that, if he colored them.

THE BEAUTIFUL-UGLY

Will thought about it and one morning, with Connelly deeply ensconced in her studies at Austin, called Johns.

They talked about old times for a while and then he told him what he wanted.

Johns was happy to accommodate and told him, "C'mon up, son. But don't forget my analogy of a goldfish swimming in the pool of piranhas. And don't be surprised if they're not very receptive while stripping you to the bone. Surviving prison, that entire protracted agony, was great preparation for entering the New York art scene."

It took Will a couple of weeks to obtain permission from his parole officer in San Antonio to fly to New York. Once he had this, however, it all began to move very quickly. Liz purchased him a large leather travel portfolio, and the day before he left, they again went through the works, selecting two from each of their three categories; then slipping them carefully inside the lined case.

The next morning, carrying the portfolio on the plane with him, Will flew to New York City. Over lunch, Johns told him the curator that would be coming by his studio that afternoon to look at his wife's paintings was Francois Vergne, from the Whitney, and that his bark was not nearly as bad as his bite.

"I had to cash in all my chits to get him over there," Johns said. "His latest show's got some bad reviews and he, unfortunately, is pissing blood these days. He let me know he certainly didn't have the time, but would swing by on his way over to somewhere else."

Will lowered his head, poking at his food. "Well, I appreciate it, Winston. Anything you can do."

Johns' laugh was a little morose. "It's got nothing to do with me. Either it's there or it isn't, and Mr. Vergne will not be shy telling you which is which."

After lunch, as a bleak gray snow began to fall, they went for a walk. Will was nervous and, although not a smoker, he purchased a pack of cigarettes from a drugstore and lit one up as they walked along. He threw the cigarette and pack away halfway down the block.

Johns told him, "You need to settle down. If Vergne sees you like this he might go into a feeding frenzy."

There was a bookstore they passed. Will went back and bought her a selection of Katherine Mansfield stories he knew she loved. Now carrying the small book in his coat pocket he felt better, and they slowly made their way back to Johns' SoHo loft where Francois Vergne was sitting in the back of his snow-encrusted Town Car, waiting on them.

"Oh, *Christ*," said Johns. "He's early."

Will saw a small nervous man, wearing a black cashmere overcoat and peach silk scarf, alighting like an attack wren upon the sidewalk, and felt his stomach sink. Vergne nodded curtly when Johns introduced them, though first staring with open incredulity at his scuffed Justin boots and Carhartt coat and tattered Knudsen hat. Then he glanced at his watch, announcing: "Three minutes, Winston."

They tromped somberly up the dark stairs and finally entered the spacious, gray-lighted loft. No one said a word as Will hurriedly fumbled, unzipping the portfolio, and taking out the six paintings, one by one; again, encountering that feeling of near vertigo of color and form, washing over him, seeing them there in their new setting. He leaned them against the wall, glancing up once at Winston and Vergne, and then stepped awkwardly to the side, out of the way.

Francois Vergne stepped forward before the paintings and stood there, chin in hand, contemplating.

A full minute passed in complete silence. Will slowly sucked in his breath and exchanged glances with Johns.

Johns shrugged.

Another entire minute passed interminably by with Mr. Vergne still there, seeming a small abandoned statue, when Will heard the faint sound of what could well have been the deadly sigh of discontent, and Vergne said quietly, "When may I meet her?"

Will glanced aside at Johns and back, swallowing. "She won't come here."

Francois Vergne now looked over at him severely, as if he might suddenly snap or peck at him, and then offered, painfully, what Will figured was his version of a smile. "Good. Let her paint." He looked back at what was before him, his eyes coming to rest on the mother-and-son nude in the light and dark shadows of deep cerulean smoke. "We'll go there."

EPILOGUE

♀ FOURTEEN YEARS GONE

In that twentieth summer of her life she rode with her husband and son up the Lost Woman shed to watch the sun go down over the unfathomed hills. A party, meanwhile, was still in progress at the house, celebrating that day's publication of *Settler Girl: the Journal of Melissa Montgomery Parker*, edited by Elizabeth McCullough, PhD, University of Texas, with original watercolor drawings by Connelly Pierce-Walker. Though Connelly told Will she was tired of the attention and just wanted to ride somewhere.

They spent the better part of an hour sitting beneath Melissa's now infamous oak tree, watching the approaching twilight, before Will Jr. pointed and said, "Oh, look, Daddy!"

"It's just an old firefly, boy," Will said, starting to rise up and snatch it from the air.

"No," she said. *"Don't."*

Will looked at her. "I was just going to show him how you can—"

"Yes, I know," she said. "But, if you do that, then it won't be able to find its way home. It'll be lost, Will. Forever lost."

"What?" he said. "Who told you that?"

"Someone. Long ago."

Will only shrugged. "So we ready to be getting back?"

On the ride back, Connelly thought about that little moment of forgiveness with the firefly, and then thought how, perhaps, her own life had been that—and act of ongoing forgiveness to herself, as well as to others—and what she had to do, in order to go on with it. And, for just a moment, she wondered if that had been the best way, deciding finally it didn't matter. The important thing was she *had* gone on with it, regardless. She had found a way, over and over, to forgive, in order to simply *be*. And that was enough. With fourteen years gone since the day her parents were lost, and she went searching.

That was enough, she decided. That was all.

Until the late hour, when the magic bugs had finally availed in their search, and the rivers ran silent and deep somewhere beyond, they gathered on the verandah to hear her read from Melissa's diary, watching her open the new book, turn over the crisp pages between her fingers, and say: "Father was made to pull me aside this morn and chastise me for that, in his words, ill-thought and worse-timed comment to those gaggling ladies of our church sanctity order that he indeed, for whatever reason, found previously necessary to offer official sanction. And though I find them so many low-queened hens of sovereign arbitration, clucking about so into the private affairs of goodly, awkward men and kind women feigned to mannered etiquette, father insists their benefit and need among the more ill-kempt and off-mannered in our community; leaving me thus to say—'O, Father, as thou hast decreed, then must it be so!' Which inevitably infuriates him the while, as I am made to offer quick-felt apologies to soothe his rumpled red brow and calm those two queer crimson orbs that were prev his so wonderful and familiar and comforting eyes.

"Yet, I must admit, when he requested I make similar entreaties to those fore-mentioned ladies of the church, I threw myself begging against him not to expose me in so unkindly a manner before them and their specious judgments against all that our own all-loving, all-forgiving (as I greatly emphasized) God hath wrought. Tho, as feared, my pious argument held little effect on him, and I was made to walk stiff-jointed, with a vertiginous swirling inside my head, before them; and then seeing them there, sitting and leaning together in their soft-clucked row, as if well-sweated, brown-shelled eggs would suddenly and magically roll forth from 'neath their feathered hems…waiting…as I finally—tho foul throated and sour tongued—did apologize and offered them a piqued curtsy and made my stumbled flight.

THE BEAUTIFUL-UGLY

"Thereafter, our wagon ride home was a sullen, long affair, with mother first peeking back at me and then father, who sat before me stiff-backed and holding out the reins before him as if a dozen tender lambs were yoked to that gathering weight behind, and he dared not so much as twitch the tethered lines between, less they jerk him forth in some violent recompense.

"Then, arriving at our home, as I could no more break dinner bread nor have genial conversation with that man, I went walking behind the cabin on the little hillock where that cluster of scaling birch offer their mote of privacy, and I did sit there and visage him in private agony behind, and me in my own sweet steaming agony therein. Tho anon I began to remember the time, when only a child of four or five, I fell on the shale pile behind our Pittsburgh home (alas, do I still miss the pink and yellow of its gingerbread trim), and did he make such a fuss, coming and picking me up and pretending to doctor me, offering me up his kisses and coos. And the time on the riverboat, indeed coming downriver toward and into our unknowing frontier, when that derelict wharfsman in New Orleans did accost me in a manner I was heretofore unfamiliar, and father defended me, telling him to mind his lines as the vermin were boarding tail to nose in a row behind him even then, and escorting me away.

"And thinking thus, I soon rose up and returned in evermore fervent steps to our little abode, where I saw him at his sermon desk, bent and worried as ever over the manners and morals of his people; fumbling with the next words he must say to them that would change them, their piteous lives, forever; and my heart nearly broke inside me at the witness of his impossible task. So I ran to him across the strawed earth and threw my arms around him, truly apologizing for my misbehavior, and promising to astonish him with my future demure.

"Thence, we sat laughing and arguing together, as was our practice, with my brothers running to and fro into the evening sun, and mother smiling and bringing me my late plate of peppered pintos and cornjack with blackboot sorghum, and smiling the while that good order was restored amongst us.

"Then father said, Mellie, my flock is dwindling, and what can I do to save my flock? And I said Father, indeed, to beat the beaten will not make them love you the more. They work so hard in their fields and pastures and over their kettles of lye, oft stopping only to bury their dead, before continuing on with their labors. Ere, don't begrudge them their nip of hardened cider or to puff their pipes in solemn reflection or to sweat out a well-flung dance in the wee morning hours. Instead, offer them a tincture of hope, Father, I told him, and, by all means, give them forgiveness. As only those two can chance the needed comfort in our untidy lives. And he said, Oh yes, I see your thought's light, and do confess to pounding the pulpit a-mite on occasion.

"Thereupon, leaning together, we scribed those first words of sweet promise he would deliver a-morrow's sermon, thusly: *That as long as the night rain falls, and the yellow sun rises, and the green river runs down to the sea…*"

ABOUT THE AUTHOR

James Snyder was born in Memphis, Tennessee and fell in love with the cadence and sound of storytelling as a child, listening to the meandering tales of his Southern grandmothers and great aunts. While still a child, his family moved to Napa Valley, California where he attended middle and high school, and began taking writing classes at the local college. He left after a year to join the military, and was a soldier with a tactical mobile operations unit in Germany. It was there, while pulling a Harz mountaintop guard duty one night during a snowstorm, he had the chance encounter with another soldier that ultimately became the genesis for his debut military thriller *American Warrior*.

Other works include the suspense thriller *Desolation Run* and his collection of short stories, *Tales of the Late Twentieth Century*. He is currently working on a historical thriller, based upon infamous events that occurred in New Orleans at the close of the 19th Century, and that nearly resulted in war between the United States and the Kingdom of Italy.

Berlin Diaries is his blog at JamesSnyder.net where he further discusses the backgrounds of these and other writings.

He currently lives in Texas.

Printed in Great Britain
by Amazon.co.uk, Ltd.,
Marston Gate.